Blood-Soaked Earth

LEGENDS OF THE DESERT, BOOK 4

BLOOD-SOAKED EARTH

THE TRIAL OF OLIVER LEE

W. MICHAEL FARMER

FIVE STAR
A part of Gale, a Cengage Company

Farmington Hills, Mich • San Francisco • New York • Waterville, Maine
Meriden, Conn • Mason, Ohio • Chicago

Five Star Publishing, a part of Gale, a Cengage Company

LIBRARY OF CONGRESS CATALOGING-IN-PUBLICATION DATA

Names: Farmer, W. Michael, 1944– author.
Title: Blood-soaked earth : the trial of Oliver Lee / W. Michael Farmer.
Description: First edition. | Farmington Hills, Mich : Five Star, 2019. | Series: Legends of the desert ; book 4
Identifiers: LCCN 2019002601 (print) | ISBN 9781432857431 (hardcover : alk. paper)
Subjects: LCSH: Lee, Oliver, 1865–1941—Fiction. | Fountain, Albert Jennings, 1838–1896—Fiction. | New Mexico—History—19th century—Fiction. | GSAFD: Legal stories. | Historical fiction.
Classification: LCC PS3606.A725 B585 2019 (print) | DDC 813/.6—dc23
LC record available at https://lccn.loc.gov/2019002601

First Edition. First Printing: September 2019
Find us on Facebook—https://www.facebook.com/FiveStarCengage
Visit our website—http://www.gale.cengage.com/fivestar/
Contact Five Star Publishing at FiveStar@cengage.com

Printed in Mexico
1 2 3 4 5 6 7 23 22 21 20 19

For Corky, my best friend and wife.

TABLE OF CONTENTS

ACKNOWLEDGMENTS

Many friends and associates have supported and encouraged me in this work. There are several who deserve special mention.

Melissa Watkins Starr provided editorial reviews and many helpful questions, suggestions, and comments to enhance manuscript quality. Her excellent work is much appreciated.

Bruce Kennedy's knowledge of the southwest, invaluable commentary, and research made many useful contributions to this story. I thank him for his support.

Pat and Mike Alexander graciously opened their home to me during return visits to New Mexico for research and book tours, and they provided company on long roads across endless deserts and prairies and tall mountains. Friends such as these are rare and much appreciated.

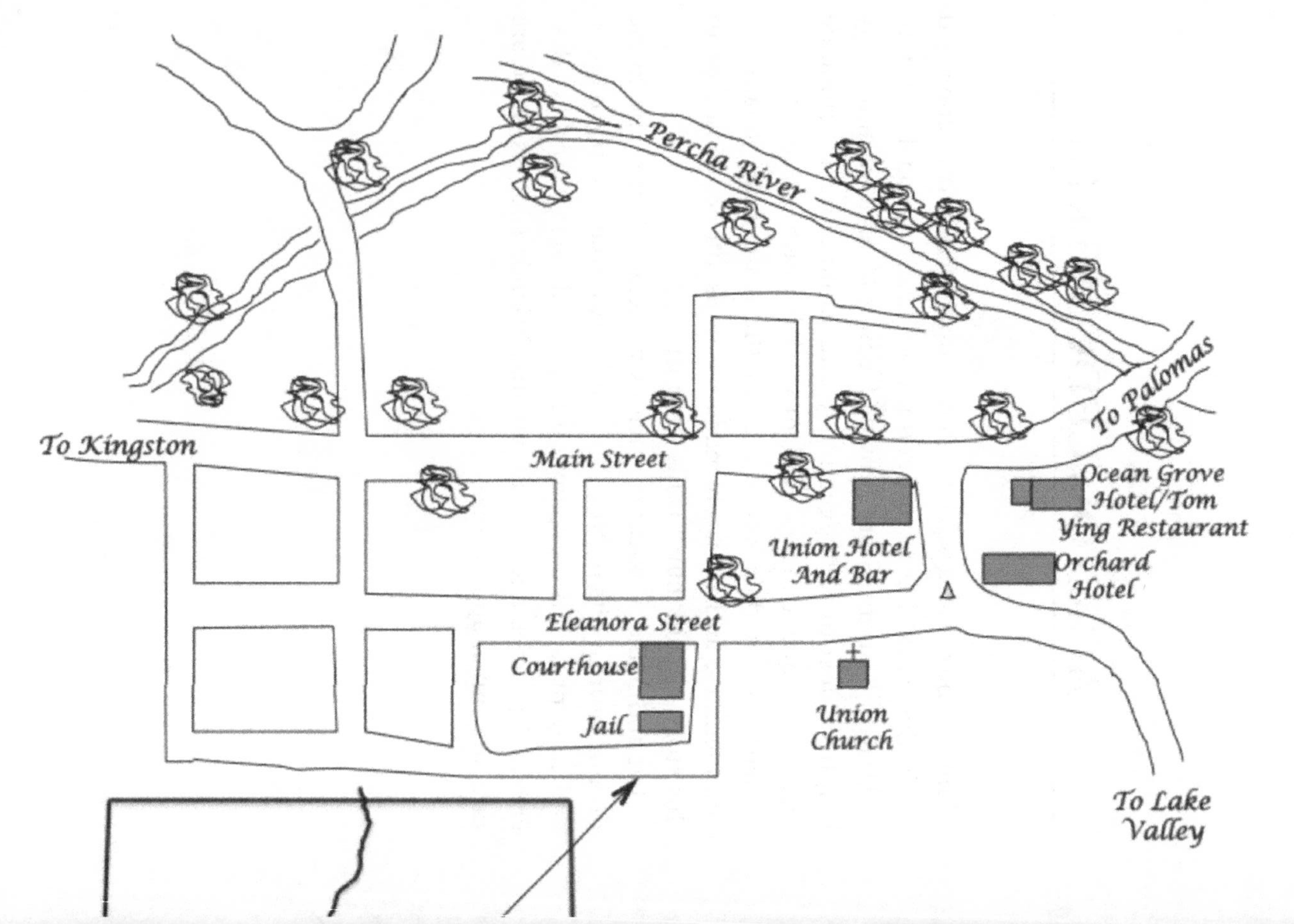
Percha River
To Palomas
To Kingston
Main Street
Ocean Grove
Hotel/Tom
Ying Restaurant
Union Hotel
And Bar
Orchard
Hotel
Eleanora Street
Courthouse
Jail
Union
Church
To Lake
Valley

Hillsboro, New Mexico Territory, 1899

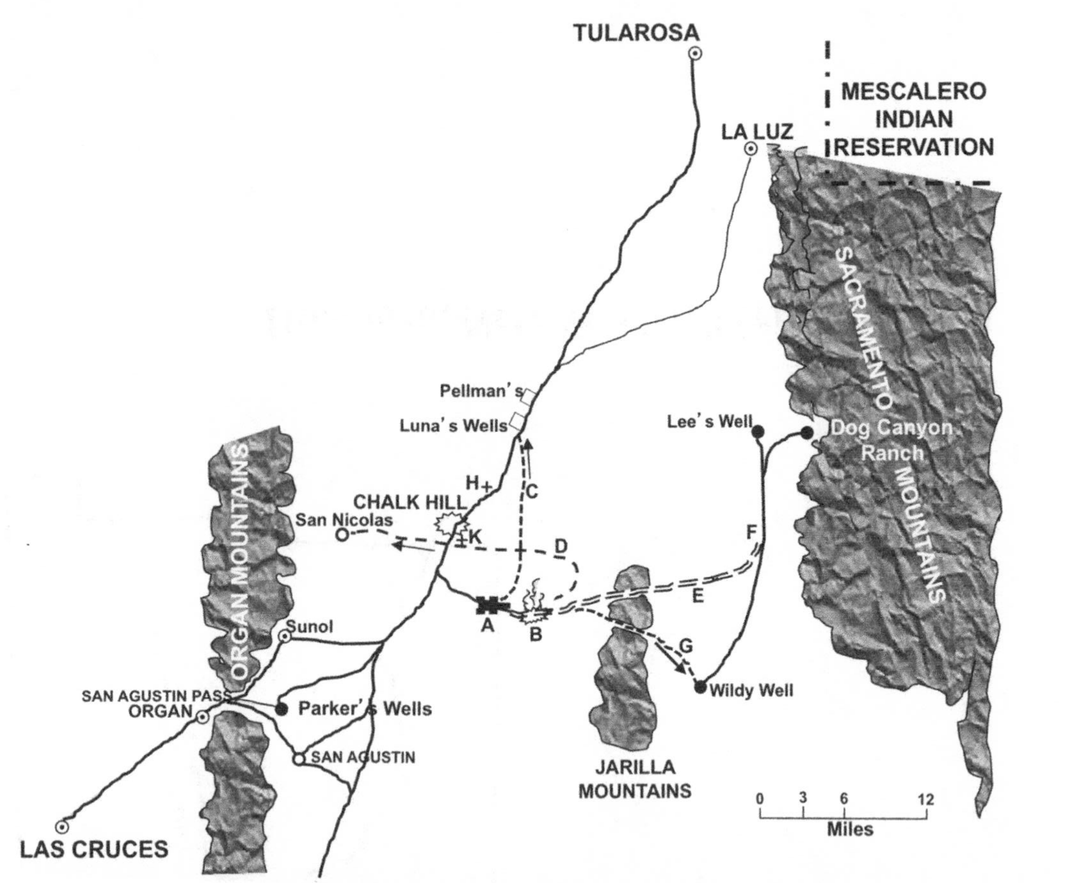
TULAROSA
LA LUZ
MESCALERO
INDIAN
RESERVATION
SACRAMENTO
MOUNTAINS
Dog Canyon
Ranch
Lee's Well
Pellman's
Luna's Wells
H
C
CHALK HILL
San Nicolas
K
D
F
E
A
B
G
Wildy Well
ORGAN MOUNTAINS
Sunol
SAN AGUSTIN PASS
ORGAN
Parker's Wells
SAN AGUSTIN
JARILLA
MOUNTAINS
0 3 6 12
Miles
LAS CRUCES

Carl Clausen Map of Crime Scene

Based on map used in the courtroom drawn by Carl Clausen of the scene of the Fountain disappearance. (See Additional Reading List, Sonnichsen, p. 126, for original version.)

A –Fountain buckboard found
B—Dry camp where fire was built and child shoe tracks were found
C—Route of horse led by Fountain
D—Route of white horse driven by Fountain
E—Route taken by mounted men leading Fountain's black mare
F—Intersection of trail with road between Dog Canyon and Wildy Well where posse met cattle herd
G—Trail of single horseman through second Jarilla pass to Wildy Well
H—Place where mail carrier, Barela, meets Fountain, 1 February 1896
K –Blood spot on edge of road

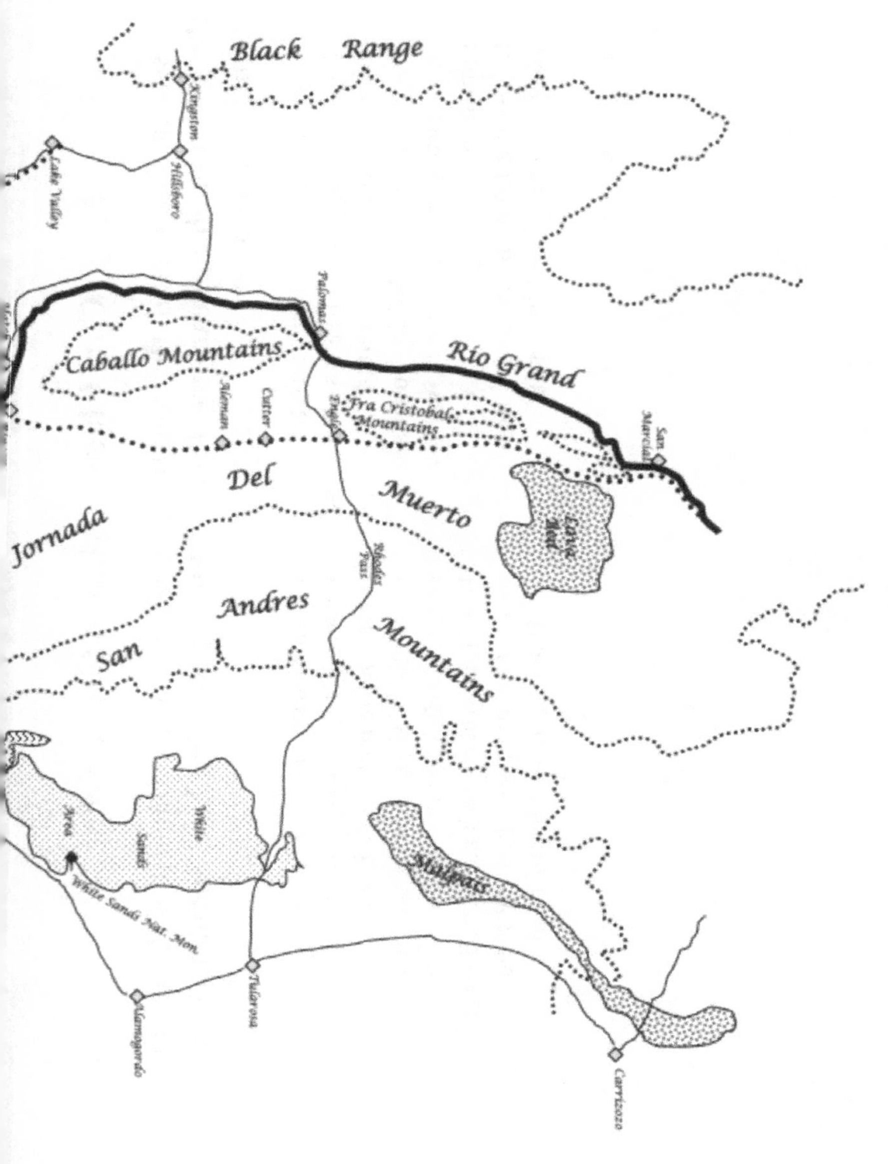
Black Range
Kingston
Hillsboro
Lake Valley
Palomas
Rio Grand
Caballo Mountains
Aleman
Cutter
Fra Cristobal Mountains
San Marcial
Del
Muerto
Jornada
Lava Bed
Rhodes Pass
Andres
San
Mountains
White Sands Area
White Sands Nat. Mon.
Malpais
Tularosa
Alamogordo
Carrizozo

A Land of Blood-Soaked Earth
Area of the Trial for Oliver Lee and James Gililland

FICTIONAL AND HISTORICAL CHARACTERS

Fictional Characters

Quentin Peach
Arch Clayton
Peyton Seymour
Persia Brown
Tomás Greco
Nadine

Historical Characters

The Accused

Oliver Milton Lee
James R. Gililland

Prosecuting Attorneys
Tom B. Catron
Richmond P. Barnes
William Burr Childers

Defense Attorneys
Albert Bacon Fall
Harry M. Daugherty
Harvey B. Fergusson

Prosecution Witnesses

Former Governor "Poker Bill" Thornton
Antonio García
Albert Fountain
Theodore Herman
Saturnino Barela
Catarino Villegas
Major Eugene Van Patten
Jack Maxwell
Santos Alvarado
Justice of the Peace Humphrey Hill
James W. Gould
Frank Wayne
Charles S. Lusk
Patrick Floyd Garrett
Dr. Francis Crosson
John Meadows
Carl Clausen
Captain Thomas Branigan

Jack Fountain
Nicholas Armijo
David H. Sutherland
James Gould
Riley Baker
W. T. White
Irving Wright
Deputy Ben Williams
William Henry Harrison Llewellyn
José Espalin

Defense Witnesses

Deputy Tom Tucker
Pedro Gonzales
A. N. Bailey
Joe Fitchett
Dan Fitchett
Sheriff George Curry
Bud Smith
Joe Morgan
Albert Blevins
Mary Lee
Oliver Lee
James Wharton
John H. May
Phillip S. Fall
Print Rhode
Albert Fountain

Historical Characters at the Trial or Living in Hillsboro

Sadie Orchard
J.W. Orchard
Boots
Todd Bailey
Eugene Manlove Rhodes
Jack ("Good Eye") Tucker
Bill McNew
Myrtle McNew
Ely McNew
Tom Ying
Belvedere Brooks
Henry Stoes
Sheriff Max Kahler
Winnie Rhode Lee
Hughes DeCourcy Slater
William Carr
Nettie McNew
Oliver McNew
Jim Madison
Judge Franklin Parker

Historical Major Suspects in Addition to Lee and Gililland

Ed Brown
Emerald James
Green Scott
Bill McNew
José Chavez y Chavez
Bill Johnson
Brady

Other Historical Suspects in Addition to Lee and Gililland

William Carr
Charles Burton
Jack Tucker
Todd Bailey
Powder Bill
Albert Bacon Fall
Joe Morgan
Spence Brothers
Bob Gray
Bill Sykes

PREFACE

"The pursuit of truth, not facts, is the business of fiction."
—Oakley Hall, Prefatory Note to *Warlock*

In 1899, the Territory of New Mexico tried Oliver Lee and James Gililland for the murder of eight-year-old Henry Fountain. The territory claimed Lee and others murdered Henry's father, Colonel Albert Fountain, and that Henry was an innocent victim. Albert Fall, lead defense attorney, who never lost a capital murder or cattle rustling case, assailed the physical evidence and the capability and integrity of every territorial witness including Pat Garrett, famous for tracking down and killing Billy the Kid. All the evidence presented by the territory was circumstantial. A sample of "blood-soaked earth" taken near the assumed scene of the murders, which could not be associated with either victim or even proved to be human blood, is emblematic of the totality of evidence in the case. Since no bodies were ever found, the territory could not prove satisfactorily that there had in fact been a murder, much less who committed the murders. Only hints of what might have been are seen through the mists of time and imagination.

The story of the trial was first published in 2009 as *Conspiracy: The Trial of Oliver Lee and James Gililland. Blood-Soaked Earth: The Trial of Oliver Lee* retells the story from a different perspective to make it more accessible to a wider audience and, like *Conspiracy,* focuses on true events that became part of the

Fountain and Lee legends.

The story presented here is a portrait of an historical event. Along with the actual historical events and characters, it is painted using events that never happened, characters who never lived, and dialogue that was never spoken. It creates for the reader, on the canvas of the facts of the trial, the personalities, politics, and conflicts that led to the Fountain murders and the Lee and Gililland trial. It is a portrait upon which readers can gaze and draw their own conclusions about the guilt or innocence of Oliver Lee and James Gililland.

W. Michael Farmer
Smithfield, Virginia
January 2018

Prologue

Near White Sands, New Mexico, 1 February 1896

A buckboard drawn by a black horse and a white horse rattles down a deep-rutted road toward a long line of steep, rough-cut mountains in the far distance. A man in his late fifties is driving, a rifle across his knees, his face grim, his eyes scanning the roadsides. By his side, a little boy hunches down in his coat, his hat pulled low on his head as far as it will go, his collar pulled to his ears. The man speaks to the child, who nods he understands as they huddle close together in the freezing wind rolling off the mountains around them. The afternoon shadows are long in the mesquites, creosotes, and yuccas.

Three riders, two on one side of the ruts, one on the other, are a half-mile ahead of the buckboard, as though leading the man and boy toward the mountains. In the distance, by the side of the road, a big, green bush trembles in the wind. A man on his knees hides behind it, staring through a hole in the fluttering leaves. He holds a lever-action rifle, its hammer pulled back, ready to fall on a waiting bullet. Down in a shallow gully a few hundred yards behind him, another man waits on a horse.

When the buckboard is not more than fifty or sixty yards away, the shooter aims and fires twice. His shots, fast and deadly accurate, hit the driver's chest. The driver falls backwards, as though struck by a mighty club, and his hands let the reins slide free. Stunned, the child stares in horror at the blood pumping from the wounds in his father's chest. Then, as if waking from a dream, the boy leans forward to grab the reins. The team, startled by the unexpected gunfire, has sprung into a pounding run, driving the buckboard wheels against the sides of the ruts, causing the buckboard to sway crazily back and forth.

The boy and the man are thrown out of the careening vehicle, and the man lands by the side of the road, blood from his wounds pooling in the sand. The tumbling child's head strikes a churning wagon wheel. He lies unmoving, his eyes staring at the deep, blue sky, seeing nothing.

Chapter 1
The Assignment

San Francisco, 21 May 1899

"Peach!"

My desk editor has the lungs of a bull moose. You can hear him for miles—even in the *San Francisco Examiner* newsroom full of Blick electric typewriters rattling off Mr. Hearst's version of Och's mantra, *All the News That's Fit to Print.* I hear him yelling for and at reporters every day, all day long and into the night. Still, when he bellows, I jump. Grabbing a pencil and pad, I take long strides toward his office.

Chewing on his half-smoked Havana cigar, he growls, "Close the door! Take a seat!" I sit on the edge of a chair in front of his desk. Making a tent with his hands, he stares at me across the top of his Franklin glasses and asks, "Peach, are you a Republican or a Democrat?"

"Roosevelt Republican. Mark my words. After San Juan Hill, old Teddy's going to be—"

"Ever been to the Southwest?"

My head wags left and right. "Uh, no, sir, I took a ship around the horn from New York to get here."

He sighs and nods. "I don't suppose you've heard of the Fountain murder trial that's about to start?"

The Fountain murders? The name, Fountain, has a familiar ring. Staring at him blankly for a moment, my mind scrambles to find the scrap of information needed to keep me from looking like an uninformed moron. I raise my right index finger.

"Hah! Yes! The Fountain murders . . . New Mexico Republican . . . territorial legislator . . . attorney . . . disappeared near White Sands with his eight-year-old kid . . . believed murdered by one of his Democratic rivals, some rancher he was set to prosecute for stealing cattle. The guy who killed Billy the Kid, Pat Garrett, was hired to catch the killer. So there's going to be a trial? Garrett caught him, huh? When's the hanging?"

He nods slowly, staring at his Havana rolling between his thumb and fingers.

"That's right, except you got a couple of facts wrong, about par for a kid learning the trade. Here's the deal. Fountain and his son were never found. All the evidence on the men accused is circumstantial. The lead prosecutor is a big-shot Republican named Tom Catron. Catron's so anxious to get a conviction, he's said he'd be willing to act as lead prosecutor at no charge to the government."

He takes a long draw on the Havana and blows the smoke toward the ceiling. "My spies tell me the defendants will be tried for the murder of the little boy. If that's true, it's a smart move. Catron has to be calculating he'll get a lot of sympathy from the jury that way. Besides, if there's not a conviction for the child, the territory can try the accused again for the murder of Fountain—a clever way around double indemnity, don't you think? The lead defense attorney is a prominent Democrat named Albert Fall, who regularly kicks Republican tail in territorial politics. The defendants have helped Fall whenever he needed a little political muscle. He owes them big time."

Chief has my full attention now. "When did Garrett catch what's-his-name?"

Chief's voice drips with sarcasm. "Garrett never caught anyone. Oliver Lee and James Gililland, after being on the run for about a year, turned themselves in to Judge Franklin Parker in Las Cruces, New Mexico. Garrett claims he has a witness who'll prove Lee and Gililland did it. It's rumored the witness is afraid to testify and has gone into hiding.

"It's the biggest trial in the Southwest, maybe even the entire country. Some claim it's the trial of the century! Hell, who knows what it might become?

"The facts are it's being held in Hillsboro, a little mining town about a hundred twenty miles north of El Paso. Reporters from all over are running to cover it. A new telegraph line has even been run up there from the main wire, and there are two operators on duty so reporters can do same-day stories on what's happening.

"If Lee and Gililland are convicted and hanged on circumstantial evidence, there'll be a real blood feud between Republicans and Democrats, not just an occasional murder. McKinley will have to call out the army to stop the fighting. New Mexico statehood will be set back for years. This story might sell lots of papers for a long, long time."

"What do you want me to do, Chief?"

He pauses, staring at me for a second or two. "Mr. Hearst's interest in politics is increasing every day. With its political implications and possibilities, he thinks this trial deserves special attention. We already have Seymour headed that way. His instructions are to send me a story summarizing the trial proceedings every day."

I begin to think this will be just another flunky job to support one of our senior reporters, but the old man keeps talking. "Now you know Hearst papers have a reputation for taking the bull by the horns. Remember how we sold papers like there was no tomorrow after our reporters freed that woman in Cuba? It'd please Mr. Hearst and sell a lot of papers if we had a man at the trial who found out where the bones of Fountain and his kid are hidden and who's guilty if Lee and Gililland aren't.

"Peach, you're a bright boy. That memory of yours amazes me. You don't rub people the wrong way. In fact, you're about the only reporter I know with whom people actually want to interview. Pack your bags! I want you in Hillsboro as soon as you can get there. You focus on the big picture, the real scoop, and the personalities involved. Follow all the leads you can. If you need detective support, let me know. Send your wires directly to me, and keep Seymour out of it. Son, this is your big chance. Don't blow it!"

"Yes, sir!" Leaping out of the chair, my mind roils with things that have to be done before leaving. Nearly out the door before remembering to thank him, I look back. He's already hunched over his desk, paying no attention to me, focused on a new sheet of copy.

Chapter 2
Stage to Hillsboro

Southern New Mexico, 25 May 1899

Air blowing in the windows comes from a blast furnace and is filled with gritty, black cinder dust from the engine's smokestack. The dust sticks to every exposed fiber. Riding this train is a miserable way to travel, but at least it must be fast and smooth compared to bumping along rocky, rutted roads in a stagecoach. The train begins to slow, passing along the edge of a valley formed by rugged, grass-covered hills. The conductor passes through my car, his deep, gravelly voice booming, "End of the line! Lake Valley! Lake Valley next stop!"

Bags are pulled from nearby empty seats or from overhead. Five passengers boarded in Las Cruces, and another three or four at Nutt Station, twenty miles back. Four of the Las Cruces passengers seem to know each other, smoking and carrying on convivial conversation that teases and jokes as we roll north. One is a big bear of a man wearing a heavy, long-barreled revolver in an oiled, leather holster on his hip. His only luggage is a saddle, a blanket roll, and a long, big-bore Winchester. His friends also carry rifles and revolvers. Browned by the sun, their hands scarred and callused, they toss an occasional glance toward a fifth man who also boarded in Las Cruces, a man in his early twenties. He has a nicely trimmed, black mustache. He, too, has rough hands and a sunburned face, but he wears a frock coat and carries no revolver. The others say nothing to him as he stares out the window, minding his own business.

The train starts down a shallow grade as it comes around a ridge. The little village of Lake Valley flows into view off to my left. Looking across the long, sweeping arc of the tracks, I see a stage waiting by the depot loading dock. The rails continue past the depot, appearing to merge into a single ribbon of steel jamming into a hillside scattered with sun-bleached, gray buildings beside mineshaft tailings.

Groaning from jerks, rattling connections between cars, and wheels being braked, the train slows to a stop at the depot platform. Several of the passengers are already beside the rails and sprinting for the stage. Most are well dressed, probably businessmen or reporters; others, possibly miners, wear lineman caps and canvas overalls. The stage leaves, passengers filling the coach inside and out. I start to run after it but see that the Las Cruces men who rode in my train car are relaxed, taking their time, so I relax too. The remaining passengers head directly toward the forlorn village main street and several houses or stores scattered along its sides.

As we enter the depot, a tall thin man with a huge hooked nose calls to us from the clerk's cage, "Howdy, boys. Second stage's running a little late. Just take a seat and make yourselves to home. She ought to be along in a bit."

We find chairs and barrels to sit on in the cool shadows. The big man throws his saddle down in a corner, and, using its well-worn, polished leather for a pillow, stretches out with a sigh. Siesta time. Watching him pull his hat down over his eyes, I notice a mangled ear with its top gone. The quiet man sits on a banker's chair looking out the door. The light catches one side of his face, leaving the rest in deep shadow, his jaw muscles sometimes rippling from clenched teeth. One man pulls a pipe, another a piece of thin paper crimped down the middle to hold threads of tobacco. The cigarette smoker is missing an eye and looks hard and rough. Everyone waits, saying nothing, lethargic in the black heat.

Soon a stagecoach appears in a cloud of dust from behind the hill. Sounding the distant tinkle of steel trace rings and chains jangling against doubletrees as it races down the road, it pulls up the rise toward the depot. A voice urges on the four-horse team in a torrent of profanities my grandfather, who sailed on whalers, would have been proud to claim. The driver is small and wears a black top hat mottled gray from dust.

My jaw drops when I see the driver is a middle-aged woman dressed like an Easterner, who might be going on a fox hunt, except the middle of her skirt is pulled up between her legs. It's not ladylike, but it lets her use the foot brake without entangling her dress. Her face is hard, but she has kind eyes and a smile that would make any man feel comfortable and welcome.

The big man with a saddle sees my face and laughs. "You being from the city and all, I don't reckon you ever heard of old J.W.'s wife. That there is Sadie Orchard, only woman stage driver in New Mexico Territory—hell, maybe in the entire West fer all I know. Her and J.W. got a couple of Concords an' run hotels an' other 'stablishments up 'ere to Hillsboro." His grin widens, and he nudges me with his elbow. "If you get a little lonely in the evenings, Sadie can fix you up with some fine female companionship, if you know what I mean."

I smile and nod, wondering what kind of woman would want to make her livelihood with rough cowboys and miners here in the big lonesome. Sadie climbs down from the driver's bench, peels off her lambskin gloves, and uses them to slap the dust out of her shirt and skirt. She looks us up and down.

"Good afternoon, gentlemen!" she says in a Cockney accent. Nodding toward the man with the saddle, she breaks into a smile. "Tom Tucker! I ain't seen you in years. Guess the last time was when you come to stay awhile with Nadine. How are ya?"

Tom is a little shy around her. "I'm fine, Miss Sadie, jes fine. You remember my brother Jack?"

"Of course I do. Hallo, Jack! I know Will Carr, too. Last year Mr. Pat Garrett tried to put you in jail to squeeze a tale out of you to prove Oliver Lee's guilty. Pretty sorry business that. Boys, the Republicans are after Lee. The bastards want to hang him. The sonzabitches don't care if he's guilty of murdering Fountain and that poor little boy. They just want him gone. I got a mighty low opinion of them Republicans. By God, Fall better see to it the Democrats don't lose this trial, or he'd best never show his face around here again. All you gentlemen going up for the trial?"

We nod, except for a quiet man who stands staring up the road, obviously pretending to ignore the conversation.

Tom Tucker says, "Yes, ma'am, Miss Sadie. Jack, Will, Jim, and me is gonna be witnesses fer Oliver an' Gililland at the trial."

She eyes the fourth man. He looks like a typical cowboy. A shock of hair hangs from under the crown of his hat. His clothes are in better repair than the others, but, like the others, he's brown from long hours in the sun.

Sadie says, "Ain't you Jim Madison? You're the one Mr. Garrett almost shot when 'e creeped into your bedroom an' stuck a pistol in your ribs, tryin' to sneak up on Oliver and Gililland."

Madison grins and nods. "Miss Sadie, you shore got a memory fer names and faces. Why, I ain't been to your place since I married five years ago."

"Mr. Madison, I never forget a face, a fancy woman, or a good story. Well, good for you, boys, doing your civic duty. The Lee camp is just down a little way from my place, and it's got plenty of tents and places to sleep. They've a chuck wagon set up to feed their folks, too. You gentlemen will have a damn fine place to hang your hats when you ain't in court or the saloons."

She crosses her arms and nods at the quiet man. "Who are you, sir? You going to the trial, too? Don't think I've ever had you as a passenger or in my hotel before."

Keeping his distance from the rest of us, he looks her in the eye and speaks with respect. "No, ma'am, I don't think I've ever been on your stage or in your hotel. My name is Jack . . . Jack Fountain. I'm going to be a witness at the trial, too."

Even though it must be over a hundred degrees, the air is suddenly very cool. Grins disappear from the faces of Will Carr and Jack Tucker. Their hands move to give their revolvers company. Tom Tucker stays relaxed and spits a bit of tobacco off his lips. Madison winces like he's been slapped, hooks his thumbs into his belt, and stares at Fountain.

Sadie doesn't blink and shakes her head. "Mr. Fountain, we're all mighty sorry that your father and little brother disappeared. Now, boys, before we get on board, we're all gonna let the jury decide what's right, ain't we?"

We all nod. She looks at me. "That's a fine boater you got on there, governor, but out 'ere it ain't worth spit for shade. You're either a drummer or a reporter."

I grin. "Yes, ma'am. Name's Quentin Peach, reporter with the *San Francisco Examiner.* My assignment is to get all the facts and keep our readers well-informed."

She eyes me a moment and smiles. "Just be sure you do, sir. Too many reporters make things up like they think it ought to be, not like it is. You need a place to roost in Hillsboro? I think we have a room left in our hotel, the Ocean Grove. Better take it, or you're likely to be sleeping in a tent!"

"Yes, ma'am! I'll take it. Be glad and grateful to get it."

"Okay, Mr. Peach, you'll get the room. Gentlemen, the fare

up to Hillsboro is two dollars one way or three-fifty round trip. I'll get the team changed, and then we'll be on the way. Go on; get on board. We'll leave in about five minutes. Got to git back before dark."

As she speaks, a boy in raggedy overalls brings a fresh team up the hill from a livery barn near the depot. He makes quick work of changing teams. We dig in our pockets and wallets for the money it takes to ride.

We climb inside the coach. The Tuckers and Will Carr sit facing backwards. I sit between Fountain and Madison on the other side. It isn't long before Sadie pulls open a coach door, sticks in her hand, and says, "What'll it be, gentlemen?"

I'm the only one that asks for a round-trip ticket. She thanks us and closes the door. The stage creaks as she climbs up on the driver's bench and takes the reins. Yelling, "Gid up, Dick. Hey, Nellie!" she clicks her tongue and ripples the lines across the backs of the team. They lunge off in a fast trot, jerking me back against the seat.

Behind the hill, the team struggles up and across a couple of high, winding ridges before the road weaves down washes and across long stretches between rolling hills. Through the shimmering mirages off to the west, the Black Range hangs omnipresent, suspended above the grassy hills.

CHAPTER 3
STORIES ON THE STAGE

Tom Tucker sits with his arms crossed, clamping the barrel of his Winchester against his thick, muscled shoulder, the stock planted between his boots. He keeps a steady eye on Jack Fountain, who, ignoring the rest of us, stares west at the Black Range. Will Carr and Jack Tucker smoke and stare at the high hills out to the east. Madison stares out the window, the wind catching the brim of his hat and bending it back.

I covertly study all the men in the coach as Sadie makes the team pound down dry washes and up hills scarred by deep road ruts. Given how the opposing sides must feel, I hesitate to ask them for interviews in front of each other. Then I think, *Can I afford not to risk it?*

Knowing this is my big chance, I swallow my reticence and stick out my hand to Jack Fountain. "Mr. Fountain, my name's Quentin Peach. In case you didn't hear me tell Mrs. Orchard, I'm a reporter for the *San Francisco Examiner.* I'd like to ask you a few questions."

Fountain shakes my hand and studies my eyes, ignoring the stares from the Tuckers, Carr, and Madison. "Jack Fountain, Mr. Peach. For a reporter, you're not as obnoxious as most. All right, what can I tell you?"

"Call me Quent. When did you first learn your father was missing?"

Jack stares out the window. "It was a Sunday, the second of February, three years ago. The sun was just setting. My mother, my brother, Albert, and his wife, Teresa, and I had been waiting since morning mass for my father and little brother to get home. Knowing that threats had been made against my father, we were all worried.

"It was nearly dark when we heard a wagon pull into the yard, but it was Saturnino Barela, the wagon driver for the Las Cruces mail run.

"Saturnino's a big bear of a man, and I don't think he's ever used a razor. He looked desperate as Albert and I stepped outside into the cold, pulling the door behind us. Saturnino asked if our father was home.

"Albert shook his head, and Barela groaned, '*Madre de Dios!* They are ambushed!'

"My mother, who had followed us outside, put her hands to her face and sobbed. Teresa came running to support her and helped her back inside. Albert asked Barela to tell us what he knew.

"Saturnino said that he'd stopped and talked with Father on the road to Las Cruces Saturday afternoon, when Father told him three men had stayed on the road in front of him all day. Saturnino had seen them, but they rode off toward El Paso before he reached them. He said they looked like Texas cowboys to him. Saturnino said he begged Father to turn back to Luna's Wells with him so they could ride to Las Cruces together on Sunday, but Father told him no, that my mother was expecting him and that Henry had a cold. Besides, Father never backed up for anyone for any reason.

"Saturnino said he left Luna's Wells on Sunday morning as soon as possible. When he got just beyond Chalk Hill, he saw where the buggy Father was driving had turned off the road and headed out into the desert. He followed the tracks for thirty or forty yards when he saw tracks from other horses. Afraid that Father and Henry had been attacked, he quickly drove back to

Las Cruces, praying they were home safe.

"Albert thanked Barela for coming to tell us and asked him to find Major Llewellyn and tell him what he'd told us, and to tell him that we were leaving as soon as we were saddled. Albert then turned to me and said, 'That sorry bastard Oliver Lee isn't going to get away with this! He's gone too far this time.' He asked me to ride over to the house of Teresa's father, Antonio García, to tell him what had happened and that we were riding out as soon as I got back. He said he'd try to comfort Mother and make sure she understood we were off to find Father and Henry.

"I looked at Albert and shook my head. I said, 'Don't you think we ought to get supplies first and wait for Llewellyn's posse? They'll be coming as soon as they can get organized.'

"He said, 'Hell, no, Jack! Every minute counts! Father might be wounded and Henry freezing to death. We've got to go now!' "

Out of the corner of my eye, I see Tom Tucker shaking his head as Jack continues his story.

"As soon as I told Antonio what had happened, he told one of his sons to go saddle his horse. His sons and three or four neighbors said they were coming, too.

"Nobody was thinking straight that night or even the next day. It was like we'd all panicked and lost our minds. We left home in a long lope. It was freezing cold, and the wind cut right through us. All I had was a full canteen, a loaded rifle, and some *sopapillas* left over from lunch. Albert, Antonio, and the rest of them weren't much better off. We were fools that night, but our hearts were in the right place."

"Why did your brother believe Oliver Lee had murdered your father and brother?" I ask.

I glance at the Tuckers, Madison, and Carr and notice they're paying close attention to everything Jack says.

"Several reasons, but mainly because Lee threatened to shoot Republicans campaigning against Albert Fall when he ran against Father and because, before leaving for Lincoln, Father had told my sister Maggie and Albert that he believed he had enough evidence to convict Lee of cattle rustling, and Lee knew it. Lee's always ruthlessly protected his empire. He'd killed men before, and we didn't doubt he'd do it again. We just didn't believe he'd be brazen enough to murder Father when our eight-year-old brother was with him."

"So, what do you believe? Did Lee murder your father and brother?"

Jack stares at the men sitting across from us, their pistols in easy reach. He says, "I'd say he did. But Father'd want us to hear all the evidence first to be sure."

I watch Tom's eyes narrow, but his hands stay relaxed, keeping their place on the rifle barrel. I ask, "If Mr. Lee is found not guilty, will you try to take the law into your own hands?"

Jack looks out the window for a moment, and then back at Tom. "I'm just a kid. I'm not going to kill anybody, even if they deserve killing. But I will say that if Father's bones are ever found and identified, there is one man I'd kill first."

"And who is that, Mr. Fountain?"

He says through clenched teeth, "Albert Bacon Fall."

A smile cracks the lips of the men facing us. "Fall?" I ask. "Lee's attorney? Why would you want to kill him?"

Jack's voice is cold. "Fall is the Democrat brains behind my father and brother's assassination. If Lee murdered them, it's because Albert Fall told him to do it."

Tom leans back in the seat. The other three stare out the window and say nothing.

"Mr. Fountain, what happened when you got to where your father drove his buggy off the road?"

He shakes his head. "Call me Jack. I know you're just trying to do your job, but I've said too much already. You'll find out at the trial."

I nod and look over at Tom Tucker and the others and stick out my hand. "How about you boys? Can I ask you a few questions?"

They each shake my hand. Tom smiles. "Don't reckon they's any harm in that, Quent."

The stage slows and stops next to a corral with a fresh team already harnessed. Sadie calls down to us, "We'll have the teams changed in five minutes. There are facilities out back, but hurry."

Jack Tucker and Madison climb out and run for the outhouse. The rest of us keep our seats. Tucker and then Madison return just before the new team is ready to go. We're off with a jerk, leaving the stationmaster in a white dust cloud.

"How do you fellows know Oliver Lee?" I ask.

Tom cuts his eyes to Jack and back to me. "I come over from Arizona and started ridin' with Oliver back just before the Cooper-Good Range War in '88 or '89. He needed some good gun hands in them days, and I weren't bad. Old Good-Eye Jack there's my brother. Him and Will come along a few years later, and ol' Madison there, he's Lee's man over to the Wildy Well ranch. Like Miss Sadie said, he's the one who nearly got his tail shot off when Garrett sneaked into his bedroom and jammed a pistol in his ribs a-thinkin' he's Oliver."

Nodding, I think I'm riding in a wagon full of front-page stories. To put them at ease, I give Tom another easy question.

"If you don't mind my asking, how did you lose the top of your ear?"

He grins and rubs it with his big beefy paw. "Aw, it got shot off when I's in the Tewksbury-Graham feud over to the Tonto Basin in Arizona. That's before I come over here. It weren't nothin', but it hurt like hell for a while."

"Well, do you all still work for Oliver Lee?"

"Yes, sir, some of us do. These boys is top hands. George Curry hired me a few months ago as a deputy for Otero County. The county is new, you know."

I look out the window for a moment and say, "I understand Lee and Gililland were on the run for a while before they turned themselves in. If they were willing to come in on their own, why has it taken so long to have a trial?"

I see Jack staring at Tom and the others, waiting for an answer. Tom nods toward Jack and says, "I'll let Mr. Fountain there correct me if what I tell ya ain't true, 'cept, of course, that ol' Oliver and Jim ain't guilty."

Jack crosses his arms and waits. Tom continues, "Weren't long after the Fountains disappeared that Governor Thornton gits ol' Pat Garrett to come out of retirement and take the case. 'Bout two years later, he takes all the evidence he's got to a gran' jury, expectin' to indict Lee and some of his friends. The gran' jury says Garrett ain't got spit fer evidence an' adjourns.

"The same day, with the help of Llewellyn and Branigan, Garrett gits a bench warrant for Lee and his boys on the same evidence the gran' jury threw out. Right away, Garrett, he uses that bench warrant to throw Will here"—Tom waves his hand at Carr—"and Bill McNew in jail. Garrett won't go after Lee, jes sits in Las Cruces with his warrants doin' nuthin' and waitin'.

"In July '98, ol' Garrett decides to make his move. He takes a posse over to Wildy an' tries to pull the same trick on Oliver he pulled on Billy the Kid—kill him in his bedroom in the dark of night. 'Cept it weren't Oliver in bed, it's ol' Madison there and his wife. Oliver an' Gililland, they's a-sleepin' up on the roof. After Garrett figured out where they was an' started shootin' at 'em while they's a-sleepin', Oliver got the best of Garrett in the shootout an' run him off. Oliver and Gililland killed Kent Kearney, one of Garrett's deputies, when lead started flyin', but even Garrett says Kearney shot first before telling 'em they's the law.

Oliver learns fast. He told us that little shiteree taught him that Garrett was gonna kill him once he had him unarmed. Oliver said he'd never let Garrett take him in.

"So Oliver an' Gililland hid out fer nearly a year till Fall fixed things up fer 'em so it's safe to come in. And that there is why it's took so long to have a trial."

Jack Fountain stares at Tucker but says nothing. I say, "Thanks, Mr. Tucker, you've been very helpful." He nods and grins but says nothing more. I put my pad and pencil back in my coat pocket.

We stop for one more change of horses before continuing to rock along through the afternoon heat. Nothing more is said until Sadie guides her team down a short grade into Hillsboro.

CHAPTER 4
HILLSBORO

As we come down the ridge road, I see tents and canvas lean-tos set up on a raised flat place in a line of trees edging a small stream. The stream is the Middle Percha River, but the locals just call it the Percha. Tents, two or three blocks down the road from the intersection where we stop, surround a chuck wagon and a cooking fire. A Negro, his shirt soaked in sweat, works over heavy, iron Dutch ovens, huge skillets, and a side of beef his helper slowly turns over a bed of coals. The smell of smoke from fat dripping on the coals makes my belly roar with hunger.

Off to the side of the tents, a corral formed by ropes and wagons holds a herd of horses. Long, mostly adobe or stone buildings line the roads forming the intersection where we stop. Sadie calls down, "That's Lee's camp over by the Percha! Appears Eb'll have supper ready in a bit. You'd better hurry, boys, or there won't be anything left!"

Tom Tucker and Madison throw open the stage doors. The Lee men tumble out of their seats and stretch. Every muscle in my backside aches.

Carr steps up on the stage wheel and tosses gear down to waiting hands. They wave to friends headed down the street toward the great smells coming from the chuck wagon fire, tip their hats to Sadie, and thank her for the "fine ride."

Sadie smiles and pushes back her top hat. "Plenty of 'fine riding' you can do here at the Ocean Grove when you're in need, gentlemen. The Ocean Grove is the second building down the street to the right, Mr. Peach."

A man with a deputy sheriff's star on his vest sits in a straight-back chair tilted against the wall near the Union Hotel's door across the street. He brings his chair down and stands, shifting his revolver into easy reach, and walks over to the stage. Jack follows me out of the coach and starts to pick up his bag.

"You Jack Fountain?"

Seeing the man with the star, Jack pauses, a frown of concern framing his face. "Yes, sir."

"I'm Morgan Stoddard, deputy for Max Kahler, sheriff of Sierra County. Judge Parker wants to see you."

"Okay. I'll look him up first thing in the morning before the trial starts."

Stoddard's eyes hold a hard, no-nonsense squint. "I don't think so, Mr. Fountain. Judge said to bring you to the courthouse soon as you got off the stage. Let's go. Now!"

"Yes, sir. Just let me get my bag, and I'll come right along with you."

"I'm a-waitin'."

Jack gives my hand a firm shake, nods to Sadie, and carries his bag over to the Union to drop off with the clerk. Joining the deputy, they start up the hill to the next street.

"What was that about, Miss Sadie?"

She shakes her head. "I don't know, Mr. Peach. I'm sure it's nothing serious."

A block up the hill we've just come down, I see a large, two-story, brick building with a tower on one corner. A block east from the big, brick building stands a small church. Miners, cowboys, businessmen, women, and children filling the sidewalks make Hillsboro feel crowded and full of energy.

The Ocean Grove is a long, one-story, adobe house with a porch on the west end that holds two or three straight-back chairs. It's deep toward the back and has a backyard surrounded by a tall, weathered plank fence.

Inside, the Ocean Grove is cool, dimly lighted, and very pleasant. Indian blankets in dark earth tones decorate the plastered walls, and there are a couple of plush chairs and a registration desk in the front room. An open doorway to the right leads to a restaurant in an attached building.

The young man working at the small desk asks me to sign the guest book and gives me the key to a room down a long hall ending with a door to the outside. I ask for a hot bath in the morning. He tells me it'll be six bits, says the tubs are out back inside the fence, and hot water can be had for the asking any time after six, but if I'm not prompt, I might have to wait.

My room is small but comfortable. Shaking the dust out of my clothes, I wash up using the bowl and basin on the washstand and hang my change of clothes in a battered armoire. Refreshed, it's time to go exploring.

Assay offices have a steady stream of miners and prospectors stepping in and out of their doors. I hear bell-like rings of hammers on anvils from two or three blacksmith shops. Women, most in plain dresses and bonnets, gossip in front of mercantile stores or study dresses and primp at their reflections in store windows. Saddle horses and mules are tied to hitching racks in front of saloons up and down the street. From the saloons come the tinkles of out-of-tune pianos or the squeak of fiddles mixed with the raucous laughter of rough men and the giggles of fancy women.

The Union has a steady stream of men and well-dressed women passing through its ornate, heavy wood doors. A little farther along, Tom Murphy's Parlor Saloon patrons are mostly well-dressed gentlemen. An odor of bay rum and lilac water mixed with tobacco smoke floats out the saloon doors.

Up the hill from Main Street to Eleanora Street stand the impressive two-story brick building and proud little church. The big red brick building looks new. I ask a passing miner what the building is. Smiling, he tells me it's the Sierra County Courthouse. It's built on a large, level space created by filling in a rectangular area surrounded by rock walls, about six feet high in the front and decreasing on the sides as it goes uphill to about two feet high.

Approximately thirty feet behind the brick building is a squat, one-story building with walls of red, brown, and black rock. There are bars on its windows and a heavy, iron latticework door in the center. The Sierra County Jail sits up above the flat space for the courthouse and has a narrow walkway across the front. Steps lead down from the iron latticework door to a walkway across the narrow yard and into the back of the courthouse.

A few men, wearing wide-brimmed cowboy hats, white shirts with string ties, suit coats, and polished boots, stand near the jail door, which is guarded by a couple of men with shotguns. The guards are laughing and joking with them.

I walk around to the front and enter the courthouse's large, arched door. Walking down the cool, dark hall, I pass a door with a *County Clerk's Office* sign and, a few steps farther on, one marked *County Treasurer's Office*. The second floor is reached by climbing a stairway near the back of the building. On either side, at the top of the stairs, are doors marked *Jury Room.* The hall leads to a courtroom. Looking through the open doorway, I see the room is larger than I'd expected.

Behind and to the side of the judge's platform is an office door sign that says *Judge Frank Wilson Parker.* Wandering into the courtroom and looking around, I pause, listening for voices in the judge's office, but hear none.

A steady stream of activity can be heard in the hall downstairs: clerks trotting between offices with papers in hand, doors opening and closing, and the snap of typewriter keys. Back downstairs, there is a steady stream of people in and out of the sheriff's office at the back toward the jail. Looking up and down the hall, I don't see Jack or the deputy sheriff.

Chapter 5
Jack and Albert Fountain

Dusk is falling as I finish my walk around Hillsboro. Worn out with the day's travel, my stomach growling, I'm drawn to a little cantina between a hardware store and an assay office. I order *huevos rancheros* and have a cup of milky white *pulque,* a kind of beer made from the agave cactus. I've drunk *pulque* in San Francisco and developed a liking for its slightly bitter taste.

It's not long before the waitress sweeps in from the kitchen with a big, plate of fried eggs on top of layers of tortillas covered with dark green chili sauce. Nothing gets left on the plate down to the last spoonful of brown beans. In bad need of a cold beer to quench the fire still smoldering in my throat, I leave two bits for the meal and head across the street to the Union Hotel bar.

The mug of beer at the Union goes down in welcome relief, and I see the bar's whiskey supply is well stocked and managed. The Union's bar is civilized enough to do well anywhere. I find a corner table to sit and sip my beer, study the crowd, and work on the story, based on what Jack Fountain and Tom Tucker told me.

The scrape of a chair sliding on the floor brings me out of the depths of concentration on my writing. It's Peyton Seymour. "See you made it, kid. The old man told me you were coming." Pointing his thumb toward his chest so there'll be no misunderstanding, he says, "He wants me to concentrate on the trial and you to focus on background."

"Seymour! Good to see you! Sit down! Want a beer?"

He looks like he's had a few too many already as he slumps in the chair, hanging one arm over the back to keep from sliding to the floor. "Sure! A cold one will hit the spot."

I wave a Mexican waiter over and order another beer. The waiter disappears in the crowd around the bar and is back in a blink. Seymour nods his thanks, hoists his mug, and takes a long, slow slurp. "Damn, that's good! Well, the trial is supposed to get started first thing in the morning. The prosecution asked for a continuance because their star witness, some cowboy named Jack Maxwell, disappeared. Rumor has it he's hiding out somewhere near Alamogordo. Garrett and a posse left town this morning to look for him. Judge gave the prosecution until tomorrow morning, and then jury selection starts. I bet Fall is praying Maxwell stays gone. It'd sure make his job easier."

"What makes Maxwell so important?"

"Gossip has it that he can break Lee and Gililland's alibi. I hope he shows up. I'd like to hear that story."

"Who have you interviewed, so I won't be covering the same sources as you?"

Before he answers, he sees a couple of reporters and says, "Those fellows are from Austin and Santa Fe—supposed to be real close to the Fountains. They might even get an interview from one of the Fountain brothers. Word is the Fountain side won't talk to reporters. Got to find out the latest. See you in the morning, kid."

Seymour joins his buddies, disappearing into the hotel. I smile, wondering what he'll think when he finds out I've already talked to Jack. Work on my story fills another hour or so. As the grandmother clock behind the bar strikes nine, I glance up to see Jack Fountain come in with a man who favors him but is several years his senior. Jack sees me, and I wave them over.

Jack sticks out his hand. "Quent, this is my brother Albert. Albert, Quentin Peach. We rode in on the stage with some of

Lee's men."

I take Albert's hand. "It's a pleasure to meet you, Mr. Fountain, and please, call me Quent. Jack told me about you on the ride over. Sit down, gentlemen. Let me buy you a drink."

Albert smiles and pulls out a chair. "It's a pleasure, Quent. Please call me Albert. Our father ran a newspaper in Mesilla, and my brother Thomas and I used to help him in the print shop. We're enthusiastic supporters of newspapermen, but the reporters here are such fools and idiots!" He flashes a quick smile and holds up his hand. "No offense intended, and present company excluded."

I grin. "None taken! It's not an unusual description for a reporter. Tell me why you think the reporters here are fools and idiots."

Albert smooths back his big shock of black, curly hair and eyes me. "Ever had any dealings with Albert Fall?"

I shrug my shoulders and shake my head. "Never met the man."

"Count your blessings. Fall has the press wrapped around his little finger. He's slick and a good attorney. He's manipulated reporters into believing Oliver Lee and his gang are Jesus Christ and the Apostles, when, in fact, they're no-good bastards. Fall will do anything to get them off, and the idiot press will praise him for it."

"I can understand how you must feel. I just hope you understand that for me to do my job, I need to talk to both sides. Beer okay with you fellows?"

"Yes, sir!"

I wave at the Mexican waiter, hold up three fingers, and mouth *beer*.

"Jack, if I'm not being too nosy, what was that business about Judge Parker insisting on seeing you right away?"

He smirks, rolling his eyes. "It was all Fall's doing. It was just a play for a little sympathy and additional newspaper reports to influence potential jurors. He told Parker I had threatened to kill him and that he feared for his life. What bull! Fall isn't afraid of me. Parker wanted to know what I said about killing Fall, so I told him." Jack crosses his arms and sits back in his chair, looking at me.

"Come on Jack. What did you say?"

He grins. "Pretty much exactly the same thing I said about him on the stage this afternoon—that I wasn't going to kill anyone, but if they ever found Father's bones, the man I'd go after is Albert Bacon Fall!"

"What'd Parker do?"

"He told me to stay out of trouble and made me post a five hundred dollar bond to be sure I did."

"Judge Parker must think the Fountain side is after blood. I went walking around town this afternoon and saw armed guards at the jailhouse door."

The brothers look at each other and shake their heads. Albert says, "Just another Fall move to gain sympathy for Lee and Gililland. He's claiming there are death threats against him, Lee, and Gililland. Since Lee can't have a firearm in jail, the judge is letting him have guards—of his choosing, I might add—at the jailhouse door. Lee claims Pat Garrett will shoot him in the back if he has a chance. Bull! Do you have any idea who's guarding Lee?"

I shake my head.

"It's Gene Rhodes! He helped hide Lee and Gililland when they were on the run from Garrett, and he even rode with them on the train when they came down to Las Cruces to turn themselves in. Now he's sitting at the jailhouse door with the authority to shoot anyone who tries to get in. It's a damn outrage! Rhodes ought to be in jail for criminal complicity in hiding those outlaws. Not only that, Lee is officially in the custody of George Curry, the new sheriff of Otero County. Curry and Lee have been friends for years. You know who Curry's deputy is?"

I shake my head.

"Tom Tucker! He used to work for Lee. There's a warrant out for his arrest for murder! But you know what?"

I shake my head.

"He'll get off. Claim it was self-defense while he was carrying out his official duties as a law officer." Albert takes a swallow of beer and pounds the table. "I'm telling you, Quent, the Federal government ought to come in here and put the whole territory under martial law. Why, every time Garrett or Catron comes up with a witness who will hang Lee and his gang, the witness unexpectedly dies, disappears, or suddenly refuses to testify."

He holds up his hand, his fingers spread, and begins to count, folding down a finger with each name. "First, Les Dow, who had cold, hard evidence that was used to get indictments against Lee and McNew for cattle rustling, was gunned down in the dark at Eddy by person or persons unknown.

"Second, Kent Kearney, who heard Gililland tell him that Father's murder was a really slick job and things were a lot quieter now that he was gone, was killed in a shootout with Lee and Gililland.

"Third, T. J. Daily, a witness who lives in Larimore, North Dakota, wrote Catron that he used to work for Lee and that, while he was at Lee's ranch, he found out what had happened and who did what. Daily claims to know where the bodies are. He was run out of the country by Lee's gang. He wrote Catron that he was ready to testify. Now he's changed his mind. Says he's afraid to leave North Dakota.

"Fourth, Pat Garrett found three Mexican witnesses who were down in an arroyo cutting up a beef when they saw the riders pass by with the bodies. They've disappeared into

Mexico—nobody knows where. Finally, there's the old Indian who was with Mr. Van Patten's search party and who later found the Mexicans. He got the story out of them. Now he's disappeared, too."

Albert pounds the table again, making the empty beer glasses jump. "But maybe, just maybe, Garrett has the man who'll hang them all because his story, according to Catron, will destroy Lee's alibi."

I shake my head. "Lee and his men sound like bad outlaws, more like what we'd call gangsters back East. Men who are so powerful they do what they want, when they want, and kill anyone who gets in the way."

Albert and Jack nod in agreement. Albert reaches across the table and takes my hand as he stands up. "That's exactly right, Quent. It's been a pleasure meeting you, and we thank you for the beer. Guess we'll see you at the trial."

"You can count on it. Good luck!"

Chapter 6
Sadie's Witnesses

A lantern casts its pale yellow light over the porch of the Ocean Grove. Sadie, wearing pearls and a stylish dress, sits in a rocker, sipping from a china cup. As I ascend the porch steps, she smiles and motions me over to a straight-back chair beside her. "Good evening, Mr. Peach. Come join me and tell me what you think of our fine little village. Can I pour you a spot of tea?"

I ease down on the chair beside her small tea table and take in the peace of the evening. "Yes, ma'am, tea would be welcome. Aren't you up late?"

"I never go to bed until all my ladies are in for the evening. Still waiting on Ruth. I'd be pleased to send her down to your room when she gets back if you're lonely. She's a real beauty, she is."

I shake my head. "I'm not lonely now, but I might be talking to you about some company before the trial is over."

"Well, just let me know, and I'll fix you right up. You found any interesting stories?"

"I just had a good talk with Jack and Albert Fountain that might lead to something. They're convinced Lee's attorney, Fall, has the press wrapped around his finger and is faking death threats to gain sympathy with potential jury members. Jack is sure Fall is the brains behind the murders and that Lee will do whatever Fall tells him. After listening to the Fountains, I'm curious why you're so certain Lee and his men are innocent."

Sadie stares off toward the lights on Main Street before looking in my eyes. A minute passes. "All right, I'll tell you what I think, but you can't ever quote me on anything. If you do, it'll ruin my business. You and I will be on the outs, and I'll swear by all that's holy that I never told you any such thing. I'll say that you're just a lyin', no-good newspaperman who got himself killed because of those lies." She smiles. "We do understand each other, don't we, Mr. Peach?"

Defensively, I raise my right hand, palm up. "Yes, ma'am! I promise I'll never use your name on anything I write." Her eyes tell me this is one promise I'd best keep. I take out my notepad and push back my boater. "All my friends call me Quent, and I wish you would, too."

She smiles. "All right, Quent. So why am I so sure Lee and Gililland are innocent? First of all, I know a lady who can prove the territory's key witness is lyin' through his teeth. She even filed an affidavit as to what she saw right after the murders, believin' it'd likely show Lee and his boys were guilty. What that deposition shows is that they couldn't have been out killing Fountain and the little boy the way Jack Maxwell claims, because they were all the way over on the road to Tularosa around dawn the day after the Fountains disappeared. They couldn't have had time to travel that far if they'd killed the Fountains. Pat Garrett claims her deposition is a lie 'cause it ain't consistent with Maxwell's statement. Garrett and that hothead, Charlie Perry, sheriff over at Roswell, they're hot to collect all the reward money they can for convicting Lee. I suspect Garrett needs that money bad 'cause he's always in a credit hole up to his eyeballs from gamblin'. He'd starve to death if he had to play poker for a living."

"Who is this lady?"

"Eva Taylor. She worked for me a time or two after old Taylor left her high and dry. She ain't got the best of reputations. But she ain't got no reason to lie, either. She's just trying to do what's right. There's another reason Garrett can ignore her sworn testimony. He knows them prosecution attorneys will never consider it—even if it means hanging innocent men."

I drain the rest of the tea from my cup and ask, "Why won't Albert Fall use Eva's testimony to rebut Garrett's witness?"

"Jury'll think he's paying a loose woman to lie for his clients. Fall ain't likely to use her testimony unless Catron has him cornered, and that ain't goin' to happen."

"Where's Eva Taylor now? I'd very much like to talk to her."

Shaking her head, Sadie says, "I don't know. Last I heard, she was headed up north somewhere, maybe up to Denver."

I write myself a note to ask Chief about tracking her down.

Slowly rocking, Sadie stares off into the night. She cradles her cup in her hands and speaks as if she's thinking aloud. "After a man's been pleasured by one of my ladies, he'll tell her things he wouldn't dare say out loud anywhere else. Part of what my girls earn comes from helping their customers unburden their souls as well as their bodies."

I'm burning with curiosity as I flip to a fresh page in my notepad. "What have your girls heard?"

She nods. "Tales about a meeting of some ranchers in late '94 over around Socorro. Ed Brown and Slick Miller called the meeting, but Fountain sent Miller to prison a few months later. Lee, McNew, Gililland, and several others from around Tularosa were supposed to have been there, but for the most part, it was just ranchers from around Socorro. They were worried about bein' framed and sent to prison. Fountain had 'em by the short hairs. He'd already sent a bunch of their friends to the penitentiary.

"During their meetin', the ranchers picked out a couple of places where they could ambush Fountain and MacDonald, who's the president of the stockman's association and who's payin' Fountain. They talked about how to hide Fountain's body so it would look like he just up and took off somewhere. He did that once, you know—just disappeared for a couple of weeks and then came back. Never did say where he went. After they figured out what they's gonna do, Brown said that each of 'em had to get Fountain's blood on their hands and swear never to talk about the meeting on penalty of death.

"Lee said, 'You boys are crazy. Killin' Fountain won't solve nothin'; it'll just make things worse. There's better ways to stop him. Fall can pull the political levers and beat the Republicans, speculators, and Catron's ring at every turn. That'll take the wind outta Fountain's sails. You go killing Fountain, and you'll bring down the thunder.'

"Then Gililland said, 'Now, Oliver, this is a slick plan. Old Fountain's framin' folks and throwin' 'em in jail right and left. We gotta back these boys. This'll make things quieten down.'

"Oliver replied, 'No, these boys are makin' a big mistake.' Then Lee started to leave, and Ed Brown got burning angry. He told Lee he couldn't back out because he knew too much. Lee told him he wasn't backin' out because he never was in, never heard a word that was said, never was interested in hearin' it. Brown was reachin' for his pistol, but Lee already had his in his hand, cocked and pointed right between Brown's eyes. Lee told him to forget about it, that he and his boys ain't been there and ain't heard nothing. All Brown could do was sputter that Lee was goin' to get in trouble tryin' to go it alone."

Sadie pauses and looks at me. "So what do you think happened?"

I shake my head as I scribble my notes.

"The Fountains were murdered at one of the places Brown's crowd planned to use. Tracks led away from the murder scene straight for Lee's ranch on the other side of the Jarilla Mountains.

"Quent, Lee ain't stupid. He'd never leave tracks back to his own ranch house or ask his women to lie for him—'cause they wouldn't. They won't lie for anybody.

"All this may sound mighty incriminatin', but it ain't proof those boys at the Brown meetin' did it. I know you understand that."

I nod as Sadie continues. "Four or five months after the murders, Sheriff Bursum over to Socorro and a Pinkerton dick named Sayers had Brown in jail and were trying to get 'im to confess to the murders or tell who did 'em.

"About that time a man named Brady—I don't think that was his real name—showed up here. Brady wanted to buy a few days with Nadine. He had plenty of money, and we made a right nice bundle off him.

"Nadine was scared to death of him. He kept having bad dreams, wakin' up in a sweat, and grabbin' his gun to shoot whoever was after him. Almost shot her once. Nadine was ready to leave, but he begged her to stay. He told her he was friends with a man the law was tryin' to break, and he kept dreamin' the law was chasing him hard. Promised he'd leave his gun unloaded, so Nadine stayed with him.

"After he left, we kept our mouths shut. I don't want any hired guns after me and my girls.

"Brady stayed with Nadine for three days. He told Nadine he was goin' to California, but I know for a fact he headed straight for El Paso and the border."

I purse my lips in a silent whistle. "So you think Brady and Brown were part of what happened to the Fountains, and Brady disappeared into Mexico a few months later? Do you think Brown would talk to me?"

Sadie grimaces. "Brown and me have had a few words in the past couple of years. He has a niece who works over at the Black Range Café. She's a good girl, and I've helped her out a time or two. Before she showed up in Hillsboro, she was livin' on Brown's ranch when the Fountains disappeared. Brown's been tryin' to make her come back. He told her she'd be mighty sorry if he ever hears she's tellin' tales about his business. I told him if he knew what was good for him, he'd leave her alone, and he has, so far." Sadie looks in my eyes and squeezes my arm. "Quent, stay away from him. Brown hires assassins to get rid of people he don't like, and I'm sure he ain't about to talk to no reporters.

"What me and the girls think don't mean nothin'. To lawyers it's just hearsay evidence from whores. Even if I told what I know, they'd still have to find Brady and break him or Brown. Bursum and the Pinkertons couldn't break Brown. What I do know is that those boys on trial now ain't guilty of killin' little 'enry Fountain."

I frown and ask, "Aren't you worried they'll be convicted if you remain silent?"

"Yes, I've lost some sleep over it, but Albert Fall is a fine lawyer. Moreover, even if they're convicted, they'll never go to jail."

"What do you mean?"

"About a week ago, a cowboy spent some time with Nadine."

I smile and shake my head.

"He told her that him and two other boys had stationed relays of fast horses from Hillsboro all the way across the border and down into Mexico. It's nothin' Lee and Gililland knows about. If the verdict goes against 'em, those boys are going to break 'em out of the courthouse right then and there and point 'em south."

I shake my head. "Who told Nadine about this plan?"

Sadie smiles. "She ain't saying."

"What do you think about Fall claiming someone is paying assassins to kill him, Lee, and Gililland?"

She frowns and shakes her head. "Fall ain't above playing for sympathy if he thinks it'll do him some good, and if Fall has even a hint there's a threat while his clients can't defend themselves, then he's going to do everything in his power to be sure they're safe. That includes telling God and everybody else they need protection."

"So you think the threat is real? If someone really wanted to kill them, why would they warn them?"

I see the corners of her lips turn up. "It's obvious you don't know the code."

"What code?"

"The one all these fellows live by, just like it was a law made in Washington. It came in here from Texas with the cowboys. The code says that before you can kill your enemy, you have to warn him so he has a chance to leave the country. If he don't, he's fair game anytime, anywhere, in any way, except when you're on neutral territory. Fall's been warned, and he's still here. He's fair game now. Fall ain't takin' any chances. There're men here who'd take great pleasure in killin' Fall—old Ben Williams, for example—but they ain't the ones that'll get him. It's the ones that ain't warned him an' don't live by the code he's worried about."

I try to remember all the names I've heard that might fill that bill but draw a blank. "Who are you talking about?"

She casts a baleful eye at me. "The ones that's been losing to Lee when they tried to move in on his operation. The ones who want to use the murder of his attorney to knock him out of operation or make him so weak he won't challenge 'em and will leave the country. The big-time businessmen and speculators, Republicans all, that's who. They play dangerous and dirty when they're crossed."

"Who specifically?"

She shakes her head and stares again off into the darkness. "I ain't goin' to say no more about it. You just find out for yourself. I know you will. Just be real careful not to get between blood enemies with guns, or you might get shot."

We sit in silence for a while, and then I ask her something I've been puzzling over most of the evening. "How do I get into the jail to interview Lee or Gililland? From what I saw, only people who know them get in the jail."

She laughs aloud. "You've come to the right place for that one. I'm providing the meals for Lee an' Gililland from right here at the Ocean Grove Restaurant. I'll ask Fall if it's all right, and he can tell Lee and Gililland that it's all right to talk to you. Tell me when you want to talk to 'em, and I'll tell my cook, Tom Ying, that he don't have to find nobody to carry that meal up to the jail. How's that?"

"Wonderful! That'd be a great help. Thanks very much."

An attractive, well-dressed, young woman with bright red lips comes down the street toward the porch. "Ah, here comes Ruth now, the last chick in from the fox's den. I'll be telling you good night and good luck."

"Thanks for all the information, Sadie. See you tomorrow."

"Yes, sir, I expect you will. Remember, luv, don't you go tryin' to get no story out of Mr. Brown."

"Yes, ma'am. That's good advice."

Chapter 7
Persia Brown

The next morning, I go a couple of blocks up Main Street and find a small restaurant wedged between the telegraph office and a mercantile store, where the smell of frying steaks mingled with bacon and fresh bread fills my nose. It's time for breakfast at the Black Range Café.

Three cowboys sit at a table near the door and sip coffee from big white mugs. Smoke from their cigarettes curls toward the low ceiling. Amid a rattle of pots, a young woman appears from a doorway. Her long, black hair is pulled into a bun on the top of her head. Her lips, dark almond eyes, and smooth skin make me think about things other than breakfast.

Small bosomed and willowy, she wears a long white apron over the front of her calico dress. Without apparent effort, she carries a large tray covered with big plates filled with eggs, fried slices of baked bread, steaks, bacon, beans, red chili sauce, and sliced tomatoes. Seeing me, she smiles, showing beautiful, straight, white teeth, and nods toward a small table by the window as she heads for the cowboys' table.

They sit up straight, and one of them greets her with, "Boy, howdy, Persia, you got here just in time. Thought we's gonna have to salt our boots an' start a-chewin'."

She laughs with them and says, "It's worth waitin' on, boys. Dig in!" Then she picks up her tray and shifts to my table. "Howdy. Welcome to the Black Range Café. Name's Persia Brown. Friends call me Persia. What can I get for you?"

"Hi, Persia. My friends call me Quent. I'll have a plate of what you just brought those gentlemen there and a mug of coffee."

She lights up the room again with her brilliant smile. "Yes, sir. I'll be right back with your coffee."

One of the cowboys hears me and grins. "Mister, you're a-needin' glasses if you think these here jaspers is gentlemen." They all laugh and so do I.

Persia returns with a steaming mug of syrupy, black coffee and a linen napkin wrapped around plain flatware. The cowboys are quiet as they shovel down their breakfasts. The light steadily brightens on the street. More shops begin to appear in the increasing light, and as they open, customers appear. A nattily dressed man stops next door and unlocks the Western Union office.

Soon my plate appears on Persia's tray. She refills my cup and collects empty plates from the next table as the cowboys finish a last cup, pick their teeth, and roll cigarettes. Snatches of their conversation catch my attention.

"You feel right about where we got the horses stashed?" "Todd, when're you gonna tell Oliver and Jim?" ". . . ain't nobody gonna catch 'em." ". . . ain't no telegraph thataway." ". . . ain't gonna wear mine in a holster, fits in my boot just fine, ain't no deputy gonna see it till it's too late."

Sadie's story sets my thoughts in a whirl. I realize these are the boys planning to spring Lee and Gililland. A couple more slurps of coffee, clinking coins tossed on the table, and they're out the door, mounted, and riding off down the street toward Lee's camp.

Persia is busing their table when I wave her over and tell her I'm ready to pay for my breakfast.

"That'll be two bits."

I drop a quarter and a nickel into her palm. "Yes, ma'am.

Pleasure to meet you, Persia. Do you mind if I ask you a personal question?"

She blushes. "Depends on how personal it is."

"You said your name was Brown. Are you any relation to Ed Brown? I think he has a place over by San Marcial?"

She makes a face. "He's my uncle. Can't say I'm proud to claim it though. Why?"

"Just curious. I've heard he might know something about the Fountain murders."

The creamy skin on her neck turns a delicate pink. Shaking her head, she stares at a knot in the plank flooring. "There's nothing I can say about that. He's mean and vengeful. Before Daddy died, they got into it over Ed using hired killers."

"I'm staying down the street at the Ocean Grove Hotel." I hand her my card. "I'm a reporter for the *San Francisco Examiner*, doing background stories on the trial. I'd very much like to chat with you about what you know about your uncle, even if I can't quote you. May I take you to supper this evening?"

She smiles. "All right, as long as we don't eat here. I have a little room in the back. I'll meet you here in the café at seven. How's that?"

"That's just fine. I'm looking forward to the pleasure of your company."

CHAPTER 8
EUGENE MANLOVE RHODES

Tipping my hat to Persia, I walk out the door, take a few steps, and enter the Western Union office. A man in a white shirt, garters around his sleeves, is busy sorting through a stack of papers. He looks up as the bell over the door tinkles.

"Morning! Be right with you."

"No hurry, take your time."

The place is large for a Western Union office. Four chairs line one wall, and there are two tables with chairs where customers can sit and write. Two silent key stations sit side by side behind the counter as the clerk quickly works through the stack of papers until he finds the one for which he's searching and sets it aside.

"Now, sir, what can I do for you?"

I hand him a business card. "My name is Quentin Peach. I'm a reporter for the *San Francisco Examiner.* I'll be sending reports back to my editor on the trial and will probably be here about this time every morning."

He shakes my hand, his brow forming puzzled wrinkles. "Belvedere Brooks, telegraph operator and general flunky for my uncle, who's a big cheese in the Western Union operation. Seems like I remember the *Examiner* already has a reporter here. Yeah, his name is Seymour, isn't it?"

"That's right, Seymour works for the *Examiner,* too. He's covering the trial, and I'm assigned to do background stories. My editor wants me to open an account with you that's different from Seymour's. Fifty dollars enough to establish an account for my reports?"

"That'll work. We'll keep a running tab for you. When it gets down to ten dollars, I'll let you know. Anything to send now?"

In my portfolio is a short summary of yesterday's interviews and a request to track down Eva Taylor. "I'd appreciate it if you kept these reports confidential—even from Mr. Seymour."

He grins. "Not to worry. Western Union and my uncle require me to keep information from all our clients completely confidential. I'll transmit it myself and personally handle all the paperwork."

To keep an eye on the comings and goings, I find a bench at the courthouse and jail. One of the guards from yesterday afternoon, who appears to be in his late twenties, sits on the steps below the jailhouse door. A shotgun leans against the step walls close beside him. He stares at a small notepad on his knee, a stubby, yellow pencil clenched tightly in his fingers. He jots down a line, pauses, scratches through a few words, and then writes more. His hair is cut short, and with the exception of the intense concentration with which he writes, he looks in every detail how city folk imagine a cowboy.

It's a few minutes after seven. I read the *Sierra County Advocate* and am surprised at how evenhanded the reporting is for both sides preparing for trial.

A wagon pulled by a beautifully matched team rattles up to the narrow walkway in front of the jail. A man and an elderly, gray-haired lady sit on the front seat; a young woman sits on the second bench with a little girl beside her. Two children, an older girl and boy, ride on the tailgate. The man steps down, graceful as a cat, from the wagon's front bench. The air is so still I can hear every word that passes between them.

"Mornin', Gene. Writin' a new story?" the man asks as he

clips stanchions to the horse's harness.

The jail guard has a lisp, but he speaks educated English. "Howdy, Bill. Just a little poem for my girl up in Apalachin, New York. Mornin', Mrs. Lee and Mrs. McNew. How're you children doing back there?" The adults greet him as the kids giggle and climb off the wagon. Sitting on the back seat, Mrs. McNew, who everyone calls "Nettie," hikes her dress and climbs down from the wagon without assistance. She herds her children through the jailhouse door held open by the guard. He closes the door behind them and sits back down on the steps, sees me, nods, and resumes his writing.

I fold my paper under my arm and stroll over to him. He doesn't look up from his writing as he says, "Howdy. Curiosity get the best of you? Can't let you in the jail right now."

I stick out my hand. "Actually, I just wanted to ask you a few questions. My name is Quentin Peach. I'm a journalist for the *San Francisco Examiner* writing background stories for the trial. There's another fellow from my paper, Peyton Seymour, who's covering the trial proceedings."

He takes my hand and gives it a cordial shake. "Howdy, Mr. Peach. Mine is Eugene 'Odes. Just Gene to my friends. I lisp some and can't even pronounce my name correctly." He writes *Rhodes* on his notepad and shows it to me. I nod, and he continues, "I met your *compadre,* Seymour. Can't say I like him much. He gets obnoxious pronto. Thought I was going to have to toss him off the steps here a day or two ago."

I nod. "Yes, sir, Mr. Seymour can be a little pushy sometimes. I'm just here for stories that'll help our readers understand what's really going on. What with New Mexico pushing to become a state, there's a lot of interest about how and why the Fountains were murdered. I was just wondering if you might tell me who those folks were who just went in the jail."

"Don't guess there's any harm in that. The gentleman with

the ladies is Bill McNew. He just got out of jail after a trial in Silver City about a month ago. Pat Garrett held him illegally in Las Cruces for almost a year. Claimed Bill was in on murdering Fountain and his son. That arrest left his wife, Nettie, who's also Oliver's niece, alone out in the middle of nowhere, while she was pregnant and due to deliver in a couple months. She lost the baby 'cause a storm blew in on 'em and gave it pneumonia.

"When Bill went to trial over in Silver City, the territory decided they wouldn't prosecute him. After all Nettie went through, they wouldn't prosecute—they even asked Judge Parker for a three-month extension. Damned, no-good Republicans!"

"Well, that's awful! Why'd Garrett do that? I thought he was a good lawman."

Rhodes sticks out his lower lip and shakes his head. "Not in this case! I think he's right decent overall. I like him fair enough. But he's sure got a blind eye when it comes to Oliver Lee."

"Why is that?"

Rhodes shrugs. "My guess is Garrett's got a bigger hunger for poker than I do, and, Mr. Peach, that's pretty big. He stays near broke most of the time. I think maybe the thought of all that reward money has made him blind and crazy."

"I got you off track. Who's the other lady?"

"She's Mrs. Mary Lee, Oliver's mother. This trial business has been rough on 'er, too. The three children are the McNews'."

"Do you suppose those folks would talk to me? Maybe on Sunday?"

"Mr. Peach, I can't speak for those folks. Mrs. Mary and Mrs. Nettie, they'll be in church on Sunday. Maybe they'd talk to you after Sunday dinner. I'll ask 'em, if you like. You know, sorta introduce you and all."

"Gene, I'd very much appreciate it if you would. And, please, it's just Quent."

"Okay, Quent, I'll see what I can do."

"Just one more question. You know anything about the story claiming Ed Brown is one of the killers?"

Rhodes crosses his arms and stares at me for a moment. "No, not directly, but I've heard the same tales and wouldn't put it past him. I don't like him, never have. He's a mean *hombre.* But he's smart enough to hire killers to do work for him. I think Oliver and Jim know something about Brown and the Fountains, but they'd hang before they'd say anything. There's a lot more going on in this trial than most folks realize. Fall knows, but he's playing his cards close to the vest, so it's not for me to jaw about things when I don't know all the facts."

"What about the death threats Colonel Fountain was getting about the prosecution of Lee and McNew? Seems like the only ones to gain from him dropping the case are Lee and McNew."

Rhodes smiles. "It's a setup. Anybody who knew Colonel Fountain knew he wouldn't back down because of threats. It'd just make him bear down that much harder. Lee and McNew didn't make those threats. Lee's too smart, and McNew and Gililland do what Lee tells 'em.

"I think whoever sent those notes was setting Lee up. Brown might have been in on the killing, but I ask, who had the most to gain if Lee and his boys lose their ranches? If Colonel Fountain is killed while prosecuting Lee, who's going to be blamed? Lee and his boys. If Lee and his boys are hanged for killing the Fountains, who gains the most? The Blue Water Company, which wants Lee's water rights; and Mr. Catron, who wants to put away a political enemy. Who's doing his damnedest to be sure Lee and his boys are convicted? Who's offered to work the case for no pay? Mr. Catron, that's who. This trial is part of a game, Catron's game."

I frown, trying to sort this all out. "But what about all the incriminating witnesses disappearing? Fountain's range detective, Les Dow, shot down by person or persons unknown in the dark of night, the witness in North Dakota, and the Mexicans who are afraid to testify?"

Gene crosses his arms and cocks his head to one side. "If Dow framed Lee and McNew, Lee and McNew would want his head. They're known all over this range as dangerous men, good with guns, deadly, afraid of nothing. Still, if they killed Dow, it would have been face-to-face, not in the dark. On the other hand, if a good attorney like Fall gets Dow on the stand and makes him spill the beans on who paid him to frame Lee, then the men behind the frame-up are in big trouble. They don't need Dow to testify, and his very presence at the trial puts 'em at risk. Now, who do you think killed Dow?

"If they're so important, why aren't the Mexicans and the witness in North Dakota here to be cross-examined by Albert Fall? Probably the same reason Les Dow isn't here. Suppose Fall isn't here. Suppose Fall gets killed. You reckon those witnesses would appear? You're a smart man. You figure it out."

"Very interesting conspiracy theory, Gene. I'll look into it. Thanks for talking to me."

Gene looks at the ground and shuffles his feet. "I've got a request."

"Sure. Anything I can do."

"Well, I'm working on becoming a writer. I've written stories about this country, but haven't published any yet. Would you read one and tell me what you think?"

"I'd be happy to read it. I'm staying at the Ocean Grove, or you can give it to me any time while I'm here at the trial."

A big grin spreads across his face. "Thanks, Quent! I'll get it to you soon as I can find some free time to write you out a copy. I'm much obliged."

I nod and glance over at the courthouse. "Looks like it's getting busy. I'd better get over there if I want to get a seat."

"Yes, sir. It's gonna be a show, and tickets are going fast. See you later."

I salute him with a tip of my hat and walk around to the front of the courthouse. Rhodes has given me a big bone to chew. *Is this trial about a big conspiratorial land grab? Is it just local gangsters throwing their weight around and trying to blame the powerful? Is it one gang trying to get revenge on another? Are Lee, McNew, and Gililland truly innocent?*

Chapter 9
The Trial Begins, 26 May 1899

The courtroom is packed. An occasional breeze pushes in fresh air. Hand fans from the funeral parlor are in motion. I wonder how hot it will be at noon. There is a low hum of conversation between neighbors.

Checking my watch, I see it's a few minutes before nine. As we wait, I scribble notes on what Gene Rhodes and Sadie have told me. Their stories are not at all what I expected after talking to the Fountain brothers.

The hum of conversation falls silent and heads turn. From the short hallway at the top of the steps, a man calls, "Excuse us! Make way, please! Excuse us!" Sheriff Max Kahler and the same deputy who escorted Jack Fountain to see Judge Parker come up the aisle followed by two men. One is in his mid-thirties. He moves with easy grace and gravitas. He's handsome, with eyes that droop at the corners, a full mustache, and short, well-groomed hair. There is a no-nonsense look about him. This is Oliver Lee, and women's eyes follow his every step.

The second man, James Gililland, maybe in his late twenties, pulls at his stiff, white collar and tie with a finger. He appears uncomfortable in a suit, but he winks and grins as he gives little hand waves to acquaintances on either side of the aisle. He is tall and has a muscular upper body and a face framed by carefully combed hair.

The sheriff escorts them through the swinging gate in the dividing rail. They stop at the defense table in front of five chairs next to the rail, pull back two middle chairs, and sit down. Three well-dressed gentlemen carrying attorney cases soon join them. The tall, distinguished-looking Albert Fall takes the chair to Lee's right next to the rail gate. He has a big, bushy mustache, a full head of long, curly hair, and eyes that quickly sweep the bench rows where prospective jurors slouch. The other two defense attorneys, Harry Daugherty and Harvey Fergusson, appear a bit younger than Fall and are all business as they acknowledge the defendants and sit with Lee and Gililland. Daugherty is a former district attorney in Socorro, and Harvey Fergusson is an Albuquerque attorney.

The prosecutors follow the defense attorneys. In the lead is an older, heavyset man with bushy, gray eyebrows that match his mustache. His rumpled suit looks like he slept in it. His shirt and string tie are not much better. This is Tom Catron. The other prosecutors, W.B. Childers, an Albuquerque attorney, and R.P. Barnes, district attorney from Silver City, are younger and have a hungry look.

The McNews and Lee's mother enter and find the bench space saved for them behind Lee and Gililland. McNew's ice-blue eyes survey the courtroom and rest momentarily on me before moving on. His eyes hold a fearless, aggressive quality that would make anyone want to stay out of his way. A man wearing a sheriff's star opens the gate and steps past the rail. Not far behind is Tom Tucker, who nods at me in recognition from our stage ride. Tucker finds a seat in a row reserved for witnesses. The sheriff is clean-shaven and tall. He has a shock of curly, dark brown hair. Since Tucker appears to be his deputy, I assume the man is George Curry, sheriff of Otero County. He has official custody of Lee and Gililland, but he now acts as a deputy for Sheriff Kahler, since the trial is in Sierra County.

Glancing around the courtroom, I see Seymour and his reporter friends leaning against the wall on the other side of the room. Seymour sees me, grins, and flicks a forefinger salute off his brow. I smile and nod back.

The court clerk and stenographer take their seats. Sheriff Kahler stands and calls for the crowd to come to order and to stand as Judge Franklin Parker enters and sits down. I see a number of distinguished-looking people sitting in the witness rows. The Fountain brothers sit on the far side of the room, arms crossed. Around them are other members of the Fountain family and their friends. I wonder what the brothers must be thinking. I recall the old cliché: the wheels of justice grind slowly but exceedingly fine. I hope it's true.

My attention moves back toward the bench. The bailiff reads the indictment for Case No. 2618, Territory of New Mexico versus Oliver M. Lee and James R. Gililland, who are accused of murdering Henry Fountain.

Judge Parker asks how the defendants plead. Fall stands and states in a voice loud and unequivocal, "Not guilty!"

Many smile and nod, except the group supporting the Fountains. Judge Parker asks, "Mr. Catron, is the prosecution ready to proceed?"

Catron stands slowly and nods with great dignity. "The territory is ready, Your Honor!"

"Mr. Fall, is the defense ready?"

Fall speaks in measured tones. "The defense is ready, Your Honor."

"Very well. The clerk will call the names on the venire. Gentlemen of the Defense and Prosecution, select your jury from the good citizens of Sierra County. Remember that your preemptory challenges are limited and cannot be rescinded once made."

The clerk begins his list. The third man called speaks only Spanish. The judge holds a brief sidebar while he and the attorneys confer on an acceptable translator. A young man named

Chavez is summoned from the prospective jurors. He's of medium height and appears friendly and easygoing. He speaks with the judge and attorneys at the bench and takes a seat next to the witness chair. The judge bangs his gavel and tells the clerk to resume calling his list of prospective jurors.

It is a show worth watching as Fall and Catron interrogate ranchers, farmers, miners, skilled craftsmen, businessmen, cooks, and prospectors. Each side probes for bias for and against the defendants, looking for neutral points of view or slight advantages they might exploit for their side of the case. As potential members of the jury are called, Lee often whispers to Fall, who nods and makes notes before he questions the prospective jurors. Gililland pays little attention to who is selected for the jury. By eleven-thirty, a jury of eligible men is obtained and peremptory challenges begin.

By noon, eleven jurors have been seated, and each side has fourteen challenges left. The jury pool is almost gone. Judge Parker calls a dinner recess until two and instructs Sheriff Kahler to begin summoning another venire.

The courtroom empties. Outside, the men cluster into groups of four or five for a smoke. Women herd children, who've been playing outside, home to eat and to do chores. I stay seated to watch Sheriff Kahler and his deputies lead the prisoners back to jail. Oliver Lee has attracted my attention. Lee is all business. Lee's charisma invites immediate respect or, perhaps, fear. Gililland reminds me of a big, gangly kid.

Chapter 10
Ben Williams

Last to leave the courtroom, I see the groups of men having a smoke in the shade on the north side of the courthouse begin to break up. Jack Fountain walks away from a man sitting on the foundation wall near the steps behind the courthouse. Wearing a flat-brimmed hat and gentleman's coat, the man rests his elbows on his knees as he smokes a cigar. His belly hangs over a gun belt filled with cartridges, the butt of a revolver peeking out the edge of his coat. He has a plain, hard face with close-set eyes, a face easy to remember, and his hair is very short. I walk over to chat. From the once-over he gives me, I figure he is or was a lawman.

I stick out my hand. His grip is firm, muscular. "Hello, I'm Quentin Peach, a reporter with the *San Francisco Examiner.* I saw you up in the courtroom and wondered if you'd mind answering a few questions."

He blows a puff of blue smoke up into the still, noon air and nods. "Howdy. Figured you was a reporter. Name's Williams, Ben Williams." His chest visibly swells. "I'm going to be a witness here in a day or two."

"Well, then, you're a man who ought to be interviewed. Shall we sit here, or can I buy you dinner while we talk?"

"We can talk here. Don't usually eat much dinner anyways. What do you want to know?"

I pull out my pad and pencil. "Are you a witness for the defense or prosecution?"

He grins. "Mr. Peach, if you knew anything at all about this case, you'd know I'm a key witness for the prosecution. I've had a lot of experience with Lee's gang and their bastard attorney. I was working undercover as a range detective for Colonel Fountain when he and little Henry disappeared."

I give him a big smile. "Wow! Tell me about yourself and your experiences with the Lee gang."

He takes a long draw on his cigar and stares at the ground.

"I've been doing law work most of my life. I've always been pretty good with a gun and a hard man to whip in a fight. I had to prove that quite a few times. In one of my first jobs, I had to make collections and repossessions for defaults on installment payments to the Singer Sewing Machine Company."

I frown, and he laughs. "You think collecting on sewing machines ain't dangerous? Reckon it is kind of comical, but I'll tell you, Mr. Peach, nothing makes them women living in the big lonesome madder than when some sonovabitch comes along and takes away their sewing machine. That machine helps 'em make nice clothes for themselves and their families. They ain't got no control over a drought killing their crops or if their cattle's been run off. And it ain't their fault their man can't make the payments. They say they'll pay when they get the money, but ol' Singer says, 'No, ma'am, you got to pay on time or that sewing machine comes back to me.'

"That ain't fair in their eyes. Makes 'em see red thunder. Why, they'll shoot you with both barrels of a ten-gauge Greener when you're standing at their front door and not blink an eye. And you can make book that, when they get upset about losing their sewing machines, their menfolk won't hesitate to kill you, either. Why, you'd think you's about to steal one of their children.

"It was damned dangerous work, and I learned a lot about dealing with people. First rule is, you got to be tough, look like you mean business, and, aye God, never back down. Killin' one or two if you have to is better than gettin' your own tail shot full of holes and maybe having the whole family hanged if they kill you."

He stares off in the distance, perhaps lost in the mists of remembrance as his mind turns to another page in his life. "I was a United States deputy marshal for a while, too. About ten years ago, I was the chief deputy for Doña Ana County under Sheriff Lohman over in Las Cruces. Old Lohman didn't even like the country and had so many other irons in the fire a-runnin' his store in Las Cruces, that pretty soon I was doing the sheriff's job.

"The damned Democrats won the election in '92, and Guadalupe Ascarate became sheriff. He's a pretty good man, better'n old Lohman ever was. Only problem was, he did ever'thing that sonovabitch Fall told him to do—fired me and made Joe Morgan, McNew, Lee, and Gililland his part-time deputies. I was a marked man after that.

"It's a Cruces ordinance that only the law can pack iron in town, but I'd been the law and had men wanting to put a bullet in me for putting 'em in jail. And I'd been hired as a range detective by the stockman's association to do undercover work for Colonel Fountain. I did that while I was working as a cattle inspector for the New Mexico Sanitary Association. Point is, I needed to pack my gun while I was in Cruces, and it should have been all right. At first, old Ascarate didn't care. But Fall and them damn deputies did, and Ascarate wouldn't tell 'em otherwise.

"Every time I wore my guns in Cruces and Lee was around, he'd come take 'em off me, grinning all the while. He'd taunt me, too, sayin' something like, 'Come on, Williams, don't you want to try me before I take that gun away from you? You know if you shoot me, it'll be self-defense. Go on. Pull that smoke wagon.' I wanted to put a bullet in that sorry sonovabitch mighty bad, but I never tried it."

Williams's eyes, cold and flat, make me shiver inside. I wouldn't want this man staring at me across the business end of a gun. "Why didn't you try? You look tougher than him, more experienced, able to handle yourself."

"I am. But maybe you don't know about Lee's skill with guns. Rifle or revolver, it don't make no difference. He's fast, and he hits where he points his gun. I'm good, but he'd have blowed my brains out before I could even touch my piece. He's a dangerous killer. Ever'body in Cruces is afraid of him 'cept Fall, and that's the way they want it. Why, ever' time Lee went to court, he got off, and he didn't go at all as long as he was a deputy. Them other two—McNew is related to Lee 'cause he married Lee's niece, and Morgan is Fall's brother-in-law—they're meaner'n snakes and do exactly what Lee and Fall tells 'em. I'd kill all four of the bastards if I had half a chance."

His eyes squint into a far-away, dreamy look. "I had a chance to do just that a time or two after the colonel was murdered, but they got away. Pat Garrett, he knows a good man when he sees one. He hired me as a deputy when he became Sheriff of Doña Ana County. Fall and those other bastards knew I was after 'em and was gonna make things right for all the evil things they done. Garrett even told Lee he'd best not surrender to any posse I led."

My stubby pencil races to fill my note page. "Hope you'll pardon my saying so, Mr. Williams, but you seem to be in an awful rage just because Lee took your gun when they saw you in Las Cruces. Were there other things they did that stoked the fire in your eyes?"

Taking a last draw off his cigar and crushing the butt under his heel, he says, "Hell, yeah. Those bastards kept pushing it. Wouldn't cut me no slack. Me and Fall almost got into it a time or two, and I told him if me and him ever squared off alone, I'd kill him.

"One October night in '95, I was walking down the street going home after some detective work for the colonel over in the basin. We was getting mighty close to putting the clamps on Mr. Lee for stealing a big part of the Blue Water herd. It was darker than a coal mine, and I was just walking along, minding my own business. 'Bout the time I got to Deacon Young's law office, I come face-to-face with Fall and Morgan. They surprised me, and outta pure reflex, I reached for my pistol.

"I think Fall already had his out and was waiting for me to make a move, 'cause I know damn well I'm faster than he is. He started shooting, and one of his shots hit me in the left arm just above my elbow. It busted the bone—hurt like hell—and my left arm ain't been worth a damn since, never will be. That sonovabitch Morgan stood behind an awning post at the edge of the sidewalk and fired for my head."

He tilts forward and points to an ugly scar across the side of his head just above his ear. "Grazed me right there. I'm mighty lucky I ain't dead. He was so close, I got powder burns, and my face hairs was singed. I managed to get my pistol out with my right hand and get off a few shots myself, even put a bullet in Morgan's left arm. The sheriff come running, and the saloons emptied soon as the shooting started. It was all over purty quick, but when you're in a shootin', aye God, it feels like it's a lifetime."

I stand there, my pencil frozen to the paper. I've never heard a firsthand account of a gunfight, and it had never sunk in, for all the tales I'd heard, just how violent it sometimes is in the West.

Williams grins at me. "What's the matter, Peach?"

I shake my head. "This is violent, hard country, isn't it? What happened after the shooting stopped?"

"Fall and Morgan were the first to shoot, and they admitted they wanted to have it out with me once and for all, so Ascarate arrested 'em. A special session of the Doña Ana Country grand jury was convened to hear the evidence. A bunch of witnesses testified. Old Fall and Lee had 'em scared to death. Next thing I knew, they indicted me as the principal in the shooting, and Colonel Fountain as an accessory before the fact 'cause I worked for him! I'm telling you, it was a goddamn outrage. When the indictments got to Judge Bantz over in Silver City, he threw 'em out and said it was the damnedest thing he'd seen in all his years on the bench.

"I was gonna be laid up a right good while with my busted arm and decided the best thing for me to do was stay down to El Paso until I was healed up good enough to take care of myself in Cruces.

"Les Dow, one of my partners in Colonel Fountain's range detective work, come to see me ever' week or so. He told me he'd figured out how to get those bastards, Fall and Lee. He said all he needed was one hide that showed Lee'd been running brands on the Blue Water stock, and he knew just how to set it up. Once we had that evidence, Colonel Fountain was ready to put the clamps on 'em. Throwing those sonzabitches in jail for the next thirty years would set accounts right for all the evil they done me. I was just starting to get around some when word come that Lee had murdered the colonel and his little boy. Aye God, I put on my pants and headed for Las Cruces. There was gonna be hell to pay for what they done, and I was gonna be part of the collecting agency."

I spend a minute or two scratching down what he's told me, and then I review it with him. He nods that I have it right.

"I understand Mr. Dow was killed over in Eddy. How did he plan to get the hide that would prove Lee was changing brands?"

Williams laughs. "It was a pretty slick trick. Them Texans was always taking each other's cattle—you know a calf that ain't running with his mammy and never been branded gets branded by whoever can catch him. That there is the code them idjits live by. They never eat their own cattle. Old Dow found this calf that had this here odd-shaped spot on his forehead and already had a Blue Water brand on him. That spot made him real easy to pick out in the biggest of herds. Les, he had that brand fixed up to look like Lee's, and then run it in with Lee's stock just before the big fall roundup."

My disapproval must show on my face because Williams asks, "What's the matter, Peach? We knew that's what those thieves was doin', and they was damn good at it, too. We couldn't kill a few hundred head of stock just to find run-on brands, although we must have looked through a thousand hides around the butcher shops in Tularosa and La Luz. We decided Lee and McNew was running the Blue Water stock across the border and selling 'em down in Mexico for next to nothing. So Dow made us an example, that's all, to show ever'body what we was sure they did."

"Well, if you were so sure Lee was guilty, why didn't you use the evidence you'd found that convinced you?"

"Aw, Dow had a hide he'd got off a Mex family that had bought a couple of steers from a Lee man. It had a Lee brand on the outside, but there were the marks of a Blue Water brand bigger than life on the flesh side. Fowler, the other detective working with us, saw it, too. Damn if Dow didn't go and lose it. Couldn't find it nowhere, so old Les just made us up another one.

"He waited until the big roundup was just over and all the cattle had been separated by brands. For some reason, Lee didn't come to the fall roundup in'95. McNew went in his place. Didn't make no never mind since they was all in the same gang, and I was gonna fix McNew, too. Old Les, he found the steer with the special markings and bought it right off McNew for ten dollars more'n it was worth.

"While McNew was a-sittin' at the coffee pot, Dow took the steer and had it slaughtered and skinned. Sure enough, there was the Blue Water brand on the underside. Haw! He had the bill of sale from McNew, the hide that went with it, and witnesses who saw McNew sell the steer to him. He went and put the cuffs on McNew right then and hauled him off to Lincoln—wouldn't even let him stop at Lee's ranch to tell what happened.

"McNew posted a bond and come back to the grand jury when it met. At the grand jury, he swore up and down he was framed. But, aye God, we had him cold! He wasn't gonna get away with that one, and then, a week later, the sonzabitches murdered the colonel and his little boy and stole all his papers."

I think, *No wonder Lee and McNew believed they were being railroaded.* "Let me ask you another question, if you don't mind."

"Shore. If I know the answer, I'll tell you."

"What do you know about Ed Brown?"

He smiles, spits on the ground between his boots, and shakes his head.

"Brown's murderous and crooked as a snake, but that don't mean nothing in this case. Slick Miller tried to get out of jail by telling Governor Thornton a tale about Brown being in on the colonel's murder. Thornton brought in a Pinkerton—I think his name was Sayers—and him and the sheriff up to Socorro put Brown in jail on another rustlin' charge and tried to break him.

"Man sits in jail a month and don't tell you nothing—either you ain't gonna break him, or he ain't guilty. They never did get Brown to 'fess up. Brown's just a blowhard, likes to think he's mean, but he couldn't hold a candle to Lee and his boys. Believe me, Mr. Peach, there ain't nothin' to the rumors floatin' around that Brown did it, nothin' at all."

He pauses and says, "Think I'll trot myself down to the Union bar and have a shot or two of bourbon before court starts again. Come on. I'll buy you a drink."

I shake my head. "Thanks very much, Mr. Williams, but I need to get my notes together. Maybe I can buy you a drink here in the next day or two."

He stands up and knocks the dust off his pants. "That'll work. See you later, Mr. Peach."

Court starts promptly at two o'clock. The names left on the first venire quickly evaporate as the obviously biased are eliminated by preemptory challenges by one side or the other. Judge Parker adjourns court until nine the next morning, when Sheriff Kahler is expected to have the second venire ready.

The packed courtroom again empties in a rush. Reporters are first out the door and race for the telegraph office. Walking down the hill toward the Ocean Grove, I feel drained and weary. My brain aches from trying to tie together all the loose threads of information I've found, and the first trial witness has yet to take the stand. A double shot of Tennessee sour mash from Tom Murphy's Parlor Saloon will help me concentrate while writing. My hope is Miss Persia Brown can help me understand what Ben Williams denies about Brown and what Sadie and her girls heard in the months following the Fountain murders.

Chapter 11
Supper with Persia Brown

The double shot of Tennessee sour mash goes down smooth and easy. I turn the glass and set it upside down with a solid thump. Winding my way out of Tom Murphy's, I wave at the girls working the early shift, who wave back with perfumed handkerchiefs, hoping for a little early business. The alcohol burn reaches my belly, and I feel the fatigue from the day start to drain away. In my room, I throw off my coat, loosen my tie, and roll up my sleeves. Pulling up a chair next to the washstand and setting the bowl and pitcher on the floor, I begin a report for Chief.

Shadows are growing long when I finish the first draft. The air is warm and peaceful as I stretch the kinks out of my back and pace back and forth, proofing my work. My pocket watch says ten minutes after six, so I have time to shave, slap on some bay rum, and step up to the Black Range Café for Miss Persia Brown.

Persia is radiant. It's amazing what a little blush, red lip rouge, and a blue satin dress trimmed with ivory lace does to make a pretty waitress look elegant. I'd be proud to escort her to any social event in San Francisco or New York.

Sweeping off my boater, I bend across my arm, bowing to her in my best big-city gentleman's salute. "Miss Persia, you are magnificent! Why you're the most beautiful lady this side of the Mississippi. Please allow me to escort you to the best meal this fair village can offer."

She blushes and holds out her warm hand. My kiss on her fingers is an etiquette far beyond what she's accustomed to, and it makes her giggle. "Why, Quentin Peach, I believe you must be the best-mannered gentleman in Hillsboro. Sadie told me to expect that you'd know how to treat a lady."

"Sadie?"

The giggle grows to a sweet, throaty laugh. "Yes, she helped me decide what to wear and then loaned it to me."

"Sadie is a kind lady, isn't she? Shall we go?"

"Yes and yes." The sparkle in her dark eyes is mesmerizing. My inquisitive reporter's mind goes blank as she takes my arm and we meander up the street in the deepening twilight. I feel disoriented, light-headed.

We enter the Double Eagle Restaurant up the street from the Union Hotel. A tinkling bell announces our entry. The dining room is clean and filled with tables covered by red tablecloths with candles in crystal holders. The headwaiter, the only waiter, is a short man with black hair and a pencil mustache. He grins broadly and motions us in. "Persia! You look *magnifica, muy bonita!*"

Persia smiles and lowers her eyes. "Why, thank you, Miguel." She gestures toward me. "Miguel, this is my friend, Mr. Quentin Peach, a reporter from the *San Francisco Examiner.*"

We shake hands. He has a firm, goodwill grip. "A pleasure to meet you, *señor*!" The room is filled with delightful smells of roasting beef, frying onions, and fresh-baked bread. Miguel's smile broadens. "Miss Persia, I will see that Antonio makes his best meal for you. Come to thees table back here in the corner and enjoy a leetle privacy."

He nods and sweeps open his arms to make a little bow. "Excuse me while I order your supper." He seats us and heads for the kitchen door.

There is a brief, awkward silence as we study each other and smile. I know I'm breaking every rule about reporters by becoming emotionally attached to a story lead, but I can't help it. Persia is a diamond in the rough. In the back of my mind are images of what great times we might have while I'm here. "How was your day, Persia?"

She shrugs. "Busier than usual. I was running in and out of that kitchen all day. I haven't worked that hard since I helped Daddy on his ranch."

"Tell me about your daddy."

On the edge of tears, her eyes blink as she stares at the tablecloth. "Daddy, Ma, and I moved out here from Kansas about 1887. I was six or seven then and don't remember much about Kansas or the move. Uncle Ed had already started a ranch over around San Marcial, not too far from Socorro. I remember Daddy complaining that Uncle Ed had talked him into coming out here to start a ranch next to his and then tried to steal him blind with cattle and land.

"We did all right until the drought came in '89.The cattle started dying off, and Uncle Ed started stealing every maverick. By the end of '90, half of Daddy's herd had disappeared, and Uncle Ed's had grown.

"They were near to shooting each other. Probably would have, too, except one day while riding down a steep arroyo bank, Daddy's horse fell on him and broke his hip. He lay there for two days before we found him, nearly dead from lack of water and the pain making him babble out of his head. Doc Crookshanks just shook his head, said there was nothing he could do. The break would just have to heal itself."

Persia sighed. "Daddy never did walk again without crutches. The rains came in '92, but they were too late to save us. All our stock was gone. The hands had left, and we were facing starvation. Uncle Ed offered to buy Daddy out for ten cents on the dollar. Daddy figured it was enough to get us a place in San Marcial, or maybe Socorro, where he could find work as a clerk in one of the stores.

"We moved up to San Marcial and found a nice little house in town. Daddy went to work for a dry goods store, and Ma worked as a seamstress. We'd lived there for a month when Daddy took Ma for a wagon ride down by the Rio Grande on a Sunday afternoon. They were going to take me, but Juanita Torres and I were best friends, and I wanted to stay and play with her, so they went by themselves."

Persia pulls a lace handkerchief from her sleeve and dabs at her eyes. "When Daddy and Ma weren't back by dark, I was in tears, afraid something bad had happened to them. *Señor* Torres, Doc, and a couple of other men went looking for them. They were back early the next day. I remember seeing Doc drive our wagon back into town hitched to his horse. He had the saddest look on his face I'd ever seen. There were two bundles in the back of the wagon wrapped in blankets, and Daddy and Ma were nowhere to be seen. I knew what those bundles had to be, and I cried all day and into the night."

She pauses, looks at me, and then shakes her head. "When I was done, I didn't cry anymore, not even at their funerals. Uncle Ed took me in. He made me Delia's helper. She's his wife, and she was kind to me, too. After a few years, I started catching looks from him that weren't from no uncle. That's when I run off, and Sadie helped me get work here in Hillsboro."

I felt terrible that Persia had endured such outrageous fortune. "What happened to your folks?"

"They both were shot square in the chest. They never had a chance. Whoever did it wanted the horse and didn't want them to tell who took it. Doc said Apache Kid probably did it."

"Apache Kid? I've never heard of him."

"He's a bad outlaw, a renegade Apache who wears a three-piece suit. Some say he's been killed, but others claim he's just hiding in Mexico, waiting to come back and steal women and horses." She shrugs and shivers. "I just hope I'm not around when he does come back."

Miguel appears with a teapot, two elegant bone china cups and saucers, and a selection of cheese and crackers such as would be common in the best of restaurants in San Francisco.

Persia pours tea with the perfect manners of a well-bred lady. "Now, Quent, tell me about yourself."

I feel my face grow warm. It's hard to be suave around direct women, and I know if I try to pad my resume, she'll catch me in an instant. "There's not much to tell. I was born in Virginia. My father, who made a fortune running small cargo boats up and down the rivers in southern Virginia and North Carolina, sold his business and moved to New York City to start a trans-Atlantic shipping business. He did well for a while and then lost one of his ships in a hurricane. It ate up a good part of his money. Lucky for us, he was smart enough to keep a reserve that allowed him and my mother to continue living comfortably and for me to attend Harvard.

"After graduation, I was hired as a reporter at the *New York Journal* and worked there for a couple of years. They only let me write society-page stories or, if I was lucky, cover an innocuous political event. Wanting to be where the action was, and since Mr. Hearst owns both the *Journal* and the *Examiner,* I transferred to San Francisco and went to work for the *Examiner.*

"It didn't hurt, either, that Mr. Hearst and my father were good friends. My editor in San Francisco has sent me out on some good stories, and I've even had a column or two. He sent me here to try and figure out who committed the Fountain murders, where their bodies are, and to cover the probable riots and shootouts if Lee and Gililland are convicted."

She takes a sip of tea and smiles. "I don't mean any

disrespect, but those are mysteries experts haven't been able to solve in over three years. I'm sure you're an excellent reporter, but why would your editor send you rather than someone who has years of experience?"

I bristle a bit. "He said it's because I have an excellent memory and people aren't reluctant to talk to me."

She smiles and tilts her chin up. "No offense intended, sir, just curious."

My face feels flushed again. "I'm sorry for appearing testy. I'm just tired of being taken for a naive kid."

"It's an advantage, so use it. No apology necessary. Ah! Here comes Miguel with our suppers."

It's simple fare: grilled steaks, potatoes, and brown beans with chilies. Over the delectable meal, Persia tells me about her life in Hillsboro. Under Sadie's wing, she's learned to fend off unwanted advances from men, use a modicum of polite society manners, and keep her ears open for useful gossip. I tell her about stories I worked on in San Francisco while the Spanish-American War was in high gear.

Chapter 12
The Warning

Relaxing in the glow of each other's company, we wait for Miguel to bring us dessert. Hoping I'll be able to kiss those heart-shaped lips before the night is over, I try to think of a clever excuse for asking Persia for a walk in the moonlight.

The café door opens. A tall, muscular man with big hands and a thick neck steps inside the café. He's wearing stovepipe chaps and a holstered revolver, butt first. His wide-brimmed hat keeps his face in shadow. He pauses in the doorway, looks around the room, and then walks straight to our table. Standing back in the shadows, he makes it hard to see his face in the table's flickering candlelight. I glance at Persia. She squints at him in recognition, her mouth a tight, straight line, her jaw jutting a little forward in defiance.

He nods at her. "Howdy, Persia." His tobacco rasp is soft and whispery, a snake's hiss. He looks at me. "You Mr. Peach?"

"What can I do for you?"

"There's a feller outside got somethin' to tell you. He asked me to come in and tell you he needs to see you now."

I feel Persia give my shin a little kick under the table and see her head make an almost imperceptible shake. "Well, sir, I'm still having supper with this lady. He'll have to wait. Tell the gentleman I'll talk to him later this evening."

"No, sir, 'fraid not. He knows it's bad manners to interrupt a gentleman's supper, especially if it's with a lady, but you seein' him later won't work. He's leaving town in a little bit and says it won't take but a couple of minutes."

My curiosity grows even as I feel Persia give my forearm a squeeze of warning. I study his weathered face and see the hard glimmer in his eyes. Warning bells go off in the back of my mind, but I think, *No risk, no gain.*

I toss my napkin on the table. "All right. Please excuse me, Persia. I'll be back in five minutes."

Frowning her disapproval, she says nothing.

I follow the cowboy outside. No one is there. "Well? Where's your man?"

"He's right up there across the street around the next corner. Come on."

He leads me across the street and up the boardwalk past dark store windows. Turning up an unlighted street, I see the outlines of a couple of men. They stand by horses tied to a hitching post near a rock wall. Their cigarettes cast faint, yellow light on their faces in the deep blackness under a big cottonwood.

The warning bell in the back of my mind gets louder. The certainty of my playing a fool grows, and the temptation to run back to the lighted street is strong. Something in my core makes me steel myself and advance. The man who came in the restaurant stays just behind my left shoulder. Tension crackles in the air, a dead calm before a storm.

The full face of the man in front of me is still in the dark after the others step out of the shadows to meet us in the low glow of lights from Main Street. I can see he's wearing big batwing chaps, a red bandana, a leather vest, and a fancy gun belt that holsters a Bisley. The glow from the end of his cigarette shows dark hair and a heavy, black mustache. He hasn't shaved in a while but smells of lilac water and whiskey, as if he's just been cozy with a professional lady. His eyelids are narrow slashes as he watches me approach.

The second man stands back to his right. A sombrero hangs

on his back. His hair is shiny and black, and he wears a fancy short jacket and pants with gold braid down the sides. I can see light reflecting off a couple of gold teeth in his grin. His silver-trimmed holster holds a nickel-plated Smith and Wesson Model 3. Even in the low light, his smirk reveals a short, jagged scar across his cheek.

Batwing Chaps tips his broad-brimmed hat back on his head and looks me up and down. My eyes lock on his. I focus on his face and try to show no fear.

"You Peach?"

"That's right. Who are you?"

He blows a long stream of smoke into the air, taking his time as he sizes me up.

"Man there who come and got ya, that's Arch Clayton. He's a right powerful feller. One time I seen him break a man's back in a fight. The man behind me is Tomás Greco. Tomás is a genuine, blow-your-balls-off *pistolero.* He'n shoot the eyes out of a lizard at thirty feet so fast you can hardly see his hand move. Tomás, Arch, and me work together now and again."

"I'm delighted to hear that, but I still don't know your name. I have a lady waiting back in the restaurant and promised her I'd be back in a couple of minutes. I'm ready to listen or leave. What is it you wanted to tell me?"

"Now that's what I like! A man who gets right to the point, even if he's a damned fool reporter. Name's not important. I hear you been sniffing around and listening to tales about other folks besides Lee and his boys murderin' the Fountains. Whatever you heard is goddamn lies. Trial's gonna show that no-good sonovabitch Lee murdered 'em. You just forget the idea that anybody else had anything to do with it. Leave Persia alone! She don't know nuthin'."

He takes a long draw on his cigarette and blows the smoke up into the trees. "Now you understand this, boy. If you don't pay no attention to what I'm tellin' ya, old Greco, Arch, and me are gonna see that you go back to San Francisco in a coffin."

Greco smiles as he rests his hand on his pistol, his thumb ready to cock the hammer. Clayton stands close behind me, the stink of his whiskey-soaked breath in my nose. "Do I make myself clear, reporter? Or do we have to give you a little taste of what's coming if you don't stop sniffin' around Persia and tryin' to get Lee off?"

My mouth is dry, my knees are turning to water, and I can feel the sweat running down my neck. I want to run, but my feet won't move. I hear my voice from far away. "Yeah, I get your message loud and clear. Threats—"

There is an explosion of light in my head that blinds and confuses me. Falling to my hands and knees, I feel sharp hammers of pain pound my kidneys and ribs. I fall into velvety blackness.

My head is pounding, vomit on the edge of my throat. It takes a few moments to realize that I'm in my room at the Ocean Grove with sunlight streaming through the window. Persia sits next to my bed. She holds my hand, her eyes red and cheeks tear-stained. I hear her voice from far away.

"Quent, you're awake! Thank God! Doc said you'd come around."

Sunlight on the window. It's midmorning! Through my headache, I realize I'm missing the trial and curse under my breath. I start to sit up. There are sharp jabs of pain across the small of my back and on my right-side ribs. I ease back down on the pillow, feeling a goose egg on the back of my head. It's big and tender.

I look into Persia's eyes. Scenes from the night rumble through my memory: Persia smiling in the restaurant candle-light, dark figures surrounding me, fear, a flash of light, and total darkness.

I manage to croak, "Water?" She rushes to a pitcher and fills a glass. I fight through the soreness in my side as she helps me sit up. I gulp it down and ask, "How'd I get here?"

"When you didn't come back after a few minutes, I knew for sure something was wrong. I found you passed out and lying in the middle of the street. You looked like somebody beat the hell out of you. A couple of fellows I know helped me get you back to Sadie's. She showed me your room and sent for Doc. He said no bones were broken and that you'd be all right, just sore for a while. He left some laudanum if you get to hurting too bad.

"I tried to tell you not to go with Arch. He works for anybody that needs dirty work done. You should've listened to me." I see a trickle of tears start down her cheeks. "Who else was out there?"

I remember her trying to warn me. "Tomás Greco and another one who never said his name. He said I was to stay away from you and not go around asking questions about anybody else murdering the Fountains. Looks like he has friends who keep him well informed. Maybe he was your uncle."

"Could be." She nods. "Probably was. What did he look like?"

"Dressed like a cowboy, black hair, mustache, red bandana, medium height and weight."

"It doesn't sound like him, but Greco and Clayton came by his ranch often when I worked in his kitchen. He had sources of information you wouldn't believe. Why, I even saw him once with papers stolen from the governor's office in Santa Fe that had *Governor's Eyes Only* marked on the folder."

"That's right! You were staying with him when the Fountains were murdered. You must know enough to get him in a whole lot of trouble, maybe even hanged. Has he tried to get rid of you?"

She smiles and slowly shakes her head. "When I told Sadie

he'd probably have someone kill me right here in Hillsboro, she sent him a note saying I'd better stay healthy or evidence was going to the law that would get him locked up for years—maybe even hanged. Whatever it was, it scared him enough to stay away from me, at least until now. Whoever beat you up doesn't want the water muddied up by the facts. What are you going to do?"

I squeeze her hand and whisper, "I'm not backing off. You warned me. I know I was a fool, and I'm lucky to be alive. But I have a little code I try to live by that I learned from my grandfather: I won't be wronged, and I won't be insulted. If I find those men, we'll settle up, even if it kills me."

She bites her lip and whispers, "It probably will."

I drink more water before staggering to the facilities out back, every step an exercise in pain. When I make it back to the doorway, Persia helps me sit down on the edge of the bed. The room starts to spin as I lie back. She gives me a swig of laudanum. I drift off on a sea of warm unconsciousness.

By midafternoon, I'm awake and rested. The memory of my beating leaves a taste of bitter gall the water can't wash away.

There's a light knock on the door. Persia opens it to Sadie and a tall gentleman in a frock coat behind her, Albert Fall.

Sadie asks, "Quent, may we come in for a little while?"

"Of course. I'm feeling much better. Thanks for all the help you've given me."

"Ah, it ain't nothing. Quent, I'm sure you recognize Mr. Albert Fall, Oliver's lead attorney. He wanted to wish you well and ask a couple of questions if you're up to it."

"Absolutely."

Stepping from behind Sadie, Fall comes over to my bed and sticks out his hand, his eyes taking in everything about me. "Sadie tells me some assailants beat the hell out of you because you were asking questions about other folks besides Lee and Gililland murdering the Fountains," he says, his voice a soft rumble ready to explode.

"Yes, sir, that's right. Arch Clayton, Tomás Greco, and someone who never said who he was. He told me to quit asking if someone else murdered the Fountains and to stay away from Persia. Makes it sound like Mr. Brown was behind it."

Fall squints and nods. He pulls a cigar from a vest pocket. "Mind if I smoke?"

Sadie and Persia shake their heads, and I wave him on. Lighting his cigar, he takes a puff or two while he eyes me.

"What you've told me fits with other facts of the case. It could have been Brown or any one of several others. Brown's mean. He's a two-bit outlaw who tries to hide his nefarious ventures behind his ranching business. I don't know how he managed to escape Fountain's sweep of Socorro operators in '94. Brown likes to hire Mexicans to do his dirty work. My money says revenge'll kill him someday." His eyes never leave me as he takes another puff on his cigar. "I'm curious, Mr. Peach. How'd those men get the drop on you?"

"Arch Clayton came in the restaurant where Persia and I were having supper. He said a man outside had some things to tell me before leaving town. Like a fool, I went with him, even though Persia tried to warn me. I didn't have a weapon. So I guess it was easy enough to give me a few warning licks to back off."

"Son, you're in serious danger of being killed if you hang around here, especially if you don't carry a weapon. This is free advice: either get yourself a weapon or be on the morning stage."

"Mr. Fall, I'm not leaving. I boxed and was on the pistol team at Harvard. I can take care of myself."

He nods, smiling. "I'm sure you can in your social class, but the men who beat you won't hesitate to kill you. You're a threat.

They don't live by any Harvard gentleman's code of honor. Now, before I go, can you give me a business card so I'll know how to contact you, if I need you, to tell what happened at the other trials?"

"Other trials?"

"Oh, yes, there'll be other trials. Lee and Gililland will stand trial in Alamogordo for the murder of Kent Kearney at the Wildy Well shootout." Taking another puff of his cigar, he blows the smoke toward the ceiling. "And the prosecution wants to try them again in Silver City for the murder of Colonel Fountain. When that trial comes up, I'll probably call you as one of my witnesses to show there were other possible, even more reasonable, suspects than my clients."

"You can count on me, Mr. Fall. What happened in court today?"

He smiles, rolling the cigar between his long thumb and fingers. "Well, we went through the second venire like grease through a goose. We still had only eleven jurors by eleven-thirty. Judge Franklin ordered the sheriff to call talesmen. Of course, I vigorously objected since, for this trial, that is totally illegal, but he overruled me. Out of the talesmen, we finally found a juror to whom neither Catron nor I objected, so a jury was finally formed.

"Garrett still hasn't found the prosecution's key witness, Jack Maxwell, so Catron asked for a continuance until Monday morning. Parker gave it to him, but he warned him that, starting Monday, witnesses have to be called, regardless of whether their key witness is found or not. Starting at nine in the morning, Parker will have the witnesses sworn, the jury impaneled, and we'll finally get to the end of this nonsense of Lee being Fountain's murderer."

"Do you think they'll find Maxwell?"

Fall shrugs his shoulders and smiles. "Don't know. I hope so.

He's a demonstrable liar, who'll be a better witness for the defense than the prosecution. I'm looking forward to cross-examining him." He shakes my hand. "Mr. Peach, it's been a pleasure meeting you, and I hope you're feeling better soon. I'll look for you at the trial. Let me know when you want an interview, and I'll try to ensure the defendants are available. Good evening."

Sadie steps to the side of my bed. "Quent, I'll send you two some supper if you feel like eating."

"That'd be wonderful. Are there any stores open on Sunday where I can buy a pistol?"

"Only thing open on Sunday are the saloons and restaurants. You'll have to wait until Monday to buy a pistol."

Chapter 13
The Bodyguard

As the evening shadows grow, Persia lights the lamp in the corner of the room and brings me more water. Then Ruth brings a large tray holding our supper. The smell of fried meat, vegetables, biscuits, and hot apple cobbler makes me ravenous. I wolf it down. Persia just picks at her plate.

I finish and lie back on the bed, sore but feeling much better. Persia carries the dishes back to Tom Ying's kitchen and returns. She sits down beside me, gloom covering her face. "Why are you doing this? Please get on that stage tomorrow. Someone is going to kill you if you don't."

I take her hand. "Don't worry. No one's going to kill me. I have to find out who murdered the Fountains. This is my chance to get some recognition as a writer. I'm not losing it because I can't master my fear. Besides, there's a score to settle—one way or the other. Just have a little faith in me. Can you do that?"

Staring at the floor, she nods. "All right," she croaks. "I'm counting on you."

I squeeze her hand. "Now help me do my job. Before those men beat the hell out of me, the lead dog called Lee a sonovabitch. Did you ever hear your uncle say if he disliked or maybe even hated Lee?"

She frowns and nods. "Oh, he hated Lee all right. At his meeting with the ranchers, Lee and his boys didn't support the plan to kill Fountain. Lee said it was a fool idea. What's worse was when Ed was on trial and about to be sent to prison. Lee didn't support him like the other ranchers when he had to scratch up two hundred dollars for Elfago Baca to fix the jury. When Ed and his boys were sitting around the table after dinner, I'd hear him talk about how he was going to set things right with Lee so that Lee'd never know who'd done him in. Said he had it all figured out."

An image of Ed Brown as a shrewd manipulator, fast on his feet and a first-rate liar, forms in my mind. Something Chief told me at the *Examiner* floats to the top of my memory: "You want to know who did a crime, particularly murder? Just listen to who talks. The one who's guilty always talks. That's their real reward for killing someone, the notoriety that goes with how clever and powerful they were in doing what they did and how they got away with it." Ed Brown was a talker.

The sudden need for sleep fills my consciousness. I lie back on the bed to rest for a few minutes and drift into a nap. My dreams are filled with images of my being chased by a bully and his gang to beat me up and take my money. Only thirteen, I wanted to stand and fight, but I was afraid to face them alone. I knew I was a coward because I ran. Somehow, my father found out what was happening and paid the constable a visit. The bully and his boys soon disappeared, and I was never bothered again. I swore to myself that I'd never run from a threat again and looked forward to the day when I'd have a chance to prove I wasn't a coward. It never came until now.

There is a gentle shake on my shoulder. I swim to the surface of consciousness. Sadie smiles at me as I rub the sleep out of my eyes. "What time is it, ma'am?"

Sadie pats my shoulder. "It's getting on to midnight. There's nothing to worry about. Just checking in on you. How're you feeling?"

"I'm better, feeling much stronger. I'm just a little tired."

"Good. I brought you a present." She pulls her right arm

from behind her back and holds out a shoulder holster with a pistol in it. "I've had it for a while now and never used it. A Pinkerton left it with me when he decided he'd rather prospect for gold than chase criminals."

The holster shines with polish and long use. The pistol is a clean, lightly oiled Smith and Wesson .44 caliber Model 2 revolver, its barrel short for easy concealment. It has a comfortable, yet awkward, feel in my hand. I shot a Bisley Colt when I was on the pistol team at Harvard. The Bisley handle is humpbacked and a lot closer to the trigger guard than the long, stretch grip of the Smith and Wesson.

"Thank you, Sadie! I'm very grateful for all the kindnesses you have shown me."

Sadie nods. "We're gonna have to figure out how to keep you from getting killed if you're stayin'."

I sigh. "Yes, ma'am, I know. I've thought about it a lot. I think my best chance is to arm myself and dress like one of the locals, maybe a miner or a cowboy. What do you think?"

Sadie says, "I think if you don't look like a reporter, you ain't gonna get no interviews. If you dress like a cowboy, them boys is going to want to know who the stranger is at the trial and what outfit he rides for. You'll be a marked man in minutes. If you dress like a miner, you'll stand out 'cause educated miners are few and far between, and you ain't got miners' hands or social manners."

I see her eyes sparkling. "You're probably right. What's your recommendation?"

"A bodyguard!"

"A bodyguard? I can't afford one, leastways not one that might do me some good."

"Now look here, Quent, as long as you stay in plain sight during the day, they ain't gonna try anything. It's early in the morning and right about or after sundown that they'd try to do you. That's about the only time you'd need a bodyguard. And you don't have to worry about money. I've got it covered."

I can see she's about to laugh aloud. "Who and what on God's green earth are you talking about?"

"Tom Tucker. He's a deputy for George Curry, and he ain't reluctant to shoot if it needs doin', and he's faced flying bullets before. He's got a powerful itch when it comes to women. If I promise him a romp or two with Nadine for a little bodyguard work, he'd beg to keep an eye on you. Ain't nobody going to come around the Ocean Grove or the Orchard. Judge Parker, the jury, the attorneys, and the clerk are staying in my hotels for the trial. It'll be the natural thing for Tom to hang around like he's keepin' an eye on 'em. He'll just keep a special eye out for funny business as far as you're concerned. You won't even know he's there, but he'll keep your back covered. That ought to increase your chances of survival quite a bit."

I remember Tom from the stage ride up from Lake Valley. I like him. He won't take anything off anybody. "I'll have to send you the money for his work when I get back to San Francisco."

Sadie laughs. "Good! I'm sure Nadine'll be glad to hear that. Tom's getting a down payment on his bodyguard fee right now."

"Sadie, how can I ever thank you?"

"Just be sure you get your facts straight and tell the truth."

"I'm bound by honor to do that." She sweeps out the door, a hand trailing her wave goodbye.

Chapter 14
Tom Catron

The Ocean Grove Restaurant, barely awake after a frantic Saturday night, has two tables already occupied. A cowboy sits and slurps coffee from a big, white mug and massages his neck muscles with his free hand. The look of pain on his face says his hair hurts, that he's a victim of a few too many glasses of Forty Rod Whiskey the night before. At the second table sits a heavyset man dressed in a rumpled business suit, his thick thatch of coarse, gray hair falling over the collar of a wrinkled white shirt. Unlike the cowboy, he eats from fine Prince Albert china while staring at a folded newspaper. He sips his coffee with his pinky extended like an aristocrat, occasionally raising his bushy brows, frowning, and snorting at something in the paper.

I can't believe my luck and whisper to Persia, "That's Tom Catron, the lead prosecutor. Maybe he'll give me an interview. Do you mind waiting a bit longer for breakfast?"

Smiling, she waves me forward as she heads for a table. Before I can say anything, Catron senses my presence and looks up from his paper.

"Mr. Catron?"

"Yes, sir! What can I do for you, young man?" His booming voice in the nearly empty room reminds me of Chief and makes me flinch in spite of myself.

I hand him my business card. "Sir, I'm Quentin Peach, reporter for the *San Francisco Examiner.* I was wondering if I might have a few minutes of your time to ask you some questions about the Lee case?"

He stares at me a moment, a look of disbelief on his face. "Hell, no!" he growls like an angry dog. "Do you think I'm crazy? I'm not talking to any goddamn, still-in-diapers reporter. You're all a bunch of no-good liars. Fall has every one of you on a leash like a bunch of hounds. Get away from me! You're ruining my breakfast!"

I'm stunned almost speechless by his unexpected outburst. "Sir, I . . . I don't know why you're angry at reporters. Let me assure you that I have no extraordinary motives. I'm just after the truth. I very much want to hear both sides. I don't have a paper deadline to meet like Mr. Seymour, who's covering the trial for the *Examiner.* My editor sent me here to get background information and try to find the truth. I hope you'll reconsider talking with me. You have my card. Mrs. Orchard is putting me up here with you in the Ocean Grove, and I'll be happy to talk with you any time. Sorry to disturb your breakfast."

He waves his hand, growling, "Just get the hell away from me."

I turn to the table where Persia sits, her eyes the size of quarters. After I ease down in my chair, she whispers, "What was that all about?"

"I don't know. Fall's been working with reporters for a couple of months, letting them have access to Lee, Gililland, and McNew. I'm sure he's trying to establish what fine, upstanding gentlemen they are to potential jury members. It makes the prosecution look bad. Evidently, Catron thinks reporters aren't giving his side a fair shake."

A tall waitress, skin as brown as milk chocolate, appears with cups of coffee in the restaurant's fancy china. We order, and soon plates of steaming steaks, fried eggs, and buttery skillet toast are in front of us. As we eat, Catron keeps glancing our way. As the waitress carries away our dishes, he pulls a crook-stemmed burl pipe from his jacket pocket and loads it, staring at us. I glance over at him as he sits and puffs, his arms crossed. When the waitress refreshes our coffee, he makes small waving motions to me through his cloud of white smoke.

"Looks like he has some more cursing to do. Go on back if you want. I'll probably be along in a couple of minutes."

"This is better than watching the boys try to ride steers over in the corral. Go ahead. I'll wait."

I take my coffee and approach his table.

"Sorry I was short with you, Mr. Peach. Your brothers in the press have been giving the prosecution attorneys a mighty hard time. You look like a bright young man. I'll trust you to tell the truth. Sit down and ask your questions. I'll tell it to you as straight as I know how."

"Thanks very much, Mr. Catron. I assure you, you won't be misquoted."

He nods and surrounds us with a big puff of smoke, making my eyes water. I pull out my pad and pencil and look him in the eye. "Is it true that you said you'd try the territory's case for nothing?"

He frowns, suspicious again. "Yes."

"Why?"

"Because I'm the best attorney in the territory, and Lee is a blight on the territory's honor, that's why. He deserves to be convicted, and, if not hanged, sent to the penitentiary for the rest of his natural life. Satan will take care of him in the next life."

"Why are you so sure he did it? All the evidence is circumstantial."

Catron crosses his arms again, puffs on his pipe, and considers his answer. He holds up a fist the size of a small ham and raises his thumb.

"First, he had motive. Fountain and Lee were mortal political enemies. Fountain was on him like stink on a skunk and was about to send him and his men to prison. Deservedly so, by God! Lee was stealing companies like Blue Water blind!"

He held up his forefinger. "Second, he had opportunity. Fountain was fool enough to ride with only little Henry for protection right past Lee's ranches on the way home after getting him indicted on cattle theft in Lincoln." He held up his middle finger with the first two. "Third, he's a deadly killer. Just ask Charley Rhodius or Matt Coffelt what Lee does to men who cross him. They found seven bullet holes in Rhodius's body, and Lee admitted he killed both of them. Damned if he didn't get off for those killings. He's a deadly gunman, no doubt about it. People are scared to death of him in Las Cruces, Alamogordo, Tularosa, just about anywhere he's known. Somebody gets up enough courage to say they'll testify against him, and they unexpectedly die, disappear, or lose their memories. Hell, he even tried to kill Pat Garrett, and he murdered his deputy when they were legitimately trying to arrest him and Gililland in July of last year."

Catron, already red, turns even brighter as his anger grows. "Then Lee, by God, has the unmitigated gall to dictate the terms of his surrender to George Curry, and Curry, who owes him money, accepts them! Just thinking about that sonovabitch infuriates me! I tell you if there was ever an outlaw who deserved the rope, it's Lee, and, by God, this time, he's going to get it."

Scribbling my notes, I hear the roaring anger and frustration in Catron's voice and hope it's captured in my story.

"Mr. Catron, I understand Mr. McNew was kept in jail over in Las Cruces for nearly a year before he was brought to trial in Silver City for the murder of Colonel Fountain. And then you let him go. What forced you to do that?"

Catron takes a couple of deep draws on his pipe. "Yes, sir, we did have to let McNew off, even though he deserved to be hanged, too. It was a tactical decision to ensure we had our best chance to hang Lee, who was the leader of the gang that killed Albert and little Henry."

I frown and ask, "How so?"

"It's simple, Mr. Peach. We have witnesses and a good strategy. It is, however, a circumstantial case. We need to make as powerful a presentation of our evidence as we can. If we gave Fall and his henchmen, Daugherty and Fergusson, an opportunity to see our strategy and evidence before Lee was brought to trial, we knew he'd have time to spread lies to counter it or see to it that Lee's people got rid of our witnesses.

"We wanted to do Lee first, but McNew was arrested first, so the judge said it was only fair that he be tried first. Our witnesses had to be brought in from Montana and other far places. We were still trying to locate some of them. The territorial budget just didn't have enough money then to bring them in, so we asked for a continuance in the McNew trial until the next term of court. It wasn't a big thing, maybe three more months of jail time is all."

I nod and Catron pauses while I finish my notes.

"I could tell Judge Parker was seriously considering our request, but Fall argued that McNew had been held in jail almost a year on a warrant that had expired when the next term of the court began three months after he was arrested. He said it was patently unfair and unjust to hold McNew even another day, much less three more months.

"He also claimed that McNew's defense hadn't had more than four or five days to prepare, which to my mind was a good thing. It kept our witnesses from being killed or losing their memories. We were all embarrassed when Fall offered to pay the territory's costs in order for McNew's trial to go forward. He was bluffing, of course."

Taking a long draw and blowing a smoke ring toward the

ceiling, he shakes his head. "The next day Judge Parker denied the continuance, but he gave us nearly three weeks to round up our witnesses and get ready for the trial then and there, but we had to keep our cards close to the vest to get Lee. We had to let McNew go or show our hand. So when McNew's trial started again three weeks later, we entered a *nolle prosequi.* We wouldn't proceed any further with Mr. McNew, even though he was guilty as hell and everyone knew it.

"Fall objected, he actually objected, to our withdrawing the case. He wanted to force us to try McNew, but Judge Parker accepted our entry. It was a bitter cup sir, a bitter cup. However, it was for the public good. It'll be worth it when we see Lee on the gallows. It will be the end, I tell you, of a gang of thieves and murderers and political graft and corruption—all by Democrats—that has kept New Mexico from being seriously considered for statehood."

As I finish writing Catron's answer, he knocks out his pipe and crosses his arms. "Sir, I understand there are a number of other suspects, perhaps as many as thirty, who said they wanted to murder Colonel Fountain. Why did you settle on Mr. Lee instead of one of them?"

Catron frowns as if he doesn't know what I'm talking about. "Son, I don't make the arrests. I just use the evidence the sheriff gives me. Mr. Garrett worked for two years collecting evidence against Mr. Lee, wound up in a gun battle with him, and had a deputy killed for his efforts. Then he chased Lee all over the Southwest for nearly nine months. I believe it's self-evident that Lee is guilty as sin. Just who do you think is a better suspect than Lee and his gang?"

I steel myself for the coming fury. "Well, how about Ed Brown?"

Catron's bushy eyebrows nearly rise off the top of his forehead. "Ed Brown? Ed Brown of San Marcial? That Ed

Brown? Why, he doesn't have enough sense to pour pee out of a boot with the instructions written on the sole. Why on earth do you think Ed Brown is a proper territorial suspect? He's just a two-bit cattle thief."

Now it's my turn to hold up a fist and raise my thumb. "First, the Pinkerton, Sayers, destroyed Brown's alibi about where he was for over seven days at the end of January and beginning of February when the Fountains were murdered. He clearly lied and tried to cover it up. He's never truthfully said where he was. He came back to San Marcial on the third of February on horses so tired they nearly died, and his boots were beat up so badly, he bought a new pair. He even claimed he'd tell who could say where the Fountains were buried if he got part of the reward."

I hold up my forefinger. "Second, a convict named Slick Miller claims Brown and some other ranchers had a meeting in '94 where plans were made to ambush Colonel Fountain. Two sites were identified for an ambush. The place where the colonel and Henry disappeared was one of those sites."

My middle finger comes up. "Third, Brown had at least as much motive as Lee because Fountain sent twenty men from Socorro and the San Marcial area to the penitentiary, and he very nearly snagged Brown in '94. Brown was anxious to get Fountain out of the way. That's why he called that meeting.

"Besides all that, as a reporter, I've heard stories from people who've overheard Brown's men talk about murdering the Fountains."

Catron smiles. "Yes, yes, I've heard some of that, too. Show me the hard evidence. All you've heard are just words in the air, not credible sworn depositions. Garrett talked to Sheriff Bursum up in Socorro and concluded there wasn't anything there of any significance, no hard evidence. Just the story of a convict who wanted to be free and would say anything to get the governor to reduce his sentence. I haven't heard any of these other witnesses you claim to have heard. Get their depositions and the territory will follow up, I promise you that."

I stare at the floor and shake my head. "I can't. They won't testify in public, and I've given my word I'll not betray who they are. They're fearful of losing their reputations for keeping their mouths shut and that Brown will have them killed."

Catron swats at a fly and nods. "Trust me, Mr. Peach. Brown didn't have the guts or skill to kill Colonel Fountain, but Lee did. Lee's guilty. Of that, I'm certain. Any other questions?"

"Not now, Mr. Catron. Perhaps I can chat with you as the trial progresses and get your impression of how things are going?"

He smiles and nods. "Why, I believe that can be arranged, as long as it's clear you're writing the truth."

"I'll do just that, Mr. Catron. Thank you for your time."

He stands, and we shake hands. He has a grip that can bend a horseshoe. I grit my teeth to keep from flinching. He plops his hat on the top of his head, grabs his paper, and sashays out of the restaurant.

Persia, holding her cup, is smiling as I sit down beside her. "That was quite a talk you had with Mr. Catron. I heard every word clear over here. He's a loud talker, isn't he?"

"Yes, so I don't have to tell you he's certain Lee is guilty."

She stares at her coffee and nods. "That's too bad. Him believing that means that Ed Brown will ride out of Hillsboro free and in the clear, ready to murder the next person who crosses him. It makes me sick just to think about it."

Chapter 15
Political Parallax

Persia and I leave our table. Outside in the soft morning air it's a quiet Sunday morning. She looks at me, indecision in her eyes. "I need to get back to the café and get caught up on my chores. Can you go rest? I'll be back to check on you this evening."

"I'm all right. Let me walk you back to the café, and then I'll come back here, rest, and write my next story. I'm sorry I ruined your weekend. Let me make it up to you and take you to supper here this evening."

She frowns. "Don't you overdo it. And don't worry about me and the weekend. I'm just so thankful you weren't hurt worse than you were, and, yes, sir, I'd be proud to have supper with you this evening." She smiles and slides her arm through mine. We step out of the stoop's shade into the brilliant morning. Content, we say nothing to disturb the morning until we reach her door.

"What time shall I call for you?"

"Come about six, and I'll be ready." Smiling, she gives me a peck on the cheek before she steps in her door. "See you then."

I walk back to the Ocean Grove whistling, even feeling a little light on my feet despite my bruised body and sore head. In the cool gloom of my room, I find my notes and move the washstand over to the window. Words fly to my writing paper in an uninterrupted stream. I finish in a couple of hours, and, proofing my work, find only a few corrections and write a note of explanation.

Sir:

I regret I'm late with this story. As you will see, circumstances beyond my control prevented me from being timely. I expect to send you other stories expeditiously as I develop more information and follow leads that are included in this one. I am staying at the Ocean Grove Hotel. If you need to contact me, please send a wire to the attention of Mr. Belvedere Brooks, head of the telegraph office. He understands my need for confidentiality. My story follows.

Very Respectfully,
QP

Political Parallax.

Hillsboro, New Mexico Territory, 28 May 1899—Who murdered Albert Fountain and his eight-year-old son Henry? Why were they murdered? Where are their bones? The New Mexico territorial government believes Oliver Lee and James Gililland know the answers to these and other questions because they are guilty of the heinous crimes and is prosecuting them.

However, after exposure to local points of view, it is clear that the least slanting of the facts, the least change in how they are viewed, can drastically change perception of the defendants' guilt or innocence. The situation in Hillsboro is a vivid example of what can only be called political parallax, a metaphor for the physical phenomenon, optical parallax. Hold a finger up at arm's length and view it with both eyes. It has depth and position relative to its surroundings. Seen with only one eye, its position shifts left or right, depending on which eye is used, and it cannot be placed in a true position of depth relative to its surroundings.

As testimony begins in the trial here in the little village of Hillsboro, New Mexico, the parallax in the views of the defendants' guilt or innocence from the same set of facts is astonishing. The change in point of view, the parallax of the facts, results from politics—the single eye of guilt or innocence depends on whether you are a Yankee Republican or a Texas Democrat . . .

My story goes on for nearly a thousand more words, relating what I had learned so far and telling of the threats and beating I'd received.

Chapter 16
"Poker Bill" Thornton

The warm air drifting in the window makes my eyelids heavy. I take a nip of laudanum and lie down. When I awaken, my watch shows it's nearly four in the afternoon. My roaring thirst needs quenching with a cold beer at the Union Hotel bar.

In the bar, I find a table where I can sit with my back to the wall and watch the room. A thin, distinguished, older gentleman sits nearby. His face is narrow and clean-shaven, his hair thin and meticulously combed. A derby sits on the table beside him. Smoking an expensive Havana, he sips a beer and watches a poker game. A steady stream of businessmen and ranchers stop, shake hands, and speak with him for a few moments before drifting off.

I ask the Mexican waiter who he is. "Oh, *señor,* that ees old governor, *Señor* Poker Beel Thornton." I don't waste any time getting over to introduce myself and hand him my card. "My name is Quentin Peach. I'm a reporter for the *San Francisco Examiner.* I'm doing background stories on the events leading up to the trial, and I was hoping you might give me your view of this case."

I wait as he takes a long draw on the Havana and blows the smoke toward the floor. Squinting through the smoke, he motions me to take a seat as he leans back in his chair and crosses his arms. "What do you want to know?"

"Sir, the outcome of this trial may affect New Mexico becoming a state for years. My paper would be very interested in your perspective of the events surrounding the case. I'm here for Mr. Hearst to get the true story of the events behind the murders, not to report the details of the trial."

"All right, I can support that." He takes his cigar out of his mouth and pokes it at me to emphasize his point. "Just be damned sure, Quentin, that you're accurate in reporting what I tell you. Deal?"

"Deal! Sir, I can assure you that I'll be fair and accurate in what I write. I understand you were quite active in getting the official investigations of the murders started. Is that true?"

He rolls the Havana between his thumb and fingers as he considers his answer. "Quentin, Albert Fountain was a territorial treasure. Smart, strong, fearless. I first met him about twenty-five years ago when I was a Santa Fe attorney. He was a major in a volunteer militia cavalry unit that operated out of Mesilla. The gangs in the southern part of the territory had become intolerable. Governor Sheldon was receiving letters and telegrams daily from folks down here who were begging him to do something, anything, even to the point of declaring martial law and sending in the army to set things right. Sheldon asked Fountain to lead the mounted militia and clean up the gangs."

Thornton takes a long draw on his cigar and blows the smoke toward the ceiling. "Fountain wiped out those gangs in two months! It was incredible. After he threw the survivors in jail, he prosecuted them and sent them off to prison faster than a dealer can toss cards. The leader of a big gang over around Rincon, named Kinney, had the *cojones* to try and hire Fountain as his defense attorney after being captured by Fountain. Kinney said money was no object and offered Fountain three thousand dollars to defend him. Fountain just laughed at him. So Kinney hired me."

He smiles, his eyes twinkling at the memory. "In those days, Fountain, Tom Catron, and I were considered the best attorneys in New Mexico. At Kinney's trial, Fountain was the lead prosecutor. He beat my brains out on every point I raised for the defense. It took the jury less than ten minutes to decide Kinney was guilty. Over the years, I've had other occasions to deal with Colonel Fountain. Whether he was for or against me, I found him to be the best, even if he did like to toot his own horn, but then, what politician doesn't?"

The governor flicks the ash off his cigar and stares out the door as if lost in his memories. In a couple of minutes, he takes a swallow of his beer and continues, "You can imagine my shock when word came that Fountain and his son had disappeared and were probably murdered. I was on the next train out of Santa Fe, headed to Las Cruces. I knew the Republicans were in a lather, chafing for action. They were convinced from the get-go that Lee and his boys were guilty. Most of them were certain Lee's attorney, Albert Fall, had masterminded the whole affair. They believed that, because Fall had made Lee and two or three who ran with him deputy sheriffs and deputy U.S. marshals, none of them would ever be tried because Fall and the Democrats controlled the sheriff and the grand jury."

Thornton lets his gaze roam back over to the poker games while I write a few notes. "Can you tell me more about the general state of the region at that time?" I ask.

"Things were in a real mess in Doña Ana County. Cattle rustling was rampant. The town folk didn't understand the code the cattlemen lived by, and there were shootings and murders everywhere."

I nod. "I think I've heard about this code before. You mean branding mavericks that weren't yours, warning your opponent before you could kill him—that code?"

Thornton takes a puff and grins. "That's right. But six years ago, the range was coming off a terrible, three-year drought. The small ranchers were just hanging on, and they were mavericking the big operator herds down to nothing. It had passed mavericking. It was pure theft.

"In turn, the big operators wanted the little operators' water rights, so they were trying to drive the little ones out of business by overgrazing the open range with their big herds. Fountain was throwing a big net over the situation, sending men to prison. There were well-earned, bitter feelings on both sides. Everybody was on edge, antsy, ready to fight over anything. One false move by your opponents, and the guns came out. Yes, sir, they were really bad times."

Thornton shakes his head and sighs. "Part of the problem in Doña Ana County was that Sheriff Guadalupe Ascarate pretty much did what Fall told him to do, and Fall seemed to take great pleasure in antagonizing the Republicans. It was apparent, at least to me, that in the election in the fall of '94, the Republican candidate, Numa Reymond, had won the race for sheriff. Evidently, the Democrats thought so, too, because they stole and burned a ballot box from Tularosa. Tularosa was heavily Republican. The votes in that box would have ensured Reymond won the election.

"Naturally, the Republicans screamed foul and took the case to court, and Fall made every legal maneuver on the books to slow down adjudication of their complaint and keep his man, Ascarate, and more importantly, the deputies he'd had Ascarate hire—Lee, McNew, Gililland, and Joe Morgan—in office. That's the way things stood in Doña Ana County on the first of February, 1896, when Fountain and his son disappeared. There was never any doubt in Republican minds as to who was responsible for the murder of the Fountains. It had to be Lee. He was deadly with his guns and didn't take bull off anybody. And, of course, to make matters worse, more than a few believed Fall masterminded the entire business."

I motioned to the waiter, ordered a beer, and then took time to scribble a few more notes into my notebook. "So riding the train down to Las Cruces, you had a lot to think about."

Thornton smiles through his cloud of smoke and nods. "You've got that one right, Quentin. I had to set the overall situation straight, and I had to find Fountain's killers fast. If I didn't, blood was going to flow in the streets, Republican versus Democrat, the cattle barons versus small ranchers. Hell, if things got out of hand, I figured it might be another fifty years before New Mexico Territory became a state."

Resting his elbow on the table, Thornton holds up a finger. "First, I had to get the duly elected sheriff installed. A new sheriff would fire the deputies accused of murdering Fountain and get serious about solving the case. That would make the Republicans calm down a little. However, Numa Reymond wasn't the man to solve the crime. He was just a little Swiss shopkeeper, someone the Republicans planned to use to control the county. I had to find an experienced, big-name lawman to take over, and I had to get Reymond to resign so I could appoint the more experienced man."

He points his finger for emphasis. "From all my correspondence, I was certain the Lee gang had murdered the Fountains. However, with Fall, as smooth and slick an attorney as there is, we had to have bedrock evidence he couldn't deny, just like Fountain had against Kinney when I was trying to defend him.

"The train I took out of Santa Fe got into Las Cruces first thing on the morning the fifth of February. I told the crowd I was offering a five-thousand-dollar reward for information leading to the arrest of the killers, and I promised a full and complete pardon to anyone connected with the crime, except, of course, the principal, who first turned state's evidence and furnished testimony for the arrest and conviction of the associates. That offer made the reporters run for their editors to make the latest edition with the news."

I smile. "I can see where it would. Did you speak with Fall?"

"When I went to Fall's office, he told me that about a year ago Fountain had disappeared and come back two weeks later. Said he wasn't so sure Fountain and his son had been murdered, that maybe Fountain had just run off because he and his wife were having problems. I told him to keep his scurrilous mouth shut.

"Visiting the sheriff, I asked how the search and evidence-gathering was progressing. He was clueless, totally useless. More and more, it looked like his deputies were the prime suspects. Next, I visited with the Fountains, expressed my deepest sympathy, and promised them I'd do everything in my power to bring the killers to justice.

"When I got back to Santa Fe, I sent letters to leaders on all sides, asking for their support. The secretary of the cattleman's association, Mr. Cree, immediately wrote me back and sent a letter he had received from Fountain in October of '95, less than four months before he was murdered. The letter said the Lee gang was behind the cattle rustling and that it might be a fight to the death to put them in the penitentiary."

I give a low whistle and drink several swallows of beer before adding to my notes. Thornton sits there scowling until I stop writing. Then he says, "I sent word to the leading lights in both parties in Doña Ana County that I wanted to meet with them on neutral ground in El Paso. They all agreed to come. Llewellyn, Van Patten, George Curry, Fall, Sheriff Ascarate, Numa Reymond, and several other leading politicos met with me around the twentieth of February. I proposed that we find a strong, experienced law officer to act as Sheriff Ascarate's chief deputy and that he be paid five hundred dollars a month until litigation straightened things out. When asked if I had anyone in mind, I said, 'Pat Garrett.' You could have heard a pin drop. I walked over and opened the door to the adjoining room, and there he stood, all six-foot-six of him. I asked him to come on in and have a seat."

Thornton crosses his arms and clamps down hard on his Havana. "Fall didn't say a word. He just sat in his chair, crossed his arms, and stared at us. All the Republicans had big grins on their faces and shook their fists in agreement. Ascarate shook his head, said he was able to take care of the sheriff's office, and wouldn't let anyone dictate who his deputies were. Reymond's eyes bored holes in Ascarate, and he said he'd drop his lawsuit about the sheriff's election fraud if Ascarate would resign and let Pat Garrett be appointed sheriff."

I try to picture the scene as Thornton shakes his head at the memory and winces. He says, "There was some argument about the legality of what I was proposing. After a while, Fall stood up and put on his big, black Stetson. He said the meeting was a political farce and that it was over as far as he was concerned. Fall's exit broke up the meeting. After we were alone, I told Garrett to be a patient, that I would get things straightened out in a few days.

"With the information I'd gathered during the meeting, I contacted Judge Bantz in Silver City and requested he expedite resolution of the question of who had been elected sheriff."

Thornton reaches for his beer and takes a long swallow, smacking his lips as he thumps the empty mug on the table. "Next, Albert Fall and I had a come-to-Jesus meeting. We were both Democrats, and I was sensitive to his concern that politics was playing a major role in bringing Pat Garrett in as a deputy. I also knew Fall was probably concerned that Garrett wouldn't hesitate to stand up to any bullying from Lee, which meant Fall's power through the sheriff's office would be gone. I told Fall he could oppose me or he could support me, but I was going to have Garrett in Las Cruces working on the case regardless. I told him that if I didn't do something quick, the President would appoint a governor who would, and he might even send in the troops and establish martial law.

"Fall said, 'Okay, I'll back you and tell my clients to do the same. Just be sure this investigation and Garrett are evenhanded, because my clients are first on the suspect list.' Then he asked, 'What are you going to do about Ascarate and Reymond?'

"I told him I'd asked Judge Bantz to legally resolve the election litigations as fast as possible, which meant he'd have to stop his legal maneuvers to keep the case from coming to trial. He agreed to let the case progress on its own merits. Assuming Reymond won the case and resigned as he promised, I planned to appoint Garrett in his place. If Ascarate won, then I had to get him to appoint Garrett as chief deputy, while I tried to figure out how to lever the sheriff out and have his deputy take over."

I finish my beer and scribble a few more notes. "So how did it work out in the end?"

"I appointed Garrett as an independent detective to work out of the sheriff's office until I could get rid of the pretenders and appoint him sheriff. He didn't care for the approach, but he wanted the fat salary and a chance to collect the huge reward. By that time, it must have been over ten thousand dollars. I think it eventually grew to about twenty thousand.

"In my hotel room the next day, I met again with Garrett and most of the others from the previous meeting. I told them what I wanted to do and invited them to ask Garrett any questions they wanted, and, if they were so inclined, to try to find a reason not to hire him to solve the Fountain murder case. None tried to stop me from hiring Garrett.

"When asked, Garrett told them he planned to start his investigation the next day, that he had a clear idea who was responsible from evidence he had already collected, and that they should expect arrests soon. Fall, sitting with his arms crossed, saying nothing, watched him carefully. I knew Garrett had made his first mistake."

Tilting back in his chair, Thornton pauses and chews on the inside of his cheek. "Soon, I sent a telegram to the Pinkerton Detective Agency in Denver, requesting they send an operative to work with Garrett to collect evidence against the murderers of Colonel Fountain and his son, and they sent John Fraser.

"After looking the situation over on the ground the posse had ridden over, Garrett decided there were more than just two or three men involved, and that he was going to need help. Charlie Perry, sheriff over in Roswell, agreed to work with him for a piece of the reward.

"Fraser reported that while Garrett wasn't unfriendly, he never volunteered any information. If Fraser wanted information from Garrett, he had to ask him a direct question, and Garrett only answered what he was asked. When Fraser got out in the country on his own, with Clint Llewellyn acting as a guide, he interviewed just about everyone who would talk to him. He developed a few new leads, but none of them went anywhere, and, as I say, Garrett never shared anything with him, so I never received much from the Pinkertons."

Thornton puffs on his cigar and speaks in his slow, Virginia drawl, so it's easy to keep up with him in my written notes. I have to ask, "Was one of those leads that never went anywhere Eva Taylor's affidavit?"

He frowns. "How'd you know about Eva Taylor?"

I shake my head. "I'm sorry, sir, but I was told about her in confidence, and I can't betray my sources, even to a former governor."

"That's all right. I understand and admire a man of his word. Yes, Eva Taylor was one of those leads. Garrett claimed he read her affidavit and talked to her. Said he didn't believe her. Fraser tried to interview her, but he couldn't find her. The stage driver who might have verified her story had moved on to another job, and Fraser didn't have time or money to track him down."

That seems to me like a lame excuse for ignoring a potentially important witness, especially if she might contradict Pat Garrett's key witness. I frown and say, "Just one more question, Governor. What do you think chances are that Ed Brown was involved with the murders?"

His brows go up, and I see his jaw muscles flexing. "You do have your sources, don't you? Maybe I should have hired you instead of Pat Garrett. Look, I'm known for playing poker. Let's just say that the odds Ed Brown was involved in the murders are about as good as winning a pot with a straight flush.

"When I got word from the warden at the state pen that Slick Miller had information about the murders he wanted to pass along to me in the hopes I might reduce his sentence, I went to see him. His story was intriguing enough that I contacted the Pinkertons again, and they sent me another of their most experienced men, a fellow named Sayers. His investigation showed Brown was lying about his whereabouts during the time the Fountains were murdered, that Brown was desperate to cover his tracks during the time he disappeared, and that Brown even claimed he knew who to ask to find out where the bodies were hidden. Sayers and Sheriff Bursum tried to bluff him into spilling the beans, but Brown was just too hard a nut to crack. The territory's attorney couldn't even get a conviction against him for an indictment that was pending for cattle theft. My guess is Brown was too smart and too fearful of Oliver Lee and his boys to break. I guess we'll never know."

Thornton stands. "That's about it, Quentin."

I nod as I close my notepad. "Thanks, Governor. You've been very helpful. Guess I'll see you at the trial tomorrow."

Chapter 17
Talks in the Moonlight

The air on Main Street is a still, luminous haze in the dying light. I take Persia's strong, rough hand in mine. We walk down Main Street and across the bridge over the Percha along the gurgling water. A bright, yellow glow is beginning in the eastern sky as a full moon gets ready to float above the range of hills. Off to our right is the Lee camp, crowded with men eating, smoking, and swapping stories around the big chuck wagon fire.

We pass several gentlemen with ladies on their arms. The men tip their hats and say "Good evening" and the ladies smile and nod. I think Persia must be friends with everyone in Hillsboro. At the bridge, we stop to lean against the side railing and listen to the night chorus of frogs and its competition from up the street—the tinkle of pianos, a mournful fiddle, and a twanging banjo.

Persia stares off into the dark and whispers, "It's been a pleasure to know you, Quent, and thanks for supper. If you've finished your interview, I should get on back home and let you talk to others."

I'm dumbfounded and feel my heart sinking like a stone in deep water. "What makes you say that? We're friends. No, we're more than friends. I have feelings I haven't yet spoken, and you've helped me more with my work than I can say. I want to enjoy your company all I can. What have I done or said that offends you?"

She glances at me, the moonlight reflecting off the little streams of water on her cheeks. "Yes, we're friends, as you say, and maybe more than friends. I, too, have feelings I cannot and will not speak. Let's be honest with each other. You're not interested in courting me; you're just after information and maybe something else."

She pulls a delicate handkerchief out of her sleeve and dabs at her eyes and cheeks. "I'm just a rough-cut ranch woman. You're not about to court me with any real intentions. You're not above takin' advantage of a lonesome girl, either. I don't want you to play at courting me for the rest of the trial 'cause I don't want to be standing in the dust of that stage when you leave, my heart breaking, knowing you won't be back." She turns to continue up Main Street.

"No, wait! Persia, please, wait."

She stops, her back to me, her head bowed, listening.

"I'm not being felicitous just to get information out of you. You're a wonderful woman—strong, smart, easygoing, and very easy on the eyes. I'd be proud to be seen with you on any street in the world, but you have to understand. A reporter's life is filled with turbulence. He's always on the go. He works awful hours, and his life isn't his own. It's no life for a wife or the mother of his children, and I know that's what you must want. I think you're wonderful, but I can never ask you or any other woman to suffer through the loneliness and uncertainty from the kind of work I do. Can you understand what I'm trying to tell you?"

She keeps her back to me. I hear a sniff, and she nods, murmuring, "Yes, I understand. Thank you for being so thoughtful about my future feelings. Come on. I have to get up early, and you have work to do." Taking my hand in a gentle squeeze, she heads up Main Street toward her room in the back of the Black Range Café.

I feel sick, depressed, thinking she doesn't want to spend any more time with me. A huge split in the earth seems to have opened between us. I wonder what I've done to provoke her into running me off.

At her door, Persia gives me a peck on the cheek. "Quent, I wish you much success. I hope this trial is your big break. Most of all, I hope you don't get killed because of it. Goodbye."

Before I can say anything, she slips inside, closing the door behind her. Morose, I walk back down Main, staying in the shadows, trying not to make myself an easy target for Clayton and Greco. I head for the Ocean Grove's porch to try to sort out my thoughts and feelings.

As I walk up, Sadie is giving instructions to the tall, good-looking, black woman who was a waitress this morning. "Now, Sam, you be sure he pays you first this time. We ain't no charity. I hate worse than the plague to go after anybody for money, especially a soldier. It's bad for business, but I've done it before, and I'll do it again if I have to."

Sam smiles and nods. "Yas'm. That boy's gonna pay me first all right, or he ain't gettin' nuthin'! See you after a while, Miss Sadie. Evenin', Mista Peach."

Sadie smiles, waves her off, and beckons me to a chair. "Well, I say! Good evening, Quent. I thought you'd be out late with Persia this evening. You two seemed to hit it off well, and I know she likes you."

I plop down on the slat-bottom chair and lean back against the wall. "I thought she did, too, but she sent me packing. Said I was just after information and not serious about courting her. Sadie, I can't court her. I don't see marriage any time in the near future because a reporter already has a mistress—his work. A wife isn't going to be happy with a man who has a mistress, even if it is only his work."

Sadie shakes her head. "That child is smarter than I thought.

Good for her." She takes a sip of tea and asks, "Have you seen any more of those men who beat you up?"

"No, not since I've been out this afternoon. By the way, I was able to interview Governor Thornton this afternoon. He says Garrett interviewed Eva Taylor, but he didn't believe her."

Sadie shifts her weight and smiles. "J.W. told me Poker Bill was on the stage this afternoon. He's a good man. Had him as a customer for my girls a time or two. I ain't surprised Garrett didn't believe Eva, especially when Poker Bill told him Lee was the murderer. Like I told you, her story don't match up with Garrett's witness tellin' about Lee and his boys doing the murder."

We pass an hour or two discussing witnesses in the trial. Sadie thinks Catron must be in a real sweat to find Maxwell. A couple of good-looking ladies stop by to give Sadie money. She pockets it and holds up her hand to stop them from leaving. "These girls have no more business for the evening, Quent. One or both of them can make you forget your troubles with Persia."

I force a smile and shake my head. "They're nice, Sadie, really nice, but not tonight. Thanks just the same."

Smiling, they nod, curtsy, and are off down the street.

I yawn and feel all the places where I was pounded as I stretch. "I'm tired and going to bed. Thanks for the company. I expect I'll see you sometime tomorrow."

"Good night, Quent. Yes, I'll see you tomorrow. Just let me know if you need anything."

Chapter 18
Testimony Begins, 29 May 1899

Seventy-five of ninety witnesses come to the front rail to be sworn. Jack Maxwell, key witness for the prosecution, is among the missing. No word has been received from Pat Garrett, who leads a posse searching for him. Fountain partisan rumors say the Lee side murdered Maxwell and hid his body in the same place as the Fountains. Lee partisans say Maxwell is deathly ill and won't be able to attend the trial. Another rumor says he's sick because he's fearful Lee partisans are looking to kill him.

After the witnesses are sworn, R.P. Barnes, district attorney from Silver City, makes the territory's case. He admits the evidence is circumstantial, and there are no *corpus delicti*—no bodies. Nevertheless, he maintains the territory will find Maxwell, and with his testimony and other evidence, prove beyond a shadow of reasonable doubt that first, Albert and Henry Fountain were murdered, and second, Oliver Lee and James Gililland were directly responsible for the murder of Henry Fountain.

Lee, his arms crossed, sits, slowly shaking his head. Gililland stares out the window. The jury listens intently. Chavez, the interpreter, speaks in a low voice, and the Spanish-speaking members of the jury hold cupped hands to their ears to hear his translation of Barnes's opening statement.

Barnes tells Judge Parker the prosecution's lead witness is not yet available and asks permission to call witnesses out of the order they were provided. Fall says the defense has no objections to calling the witnesses in any order. Judge Parker approves the request and tells Barnes to call his first witness. Barnes calls former Governor William T. Thornton. Poker Bill looks very tired, and I wonder if he's been playing poker all night.

Barnes asks Thornton to describe how he became involved in the case.

Thornton states he first learned of Albert and Henry Fountain's deaths on Tuesday, February fourth, after their deaths on Saturday, February 1, 1896.

Fall is on his feet objecting to the term *deaths,* saying that since no bodies have been found, the correct term is *disappearances.* I look over the courtroom and see smiles and nods from some, frowns from others. My gaze falls on the three cowboys I met in the Black Range Café. They sit in exactly the same spot they sat Thursday when the jury was selected. Now they lean forward, their hands clasped, elbows on their knees, listening to every word. I wonder why there is such loyalty and devotion to Lee and Gililland.

Judge Parker sustains the objection and asks Thornton to proceed with his testimony. Thornton testifies that in Las Cruces he made an investigation of the facts, as they were then known. Colonel Van Patten provided him with a package of blood-soaked earth he collected while he was with a posse at what he believed was the scene of the murder. Later Van Patten sent him hair he shaved from Fountain's white horse. It appeared to be stained with blood. Thornton gave the earth and horsehair samples to an Albuquerque chemist, Dr. Francis Crosson, for analysis.

Fall, looking over his glasses, leans back, relaxed, in his chair to cross-examine Thornton.

"Governor, who requested you come to Las Cruces?"

"I don't recall anyone asking me to come to Las Cruces.

Llewellyn and Numa Reymond asked me to offer a reward."

"Didn't Thomas Tucker send you a telegram asking that you come?"

"No, sir, I think not."

"Didn't you state that Tucker sent you a telegram?"

"No, sir. I'm certain Tucker never sent me any telegram, and I don't believe anyone else did either."

Fall takes a long minute or two to make a point of jotting something on his notes of Thornton's testimony. "No further questions, Your Honor."

Antonio García, father of Albert Fountain's wife, is called next.

Barnes asks García to describe the last time he saw Colonel Fountain and Henry and what happened during the posse's search for the Fountains. García looks ancient in years, with his thick, white hair and a face as craggy as mountain canyons. He's slow to grasp Chavez's translations of Barnes's questions.

After some preliminary give and take with Chavez, he nods and tells the packed room that the last time he saw the Fountains was when he and Albert Fountain returned runaway horses to the colonel and Henry when they were camped up on San Agustin Pass, right after the colonel left home for Lincoln.

Describing what was found two weeks later, he says the posse followed the trail of the buckboard out into the desert, and when it was found, there were numerous boot tracks around it. Some of the posse stayed with the buckboard while the rest followed the trail of the horses leading away from it: six horses in a group. The men followed the trail until it split into two groups of three. The posse followed the group that went across the northern end of the Jarilla Mountains and on into the desert northeast toward the Sacramento Mountains and Lee's Well. Within seven miles of Lee's Well, the trail was wiped out by a herd of cattle that crossed it. They then broke off the search and rode south to Wildy Well for water.

Barnes has no more questions for *Señor* García. Judge Parker recesses for dinner with court to resume at two o'clock. The courtroom slowly empties, the crowd rumbling down the stairs.

After being in the courtroom all morning, I find the sunlight blinding. I look around, squinting against the glare. Clayton and Greco sit on the far west end of the wall supporting the ground fill for the jail foundation. They both grin when I see them. The sunlight glints off one of Greco's gold teeth. He makes a finger pistol and snaps it at me. Out of the corner of my eye, I see Tom Tucker, arms crossed, leaning in the doorway of the jail, watching us, his head making the faintest suggestion of a nod. I sigh with relief, grin back at Greco, and pretend to blow the smoke off the end of my finger as though it's a pistol barrel.

Greco's grin turns to a snarl, and his eyes narrow. Clayton's smile is gone, too. He stares at me as he reaches up to scratch the stubble on his face and makes a slow slashing sign across his throat with his index finger.

Still smiling, I make a point of ignoring them. I glance around the groups of men for someone to interview, but see no one of interest. When I look back toward Clayton and Greco, they are gone, and so is Tom Tucker. I set off down the hill for the Black Range Café.

Men sit on benches outside the café waiting for a table. I see two women inside, carrying full plates to tables surrounded by hungry men and clearing tables for new customers. Persia isn't there. I ask one of the waitresses if she knows where Persia is. She shakes her head, shrugs her shoulders, and says Persia hasn't been there since before breakfast. I hurry down Main Street, looking in restaurants and cantinas. She's nowhere to be seen.

I get to the Ocean Grove Restaurant and ask a waitress if I

might speak with Sadie. The waitress smiles and shakes her head. "Sorry, Mr. Peach. Sadie drove the stage today. I expect she'll be back about three. She took Persia with her to see how well she can drive. Persia says she ain't gonna work in the Black Range Café no more and wants to be a driver like Sadie. Persia gonna start workin' here some, too. Can I get you some dinner?"

I'm so relieved I can barely nod.

Court resumes promptly at two o'clock. Judge Parker announces that he has met with the attorneys on both sides. All are anxious to expedite the trial and have agreed sessions will be held day and night as necessary and appropriate. Judge Parker has Antonio García called back to the witness chair. He's reminded that he's still under oath to tell the truth. The defense is invited to begin its cross-examination. Fall stands, draws himself up to his full height, and moves to hover, tall and intimidating, over the old man.

After two or three questions about the last time García saw the Fountains alive, Fall bores into the old man. It's not pretty. The long and tedious cross-examination is more an interrogation. Fall appears to have an expert's knowledge of the terrain over which the posse traveled, distances between locations, the nature of the locations, and trail directions. He crucifies García with a long series of questions about this key geography that makes my head hurt just trying to follow it. García is so confused and Fall so unrelenting, I feel sorry and embarrassed for the old man. At last, mercifully, Fall says, "No more questions."

Asking for redirect, Childers stands for the prosecution. He asks if García saw any loose horses near the trail. García answers he saw some, but only a long way off.

At last, García is allowed to step down. I wonder what Fall

will do to the primary witnesses like Maxwell and Garrett if he runs a minor witness like García through his meat grinder.

Judge Parker calls a twenty-minute recess. About half the crowd is quickly out the door to smoke and visit the facilities out back. Fall and the prisoners stay put. Lee sits, calm and collected, his hands clasped and resting on the table. Gililland sits slumped in his chair, staring at the ceiling. I stay where I am.

When recess is over, Albert Fountain is called. The courtroom, still as death, waits for the eldest son of the murdered man to testify. Albert, poised and relaxed, speaks easily as Childers leads him into a description of the last time he saw his father and of forming the posse that left the night Barela returned.

Albert tells of the posse riding in the freezing cold most of the night. He says that just over San Agustin Pass, they stopped at Parker's Well for a little rest, and then rode on to Luna's Wells, where they learned the colonel and Henry had passed Luna's on their trip home. He tells how, retracing the buckboard tracks from Luna's, they found a big, green bush next to the road, near Chalk Hill, with tracks behind it, likely from cowboy boots. Depressions in the sand made it almost certain someone sat and kneeled there. He says tracks leading from the bush showed where the buckboard and three horsemen left the road. As Albert describes the scene, I see phantoms of what happened in my mind's eye.

Albert continues, "There were tracks of men and horses around the spot. We found where the buggy and horses stopped. The horses stamped their feet, as if restless. Cigarette papers were scattered around on the ground. Farther on, the other searching party found the dismantled buggy. My father's valise and boxes had been opened. Horse tracks led straight toward the Jarillas."

I wonder why Lee would lead a posse straight in the direction of his ranch.

"We could identify the tracks of six horses."

I recall someone telling me that the colonel had three horses with him, two pulling his buggy and one tied behind. That meant there were at least three riders. Fountain's white mare ran off, and the horse tied behind the buggy was turned loose. García said two groups of three went over the Jarillas. There had to be at least eight horses. Where were their riders? Where was the horse for the shooter back at the green bush?

Childers asks, "Did you see any signs of the young Henry Fountain?"

Albert says, "We found the remains of a campfire where they had apparently spent the night. There were tracks from a child about eight years old."

Childers looks out across the jurors, frowns, and waits a moment before asking Albert to continue his account.

"The trail of one horse branched off and took a zigzag course as if unwilling to leave the rest. We identified those tracks as belonging to Colonel Fountain's little mare. On the trail toward the Jarillas, another horse left the rest and headed toward the pass near the southern end of the Jarillas. The main party went on over the Jarillas and east toward the Sacramentos. We lost the trail when a cattle herd crossed it just as we were getting to the west slope of the Sacramentos."

Childers produces a well-drawn map of the Tularosa Basin and asks Albert to point out the places he described. When he finishes, Childers asks him, "Were any measurements made of the tracks, so they could be compared with those of the apprehended suspects?"

Albert nods. "Yes, sir. Major Llewellyn measured the tracks at the campsite with a pocket ruler. There's no doubt that the small tracks were those of a child. They were just too small to be those of a man or even a woman."

Childers rubs his chin thoughtfully. "Could you tell if the tracks were made by the left or the right shoe?"

Albert shakes his head. "No, sir, it was not clear to me which was which."

Childers appears pleased with Albert's testimony. "No more questions, Your Honor."

Daugherty cross-examines for the defense. He begins by asking for additional details about the last time Albert saw the colonel, when he and García returned the horses that had run off while the colonel and Henry camped in San Agustin Pass on their first night on the way to Lincoln. "The country south of Luna's Wells is rough, is it not?"

"Yes, sir."

"How far from the road might you see a horseman?"

Childers springs out of his chair, objecting that the question asks for a conclusion from the witness. Judge Parker sustains.

Daugherty continues, "At the buckboard, Mr. Fountain, you say most of the little boy's clothing was gone?"

"The coat was gone."

Childers asks for redirect. "What kind of clothing was left behind at the buckboard?"

"An old suit of my father's and my brother's coat, hat, and two shawls. My father's cartridge belt was found on the buggy seat, but his rifle was gone."

I'm surprised Daugherty doesn't pounce when Albert seems to contradict what he just told the court about the boy's coat being gone.

"At this time I have no more questions of this witness, Your Honor."

"Very well. Mr. Fountain, you're excused subject to recall. You may step down. The hour is well toward suppertime. This court is adjourned until nine in the morning." Judge Parker pounds his gavel, stands, and disappears into his office behind the bench. Acting as bailiff, Sheriff Kahler excuses the packed courtroom.

Chapter 19
Todd Bailey

I scan the crowd as I clear the front door of the courthouse. Clayton and Greco have disappeared, and so has Tom Tucker. Anxious to find out how Persia did driving Sadie's stage, I head down the hill toward the Ocean Grove as fast as I can go without losing my dignity by running.

The saloons and bars on Main Street are doing a brisk business. As the sun sinks in a glory of orange and purple streaks behind the Black Range, it's remarkably quiet for a crowded street with full saloons. I reach the Ocean Grove and jerk the door open. I look up and down the hall and in the restaurant. Persia's not there.

The black woman I saw with Sadie last night is taking a turn at waiting tables until more lucrative business appears later in the evening. She smiles, motioning me to a table. Attractive, like all of Sadie's girls, she's tall and trim. Her eyes betray an intelligence most wouldn't expect after hearing her thick, Southern drawl. "You ready fo' yo' suppa, Mista Peach?"

"Thanks, not now, Sam. I was looking for Miss Brown. Is she here?"

"No, suh. Ain't seen her de whole day."

"How about Mrs. Orchard? Where's she? Did the Lake Valley stage get in on time?"

"Yas, suh. Miss Sadie, she's over to de Orchard Hotel with Mista Orchard. I think they's takin' care of some stage business over dere."

"Thanks, Sam. If you see Miss Brown, will you tell her I'm looking for her?"

"Yas, suh, be glad to tell her."

"Thanks! Don't forget now."

She smiles as I head out the door.

I step inside the Orchard Hotel door in time to hear Sadie giving J.W. the first degree.

"Damn it to hell, J.W.! This ain't no time to be swilling Forty Rod. There's lots of money to be made, and the opportunity ain't gonna come again in a long, damn time, you idiot sonovabitch!"

Then, apparently sensing my presence, she turns and says, "Oh! Hallo, Quent." She blushes and continues as if I'd overheard nothing. "J.W., this is Mr. Quentin Peach. He's a reporter with the *San Francisco Examiner.*"

J.W. and I shake hands. He's a tall, nice-looking man with a trimmed mustache and square chin. He wears canvas pants stuffed into high boots, suspenders, and a flat-brimmed hat. His face is red, and there's a strong smell of whiskey emanating from him. "Mr. Peach," he said, "if you'll excuse me, I've got to take care of some stock. Pleasure to meet you." Without another word, he ambles down the hall toward the back door.

Sadie yells after him, "No more Forty Rod, J.W.! You listen to me now!" She crosses her arms and gives me an I-told-you-so smile. "Come for a date? I think Nadine might be available sometime around eight o'clock."

"Not tonight, Sadie. I came to ask about Persia. I understand she rode on the stage with you today. How'd she do? I need to talk to her. Do you know where I can find her?"

Her smile grows wider. "Kingston."

I frown, confused. "Kingston?"

"Yes, sir. She went on to Kingston with the change-driver. I want her to learn the road between here and Kingston. It's harder to drive than the one between here and Lake Valley, and it has to be driven in the dark coming down from Kingston. She's a natural at handling a team. I expect she'n drive the route by herself in three or four weeks. She did right well today."

"Will she be here tomorrow?"

She nods. "Stage from Kingston is due in here tonight at eight-thirty. She's going to help Tom Ying in the restaurant until she's ready to drive full-time, so you can find her this evening when she gets back. She's taken a room here in the hotel. Why are you asking? What's the matter?"

"I saw Clayton and Greco today when court adjourned for dinner. I just wanted her to know they're still around and to tell her to be careful where she goes by herself."

There's a twinkle in Sadie's eyes. "Okay, I'll let her know tonight when she gets in from Kingston."

"Uh, no. That's okay. I'll tell her. I need to discuss some other business with her too."

"Oh, I see," she teases.

"Thanks. Sorry to have barged in on you and Mr. Orchard. I'm off to have a drink and some supper. Good night." She waves me out the door.

In the deepening dusk, I head for the Union Hotel and bar.

I edge my way up to the bar, order a beer, and look around for a table where there's an extra chair. I see the three cowboys I met in the Black Range Café. They're sitting in the corner of the room at a table that has an extra chair. I work my way over to them. "Howdy, boys. Remember me? Mind if I sit down?"

The clean-shaven one with the big, black hat smiles. "Howdy. Shore, sit down and take a load off."

When they learn I'm a reporter, they aren't as jovial as they were at first, but they aren't hostile. Two of them gulp down their beers and stand to leave. Todd Bailey, the one in the black hat, continues to sit. He still has half a mug of beer.

One of the others says, "Come on, Todd. Let's go git some supper. Ed oughta have the steaks 'bout ready down to the chuck wagon."

He grins up at them. "Boys, I spent good money on this beer, an' I ain't gonna leave half of it. Y'all go ahead. I'll be along shortly."

"Okay. See ya in a while. Good to meet ya, Mr. Peach."

I salute them with a raise of my mug. Bailey asks, "So, Mr. Peach, what did you want to talk to me about?"

I raise my brows in surprise. "What makes you think I want to interview you?"

"My uncle. He says reporters are always lookin' for a story. They never sit down just to chew the fat. They're always listening and asking, so be careful how you talk to 'em."

"That's good advice. Your uncle is a smart man. Who is he anyway?"

"Oliver Lee."

I'm impressed with the young man's forthrightness. I decide I won't play ignorant with him. "Look, Mr. Bailey, I heard you fellows talking in the Black Range Café the other morning. I'm certain you plan to free your uncle and Gililland if the verdict goes against them. I promise I won't write or say a word about your plans if I can have an interview with your uncle and Gililland after they're in Mexico. What do you say? Deal?" I stick out my hand.

For a long, sickening moment, he stares at me. Then Bailey grabs my hand. "Deal. What do you want to know?"

"I do special interest stories for the *Examiner.* I'm curious as to why the big businessmen and townspeople think Lee is a major cattle thief and gunman, while his friends and neighbors find it impossible to believe he'd murder the Fountains, especially the little boy. You and your friends seem like clean-cut young men. Why are you willing to help him?"

Bailey stares straight into my eyes. "I was with him on his ranch the entire day the Fountains disappeared. I know damn well he didn't kill 'em. Even if I hadn't been with him that day, I'd never believe he'd murder a kid because of what he did for my sister and me. That damned District Attorney Barnes claimed Oliver was guilty of stealing, and that's why Fountain was after him. Well, his neighbors have been around Oliver for at least ten or fifteen years, and they're here now. You think they'd be here to back him up if he'd threatened or stole from 'em? Hell no, they wouldn't!"

I concede that that makes sense.

Bailey says, "That lying jackass, Slick Miller, was making up tales to get outta prison after the Fountains disappeared. He told Governor Thornton that Oliver was in on the murder of Frenchy Rochas. That there is an out and out lie! Oliver and Frenchy was friends. Oliver and Aunt Mary took care of Frenchy after he was shot by that skunk Morrison, who tried to rob and kill him. French showed Oliver how to plant grapes and fruit trees. When Oliver was working on the water supply outta Dog Canyon, he even fixed the ditch so Frenchy had water for his fruit trees when he wanted it. The windows in Oliver's ranch house are special made. Frenchy made them for Oliver.

"Oliver's ranch depends on the water that comes outta Dog Canyon. As soon as he found somebody murdered Frenchy, of course, he laid claim to the land before them rich slicks could snatch it out from under him. That don't mean he killed Frenchy to get it. They got along fine. Respected each other, they did. That there Slick Miller ought to be shot for the lies he's a-tellin'!"

I enjoy hearing the passion in Bailey's voice. "Well, if your uncle gets along with his neighbors so well, why are the townspeople so afraid of him?"

"Oliver don't take nothin' off nobody. He ain't never backed down from a fight. He don't start 'em, but he'll shore finish 'em. In '92, them Republicans was tryin' to scare folks into votin' Republican by puttin' their militia up and down the street in Las Cruces on election day. Fall asked Oliver and some of his boys to come into town to face 'em down. He did, and the militia backed off. When Fall was a judge, he made Oliver, Jim, Billy, and a couple of others deputy marshals. They enforced the law and wouldn't take guff off nobody, so them folks knew they had to walk the line. That's why they's afraid of him. When the election for sheriff in '94 was disputed, old Fall used all his tricks to keep Ascarate in office and got him to make Oliver, Jim, and Billy deputy sheriffs."

Bailey smiles. "Made them damn Republicans so hot, they was foaming at the mouth. That big, fat prosecutor, Catron, he's a Republican. He owns more land than anybody in the territory. He got it by takin' over the property of little ranchers run out o' business by the big operators. He—"

I hold up my hand to stop him while I write. "Gene Rhodes told me the same story. He said the big ranchers tried to overgraze the free range so Lee and the others would have to pull up stakes and move on to new grass, and Lee wouldn't let 'em. No wonder the small ranchers think he's a hero. Tell me what he did for you and your sister."

Bailey stares at his beer for a while before he speaks. I see him swallow hard a couple of times. "By the time I was ten years old, my sister, Mamie, and me was orphans. There's a feller and his wife over to Commerce, Texas, where we's livin' with daddy before he died, that said they'd take us in an' be our guardian still we was grown. That bastard, he's mean and no good. Them folks didn't want no kids; they wanted slaves. Worked an' beat me half to death all the time 'cause he said I wasn't workin' hard enough. Him an' his wife treated my sister as bad or worse than me, workin' her all the time.

"I could tell the way that man was lookin' at my sister that it wasn't gonna be long before things got a lot worse for her. We had to get outta there. The only thing I knew to do was try to find my mama's side of the family and ask them to take us in. I remembered hearing Daddy tell a neighbor that we had kin, name of Lee, living over close to Buffalo Gap, Texas. So one night, when there weren't no moon, I ran away. I had fifty cents in my pocket—"

My jaw drops. "You ran away? How in the world did you find Buffalo Gap?"

He shakes his head. "I knew how to get down to Fort Worth 'cause our so-called guardians had driven some stock down there, and me and my sister were taken along in a wagon with the supplies to help out with the cooking chores. Hardest part of that trip was getting down to Fort Worth, 'cause I walked and ran the whole way. I's afraid somebody would catch me and make me go back. After I got to Fort Worth, I asked some cowboys who took me in how to get to Buffalo Gap. One of 'em was heading for the Nations over to Oklahoma. He let me ride behind him on the back of his horse part of the way."

I hold up my hand and ask, "How far was Commerce from Fort Worth?"

" 'Bout eighty miles."

"How far from Fort Worth to Buffalo Gap?"

" 'Bout a hundred and sixty."

"Unbelievable! Were the Lees still living in Buffalo Gap?"

"No, they'd packed up and left for the grass over in New Mexico. I asked one of the men working on the Lee's old place, and he said they was living somewhere close to Tularosa. So I started walking again."

"How old were you? How far is it from Buffalo Gap to your

uncle's ranch?"

"Oh, I's going on eleven. I'd reckon it's about three hundred seventy miles, give or take, as the crow flies, but I speck I walked more'n four hundred from Buffalo Gap, as much as I got lost."

I shake my head in wonder. "How in the world did you do it?"

"I almost didn't. Stole food in towns when I could. Got fellers on horses to give me a ride once in a while, even hitched on a stage for a day, but I was always heading west. The fellers on horseback and the stage driver, they told me which way to point so's I'd hit Tularosa. Lucky for me, Oliver found me on the free range when he did. I's just about starved to death. Course he didn't know who I was when he found me and carried me home to Mam Maw Mary.

"It took her a couple o' weeks to nurse me back to where I could get around some. I guess they's mighty surprised to learn I was kin. Oliver, he had a hard time believing I come so far by myself, and on foot at that. He sent a telegram to a man he knew in Fort Worth, asking him to check my story. In a week, a telegram come back that said a couple in Commerce was guardians for a girl named Mamie and that the couple claimed her brother had run off an left 'em high and dry. I cried an' begged Oliver and Aunt Mary to please get Mamie. You shoulda seen Oliver's face when I told him what that couple was a-doin' to us and what that old man was gonna do to Mamie just any time, if he hadn't already. Mam Maw told Oliver not to worry about the ranch and for him to get going. Said she'd see to the ranch till he got back with Mamie. He left that evenin'. I was so happy an' relieved I sat down and cried." He sighs and shakes his head. "Reckon I cried a lot in them days."

"Did he get Mamie before she was badly harmed?"

Bailey takes another long swallow of beer, draining his mug. "Yes, sir, he did. He was gone nearly ten days. Caught the train down in El Paso and rode it all the way to Fort Worth, where he got a horse and went on to Commerce. He first tried to play by the rules. Went to the sheriff and told him he was Mamie's uncle, but he didn't have no papers with him to prove nothing. Sheriff, he laughed at him and said that without no proof, the court would say she had to stay with the guardian. So he went to the couple that had her and told 'em he was Mamie's uncle. They weren't about to give up a slave without a fight. The old man put a shotgun on Oliver and told him to stay away from his place. That if he came back, he'd fill him full o' buckshot and the sheriff would put what was left in jail for a long, long time.

"Oliver, he went back late that night leading a horse for Mamie, eased in the house, and found 'em in bed. When the old man woke up, the business end of Oliver's revolver was stuck right between his eyes. He asked the old bastard if he wanted to let Mamie go or have a talk with that pistol. Then and there, he was right agreeable.

"Oliver tied 'em up and had to kick in Mamie's door 'cause it was locked. He told her he was goin' to take her to live with him, Mam Maw Mary, and me. She didn't give him no argument. She hopped on that horse and was gone before Oliver could blink. They were back to the ranch in a few days. Mam Maw and Oliver, they took real good care of us. Give us some schooling so's we can take care of ourselves, and now I'm helpin' Oliver with his horses."

I shake my head in wonder. "I can see why you have so much loyalty to your uncle. It sounds like he doesn't have much patience with folks who won't do the right thing."

Pulling his hat down on his forehead, Bailey stands up and sticks out his hand for a shake. "Yes, sir, that's about right. There ain't nothing I wouldn't do for Oliver . . ." He pauses for a moment, looking at me with hooded eyes, giving me a creepy feeling. "Even kill for him if I had to. Been a pleasure talking to you, Mr. Peach. Don't forget our deal!" He nods toward the door. "Come on down to the chuck wagon and have some supper with us."

I grin and nod. "That sounds like an offer I can't refuse."

CHAPTER 20
ALBERT FALL

Several men are still sitting around the campfire when Bailey and I walk into its circle of light. We come to a well-dressed figure sitting on a short-legged bench, his pie pan he used for a plate nearly empty. He wears a big black Stetson pushed back on his long, wavy hair. He recognizes me instantly and sticks out his hand.

"Well, hello, Mr. Peach. I'm glad to see you're not shot full of holes."

I take his hand, unable to keep the broad smile off my face, thinking, *This must be my lucky night!* "Mr. Fall! It's a pleasure to see you. Is this a good time for that interview you promised?"

He nods. "I think so, if it's not too long. We need to do a little more preparation for crosses tomorrow. Go get your supper. Then sit here with me, and we'll talk."

Bailey grins and points me toward the cook, who's holding a couple of pie pans he's already filled with our supper. We take our food, and Bailey heads off to sit with his friends.

I sit down by Mr. Fall. He gives his pan to the cook's helper with a request for more coffee and says, "Okay, Mr. Peach, fire away."

"Well, sir, I've heard stories that you and Mr. Lee are concerned that someone was hired to murder you. I understand the judge even let Mr. Lee have extra guards of his own choosing. I spoke with one of the guards, Gene Rhodes. Off the record, are the assassination threats true, or is the story a maneuver to keep the prosecutors off-balance and on the defensive?"

With a grunt, he sets his blue speckled cup on the ground and reaches inside a vest pocket to bring out one of the long cigars he often fires up in court. He trims it up and takes his time lighting it. When the cigar has a bright, orange coal, he speaks.

"What I'm going to tell you will probably come out in this trial anyway. Just the same, I'd appreciate it if you'd treat it as confidential information until after the trial."

"Yes sir, you have my word on that."

He nods and smiles. "I believe I can trust you on that Mr. . . . uh, may I call you Quentin? And if you please, I'm just Albert here to the boys."

I grin. "Yes, sir. My friends call me Quent. I'm honored to be on a first name basis with you."

He takes a couple of puffs as he stares out into the dark. "At one time the threat to which you refer was real. I chose to bring it to light for two reasons. First, now it's common knowledge a threat was made and who made it. If anything happens to us, the law will know the most likely suspects. That means we ought to be safe from those who wanted us dead in the first place. Second, I've played it for more importance than it probably is. I want the public to understand the hand we were dealt and why we're playing the way we are." He winks. "Do you get my drift?"

I nod. "Yes, sir, I do."

He blows a stream of smoke up into the cool night air, spits a bit of tobacco off his lip, and takes another swallow of coffee. "Numa Reymond was the candidate the Republicans ran for Doña Ana County sheriff in '94. He was totally unfit to be a sheriff. He's a wealthy storeowner in Las Cruces, and the Republicans ran him because nearly everybody does business at his store, and he keeps a credit tab on a large number of his customers. So there's a lot of voters who feel they owe him allegiance as well as money."

I take a bite of my steak and a few mouthfuls of beans cooked with green chili peppers. "If Reymond is wealthy, then why did he want to be elected sheriff? It seems like his business would suffer from his being away chasing outlaws."

Fall laughs. "Reymond planned to make a lot of money off the sheriff's job and continue to grow his store business. Even the man he planned to make his chief deputy was just a storekeeper. They planned to get some boys off the range to do the dangerous work."

He holds up a hand with his fingers spread and starts ticking off the sheriff's sources of income. "See, first the county pays him a small salary. Next, he gets another five dollars a day for being in court. Third, if the big operators want a little extra squeeze on the competition, they pass him extra cash under the table. Fourth, keeping drunks overnight and feeding them breakfast counts as two days in jail and the county pays fifty cents a day, so, less fifteen cents for breakfast, he makes eighty-five cents per drunk for a one-night stay. Fifth, he can accept scrip for back taxes at sixty to eighty cents on the dollar and hold it until it's redeemed at full value. The extra money goes into his pocket. Sixth, he pays himself 'informer' fees after reporting illegal gambling to the person in authority—that is, to himself—and he collects fifty percent of everything left on the table when he closes down a gambling operation. Lastly, the sheriff decides what cases to pursue. If he's a Republican, he's going to go after every complaint the cattle barons—Republicans, one and all—have against the little operators—all Texas Democrats—and very few of the complaints the little operators bring. That's a long pole for levering the little operators out of business so the big operators can pick up what's left."

Fall pauses to give me a moment to catch up with him in my notes. Then he says, "Reymond expected to make a lot of money playing sheriff. Needless to say, he was madder than a rabid dog when the Democrats stole the election from the Republicans—all that money gone, all that power and control gone. I really threw coal oil on the fire when I convinced Ascarate, the incumbent Reymond ran against, to fire Ben Williams and hire Lee and the others as deputies."

Fall grins. "Williams had been the enforcer in town when he worked for Martin Lohman, the Republican sheriff. As Ascarate's deputy, Lee wouldn't let Williams pack his pistol in town. Williams was a bully in his deputy days, and it was right comical to see Lee put the clamps on him. He was afraid of Lee because Lee was way too fast for him and wouldn't take any guff off him.

"The Republicans fought back with everything they had. Fountain looked like he was going to win in court and get Reymond his sheriff job after all. But even after I resigned my judgeship, I managed to get procedural delays that kept the case in court, so Ascarate was still sheriff when the next election rolled around. We were still going at it in court when Fountain disappeared. Guess that was the last straw. Reymond blamed me and Lee for Fountain's murder and for stealing big money from him because I fought the Republicans every step of the way so he couldn't be sheriff. That's when I think he or some of the other big players might have tried to hire men to kill us."

I finish my steak and beans and hand the pie pan to the cook's helper. "What makes you think he did that?"

"I received letters in June and July of '96 from Bob Burch and Jeff Aiks, who both said they had been offered money to kill me and Lee. Both letters said the same man talked to them in his store. He told them that if they were interested, he could make killing us well worth their while."

"Numa Reymond?" I ask in a low voice.

Fall takes a draw on his cigar, pauses, and says, "There's one other little interesting piece to this puzzle. W.W. Cox owns a ranch over on the east side of the Organ Mountains. He used to be close to Reymond, friends from the old days. Now he's tight with Lee for reasons I'm not at liberty to disclose. Cox told us that Jake Ryan was paid to kill Lee and me. Lucky for us, Cox stumbled on Ryan waiting to ambush Lee. Ryan managed to get away, but not before Cox made him tell him who he was waiting for and that he was going to be paid by William Llewellyn through the New York Stock Exchange."

I mutter, "Damn!"

Fall looks at me. "You got that one right, Quent. There's some extra iron in my coat pocket because of that *damn.* So I guess you can say the threats, at least the ones we know about, have gone away and that I'm using them to our advantage now. What else can I tell you?"

"I'm curious as to why you and your brother in-law tried to kill Ben Williams."

Fall stares up the hill, now lighted by a rising moon. He sighs. "Stupidity on my part. I just had a belly full of his damned bullying ways. Joe Morgan and I decided to kill him one dark night when we'd had a little too much to drink. We saw him stomping down the street and had the opportunity to catch him by surprise. I guess it was lucky for us that we didn't kill him. It was funny, though, because when the case went to the grand jury, I convinced them it was his fault, and indirectly Fountain's, because he worked for Fountain. Damned if that didn't chap both of them, especially Fountain. Guess that made my tomfoolery worthwhile."

"What did he do that pushed you over the edge?"

"Oh, while he was on a range detective scouting trip for Fountain, he shot and nearly killed a sheepherder from Mexico on the free range when the man had a perfect right to be there. Don't get me wrong. I'm not a big fan of Mexicans or sheepherders, but what he did was just too damn sorry to put up with. He had to go."

I make my notes, holding my notebook on my knee and scribbling by the light of the fire. Fall puffs on his cigar and relaxes in the orange fire's glow.

"Do you think Brown murdered Fountain?"

Fall raises a brow and gives a little nod. "I'd say so. He and a couple of his boys and two or three other men from the Tularosa side of the San Andres probably did it. They ought to be hanged, but nothing is ever going to happen to them."

"Why not?"

"Their objective was to get rid of Fountain and Lee. Kill Fountain. Have Lee take the fall for it. Why do you suppose the officially appointed investigator never went after Brown like he did Lee when there's as strong a case, if not stronger, to be made against Brown? Brown is dumb. He's a tool. Who had the most to gain with Fountain out of the way? Lee was too smart to bring down the thunder by murdering Fountain. Was Fountain's murder just to get Lee out of the way? Who had the most to gain if Lee's operation went under? Think about it. Lee had water rights to what came out of Dog Canyon. He's piping water all over that basin to raise cattle. He stands up to the big outfits and won't let them run him off like they've done to so many others. See what I mean?"

"Yes, sir, I do. Just one more question. What's the strategy for your defense?"

Fall grins, looking at me with a twisted smile. "Brute force works every time, Quent. It's simple. Discredit the prosecution's witnesses and show my clients have an unimpeachable alibi."

I stick out my hand. We shake as we stand up. "Thanks for your time."

"Thanks for your interest. Be careful wandering around town after dark."

I check the load in the Smith and Wesson holstered under my coat. A quick look at my watch shows it's a little after eight. I still have time to meet the stage from Kingston if I step along.

I reach the Union Hotel with time to spare and soon, from up Main Street, come the sounds of the stage. Persia has the lines and sits by an old codger with white whiskers and a canvas coat, who calls to the team, making them move along. My heart soars at the sight of her.

Stopping at the Union, Persia climbs down and opens the door for a couple of businessmen who step out of the cab. They head into the hotel. The driver calls down to Persia, "You done real good today, girl. You'll be driving this here rig alone purty soon. See you later."

Persia tips her hat to him as he drives off. Standing in the middle of the street, she eyes me as the stage rolls off. She crosses her arms. "You here to see me, Mr. Peach?"

I stand, motion her over, and say in my best cowboy imitation, "Howdy, Miss Persia. I see you plan to start driving the stage."

"Yes, sir, I do, not that it's any of your business. What do you want?"

I'm surprised and a little angered by her antagonistic attitude. I motion her closer. She pauses and then steps over to me so I don't have to raise my voice to speak to her. "I saw Clayton and Greco at dinner recess today. Their hints about what they wanted to do to me were obvious. I just wanted you to know they were still around and to tell you to be careful."

She nods. "I figured they would be. You ought to be on that stage in the morning before you're hurt bad or killed. I can take care of myself."

"I'm sure you can. Sadie says you'll be driving in a few weeks, and that, in the meantime, you'll be working for Tom Ying in the restaurant when you're not off learning to drive the coach."

She frowns. "You keep your nose out of my affairs. If I wind up working in one of Sadie's cribs, you'll be the first to know, I'm sure. Just write it down that it ain't gonna happen. I'd rather starve first. Don't get yourself killed. Good night, Mr. Peach." She stalks away toward the Orchard, her head high.

All I can do is tip my hat and wonder why she's so angry with me. I haven't done anything to deserve this kind of treatment.

CHAPTER 21
JACK MAXWELL FOUND, 30 MAY 1899

"Your Honor, the Territory calls Mr. Theodore Herman to the stand."

It's the fourth day of the trial. Barnes calls as his first witness the foreman of the 1896 Lincoln County grand jury. In 1896, that grand jury had indicted Oliver Lee and Bill McNew on charges related to cattle theft. The courtroom is still, every eye on Mr. Herman, and reporters write furiously to get every word of his testimony. In short order, Barnes leads Herman to the point of his testimony and the prosecution's key question.

"Now Mr. Herman, tell us the source of the evidence that came to the grand jury that reported these indictments against Mr. Lee and Mr. McNew."

Herman looks puzzled for a moment and blinks, looking at the floor. "Why, Mr. Barnes, it was clear to everybody there that Colonel Fountain brought the case against Lee and McNew and had the evidence to support it. No question at all."

"Objection!" Fall is on his feet, bristling. "Your Honor! This testimony attempts to show motive for the alleged crime and cannot be allowed!"

Judge Parker glares at Fall. "Sit down, Mr. Fall! The witness gave a straightforward answer to a question to which you did not object. Your objection is overruled."

"But, Your Honor—"

"Overruled, Mr. Fall!"

Fall sits down, his eyes on the witness. Lee keeps a poker

face. Gililland looks back at the McNews and Lee's mother and shakes his head.

Barnes introduces certified copies of the indictments into evidence and passes them around to members of the jury. When he's satisfied they've all seen them, he hands them over to the clerk. He asks Mr. Herman why they are copies. Herman points out that they're copies because the ones Colonel Fountain carried back with him to Las Cruces disappeared from the case he had on his buckboard.

Barnes smiles. "No further questions, Your Honor."

In his usual aggressive style, Fall bores into Herman, who stays steady under Fall's rapid-fire questions. He doesn't take long to ask Herman the key defense question.

"Now, Mr. Herman, what was the main piece of evidence that caused the grand jury to bring the indictments?"

"Why, the hide Les Dow had. It showed that Lee and McNew had been running brands on Blue Water cattle."

Fall's brows go up in surprise. "Oh? Les Dow brought that evidence? How did that happen?"

"Well, somehow, Mr. Dow found out the brand had been run on that particular cow. He bought it from McNew at the end of fall roundup, had it slaughtered and skinned, and there was the Blue Water brand bigger than life on the flesh side. He got the drop on McNew, put the cuffs on him, and hauled him straight to Lincoln for arraignment and charges. Took 'em three days to get there. It was a mighty brave thing Dow did. Everybody knows how dangerous a gunman McNew is, but Dow didn't care. He had McNew cold, and they both knew it. When they got to Lincoln, McNew posted bond and then contacted you to come to his defense."

Fall nods. "So let me see if I have the facts straight. Les Dow caught McNew with indisputable evidence that he and Lee were stealing cattle, put him under arrest, and rode by himself with a dangerous prisoner for three days through the mountains to get to Lincoln, posted charges against McNew and Lee, and then appeared in front of the grand jury to give his testimony and show the evidence he'd collected. I believe I also heard you say Dow's testimony and evidence was the key reason for the grand jury to return the indictment. Isn't that so, Mr. Herman?"

Herman slowly nods. "Yes, sir, that's what I said."

Fall closes his trap. "Then sir, where is Colonel Fountain in all this? How is it he is the chief reason Lee and McNew were indicted?"

"Why he, uh, he—"

Shaking his head Fall says, "No further questions, Your Honor."

I don't understand why Barnes doesn't ask for redirect to let Herman answer the question and point out it was Fountain who had hired Dow to do the work in the first place.

Barnes calls Saturnino Barela. I remember Jack Fountain's description of how big and rough Barela looks. However, I'm not prepared for the huge, hairy man who makes the big witness chair look dainty. Barela's testimony is clear and straightforward and matches exactly what Jack Fountain told me during the stage interview. The most interesting part of his testimony is that three horsemen veered off the road to avoid him shortly before he met Colonel Fountain, and that Fountain told him his suspicion of the horsemen was why he was driving with his rifle across his knees. Barela also mentions that, after the Fountains disappeared, he found a pool of dried blood beside the road where the Fountain buckboard turned off into the brush. When Barnes has no more questions, Judge Parker notes that it's near dinnertime and orders a recess until two o'clock.

I head downhill for the Union Bar, buy a beer, and find a chair in a corner where I can review what I've started for another story. The memory of the last time I saw Persia is heavy on my mind. I can't concentrate on my notes. Instead, I sit back and try to think of what I said or did that has made her so angry, and why I feel this way about a woman I hardly know. I sip on my beer for over an hour and resolve nothing before checking my watch and deciding to march back up the hill a little early to get a good seat in the courtroom.

As I'm leaving, a cowboy runs into the bar, shouting. "They found him! They found him!" The room goes quiet, and the bartender asks, "Who'd they find, Ike?"

"Jack Maxwell! Curry's deputy, Latham, found him over in Alamogordo. He's bringing him back. They'll be in tonight sometime. Garrett and the rest of his posse are on the way back, too."

The buzz in the bar grows as speculation reaches fever pitch over whether Maxwell was trying to hide from Lee or was sick. Tomorrow suddenly promises to be an interesting day.

Back in court, Daugherty's cross-examination of Barela for the defense reveals nothing new and doesn't make the hairy giant look foolish or inept. I know Fall has a job to do, but I don't understand why he pounds the minor witnesses so hard. His interrogation of the next witness, Catarino Villegas, a member of the search party, gives me an answer.

Villegas's story agrees with those of Antonio García and Albert Fountain about what the search party found. He was with Major Llewellyn's posse that followed the trail until it was destroyed by a herd of cattle crossing it.

I look up from writing my notes and see a well-dressed businessman with yellow hair filled with streaks of gray. He must be close to forty and is sitting a few places away in the same row with me. His arms are crossed, and he shakes his head often during Villegas's testimony.

Fall asks Villegas several casual questions that are easy to answer. Well into the cross-examination, Fall, still congenial, asks, "How many of you got off your horses at the buckboard?"

"Two of us."

"Did you walk around the buckboard?"

"Yes."

"You found some shawls there, didn't you?"

"Yes."

"Did you take them back to Mr. Jack Fountain and show them to him?"

"No, sir."

"Did you ride all around the buckboard?"

"We went all around it on foot."

"Are you positive of that?"

"Yes."

"And you saw three tracks there, so that you could distinguish the difference between them?"

"Yes."

"You say the horses that went over the pass were not shod?"

"I don't know."

"Who was the trailer?"

"I was one of them."

"You were one of the trailers, and yet didn't pay enough attention to know whether the horses were shod or not?"

Villegas throws up his hands and shrugs his shoulders. "The ground was hard, the tracks were barely scuff marks or left only broken weeds on the trail over the pass. They was so faint, we lost the trail a couple of times and had to go back and find it or track forward until we picked it up again. It was a very hard trail to follow, but we—"

"No more questions, Your Honor."

Barnes calls Major Eugene Van Patten. In his late fifties, Van Patten is an upper-crust businessman in Las Cruces who's lost money in cattle corporations because of Lee and his men. Van Patten states that he went out with the initial search parties.

"Major, tell us what you found."

Van Patten folds his hands and looks at the ceiling for a moment as though searching his memory. "Among other things, I found a pool of blood on the ground four hundred twenty-four paces south of Chalk Hill on the main road near where Fountain's buckboard left the road. I also found a five- and a ten-cent piece. The pool of blood was in one of the roads of the cutoff. It was seven or eight inches deep and twice or three times the size of that spittoon over there." He points to one used in the courtroom. "The blood had spattered around for a distance of six feet. The pool looked as if a blanket was dragged through one side."

All three defense attorneys are on their feet. "Hold on there!" one says, pointing his finger at Van Patten, "Don't go any further. That kind of evidence is not admissible!"

Judge Parker, scowling, raps his gavel. "Gentlemen! If you have objections, make them to the court. This mode of procedure will not be tolerated."

Fergusson and Daugherty nod and sit down. Fall remains standing. "We understand, Your Honor, and we intend to make them to the court. However, our intention was to stop this ready witness before he could place incompetent evidence before the jury."

Parker stares at Fall as the spectators sit in thick, heavy silence. "Sit down, Mr. Fall. The objection is sustained. The testimony concerning a blanket being dragged through the pool of blood is stricken from the record, and the jury will ignore that statement. Continue with your witness, Mr. Barnes."

Barnes refers to the Tularosa Basin map still tacked on the

wall from Albert Fountain's testimony and asks Van Patten to continue. Van Patten states that he found several human tracks near the buckboard and the prints of knees and several empty cartridges behind a big, green bush near the road at Chalk Hill. He says he then followed the trail of horses leading away from the buckboard to a camp that had been occupied by several men. From there, he says he followed the trail of a horse that left the camp and that, after a long, counterclockwise swing turning east to west, the horse had traveled almost due west, crossed the road near Chalk Hill, and headed on toward the San Andres Mountains, where he found the animal.

Barnes guides Van Patten back to the testimony he thinks most relevant. "Did you examine carefully the trail of the buckboard leading from Chalk Hill?"

"I did, sir. It showed there were three horses. Two were pulling the vehicle, and one was tethered behind it. After the colonel cleared Chalk Hill, three trotting horses overtook the buckboard and surrounded it."

So there had to be at least a fourth man behind the bush. Where had he come from? Why weren't the tracks of four or more horses found besides the three Colonel Fountain had?

"Do you know if Colonel Fountain had a Winchester?"

"When he left Las Cruces, he did. It was either a .44 or .40 caliber."

"Did you go back to the spot where the blood was found?"

"I did, and I got up some of the sand and later gave it to Governor Thornton. I had some of the hair from the side of the gray horse shaved off and sent that to Governor Thornton, too. It was soaked with blood."

"What was the condition of the gray horse when you found him?"

"He was jaded and had bloodstains on him. The stains were on his left side below the saddle. The horse had a sore on its back, but it wasn't a bleeding sore."

Barnes crosses his arms and nods. He turns Van Patten's testimony back to the blood spot. "Did you see any indications of anybody having been on the ground near the pool of blood?"

Fall is quick to respond. "Objection! Calls for a conclusion from the witness."

Before Barnes can rebut the claim, Judge Parker agrees. "Sustained. Continue, Mr. Barnes." Fergusson passes Fall some papers. He scans them and nods his thanks. Lee studies them with Fall.

Barnes, arms crossed, stares at Fall, and looks at Van Patten and then the judge. "No more questions of this witness, Your Honor."

"Your witness, Mr. Fall."

Fall pushes back his chair and rises to his full height, quickly glancing down at the papers Fergusson has passed him, and then locks eyes with Van Patten. "You testified in the preliminary hearing of McNew, didn't you?"

"Yes, sir."

"You haven't repeated it to the jury as you told it there, have you?"

Van Patten doesn't blink as he returns Fall's stare. "I've told it as near as I could about what happened."

Fall crosses his arms and walks up to Van Patten to stand directly in front of him. His questions are like hard jabs from a master boxer, quick and in the vitals, as he grills Van Patten about his testimony at the McNew-Carr hearing. He first asks what Van Patten said in the McNew hearing testimony and then rebuts Van Patten's testimony by reading the record back to him. Reading from the transcript of the McNew-Carr hearing, Fall asks Van Patten if he testified that he trailed Fountain's horse east from the pool of blood, then north.

"I testified that then and now."

And so it continued until Van Patten says in reply to one of Fall's questions, "I might have been mixed up then, just like you're trying to do me now."

Fall looks over his glasses at him. "I don't want to mix you up at all. I want to unmix you."

After a couple more questions, Fall asks, "When was it that you found the blood?"

"It was the tenth of February."

Fall nods. "Did you find a jackrabbit that had been recently killed there and what you claim were the brains of the child near the pool of blood?"

Van Patten clenches his fists and yells, "I did not!"

Fall looks at the jury. "It was either the tenth or eleventh then, that you found this blood. Now, who did you send it to town with, or did you take it yourself?"

"I took it myself."

"Who found the gray horse?"

"I was with the men who found him."

"Albert Fountain testified there was no blood on the horse. He was mistaken?"

"Objection!" Barnes cries. "Albert Fountain has given no such testimony in the present trial. The evidence in the McNew preliminary has nothing to do with the case on trial here."

Fall turns and points at the clerk. "Mr. Clerk, issue a subpoena for Albert Fountain, and we'll hold him as a witness for the defense."

The subpoena is written by the clerk, issued to a bailiff, who steps beyond the railing and hands it to Albert.

Fall turns to Judge Parker. "We have no more questions of this witness at this time, Your Honor; however, we reserve the right to recall."

Judge Parker nods. "So recorded. Since we are late in the day, I suggest that there be no night session." Neither the prosecution nor the defense objects to Judge Parker's proposal. "Very well, I declare this court adjourned until nine tomorrow morning."

Chapter 22
Henry Stoes

I wander out the front door of the courthouse. I haven't seen Clayton or Greco in the crowds all afternoon. Looking over by the jail, I don't see Tom Tucker where several men gather to smoke. The gentleman I saw shaking his head during Villegas's testimony sits on the retaining wall of the courthouse to smoke his pipe. It's close to suppertime, but he doesn't seem to be in any hurry.

Approaching him, I hold out my business card. "Hello, sir. My name is Quentin Peach, Quent to my friends. I'm doing background stories on the trial for the *San Francisco Examiner.* I was hoping you might talk with me and help me make sense of the testimony so far in the trial."

Taking my card and then eyeing me with hazel eyes framed by deep crow's feet, he says with a slight German accent, "Hmmph! Why is this you speak with me? You do not know me. Is this not so?"

I smile. "No, sir, I don't even know your name. I sat a few seats away from you this afternoon and saw you shaking your head during *Señor* Villegas's testimony. I concluded you might have information in addition to his. I didn't see you sworn with the other witnesses."

He clasps his hands together and rests his elbows on his knees. He puffs on his pipe, staring off toward the Black Range. Waiting for him to decide if he'll talk, I look around and see Todd Bailey and his friends leave the crowd at the front door of the jail. They untie the two horses they've left all day at the hitching rail. Todd sees me and gives a little nod in my direction. I smile and nod back.

"So, *Herr* Peach, you watch the people here carefully, yah? Good. Sit down here, please?" He nods. "I tell what I know, if you write true what I speak, yah?"

"I'll write it true, yes, sir. I'll even review my notes with you to be sure I have the facts straight. Deal?"

"Yah. Good." He sticks out his hand, and we shake as he introduces himself. "Henry Stoes. I emigrate from Austria and live in Las Cruces many years. For a long time, I run Adolph Lohman's Mercantile. Now I have a store of my own in Las Cruces. Oliver Lee and me, we are friends."

I raise my brows in surprise. Henry laughs. "Oh, yah. Oliver is friends with many in Las Cruces, if they are Democrats. Hah!"

"What's your interest in *Señor* Villegas's testimony?"

"I was with Villegas in Mr. Llewellyn's posse that lost the trail to Oliver's ranch when the cattle herd crossed it. There is much Villegas was not asked and did not tell."

I think I might have got lucky again. "You were with Villegas as one of the trackers?"

"Yah, I was in the front with Gans and Villegas."

"Tell me your version of what happened."

"Yah. I will do just that." He takes a few puffs on his pipe. "Bunglers."

"What?"

"Yah, that is what I say. Llewellyn's posse. We are bunglers."

I take out my notepad. "Can you tell me what you mean?"

"Yah. I start with the beginning, yah?"

"Yes, sir, that's always the best place to start."

"Well, Major Llewellyn formed a posse to find Colonel Fountain as soon as Barela brought the news they have disappeared. There was Llewellyn's nephew, Lew Gans, Carl Clausen—he was Colonel Fountain's son-in-law—he draws the map we use in the courtroom. There was Deputy Sheriff Casey, Luis Herrera, Major Van Patten, Captain Branigan, and me. We were all on horses. I have good strong horse and carry plenty of grain for him. Some of the others was in such hurry they carried no blankets, food, or grain—*dummkopfs.* Major Llewellyn had a buckboard bring supplies. James Baird, Fred Bascom, and Robert Ellwood, they ride on that. There was perhaps at first twenty in Major Llewellyn's posse.

"We make it over San Agustin Pass and stop at Parker's Well deep in the night. Most of the horses would not drink there because the water is no good. In the daylight, we go to Chalk Hill and find Albert Fountain there with his posse. There is five or six with Albert, including *Señor* Villegas and Antonio García, his father-in-law.

"There was maybe twenty-five or thirty horses and the buckboard used for looking for Colonel Fountain and little Henry. Do you know what a crowd like that does to the trail they follow? It is gone forever after we pass. But we look at the ground close as we search for the colonel's buckboard. We found a couple of used cartridges behind the green bush, and we found the trail of the buckboard out into the desert. We missed the blood spot—was covered with frozen sleet, yah.

"Clausen's map, it shows we found the buckboard about six miles out in the desert. It was headed straight for the Jarilla Mountains. The trail was easy to follow. I think this is too easy. It is like the kidnappers want us to follow. I tell Llewellyn this.

"He puffs out his chest, 'What are you saying, Henry? That we can't be this lucky? This is the way Oliver Lee would take the wagon. His ranch is just over the Jarillas there. You wait. We catch them no-good bastards in a while.'

"So I keep my mouth shut. Sure enough, we find the wagon.

There is blood, there is things missing, there is no sign of the colonel or little Henry. We search all around. We look at every inch of ground. One of the colonel's horses runs off from that place. We found him two or three days later, past Luna's Wells, where he watered and then headed on north for the reservation. An old Apache, to pay a debt, he gives this horse to Colonel Fountain on his way home after the colonel and Henry stay overnight with Doctor Blazer on the reservation. The horse, he thinks he goes back home after his adventure, yah?"

I nod and have Stoes wait a moment while I catch up with him in my notes.

"We decide the colonel's body is carried on one of the horses led by three men headed for the Jarilla Mountains and Lee's place on the other side. We follow the trail and watch on either side so we are certain no horse leaves the trail we follow. Three or four miles from the colonel's buckboard, we find a camp where a fire is made and four horses stand. There is the tracks of Henry's right shoe somebody makes, and mesquite sticks they use to roast bacon like the cowboys do. We find the impression of a body that lies in the sand there close to the tracks of Henry. A blind man would not miss them, yah. I think the men who make them want us to follow. I think this is smelling fishy. We should ask why they do this.

"I say this to Llewellyn. He says, 'Henry, you're a fool. You're friends with Lee! You don't want to find the bodies with Lee!'

"The way the others look at me, they think maybe Llewellyn is right. I say no more after this. I let Llewellyn decide. I was a bungler, a fool. I know we should be going in opposite direction, but I stay with Llewellyn.

"We find the trail the riders take away from the camp, then they split. One goes south for Monte Carlo Pass in the Jarilla Mountains and maybe for Wildy Well on the other side, and two go for a pass in the hills to the north. It was very hard to follow either trail. The ground was hard, and there was long stretches of rocks and gravels. We lost the trail two or three times and had to go back or go ahead until we find it again.

"We stayed the night in a little canyon to get out of the wind. Most of the men had no blankets. There was little food, and we keep the fire small, so there was not much light. We made so much coffee to keep warm that we run out of it by dawn. It was bad, very bad, Herr Peach. The horses have no water in nearly two days, some have not eaten since we leave Las Cruces, and most of the men were not much better off."

I shiver, imagining how much the posse must have suffered that night. "Please, call me Quent, Mr. Stoes. How did you manage to go on the next day?"

"Llewellyn decided only the strongest and in best shape could go on. He sends the rest back to the Fountain buckboard to drag it back to Las Cruces. Llewellyn, the leader; Gans, he has great experience as a tracker; Casey, Branigan, Villegas, and me, we take the trail to the north. Clausen and Herrera, they take the trail south toward Wildy Well.

"Clausen, he tells us later that the rider they follow doesn't know the trail. The rider runs into mesquite bushes, backs up and goes round. Clausen thinks he must be riding in the dark. I think Lee and his men ride these trails all the time. They wouldn't ride into the mesquites, even in the dark. They just give the horse his head, and he finds the way home.

"That Branigan is a good shot. After a mile or two, he sees and shoots an antelope. We sit and eat until we can eat no more. The trail is hard to follow. We lose it often and go back to find it or ride ahead until we find it again. The trail heads for the road between Wildy Well and Dog Canyon Ranch. Gans and me have grain for our horses, but the others don't. We get ahead of the others because our horses are stronger. We're maybe two miles ahead when Llewellyn calls us back. We are so close we can see the Dog Canyon Ranch buildings in the distance. Gans and me, we're angry. Our horses are dying of thirst, we're within sight of water, and he calls us back?

"When Gans and me come back to Llewellyn, Gans says, 'What's the matter? We're nearly to Lee's ranch! We can get water and question Lee.'

"Llewellyn shakes his head and says, 'The horses are about worn out, and we can't make it to the ranch. Even if we did, we're in no condition to shoot it out with Lee and his gang.'

"There was a big argument about what we do. I said to them all, 'Look! We ought to go ahead, even if we go slower. We and the horses need water bad. If we can't get to Lee's place, we sure can't get to Wildy. I come all this way. I don't want to go back now. I know Lee. I'm not afraid to ride in and talk to him. If he's not there, then we have the right to ask where he is. I want to look Lee in the eye and ask him where he was Saturday evening. He gives straight answers. This track we follow, it maybe didn't start at Colonel Fountain's buckboard. We lost the trail too many times to know for sure.'

"Llewellyn shakes his head. He won't change his mind. He says we meet Clausen coming with water from Wildy Well. We are arguing like the bunglers we are when a herd of cattle is coming toward us. I see them and say, 'Now we'll never know where the trail goes. We must talk to Oliver Lee and ask those cowboys where the cattle is from!'

"Llewellyn is nodding with certainty when he says, 'It's pretty damn certain Lee saw us coming on his trail and ran the cows down here to wipe the trail out. Come on, it's time we go round that herd and down to Wildy Well before it's too dark to see what's happening.'

"Such foolishness I never hear. It takes days or weeks to get a herd that size together on the winter range. Never can this be done in the time since we come in sight. We follow Llewellyn, hoping we find Clausen with water. We had to ride all the way to Wildy for water. My horse was so nearly gone, he had to lie down to drink. I had to dig a little trench to his head from the water trough. I was almost in the same shape. I never understand Major Llewellyn that day. It was a fool's errand what we do."

I think, *Mr. Stoes is right; they were bunglers, especially Llewellyn. For a military man, he sure didn't act like one.* "Mr. Stoes, why do you think Major Llewellyn called you back and wouldn't go into Dog Canyon Ranch or even let you go? Why wouldn't he want to ask Lee if he couldn't search for some sign of Colonel Fountain and Henry?"

Stoes shrugs his shoulders, shakes his head, and looks at the ground. "Now you see why I'm no witness with the others. Yah?"

I thank Henry Stoes for his story. I believe him. He has no reason to lie, and his story has the ring of truth. Shaking hands, I ask him to let me know if he remembers anything else. Putting my hands in my pockets, I walk down the hill to Main Street in the long shadows from the red sun falling behind the Black Range.

Chapter 23
The Dream

I'm sure first contact with the scene of the Fountain disappearances, which were most certainly murders, was an awful time for the Llewellyn and Fountain posses. Freezing cold, short on supplies, living their worst fears about what's happened to the colonel and Henry, they cover close to forty miles of trail through the desert, looking for the trail of the killers and the bodies of the colonel and Henry. They'll never get a medal for what they did then, but I think they should.

In hindsight, it seems obvious they were deliberately being led toward Lee's ranches. It's only logical that whoever was behind the murders was trying to put the blame on Lee. It seems to me that, if they turned east toward Lee's ranches, it was to gain someone time because they had to evade the posses that must surely come, and they had to dispose of the bodies. *How would they do that? Where would they go?*

I think, *if Brown were behind the murders, he would be heading for a pass through the San Andres Mountains and home. Maybe he had the bodies with him. The feint leading the posse toward Lee's place would certainly give him a sufficient lead to get back home and claim innocence.* I see there is something very peculiar about Van Patten finding Fountain's gray horse with blood on it near San Nicolas Springs on the west side. I remember Antonio García and Albert Fountain had testified the same horse had followed the road back home on his own when the colonel camped near Parker's Well only a couple of weeks earlier.

Why would the gray horse wander out into the desert looking for water rather than take the road home to water and grain? The logical answer is that it wouldn't. Horses are smarter than that.

Why would Llewellyn nearly kill his men and horses by refusing to ride to Lee's Dog Canyon Ranch for water, look him in the eye, and ask him where he was on Saturday afternoon? Why did he make his men ride through nearly twelve miles of suffering to get to Wildy Well for water?

It seems to me that either Llewellyn was so afraid of Lee, McNew, and Gililland that he didn't want to face them on their home ground, or that Llewellyn was trying to hide or avoid something else by not going there.

By the time I reach Main Street, every restaurant is filled with customers. Looking through the door of the Ocean Grove, I see Persia rushing between tables, taking care of orders.

I wish I could see her, but without her wanting to see me, it's a lost cause. I'm not very hungry anyway. The Union Hotel is crowded, too, but I find a place at the bar and order a beer. All the talk is about Jack Maxwell, why he disappeared, and what he'll say tomorrow.

I'm soon back in my room, with the window open to street sounds, frogs, and the insect chorus. The coal-oil lantern casts a mellow glow on my notes. I write for a little while, but the beer makes me drowsy. I lie down for a short nap. A dream is not long coming.

Riders appear, surround, and ease galloping horses pulling a buckboard to a halt. One gets off his horse and approaches two bodies in the road, a man in a pool of blood and a child. The dismounted rider toes them to see if they still live. Neither moves. He looks at the others and shakes his head. The shooter, riding double with the rider who waited with him, approaches from the green bush, telling the others what to do. They wait for the man to bleed out, and then tie him and the child together before wrapping them in canvas. Unhitching the white horse from the buckboard, a rider saddles it and loads it with its tragic burden. The shooter mounts and rides the white horse west toward San Nicolas Springs, where a man with two horses waits.

The man who waited with the shooter unsaddles his horse, throws the saddle in the buckboard, and harnesses his horse in place of the white horse. He drives the buckboard out into the desert toward a small range of low mountains.

A few miles from the road, they stop the buckboard, unhitch the horses, and begin rummaging through the buckboard's contents. Papers taken from a trunk and a box are stuffed in saddlebags. The murdered man's weapons are taken. The pinto tied behind the wagon is driven off into the desert. The killers leave the forlorn buckboard and ride toward a short range of mountains. It is almost dark when they stop to make camp.

After a fire is started, the rider of the horse swapped for the white horse at the road mounts his horse, and makes a long, wandering loop back west, toward the road where the white horse was loaded with the bodies. When he gets to the road, he crosses on top of the trail left by the white horse and turns east. Reaching a corral supporting a well, he turns off the road and rides north through the darkness, across the southern end of the white sands, until he reaches a hardscrabble trail and finds a man tending a small fire, making coffee. As the sun brings the dawn, two riders and a pack animal carrying a rolled canvas package appear. After coffee and bacon, the three riders follow a trail leading northwest across the eastern front of the San Andres Mountains. At a pass leading up into the San Andres, they disappear into the mountains. By midafternoon, the canyon riders have scattered north and west without the canvas-wrapped bodies.

The men left at the fire near the Jarillas burn all the papers they've taken from the buckboard. A man wraps himself in a blanket, and the other two carry him to a smooth hillock of sand. He lies there while one of them makes footprints using a shoe taken from the child's body. Then they lift the man in the blanket and carry him back to the fire, swearing and laughing at how heavy he is. The prints in the sand look exactly like what a body might make if it had been laid there. Another takes a shoe he's taken from the child's body and makes prints near the fire.

They roast bacon on mesquite sticks and make coffee as they laugh and joke about what a hard day's work it's been. In dawn's light, they ride off toward the little mountain range looming in front of them. Soon they split, one man riding toward a pass; the other two, still leading the other buckboard horse, ride for some low hills at the end of the little mountain range.

My eyes snap open. My dream leaves me feeling as though I have a heavy rock on my chest. I hear only night sounds. My pocket watch shows it's near ten o'clock. My mind spins, trying to remember my dream. Still groggy, I sit down at the writing table to capture its details. As I write, it occurs to me that Llewellyn probably didn't go to Dog Canyon Ranch because the posse might find someone else there he didn't want seen.

The dream is an epiphany. I feel nauseous thinking about the murders, but I now see clearly how they might have been committed and covered up. I'm set to wondering how I'll ever be able to prove what the dream has shown me.

I decide to step outside and get a little cool air before going to bed. I leave my pistol in its shoulder holster and step out the Ocean Grove door hoping to find some company, but Sadie is not there tonight. I sit on the steps, wishing I had a cigar or a glass of bourbon to settle my mind. My thoughts flitter about, a flock of startled sparrows, jumping from details I've imagined in my dream to the trial to Persia Brown.

Why can't I get that woman out of my mind? She doesn't want to have anything to do with me. I'm leaving after the trial, and odds are, I'll never see her again. Staring into the darkness, I toy with the idea of trying to seduce her, yet I find the thought repugnant after all she's been through. *Don't I just need to get over the infatuation I have with her?* The question hangs in my mind. Disgusted at my confusion, I go to bed.

Chapter 24
Jack Maxwell Testifies, 31 May 1899

Every eye is on the man being escorted down the aisle toward the witness chair. Teeth clenched, eyes sweeping the crowd, shoulders hunched forward, he looks more like a man being forced to stick his hand in a fire than one about to give critical testimony.

Reporters crane their necks to get a better view of the witness, Jack Maxwell. Deputies for Sheriff Curry and Sheriff Pat Garrett have scoured the countryside looking for him.

I know that a year earlier, at the preliminary hearing in Las Cruces for McNew and Carr, Maxwell, testifying through the fog of a hangover, maybe even still drunk, claimed he was at the Dog Canyon Ranch the day the Fountains disappeared and saw Lee, Gililland, and McNew, worn out and worried, ride into the ranch within hours of Fountain's disappearance. Now he is one of the prosecution's star witnesses, and he must look Oliver Lee in the eye to say what the prosecution believes will impeach the alibi of Lee and Gililland.

Maxwell, looking at the floor, is sworn in and takes his seat. Lee and Gililland sit with their gazes locked on him, their arms crossed. Fall, calm, a smile playing on his lips, eases back in his chair. Catron's brows are pinched together as he makes last-minute notes.

Childers asks Maxwell the usual, personal identification questions and then turns to his long-awaited testimony. "How long have you known Oliver Lee and James Gililland?"

Maxwell's fingers tap on the armrest of his chair. He takes a deep breath and says, "I've known Oliver Lee and Mr. Gililland for five or six years. My ranch ain't very far from Mr. Lee's."

"Where were you on the first of February, 1896?"

Licking his lips, Maxwell looks at the ceiling. "I was at Mr. Lee's Dog Canyon Ranch and spent the night there. I got there just before sundown. Mrs. Lee, Mr. Lee's mother, Mr. Blevins, Mr. Bailey, and Ed, the colored man, was there. I ate supper with them that night and slept in the house with Mr. Blevins."

Answering Childers's questions, Maxwell tells how he got up at sunup on Sunday, had breakfast with the others, and spent most of his day working at the corral. During that time, he claims he saw four men he took to be Lee, Gililland, McNew, and the colored man, Ed, come in from the northeast toward the house, riding on two horses. Maxwell states he had dinner that day with Lee, Gililland, and McNew, and then supper that night. He says Blevins was not there at dinner, but was present for supper. He claims that night Lee and Gililland took their blankets and went outside to sleep, carrying guns they usually wore, and that he slept inside with McNew.

Childers probes with a few more questions about who Maxwell can remember was at the ranch that night, and then focuses on the horses Maxwell saw while he was at the ranch. "You said you spent the day down at Lee's corral. What horses did you see there?"

Maxwell scratches his chin in thought before saying his horse and two belonging to the ranch that he thought the four rode in on. He says he didn't know what time they left the ranch. He says, "On Tuesday morning, I got up early to go to the pasture a mile away from the house to get my horse. There were five or six horses in the pasture, and they looked like they had been used recently and rode hard, judging from the sweat and saddle marks."

Childers crosses his arms and stares at Maxwell. He asks if Maxwell testified at McNew's preliminary hearing at Las Cruces before Judge Parker in 1898.

Maxwell looks at the floor and says, "Yes, sir."

Childers takes up the transcript from the prosecution's table and begins to read.

Fall is on his feet. "Objection! The prosecution is trying to contradict their own witness."

Judge Parker strikes his gavel. "Sit down, Mr. Fall! Overruled. Continue, Mr. Childers."

Childers bores in on Maxwell. "You testified in the preliminary hearing that two of the horses had been ridden harder than the others. Which horses were those?"

"I don't remember."

I see jury members slowly, almost imperceptibly, shake their heads. Childers returns repeatedly to which horses looked like they had been used the hardest, rereading testimony from the preliminary hearing, trying to make Maxwell associate the hard-ridden horses with the defendants. Fall continues to object and is overruled. All Childers can pull out of the prosecution's star witness is, "I don't remember."

Childers tosses the preliminary testimony down in disgust. "No more questions of this witness at this time, Your Honor." Every jury member, including those who depend on Chavez's translations, are frowning and looking at each other.

The prosecution's case is becoming clear. They are trying to use Maxwell not only to tie Lee and Gililland to the horses tracked toward the Dog Canyon Ranch by Llewellyn's posse, but to show that Lee and Gililland were not at the ranch when they claimed to be.

When Judge Parker turns the witness over to the defense for cross-examination, Fall is loose and easygoing as he approaches Maxwell, who chews on the inside of his lip. Lee and Gililland continue to watch him, their faces masks of indifference.

Fall asks Maxwell if his earlier testimony is practically the same as before except for dates. Maxwell agrees. Fall asks where he went after the preliminary hearing. Maxwell says he went to the Alpine Cattle Company in Colorado Springs, accompanied by Childers, who had found him the job and paid his fare.

"Did Mr. Childers say anything to you about your life being in danger if you went back to Otero County? Did you not tell Bud Smith after you got back that Mr. Childers had told you that you'd better go away as the defendants or their friends would kill you?"

Childers is on his feet in an instant. "Objection!"

Parker shakes his head. "Overruled. The witness will answer the question."

Maxwell nods. "Yes."

Fall asks if there was any conversation with Childers about the horses during the McNew case in Silver City. Maxwell replies, "No, sir."

Fall begins using his favorite counterpunches, questions that stick in the minds of the jurors and make the witness and the prosecution look bad, even if they don't add anything to the evidence.

"Did you have any conversation with Mr. Childers last night after you got here?"

"Yes, sir."

"Did he tell you what he would do to you if you failed to testify?"

"No, sir."

"What time was it you said you got into Dog Canyon Ranch?"

"Just about nine."

"And you got back on Tuesday?"

"Yes, sir."

"When did you hear of the disappearance of Colonel Fountain?"

"I disremember."

"Did you not tell Bud Smith, within a week of February 1, 1896, they need not accuse Oliver Lee or any of these boys of the murder of Colonel Fountain, for you were there and saw Lee setting out grapevines with Mrs. Lee, and the other boys were there also at work?"

Maxwell looks at the floor and mumbles that he didn't say it like that. Judge Parker asks the witness to speak up. Fall asks if Maxwell didn't say to Smith that Lee and the others were at the ranch on Saturday, and he knew they had nothing to do with Fountain's murder. Maxwell holds up his chin and, with a tone of defiance says, "No!"

"Did you tell George Curry you were at Dog Canyon Ranch Saturday afternoon and that Lee and Gililland were there?"

Maxwell denies he told anyone he was there in the afternoon.

"Is it not a fact that this is the first time that you have been able to fix the day of the week when you got to Dog Canyon or when you left there, or the day of the month?"

Maxwell claims he hadn't thought of the day of the month until he heard of Fountain's disappearance. Fall reads from the transcript of the preliminary where Maxwell states he couldn't fix the date. Maxwell admits his confusion.

"Didn't you write a letter to Jack Tucker telling him that you would make a good witness for the boys, as you could swear they were forty miles away when Fountain disappeared?"

Maxwell admits he wrote a letter, but claims he didn't make that statement.

Fall asks if Maxwell has ever been promised any remuneration for his testimony.

Maxwell frowns. "Any what?"

Fall clarifies, "Any pay."

Maxwell cocks his head to one side with a hurt look. "No!"

Fall turns to the defense's table, picks up some papers, and asks if it is not a fact that Maxwell has a written contract signed by Pat Garrett and his associate, Charles Perry, reading something like, "We the undersigned agree to pay J. W. Maxwell two thousand dollars for evidence leading to the conviction of the Fountain murderers. Said two thousand dollars to be paid upon conviction."

Maxwell is unsure about the words, but agrees he is due two thousand dollars of the reward.

Fall asks what he has to do for the two thousand dollars.

"Why, I was supposed to just tell what I knew."

"Isn't it a fact that you told Pat Garrett and Mr. Perry you knew certain facts and would not swear to them until they gave you two thousand dollars?"

Maxwell claims Garrett and Perry just gave him the contract before he told them what he knew. Fall suggests that if Garrett says differently, then he's lying. Childers objects to the comment, and his objection is sustained.

"Mr. Maxwell, before you got this contract, didn't Charles Perry tell you that you had to do something to clear yourself?"

Maxwell says Perry didn't put it to him in that way.

"Didn't you tell me Mr. Perry told you that unless you gave evidence convicting those men, you might be hanged yourself?"

Maxwell looks toward the reporters leaning against the wall and shakes his head. "No, sir."

Fall begins asking a line of questions showing Maxwell lived in Mississippi, Texas, and Colorado before moving to Doña Ana County, and that he lived in Texas under the name J.B. Alexander. Out of nowhere, Fall asks if Maxwell ever made statements showing he had committed perjury in another trial and intended to do the same in this one.

"No, sir!" Maxwell replies repeatedly, sometimes appearing

indignant, but mostly defensive.

Judge Parker calls for the noon recess, and reporters scramble for the door.

I get up with the crowd and move downstairs. I want to interview Sheriff Curry, or at least get an appointment to talk with him. Downstairs, I knock on Sheriff Kahler's door and hear, "Come!"

Inside the sheriff's office, several men stand with shotguns pointed toward the ceiling, stocks braced against their hips. Kahler is giving them instructions about where he wants them stationed around Hillsboro to keep watch and stop fights in case they break out. Kahler sees me waiting behind the men and lifts his brows. "What can we do for you?"

"I'm looking for Sheriff Curry. Can you tell me where I might find him?"

"I think he's out checking on the witnesses from Otero County. He wants to be sure they'll satisfy their subpoenas when they're called. We sure as hell don't want another Maxwell to chase down. Sheriff Curry'll be back by the time court resumes."

"Thanks. I'll talk to him then."

Kahler gives me a nod as I edge out the door. I step out the back door and look over the three or four groups of men talking and smoking in the building's shade. There's no one I know. I start for Main Street when I notice a small folded sheet of paper stuck in my vest pocket. I have no idea how it got there. The neat cursive script reads, "Forget Brown, and we'll be your friends. If you go on asking questions, you'll never leave here alive."

I jump when I feel a hand on my shoulder. It's Tom Tucker, who laughs. "Howdy, Quent. Sorry to surprise yuh. How's beans? You ain't had no trouble, have yuh?"

I give a low whistle. "Tom! Man, am I glad to see you. I just found this note stuffed in my vest pocket. I think it was put there when everyone was crowding out of the courtroom after dinner recess."

Tom reads it frowning. "Damn, Quent. Somebody is after your tail."

"Yeah, I know. That's obvious."

"No, sir, you don't understand. I stuck Clayton and Greco in jail on a charge that oughta keep 'em there at least until the trial's over. I thought that'd be the easiest way to keep you safe and collect on my ree-ward. Hell, I thought I might get a little bonus fer bein' so smart. Now it looks like I ain't gonna get no free ride after all."

I have to laugh. "You put Clayton and Greco in jail? That's pretty clever, Tom. But that still leaves whoever was with them when they beat the hell out of me."

"Aw, I'm dead certain that was old Brown. I figured he left and meant for Clayton and Greco to do his dirty work. We ain't got to worry about Brown. Whoever is up there sticking notes in your pocket is who we got to be lookin' out for."

I nod. Tom's logic doesn't leave much room to rationalize away the threat.

"I'll tell you something else, Quent. That there note reads a lot like the one passed to Fountain in Lincoln three days 'fore he's murdered."

I try to whistle again, but only air sails past my dry lips. "I'm not hungry anymore, Tom. Think I'll stay in the courtroom and work on my notes until recess is over. Cover my back when I leave here, will you?"

Tom nods. "Don't worry, old son. I got you covered. Don't lose no sleep over this. Just see if you can figure out who gave you that note."

"Right. See you later." I return to my place on the courtroom benches to work on my story and develop a plan to identify the note writer.

After the recess, Fall continues his cross-examination of Maxwell and asks if he didn't tell George Curry, in October 1897, that his evidence would clear Lee and that he had slept at Lee's place that night?

Maxwell looks at the floor, shaking his head. "No, sir."

After a few more questions from Fall, Childers redirects and asks Maxwell what he told the prosecution the night before the preliminary examination in Las Cruces. Maxwell answers that he told the prosecution he was too drunk to testify and didn't want to make any misstatements that could cause him trouble later. Childers asks if anyone instructed him to tell more than he knew, or if he had received any money other than to pay for his traveling expenses to Colorado Springs.

Maxwell sits, shaking his head. "No, sir. No, sir."

Fall is back up for a final question. "The fact of it is, you weren't frightened by these defendants at all, were you?"

Maxwell leans back in the chair and sticks out his chest. "I don't know what it is to be frightened."

Everyone in the courtroom laughs, Fall with them.

"No more questions, Your Honor."

"Witness is excused."

Maxwell creeps out of the witness chair, his gaze sweeping the courtroom. They briefly land on Lee and Gililland before he heads for the door in a fast stomp.

Santos Alvarado, who met Colonel Fountain on the road between Tularosa and Luna's Wells on 1 February 1896, is called next. Following Alvarado, Barela is called again, and then Albert Fountain. Albert is cross-examined by Fall about the testimony given by Van Patten.

Fall asks Albert about the "white horse" and the blood on its side, the same horse Van Patten had called gray, and Thornton had called white in earlier testimony. Albert testifies the horse's back was sore, showed signs of considerable sweating, and that it appeared something wide had been thrown on its back, like a blanket, causing it to sweat and its side to be dyed from the cloth. "I didn't find any blood on the horse. When I saw it, the hair had already been shaved off."

Jack Fountain is called next. His testimony matches that of the other posse witnesses, except he says he didn't see any child's tracks at the dry camp of the three men who took and then left Colonel Fountain's buckboard out in the desert. On cross-examination by Fall, Jack says he could identify the tracks of the gray horse because Antonio García had reduced a set of large horseshoes to fit the horse and had failed to put any heels on them. Fall produces a copy of the *Rio Grande Republican* extra edition published within days of the Fountain disappearance. In it, Jack was quoted as saying he had seen both his father's and his brother's footprints in the sand near the buckboard. Jack shakes his head emphatically and says he was misquoted, and is unequivocal in saying he never made such a statement. Court is recessed for supper.

Tom Tucker meets me at the door at the bottom of the stairs. "Any more notes?" I shake my head.

"Where do you want to go?" Tom asks.

"I need to get down to the Ocean Grove, see Persia Brown and get a little supper."

Tom grins. Sadie's places are his favorite spots in the village. "Okay. I'm off for the evenin'. I'll walk with you."

It feels comforting to have an experienced gunman walk down the hill with me in the deepening shadows. My mind still wrestles over the note I found. I've spent most of the afternoon half-listening to the witnesses while studying those in the courtroom, trying to identify who might have slipped it into my pocket. I still don't have a clue. It might have been anyone except those directly associated with the Fountains or the Lees.

The Ocean Grove Restaurant is packed. Persia and two other women hustle to keep customers from yelling and pounding on the table for attention and their supper. I wave her over. She hesitates, frowns, and then comes.

"What is it, Quent? We're pretty busy right now."

"Yeah, I can see that. Can I see you for a few minutes when things settle down here?"

She bites her lip and stares into my eyes. "Okay. It'll probably be an hour or more. Can you wait that long?"

I feel a little thrill course down my spine. "I'll be here. We'll wait for a table. You come and sit for a minute when you can."

"All right. I'll be there as quick as I can."

"Thanks!"

Just as I speak, a couple of men leave their chairs. Tom Tucker muscles in and sits down, waving me to join him. Two men who had been waiting for the seats glare at him and start to argue until he looks up and grins at them. They see his badge and recognize him. Without a word, they turn and leave. I sit down with him, realizing I haven't eaten since breakfast.

It's nearly time for the night session to start before Persia joins us. "Whew! Busy night! Now, what's going on, Mr. Peach?"

Tom stands and pulls at his hat. "If you folks will pardon me, I think I'll step out on the porch for a smoke. See you in a minute, Quent. Court's about to start."

"Thanks, Tom. I'll be right along." I look at her, and she smiles. "It's sure good to see you, Persia. I wish it was under different circumstances. Look at this."

I hand her the note between two fingers. Frowning, she

unfolds and reads it. "Someone besides Clayton or Greco gave you this?"

"No one gave it to me. It was slipped into my pocket sometime just after dinner recess began today. Tom has Clayton and Greco in jail until the trial is over. To top it all off, Tom says it reads like the note that was passed to Fountain in Lincoln three days before he was murdered."

Her eyes grow wide as she hands the note back to me. "Oh, Quent. What are we going to do?"

"Well, for one thing, I'm staying a lot closer to Tom Tucker until I figure out who it is. Could you come up to court in the morning session and look over who's there? You might see someone you think might have passed me the note. Right now, I'm clueless."

She nods. "Sure, I'll be there in the morning. I'll need Sadie to find someone who can stand in for me. I'm sure she'll let me off for that."

I smile. "Persia, you're a great gal. I thank you. See you tomorrow."

She reaches over and puts her warm hand on mine. "Quent, please look after yourself. This trial isn't worth your life."

"Thanks, Miss Brown. I know. You be careful, too. I'll see you tomorrow."

Tom and I quick-step it to the courthouse and find seats just as the next witness, Nicolas Armijo, who lives in the mountains, says he was a member of one of the first search parties to go out. His testimony is consistent with that of other posse members. It takes Fall less than fifteen minutes to make Armijo look like an idiot.

David Sutherland, a friend and political ally of Fountain's, is called to the stand. Sutherland, a merchant in La Luz, says he had Fountain stay the evening with him the night before the murders. Sutherland testifies as to what Fountain was carrying and what time he left on the morning of the first of February, 1896. Upon cross-examination, Fall brings out that Sutherland and Lee have not been on good terms for several years.

When the night session adjourns, I find Sheriff Curry, introduce myself, and ask if I might talk with him tomorrow over breakfast. Curry is tall, affable, and looks me in the eye when he speaks. He says he'll be glad to meet me at the Ocean Grove in the morning because he's a big fan of Tom Ying's cooking.

Tom Tucker walks with me back to the Ocean Grove. Soon, I crawl into bed, too exhausted to worry about being assassinated, even as I slide the Smith and Wesson under my pillow.

Chapter 25
George Curry

Sheriff Curry, a cup of coffee half-gone, is reading the *Sierra County Advocate* when I sit at his table in Tom Ying's place. "Morning, Quent. Give me a couple of minutes to finish this little commentary in the *Advocate.*"

"Take your time, Sheriff." I lift my hand to the waitress behind the counter like I'm holding a cup. She nods and brings a china cup of steaming black coffee to me. We order fried eggs and steak while she's there.

Sheriff Curry folds his paper, smiling. "The *Advocate* reporter is doing a pretty good job covering the trial. What can I do for you?"

"Well, sir, I wanted to get your take on the background facts relevant to the trial. You seem evenhanded in your dealings with the Lees and the Fountains."

Eyeing me, Curry frames his chin with his thumb and forefinger. "You're not going to quote me out of context or incorrectly, are you? I don't want anything I have to say at the trial to be compromised because I talked to a reporter."

I give him my standard spiel about my journalistic integrity, and he seems satisfied. "All right, Quent. What do you want to know?"

"Well, for a starter, what's your opinion? Did Lee and Gililland murder the Fountains?"

Curry looks me straight in the eye, pushes the shock of brown hair off his forehead, and shakes his head. "No, sir, I don't believe they did. It's not Lee's style. If he wasn't in on it, then the others—McNew, Carr, and Gililland—weren't either. Oh, they're capable of killing men, and they've even done it a few times after men tried to kill them, but killing Colonel Fountain with that youngster riding on his wagon—never.

"I've known Lee from near the time when he first settled here with a herd of over five hundred horses. He was so good at producing well-trained saddle horses people came from miles around and paid top dollar or traded a few cows for them. I've seen him thrash men who didn't take good care of their animals. That bull old Maxwell was putting out yesterday about seeing horses out in Lee's pasture with sweat and saddle marks on them? Not hardly. The first thing he or his hands do when they've unsaddled their horses is rub 'em down, curry 'em, and give 'em a good grain ration. Maxwell was lying through his teeth.

"And I'll tell you something else. There's a long list of men who wanted Colonel Fountain dead. It's only because Lee and his boys were presumed guilty from the beginning that they're in Hillsboro today and not somebody else. I was clerk of the District Court in Lincoln during the grand jury proceedings back in January of '96. Colonel Fountain was collecting indictments like some kid raking up a pile of leaves. I think he told me over supper the night before he and Henry left that he thought he'd have at least thirty indictments before he went.

"During those proceedings, Colonel Fountain was trying to get an indictment on a man I knew, José Chavez y Chavez. He ran with Billy the Kid for a while during the Lincoln County War days. He had a small ranch over close to Roswell and worked as a hired hand when times were hard. Colonel Fountain just missed by a technicality getting him indicted and sent to prison. It was the second time Fountain had tried to indict him and missed. Chavez y Chavez was killing mad."

I hold up a hand to get Curry to give me a chance to catch up in my notes.

When I nod to him to continue, he says, "I had a drink with Chavez y Chavez there in Lincoln the day the grand jury completed its business. He took a long swallow of bourbon and says, 'George, you saved old man Fountain's life today, but his string is about to run out.'

"I looked at him like he was crazy. 'What do you mean, I saved Colonel Fountain's life today? I didn't do anything.' He shook his head. 'I promised you I wouldn't do anything here, but if you hadn't been here, I'd have blowed his brains out right there in the courtroom in front of God and ever'body, and let 'em chase me until they hanged me. That old bastard's been after me for years. I'm sick and tired of it, and aye God, it's going to stop. I'm telling you that for a fact right now!'

"I figured he'd calm down in a day or two, and I told him plain not to do anything we'd both regret. He left Lincoln a little before Fountain did. Later he was seen at Luna's Wells the night before the Fountains disappeared. I think Chavez y Chavez was pushed too far and did the killings. Of course, he had help."

I nod as I make notes, anxious to see how close my information from other sources matches what Curry says. "Any ideas about who the others might be?"

The waitress brings us our plates of steak and eggs, pours fresh coffee, and heads back to Tom Ying's kitchen. Curry looks at me as he slices a bite of steak. "Yeah, but no proof. This is plain speculation on my part, based on what my sources tell me."

My mouth full of steak, I can only nod I understand.

"I know a man in the pen in Santa Fe who's been locked up with a few of the old boys Colonel Fountain had been sending there since the late eighties. Several of 'em had to sell their ranches because their families just couldn't make a go of it while they were locked up. They swore they were going to give Colonel Fountain the ultimate payback. They took what money they could spare after they got out and hired Bill Johnson and a man named Brady to assassinate the colonel."

I nearly choke when he mentions Brady, the same name as the man Nadine said was having bad dreams about the murders. "Any idea where they are now?"

"Brady's in Mexico last I heard. I think Johnson's up in Montana somewhere."

"Anybody else?"

Curry looks over his shoulder and around the restaurant, maybe to check who might be listening to our conversation. Apparently feeling safe, he says "Ed Brown and Emerald James are almost certainly mixed up in it. I'd bet money Brown knows exactly where the bones of the colonel and his little boy are, because he put them there."

"What makes you so sure Brown and James were involved?"

Curry takes the last of his fried toast and sops up the remains of his eggs. "I've seen the reports sent to the governor by the Pinkerton agent, Sayers, who was hired to investigate Brown's involvement in the murders. Sayers obtained a signed and notarized affidavit from a kid named William Steen, who worked in the livery stable over in San Marcial.

"The affidavit said that Brown and James rode into the livery, on the evening of the third of February 1896, on horses so worn out, they laid down in the stall and wouldn't eat for two or three hours. In fact, Brown and James wanted to leave the next day, but their horses were still in such bad shape they couldn't be ridden. They waited an extra day and left on the fifth.

"Sayers cross-checked the dates with where Brown and James stayed. They were in San Marcial like Steen said, all right. Steen noticed Brown had chopped the heels off his boots and that they hadn't had much contact with the ground—there were boot nails still sticking out of the soles. When Steen asked him if he'd heard about Colonel Fountain's disappearance and probable murder, Brown said he hadn't and went over to the dry goods store to read about it in the Albuquerque paper.

"The reason I'm telling you all this is that when Brown told Sayers where he was, he lied and was caught lying about his whereabouts several times. He swore up and down he was never in San Marcial when Steen said he was. Sayers also found Brown was lying about being on the ranges where he said he was and when he claimed he was there. Sayers, Socorro Sheriff Bursum, and the district attorney, Daugherty, tried to break him and make him talk by locking him up for a while. Didn't work. Brown was just too tough and too smart to crack that way. But you can rest assured that Brown and James were in on those murders. There's just circumstantial evidence to prove it, and not much at that, just like there is for Lee and his *compadres*. I will say, however, that I think a better case could be made against Brown, James, and Chavez y Chavez."

Now it is my turn to scratch my jaw. "Would you know any of these men if you saw them?"

"I'd know them all for sure, except for Brady and Johnson. I think they were in Lincoln with Chavez y Chavez during the grand jury proceedings, but I don't remember their faces."

"Have you seen any of the others at the trial?"

He thought for a moment. "No, sir. Can't say that I have. Why?"

"Because I've been asking a lot of people about what they thought of Brown's culpability in the murders. Three men, one of whom might have been Brown, beat the hell out of me on a side street here and warned me to leave before they got serious. Yesterday someone slipped a note in my vest pocket that said to drop my questions about Brown, or I'd never leave here to go home. Tom Tucker says it sounds similar to the note Fountain got just before he left Lincoln. I think there must be someone here who doesn't want Brown associated with the murders for fear attention will be directed away from Lee and Gililland."

Curry rests his elbows on the table and supports his chin on his clasped hands, a frown of concern on his face. "Quent, that note is serious business. You've got to be mighty careful. I can have one of my deputies escort you, if you like."

I wave him off. "No need. Sadie already has a deal with Tom Tucker to keep an eye on me."

He smiles and nods. "Tucker is the best deputy I can offer you."

"Can I ask you another question or two?"

Motioning the waitress over for more coffee, he pulls his watch, looks at it, and nods. "Sure. We have a while before I have to get back to Kahler's office to get ready for court. Fire away."

"I talked to Mr. Catron Sunday. He was outraged that Lee dictated the terms of surrender, and that you, the governor, and Judge Parker accepted them. Why wouldn't Lee surrender to Pat Garrett?"

Curry laughs, crosses his arms, and leans back in his chair. "Let me tell you a story, and then you'll understand." He looks at the ceiling, scratching his throat. "In February or early March of last year, I was in a poker game with Fall, Lee, Tobie Tipton, and Jeff Sanders up on the second floor of Tipton's Saloon in Tularosa. We were playing along steady and having a pretty good time—you know, everybody wins a little, loses a little, but nobody goes broke or breaks the bank. It was getting along in the afternoon when Pat Garrett appears in the door. We all got real quiet for a minute. Tobie hopped up, shook hands with Pat, and called him in. He introduced him around to the rest and asked him to join the game. Pat acknowledged all of us and said he'd sit in.

"We were playing stud. For a while, Garrett did all right. Nobody really got ahead for a long while. We must have played for a good twenty-four hours that way. Nobody was willing to quit until we saw how Lee's unexpected meeting with Garrett was going to end.

"Slow, but sure as water runs downhill, Garrett started to lose. He lost and lost, but he wouldn't quit, and Lee, who was winning more than the rest of us, but not by much, wouldn't quit either. This went on for a long time, and I mean a couple of days and into the early morning of the third. Everybody was punchy from going without sleep for so long. Garrett finally knocked on the table to ask for a new deck, hoping his luck would change.

"I was about to start snoring. I had to have some rest. So I say, 'I've been hearing that the Doña Ana County grand jury is going to indict somebody in this crowd for doing away with the Fountains. My guess is that somebody in this bunch may want to hire a lawyer before long, and I have an idea the lawyer he's going to hire might be sitting in this here game.'

"Nobody said anything for a minute. Then Lee looked at Garrett and says in this smooth, quiet voice, 'Mr. Sheriff, if you wish to serve any papers on me at any time, I'll be here or out to the ranch.'

"Garrett smiled and leaned back in his chair. 'All right, Mr. Lee. If any papers are to be served on you, I'll mail them to you or send them to George Curry here to serve you.'

"He lit his cigar, stood up, and excused himself, saying he had business he had to take care of. We all left after that. I think I slept for the next two days, I was so tired.

"A few weeks later, Garrett wasn't able to get his indictments, and despite what he'd told Lee at Tipton's at the end of that poker game, he came after Lee with a bench warrant and guns blazing. Fact is, in Lee's mind, he believed Garrett showed his true colors in reneging on his poker game offer. Lee didn't trust him. And you know what? I don't think I would have either."

I shake my head. "Seventy-two hours! That must have been one hell of a poker game. I can see why Lee wouldn't surrender to Garrett after he locked up McNew and Carr. It must have been a lucky thing for Lee to have Otero County split off from Doña Ana County and have the scene of the crime wind up in Otero County so he didn't have to surrender to Garrett."

Curry looks at me and laughs aloud. "That wasn't any accident, Quent. The railroads needed better management oversight in Doña Ana County. The county was just too big and the government too small to manage all the freight that was being shipped. One of the shippers asked me about making Doña Ana County into two counties. I said I'd talk to Fall, who was in the legislature.

"It didn't take me long to figure out what an advantage that would be for Oliver Lee. Fall recognized its value right off. He managed to sweet-talk Governor Otero and the Republicans into accepting the idea. He even drew up the map for the county and made sure the scene of the crime wound up in Otero County. Next thing we know, there's Otero County, and Lee doesn't have to surrender to Garrett. The rest, as they say, is history." He checks his watch. "Guess I'd better get on up to the courthouse and jail. You want to come with me?"

I cap my pen and pocket my notebook. "Sure! Thanks for the escort."

Chapter 26
Pat Garrett Testifies, 1 June 1899

James Gould, whose cousin married Gililland, is the first witness to testify this morning. He states that he was at the McNew ranch about the first of February, 1896. He says Gililland came in a few days before, got some cartridges, left, and then returned around the first, or shortly after, with McNew. He says they told him about Fountain's disappearance, which was the first he'd heard of it.

In court, Gould says, "Gililland said a posse was out hunting for Fountain. He later told me old man Fountain came from Texas in a chicken coop and had pried up hell ever since he'd been in New Mexico but wouldn't pry it up anymore. I asked him about killing the child. He said it wasn't nothing but a half-breed and to kill him was like killing a dog."

A murmur bubbles up from the crowd. Judge Parker hammers his gavel, demanding order. Gililland bows his head, refusing to look at the jury. Lee remains unblinking and steady.

Persia and Sadie appear in the doorway at the back of the courtroom and take a couple of seats two rows in front of me.

Fall cross-examines Gould and makes him admit he's not positive about the dates he's given in his testimony and that he's discussed the story with his father, Fall's point being that Gould is using part of his father's story to make Gililland look bad. Fall asks him if he and Gililland are enemies.

Gould looks toward Gililland and says, "Yes, an enemy I suppose, now."

Fall pushes on, asking if the Gould and McNew families have a long-standing feud and travel around armed in case they meet each other. Gould admits that, yes, they carry guns "just in case." Fall also leads Gould to admit he was in the Eddy jail in March of 1897.

Riley Baker, married to the sister of Gililland's wife, is called next. He testifies to knowing Colonel Fountain and that he came to know Gililland after the Fountains disappeared. Baker stares at the floor and mumbles as he gives his testimony. Jury members lean in his direction to understand what he says.

Judge Parker hammers his gavel and says, "Witness will face the jury and speak up!"

Baker speaks louder, but he won't look at the jury as he rubs his hands against his knees. He testifies that Gililland showed him the spot where he and the defendants used a field glass to watch a posse searching for the Fountains. "As we were riding through the mountains, I said to Gililland, 'I don't know who murdered the Fountains, but the murder of a child is a mighty lowdown thing.' And Gililland said, 'Oh, I don't know, a half-breed Mexican kid ain't no better than a dog.' "

Baker claims Gililland also told him, in front of Kent Kearney, that the bodies would never be found and no one would be convicted of the murder. "Gililland said things had been quieter since the old man went missing or was killed. I don't know which he said."

On cross-examination, Fall's questions lead Baker to admit to hiding on a housetop in Alamogordo on election day with his brother and Deputy Sheriff H.W. Loomis. He says they waited all day, hoping to get the drop on Lee and Gililland when they came to vote and arrest them.

"Did you have a warrant for Lee?"

"Yes, sir."

Asked if he ever received pay for his services, Baker was quick to answer that he had been paid several times, and that he was a paid a dollar-fifty per day for watching from the roof of the house in Alamogordo.

"Were you going to get any more for killing Lee?"

"There was nothing said about killing Lee."

"No more questions, Your Honor."

I watch the jury as Baker sits down. To a man, they've crossed their arms and are looking at Childers, probably wondering what he's hoped to prove with a witness who's just been shown to be a tool and spy for law officers who haven't the nerve to serve their own warrants.

Judge Parker calls a dinner recess. I wait at the end of my row for people in the rows in front of me to pass by. Sadie slides a folded note into my hand as she and Persia pass me. Persia shows me a hint of a smile. I see the sparkle in her eyes, and I'm overjoyed. Outside I find a place to stand and read Sadie's note. It says, "See me at dinner—Ocean Grove."

At the Ocean Grove, I find Sadie waiting for me in Tom Ying's kitchen. She takes my arm, and we step outside.

I grin. "Did you ladies see anyone I need to duck?"

Sadie's face is somber. "I believe I saw Brady sitting near the back. He's about forty, clean-shaven, and was wearing a brown suit with a vest but no tie. Quent, you be careful. He murdered the Fountain child. He won't think twice about cutting your throat. Persia says she thinks Green Scott is there, too. He's worked for Brown before and wouldn't hesitate to help him murder the Fountains. Scott's in his thirties and has long, shaggy, red hair. Persia says he may not look armed, but he keeps a pocket pistol inside his leather vest and a straight razor in an outside pocket. He probably doesn't have the *cojones* to kill you like Brady would in broad daylight, but if you're on a dark street, watch out."

My frivolous mood evaporates, and my mouth feels dry. "I'll try to avoid Scott and Brady, and I'll tell Tom Tucker what's up. What do you think the chances are they'll come after Persia? What can I do to protect her?"

"Don't worry about Persia. She has the little rig I wore at one time on her leg. It only has two shots, but you could drive a stage through the holes it leaves. You two just go on about your business, or they're liable to realize they've been spotted and think they need to do something about you sooner rather than later."

"Can I still see Persia? I mean without putting her in danger?"

Sadie smiles, and for a second, her eyes soften from their usual worldly glint. "I think that's up to her and our old friend, Mr. Discretion. If a man wants to see a woman bad enough, he'll find a way. Get my drift, Mr. Peach?"

I laugh and nod. "Yes, ma'am. Thanks for all your help, Sadie. Can I see Persia for a couple of minutes?"

"Wait here. I'll see if I can find her. Don't take long. She's busy."

I wait by Tom Ying's door. In ten minutes, Persia appears in the doorway and steps out, mopping her forehead with her work-dress sleeve.

"Quent? Sadie said you want to speak to me."

"I suppose Sadie told you the kinds of danger we're facing."

Persia crosses her arms. "Yes, and I knew we were in trouble as soon as I saw Green Scott. Don't worry about me. I'm ready if those no-accounts want to try something."

"I know you are. Still, it pays not to take chances. Forget Brady and Scott for a second. I was hoping that maybe I could visit with you for a while this evening."

She looks at the ground. "I don't think that's a good idea."

"Please, Persia." I know I must sound like a whiny kid, but I don't care. "I just want to talk to you for a little while, tell you what I think, and how I feel."

It seems she takes an extra-long time to think it over, and then I see a teasing sparkle in her eyes that makes my spirits rise. She nods. "All right. I'll meet you here about nine this evening."

In succession, Childers calls Humphrey Hill, who saw Colonel Fountain on the road home the first of February, James Gould, Sr., who has evidently been a blood enemy of McNew for a long time, and Frank Wayne, who lives in the Sacramentos about twenty-five miles from Lee's ranch.

Humphrey Hill is a justice of the peace and a friend of Colonel Fountain's. His testimony is similar to that of Barela and Alvarado. Gould, Sr. testifies to having a conversation with Gililland that sounds very similar to the one Gould, Jr. claimed. On cross-examination, he admits that he served three years in the penitentiary for stealing bacon in 1878.

Frank Wayne testifies that he was at the Dog Canyon Ranch before or about the first of February, 1896, looking for a pony. He claims that when he left, Lee rode a couple of miles with him and his brother and said, "You boys say nothing about what you saw here. It might interfere with some of our plans." At that, Lee whispers in Fall's ear. Fall nods and declines to cross-examine Wayne.

Charles S. Lusk is called next. He testifies he was a deputy sheriff in January of 1896 and took McNew to Las Cruces to post an appearance bond and answer an indictment found against him at the January term. On the streets of Las Cruces, he says McNew told him that while Fountain had no hopes of gaining a conviction against him and his friends who were indicted, he'd prosecute them anyway in an attempt to break them up.

Fall is on his feet. "Objection! Mr. McNew is not on trial here."

Childers volleys back, "Your Honor, there was a conspiracy between McNew and the defendants. They all stand together."

Parker looks at Childers and frowns.

"You've already dismissed Mr. McNew, Mr. Childers. He's not on trial here. Objection sustained."

Lusk is asked if he attended court in Lincoln where Colonel Fountain was prosecuting alleged cattle thieves. He verifies that he was in court at that time and is excused.

Barnes calls Patrick Floyd Garrett to the stand. The courtroom grows still and heads turn. The thud of Garrett's boots sound down the aisle, and he's sworn in. Barnes sets the stage, leading him through the usual preliminaries. Garrett says he and his family live in Las Cruces, that he is Doña Ana County sheriff, and that he didn't know the defendants until he moved back to New Mexico, but that he had known Colonel Fountain from the Lincoln County War days. He notes that Fountain defended Billy the Kid in the trial where the Kid was sentenced to hang.

Garrett testifies that after he began his investigation of the murders, he visited the scene in March of 1896 with Van Patten and other members of the posse. He says he saw the blood-stained ground where it was believed the colonel died and then, surveying the scene and the path the buckboard took, he became convinced it was a carefully executed ambush and probably required four or five participants.

Barnes asks Garrett what he did to bring in the defendants. Garrett glances toward them. "I had a warrant for Lee and Gililland in 1898 and tried to serve it, but they objected. I caught the two together at one time, but they resisted and killed Kearney, my deputy. I made several scouting trips into the mountains, but I failed to find the defendants. I also sent various other parties out to look for the defendants, H.W. Loomis, Riley Baker, and others."

Barnes paces back and forth, his hands behind his back, listening to Garrett. "When did you try to arrest the defendants at Wildy Well?"

"On July 10, 1898, I received word that Lee and Gililland were staying overnight at Wildy Well. A posse of four men and I rode nearly all night to get there. Just before dawn, we tried to arrest the defendants while they slept, but I discovered they weren't sleeping in the adobe ranch house. However, we soon learned they were on the roof. It was coming on light, and we made several efforts to get word to them to surrender. When that didn't work, I told the boys we'd have to get up to the top by ladder and call on them to surrender. Mr. Lee and Mr. Kearney shot, but Mr. Kearney shot first, and Mr. Kearney was mortally wounded."

Barnes nods. "I see, I see. Now there's the question of your contract with Jack Maxwell. What did the contract require from Mr. Maxwell, and what did it promise in return?"

I see the jury lean forward. "I made a written contract with him to furnish the evidence for the conviction in the Fountain murderers."

"Do you have a copy of the original contract with you?"

"Yes, sir." Garrett reaches in his coat pocket and hands it to Barnes. Barnes opens the envelope, unfolds it, reads it, enters it into evidence, and passes it among the jury to read. Chavez reads it aloud in Spanish to the jury members who don't speak or read English.

Turning to Judge Parker, Barnes says, "No more questions, Your Honor."

Parker looks toward Fall. "Does the defense expect a long cross-examination, Mr. Fall?"

"I expect so, Your Honor."

"Very well, it's just past five o'clock now. The court stands adjourned until nine o'clock tomorrow morning."

Outside in the long shadows between the courthouse and the jail, I look for Brady or Scott but see no one who matches their descriptions. Tom Tucker is nowhere to be seen, either. I decide to head back to the Ocean Grove before it gets dark. I'm about half a block down Eleanora Street from the courthouse, right in front of the little church, when I feel a hand clamp on my shoulder.

I jerk away, stumbling as I try to get my hand around my Smith and Wesson. By the time I can get the weapon out and turn to face my attacker, I've taken two or three steps.

"Whoa! Don't shoot! It'th just me! Gene 'odes! I'm not after you!"

I come close to collapsing in the middle of street, but I laugh instead as I lower the hammer and holster my gun. "Gene! You about scared holy hell out of me! For a minute there, I thought I was about to be shot or cut."

"It'th okay. Sorry I snuck up on you, didn't mean to. Anyways, you said you'd read some of my work. I brought you a draft of one of my stories. Will you read it?"

"Sure. I'd be honored to. Come on. I'll buy you supper, and we can talk about it."

"Thanks, but I'm guarding Lee and Gililland in a little while. Maybe in a day or two we can eat off the chuck wagon at Lee's camp."

"Sounds good. I'll try to have this read by then. See you later."

Chapter 27
The Message

At the Ocean Grove door, I see Persia working the restaurant tables. When she sees me, she smiles and continues her race between the restaurant tables and Tom Ying's kitchen.

Sadie's handsome black girl, Sam, and the girl, Ruth, are also helping with the crush of people trying to find supper. I turn toward my room. Sam sees me and holds up a finger for me to wait. She smiles as she reaches in her skirt pocket. "Mista Peach! I have a telegram for yuh. It come just a little while ago. One of Mista Belvedere's boys drop it off. We didn't know where you was, so I kept for yuh."

"Thanks very much, Sam." I give her a dime tip and head for my room. The telegram is from Chief.

> GOOD WORK. SAVING STORIES FOR SPECIAL EDITION AFTER THE TRIAL. INTERVIEW DEFENDANTS SOONEST. MIGHT USE ABOVE THE FOLD TO GENERATE INTEREST FOR THE SPECIAL EDITION. SEE POSSIBLITIES FOR A BOOK.

I think, *Quent you're about to start playing with the big boys.* Forgetting about Brady and Scott, I rush up the street to the Orchard Hotel where Fall and the other attorneys are staying. At the little registration desk, a young clerk stands guard, his hair slicked down and parted in the middle. "We don't have any rooms, sir, sorry."

I'm puffing and red-faced after practically running to the hotel. "I don't need a room. Is Mr. Fall in?"

"No, sir. I believe he's already left for supper. You might try looking at the Ocean Grove."

"That's all right. I know where he takes his supper. Is Mrs. Orchard in?"

"Yes, sir. I believe she's in the office and can't be disturbed right now."

I narrow my eyes and say, "Don't try to jack me around, boy! Tell Mrs. Orchard that Quentin Peach needs a moment of her time. Now!"

He backs up a step and turns through the curtain across the hall's entrance. In less than a minute, he's back and motions me down the hall. "Second door on your right."

Sadie sits at a big rolltop desk. I knock gently on the doorframe. She turns to look at me, wrinkling her brow. "Hallo, Quent! Everything okay?"

"Evening, Sadie! Everything's fine. You said to let you know when I needed to get in the jail to interview Lee and Gililland. I just got a telegram from my editor, and he's anxious for me to interview Lee. Can I take breakfast up to Lee and Gililland in the morning? When I leave here, I'm going to see Mr. Fall and ask if it's okay."

Sadie's frown turns into a broad smile. "Of course, you can. I'll send word to Tom Ying that you'll take breakfast to the prisoners in the morning. It's usually ready by six o'clock. Any sign of Bailey or Scott?"

"Thanks very much. No, I didn't see them."

"Be careful, Quent. They'll be on you when you least expect it. Try to keep Tom Tucker where he can cover your back."

"I will. Thanks again, Sadie. See you later." She waves me out and turns back to her ledger.

★ ★ ★ ★ ★

By the time I leave the Orchard, the sun has fallen behind the Black Range. I go up to Eleanora Street and head east toward the Lee camp to avoid being seen by Bailey or Scott.

A large crowd of cowboys and businessmen are stuffing their mouths with steak and potatoes. Looking over the crowd, it takes a minute to find Fall, who is sitting well into the shadows, enjoying a cigar.

I make my way around the men and stick my hand out. "Mr. Fall. Quentin Peach. Do you remember me?"

"Well, of course, Quent. Come for another interview or supper?"

"I certainly want to talk more with you, but I came to ask if you'd approve my interviewing Mr. Lee and Mr. Gililland in the morning after I take breakfast up to them."

Fall asks, "Why tomorrow, Quent?"

"I just got a telegram from my editor. He thinks an interview might make the front page above the fold and wanted me to get it. How about it?"

He smiles his wolf's grin. "Sure! Sounds fine to me. I'll be seeing the boys later tonight, and I'll tell them to expect you. Just remember our little deal," he says. "You tell it straight. Sure you don't want a little supper? Maybe we can talk about what you want to cover in the interview."

"It's mighty tempting, but I have a meeting I need to attend tonight. Besides, I need to make it to the telegraph office before it closes." He nods, giving me a little wave-off as I head back to town.

Belvedere Brooks is ready to close the telegraph office when I arrive. "Belvedere! Any chance of getting a short telegram down the wire before you close?"

"Howdy, Quent. Both my operators have left for the day. If

it's not too long, I can send it myself."

"Thanks. It's not long at all. Can I write it out for you?"

"Sure." He slides a blank piece of paper across the counter and says, "Your associate, Mr. Seymour, was in earlier with a long report of the day's proceedings. He wasn't too impressed with what the prosecution had today."

I nod as I print the message. "Yeah, Pat Garrett's testimony wasn't headline news, that's for sure." I shove the paper across to him. "Here's what I want sent."

He reads it aloud, "Message received. Interview tomorrow. QP." Smiling, he says, "That is short. Charge it to your account?"

I nod, thank him, and head for the Ocean Grove. It's darker on the north side of Main Street than the south. There are more trees to cast shadows from lights in windows and from the rising moon. I stay on the north side, keeping an eye on foot traffic on the south side of Main. I pass the last dance hall on the north side and step off the boardwalk onto the path that runs to the bridge across the Percha.

As my foot hits the path, a cowboy appears out of the darkness in front of me. He matches the description of Green Scott in every detail. He has the fingers of his right hand in the vest's bottom right pocket where Persia says he carries a straight razor.

He smiles and nods. "You Quentin Peach?"

I slide my hand inside my coat and around the Smith and Wesson's grips. I pull it just to the edge of my coat and pull the hammer back so he's sure to hear the double clicks from the advancing cylinder. "That's me."

He's faster than a rattlesnake. I see his hand flash out of the vest pocket as he steps forward and slashes toward my throat. At the same time, I instinctively jerk back as I pull the revolver out of my coat. The flying blade makes a clean slice through a coat lapel. On the back slash, I have the revolver up, so the back of his hand smashes into the barrel, and the impact makes my finger reflexively pull the trigger, sending a bullet toward the stars and a deafening roar down Main Street. I see Scott's teeth clenched in pain as he vanishes in the dark.

The dance hall I've just passed empties, and several men appear outside the Union Hotel bar and a couple of the saloons down the street. They look around, see no apparent fights, and go back inside.

Men from the dance hall surround me. "You okay, mister?"

"Yeah. This revolver just fell out of my pocket and went off. Nothing to be concerned about."

"You'd best keep that hammer on an empty cylinder from now on. Just load five like the rest of us," says a young cowboy.

"Right. That sounds like good advice. Thanks for your concern, folks. I'm fine."

A grizzled old cowboy with a dancer on his arm bends down and looks at the lapel on my coat. With a knowing smile, he reaches over to flip one of the dangling pieces with a gnarled old finger. "Looks like you got lost in a cactus patch. New style?"

"Yeah. Thanks." The crowd evaporates, and I continue toward the Ocean Grove. My hands tremble. I puff my cheeks, trying to settle down, but, at the same time, I feel exhilarated. I'm alive and know I've passed some kind of test I've wanted to take for a long time. When I get to my room, I have to sit down.

I check my watch. It's nearly nine. All afternoon I've tried different mental speeches of what I want to tell Persia. All the flowery words have flown away, leaving my mind blank. I only know I have a longing for her I can't explain and have never felt for any other woman.

I walk down the dimly lighted hallway, feel my way through the dark restaurant dining room, and then to the kitchen door. It's unlocked, and so is the kitchen's back door. I step out into the chorus of peepers and insects, and it's darker than a coal mine. Barely visible within ten feet of the kitchen door is an adobe tower, supporting a large water tank for the Ocean Grove. A high wooden fence surrounds the backyard. The yard is divided by a high fence separating the kitchen yard from the side with bathtubs. The moon fills the yard with small patches of light, and I sit on the steps to wait.

As my eyes adjust to the darkness, I jerk in surprise to see a figure, arms crossed, leaning against the tower. "What's the matter, Quent? Don't you recognize me?"

Persia laughs as she walks over to sit beside me. "We finished early, so I thought I'd come enjoy the evening." Easing down beside me, she stretches her legs out in front of her, crosses her arms, and smiles at me. "What's on your mind? Sadie said you didn't see Brady or Greene this afternoon."

"No I didn't, this afternoon. Look, all during the afternoon court session, I made up fancy speeches to tell you what I'm feeling. Now my mind is a perfect blank, so I'm just going to say it and hope you understand me."

She nods. "Daddy always said it's best to say things plain so there's no misunderstanding."

Taking a deep breath, I say, "Since you told me you weren't going to waste years waiting for a man you knew would never come for you and that I should leave you alone, I've wrestled with how I truly feel about you. Persia, I feel like I've known you my entire life, although it's only been a few days. I'm grateful to you for staying with me day and night when Clayton and Greco beat the hell out of me. But I'd take that beating again if you'd stay with me another couple of days.

"I was trying to tell you on the bridge last Sunday night that all reporters have a mistress: their work. I'm on call all the time. When I'm working on a story, I might be gone for days, or even weeks.

"It's not just the time away researching and writing stories that makes life hard for a reporter's loved ones. People who don't like what I write might try to destroy me and those close to me. It can be an awful, messy business."

She nods and puts her hand on my mine. "Quent, I understand. I realized when I was looking after you that I have strong feelings for you. It hurt my soul to cut myself off from you. It's just that, if I let you court me while you're here, I know the pain I feel now will be ten times worse when you leave. Don't you understand that?"

"Yes, I do. I understand very well. It's just . . . God help me . . . I can't live with you, and I can't live without you."

"Are you saying you want me to go back to San Francisco with you? That you'd marry me?"

"I don't know. I want you more than I can say. It's just that with the demands of my career, I don't think it's right for me to ask you, and when I become an established writer, I'll be a much better prospect."

She stands. "Goodbye, Quent." I hear sadness in her voice.

CHAPTER 28
FIRST OLIVER LEE INTERVIEW

Gene Rhodes has his shotgun across his lap and his notepad on his knee. Looking up, he stops writing. His hand slides to the shotgun at the sound of my footsteps in the early light. I can see him squint under the brim of his peaked, Montana-style hat. He breaks into a big grin. "Well, howdy, Quent. I haven't seen you out and about this early."

"I'm just bringing Mr. Lee and Mr. Gililland their breakfast, so I can interview them."

He nods and holds out a blue-speckled enamel cup he has sitting beside him. "I wondered how long it'd be before you got around to that. How 'bout pouring some of that nice Tom Ying coffee in my old tin cup?"

I pour him some coffee as he taps on the heavy, iron latticework door with the butt of his shotgun. I hear a clank and squeak of some kind of locking mechanism from behind the black, solid iron door behind it. The solid door swings open just wide enough for a round, Mexican face to look around its edge. "Ees breakfast already, Gene? Who ees thees *hombre*?"

Gene holds up his cup of steaming coffee. "Geronimo, this is Mr. Quentin Peach bringing us breakfast. Mr. Peach, the man inside there is the jailer, *Señor* Geronimo Sánchez. He'th got a couple of double-barreled, ten-gauge Greeners in there that'll blow you to hell and gone if you don't behave yourself.

"Geronimo, Mr. Peach here is a reporter with the *San Francithco Examiner,* and he's expecting to interview our star boarders. I hear Mr. Fall has cleared him to see the prisoners."

The heavy, iron door swings open, and Sánchez unlocks the top and bottom straps of the latticework door. With a grunt, he pushes it open. I follow him inside, and he motions for me to put the basket and coffee pot on a table. *"Por favor,* please, your weapons on the table, *señor."* I unfasten my shoulder holster and hand it to Sánchez. "Now I have to search you, *señor.*" He's quick and thorough and nods his satisfaction that I have no other weapons. He checks the breakfast basket for weapons and puts the coffee pot on the stove beside the other one.

Sánchez takes the key ring and opens the solid iron door to the west-side cells. On the cell side of the wall is another latticework iron strap door that is locked, like the front door. It's cold in the cell room. In the middle cell, the glass window covering the bars is up. A guard sits tilted back against the south wall in a straight-back chair, facing the cell bars.

The cell in the middle is occupied by Gililland, who sits on his bunk reading yesterday's *Sierra County Advocate.* Lee is in the corner cell. He stands and says, "Howdy. Mr. Peach?" Gililland lowers his paper and looks at me for the first time but says nothing.

"Yes, sir. I'm Quentin Peach. I work for the *San Francisco Examiner.* My editor sent me to do background stories so our readers can understand the facts behind the Fountain disappearance."

Lee makes a small, one-sided smile. "Fall told me you were coming and that it was all right to talk with you. I usually don't have much to say to reporters or strangers, but Fall said you'd keep your word on being true to what was said. I guess you know that if you lie, this part of the country won't be too healthy for you."

I cross my arms and nod. "Yes, sir."

He studies me for a moment. "I recall seeing you in court.

Mr. Peach, what's your take on me and Gililland? I'm just curious to see if you think we murdered the Fountain child and his daddy, You made up your mind yet?"

I nod. "Yes, sir, I've made up my mind. I don't think you had anything to do directly with the disappearance."

Lee nods and begins dressing in silence. Smiling, Lee says, "Now if you'll slide those breakfast plates in to us and bring the coffee, we can have a little talk while Jim and I eat."

I get the coffee pot from the jailer, fill the cups Lee and Gililland hold through the bars, and pass them the plates. Sánchez gives me a chair from his room, and I sit down next to Lee's cell.

Gililland asks, "Where you from? You don't sound like you're from anywhere around here."

I tell them my history and stick out my chest a little when I say, "My editor says the reports I write from this trial could make my career."

Lee slurps the hot coffee and asks, "So, Quent, what can we tell you to help make your career?"

I pull out my pencil and notepad. "What were your early years in New Mexico like?"

Lee takes a bite of biscuit and a swallow of coffee, his brow wrinkling as he calls up old memories. "My half-brother, Perry Altman, and I came over with our horses and cattle in 1884. Old Cherokee Bill showed us this canyon that was one of a few that had a good water supply and wouldn't take much fencing to hold a good size herd, maybe a thousand head of cattle."

"That was Dog Canyon?"

"Yep. My family and our colored hands, Ed and Eph, came along in wagons two or three months later. The grama grass was plentiful then, and with the water we had, the stock did well.

"Folks were still leery of strangers because the Lincoln County War hadn't been over long. They still worried about being ambushed or even shot at their front doors. Why, every time we went visiting on Sundays, there were people warning me about how powerful Tom Catron's Santa Fe Ring was, how we could expect to be threatened by men who were fast and deadly with firearms, and that we'd be given a little demonstration of their firepower if we didn't walk the line.

"I didn't want any trouble from anybody, and I decided the best thing I could do was give a little demonstration of my ability with firearms."

I lean forward and ask, "What did you do?"

"We went to the '85 Fourth of July romp in Tularosa where the cowboys were having a little shootin' contest. I wound up shooting tossed dimes out of the air with a sightless rifle, and that seemed to make an impression, so I decided I might as well drive the point home. One of 'em had a '76 Winchester. That rifle will shoot a mighty long ways if you know how to use it. I borrowed it and asked a cowboy to get on his horse and haul a pine plank about a mile away, stick it upright in the sand, and then get out of the way. I hit that plank five shots out of six with the Winchester. Then I shooed the crowd out of the way, got on my horse, and galloped around a hitching post in the middle of a corral. I used my revolver to shoot that post to pieces, and I never missed. I figured after that day, the Santa Fe Ring wasn't going to make trouble for me, not them or anybody else."

I give a low whistle. "Whew! That kind of shooting is unbelievable, not that I doubt your word. Did it make gunmen leave you alone?"

Lee shakes his head. "It kinda backfired on me. I think it made gunmen leave me alone, but it also generated all sorts of stories about what a dangerous killer I was when, in fact, I hadn't even shot anyone at that point. I didn't care then, but it caught up with me after a while."

"How's that?"

"In '86, when I turned twenty-one, I filed to homestead a quarter section where I thought I might find water and there was free range close by. It didn't take me long to figure out that in New Mexico all that free range didn't do you any good unless you owned the water to go with it. You can control hundreds of thousands of acres of land and own only a few quarter sections, if they're in the right place, and have water."

I look up from my notes and ask, "Why is that?"

"The government will give you a quarter section, which is a hundred and sixty acres, if you work and improve the land for a few years. First come, first served. I have a pretty good nose for water, either digging wells or figuring out how to get water out of the mountains to where I need it. Once you own the water rights, the surrounding land to your section is still free and open. You don't have to buy it to use it, so it doesn't take a big fortune to control a big range."

I write furiously to capture all Lee is telling me. Gililland drains his cup and yells, "Hey, Geronimo, how about some more coffee?" Lee drains his cup, and I do, too, as Sánchez appears with Tom Ying's coffee pot for refills.

"Mr. Lee, I talked with the Fountain brothers and Tom Catron, among others. They seem to want to hang you as much for supporting Mr. Fall as they do for murdering the Fountains. This trial appears to be as much a political contest between Republicans in towns versus Democrats on the ranges."

I turn my gaze to Gililland. "I've heard stories about how Fall appointed you, Mr. Gililland, and other deputies so you could legally be his enforcers. From what I heard, you apparently enjoyed your work."

I look back at Lee. "I'm curious why both of you came to dislike the Republicans in Las Cruces so much that you were willing to risk your life in a deputy's job and help Mr. Fall with his political projects as a Democrat, when you must have been busy working hard to develop your ranches."

Lee takes a couple of bites of his biscuits and gravy while he stares off into space. It's so quiet, I can hear the big regulator clock ticking in the jailor's room. I glance over at Gililland, who shrugs his shoulders. I see the guard sitting in the chair tilted back against the wall has his ear cocked to hear every word. Lee walks over to his table and picks up his pocket watch and chain. He hands them to me through the bars and points to a flattened bullet hanging from the chain. It's about three-quarters of an inch in diameter and has a rough, irregular flared edge. Turning it over, I see small pieces of grit embedded in the lead, and there's enough of the original outline left on the backside to tell it came from a .45 caliber cartridge.

As I hand it back to him, Lee says, "That's why I don't have any use for Republicans, especially those in Las Cruces, and why I'll stick it to them every chance I get. That's the bullet that killed George MacDonald."

I search my memory and come up blank. "I don't believe I've ever heard that name. Who was he?"

Lee swallows and looks away. "George MacDonald was the best friend I ever had. We grew up together. We learned to be men together, schemed our lives together, and stood together in good times and bad. He was as good with horses as I am. When my family moved out here from Texas, George came with us and helped us start the place. He had fire in his belly and light in his brains. We were always thinking up projects to get ahead. He and my grandniece, Nettie Fry, were in love and were going to marry."

I interrupt him to ask, "Nettie Fry? Is that the same lady who married Bill McNew?"

He nods. "That's right. Mama, who raised my niece, wanted them to wait until George could get their own place started. Nettie and George always followed her advice. In '88, George struck a deal with John Stuart and his brother, who owned a store over in La Luz. He agreed to be their foreman and look after their cattle in Coyote Springs Canyon. They paid him ten dollars a month more than the going rate, and they agreed that when he started his own herd, he could graze his stock with their cattle. George didn't have much money, but with a start like that, why he'd have been a cattle baron by the time he was thirty. Nettie is smart and has grit. She's hardworking and knows ranching. They were a perfect match. But there was a snake in the woodpile named John Good.

"The same Good in the Good-Cooper Range War?"

"Yeah. John Good was the patriarch of the clan. He had three sons and a son-in-law, John Taylor. Walter was the biggest, meanest, and sorriest of his sons. John's brother Isham settled in La Luz about a year after John. Isham had four sons and four daughters. Between John and Isham, they had one tough outfit. John ran several thousand head of cattle on the free range on shares. The cattle belonged to Riley and Rynerson, attorneys in Las Cruces, and Tom Catron, who was the biggest landowner in the territory and top dog Republican in the legislature. Good tried to use his clan to run everybody else off the free range. Some left, but George didn't. He and Good almost got into it several times, but they were lucky for a while, and nobody got killed.

"In June of '88, Benito Montoya came riding into my place, his horse all lathered up. Benito said he'd been out hunting for stray cows and found George's body. I told him to take me to him.

"I found George looking like he'd gone up the canyon after dinner and laid down to take a little afternoon siesta." Lee put his forefinger on a spot in the middle of his forehead. "He'd been shot right here. That mashed slug you saw on my watch chain was right behind his skull, against a rock where he'd laid his head. He never knew what hit him. I wanted to cry when I saw him. My niece, planning to buy her wedding dress, had already left for El Paso. I swore I'd see justice done for George MacDonald or die trying.

"I found the trail of the killer. He wasn't more than twenty or thirty feet away when he killed George. Then the coward got on his horse and rode for all he was worth up the canyon and over to Tularosa Canyon, where we lost the trail. He'd have gotten away clean, except he ran his horse against a Spanish dagger cactus that sliced off a piece of hide."

"So what did the sheriff do?"

Lee looked at me like I was crazy. "What sheriff? Ascarate in Las Cruces didn't even send a deputy to investigate; said it'd be a waste of time because the killer was long gone and there weren't any witnesses. After we buried George, I started doing a little detective work."

"If the killer was long gone, how'd you know where to start?"

"George's murder looked a lot like one that had happened a couple of years earlier when A.H. Howe, who owned a trading post up in Mescalero, was murdered. The story around the range fires was that José Espalin did it. When George was murdered, Espalin was in tight with John Good's son, Walter. So I started keeping an eye out for Espalin and Walter."

I underline José's name and ask, "How were you going to ever get them to admit anything?"

"About a week after we buried George, I was in La Luz to buy supplies at Sutherland's store, and I saw Walter's pinto tied up in front. Sure enough, there was a piece of hide torn off him, the place was still tender, and it was in about the right place for that Spanish dagger cut. A few days later, I borrowed Walter's horse when it was out to pasture and took it over to the Coyote Springs Ranch. The place where it had been cut was a perfect match to the size and height of that Spanish dagger spike where we found the hide. I was certain Walter Good had murdered George."

I felt my teeth clenching, wanting to hear that justice was done right then. "You're fast and deadly accurate with a gun. Did you call him out in the street and fill him full of holes?"

Lee grinned. "I wanted to, but I didn't want to start a range war with John Good and his backers. I decided the best thing was to help the law hang him."

"How'd you do that?"

"Walter had always been a blowhard. I knew he had to be bragging around the bunkhouse about what he'd done. I started visiting the cooking fires of Good's hands when they were working the cattle out on the free range. You know, just being friendly, stopping by for a cup of coffee while I was riding through looking after my own stock, that kind of thing. It didn't take long before two of them separately told me what Walter Good had been saying."

Lee paused, looking out the jail's back window. A minute went by. Two. "Mr. Lee?"

"They claimed he said, 'I caught that sonovabitch MacDonald napping, and, by God, I plugged his ass. He ain't gonna be bothering my daddy no more.' Nearly the same story came out of both of them when I talked to 'em privately. I knew those two boys would never talk in public as long as they worked for John Good, so I convinced them to come work for me. I had to keep 'em from running their mouths and ending up dead. We had a few long talks. I promised 'em on my mother's honor that I'd protect them if they'd testify in court to what they'd told me. It took a little while, but they screwed up their courage and said they'd do it.

"It didn't take the Goods long to figure out what I was up to with those two cowboys. It kind of surprised me that they didn't come after us.

"When the next grand jury session started, we rode over to Las Cruces one dark night, staying off the road to get there. Next morning, we met with the district attorney so they could tell their story. He listened, took notes, and seemed interested, but, for some reason, I felt like he didn't care. He said he'd call us when the grand jury was ready to hear our case, so we waited around the courthouse for five days. It was about dinnertime on the fifth day when the grand jury adjourned. The district attorney was the last man out of the room. I asked him when my witnesses were going to testify. He wouldn't even look at me, just shook his head, and kept walking. He said over his shoulder, 'Session's over. The MacDonald case won't be called this term.' The district attorney is the one who presents the cases to the grand jury. He was telling me he wasn't going to pursue the case."

"Did the grand jury ever review the evidence?"

"Nope. Never did."

All I could do was stare at those burning black eyes and shake my head.

"Our case died on the vine right there. I thought a long time about what I could do to find the justice George deserved. I wanted to call Walter out in the street and shoot him like the sorry dog he was. I knew as soon as I killed him, the Republicans would hang me, even if it was a fair fight. Good's cattle belonged to big-time Republicans. The sheriff and district attorney were Republicans. They were all Yankee Republicans who didn't have any use for Texas Democrats. They weren't about to prosecute one of their own."

"So what happened?"

"I'll just tell you what the public knows. You figure the rest out for yourself."

"That works for me, Mr. Lee."

"In early August of '88, Walter disappeared. Last time he was seen was when he was riding over to my brother Perry's place to pick up his pinto that had gotten out of the Good's corral and showed up in my brother's pasture. When Walter didn't come home, old John went crazy, and that was the start of the Good-Cooper Range War.

"Good got Humphrey Hill, a justice of the peace, to issue a warrant for me, my brother, Tom Tucker, and Jim Cooper, for carrying weapons.

"Good burnt Perry's house down because that was where Walter had been headed the day he disappeared, and then he had the gall to claim Perry did it to cover up a bloodstained floor. John found my brother and very nearly hanged him, but luckily, John Taylor talked him out of it.

"A fifteen-man posse started searching everywhere for Walter. Two weeks later, they found his skeleton in the white sands. The buzzards and the coyotes didn't leave much except the bones. The only way they identified him was by how big his skeleton was, his jewelry, and some new boots he wore, which Henry Stoes verified he sold him from Numa Reymond's store. Walter's loaded revolver was found next to him with two fired chambers."

Lee touched his left temple with the forefinger and index finger on his left hand. "There were two bullets holes in his skull right here. Just before Walter was buried, a coroner's jury charged Perry, Cherokee Bill, Cooper, Tom Tucker, and me with killing him. Good and his boys chased us all over the basin and the Sacramentos. They never caught us, and we scared hell out of them a few times by making our trails disappear, or riding where we didn't leave tracks and then doubling back on them so they could see us, just to let them know we could have killed them all, but didn't."

"How did the war finally end?"

"No one was killed after Walter was found. After a while,

Good just gave up and left. Moved to Las Cruces, stayed around his Republican friends for a while, and then moved on to greener pastures. We finally surrendered and went to trial. Rynerson and Wade, who were assisted by our friend Colonel Fountain, Yankee Republicans one and all, prosecuted us. It was the first time Fountain tried to prosecute me, but it sure wasn't the last. They put together what Albert Fall calls a *habeas corpus* trial. Fountain claimed to the grand jury he had evidence that showed Walter had been tied to a post in my brother's corral and shot repeatedly and he had the testimony of a colored kid who worked for my brother-in-law, Charlie Graham, to prove it. Fountain claimed the kid said he'd seen us pumping lead into Walter. When the trial rolled around, the kid swore he never said any such thing, and that was about the end of it.

"I learn real fast. I've learned not to trust district attorneys, especially if they're Republicans. They don't play by the same rules we Democrats do. Nine times out of ten, I've seen that if you don't jam the law right down their throats, Yankee Republicans will have Texas Democrats for breakfast, fried, boiled, or scrambled. They're not fair, and they're not right, but I've never lost when Albert Fall was defending my rights. That's the truth, and there's a lot of folks around where I live that'll tell you the same thing. That's why Catron hates us so bad."

"Two empty chambers in his revolver? Sounds to me like you gave Walter Good more chances than he deserved."

Lee raises his brows and looks away, a smile playing at the corner of his lips. He says nothing.

I put away my notepad and say, "It's getting late. I'd better get these dishes back to Tom Ying. Have a good day in court. See you later."

Chapter 29
Pat Garrett's Cross-Examination, 2 June 1899

The interview with Lee weighs heavy on my mind while I wait for court to begin. I think of the disgust on Lee's face when he told me of how the law made a mockery of his attempt to use the justice system after his best friend was killed.

Seymour takes his place next to a wall with the other reporters. Seeing me, he smiles and gives me a salute. I wave back. A little tense, I scan the crowd, looking for a man matching Brady's description and for Green Scott, but don't see them. I haven't seen Persia all morning, and I'm worried about her. I wish to heaven I could tell her that I want her to be mine, but reporting is my life.

Sheriff Kahler walks up the aisle, leading Lee and Gililland, who are followed by George Curry. It's not long before the judge is seated and Pat Garrett has been recalled to the stand. Judge Parker looks toward the attorneys at the defense table. "The witness is yours for cross-examination, Mr. Fall."

Fall, eyeing Garrett, walks in front of the defense table. Taking his coat lapel in his left hand, he questions Garrett about how he came to be recruited for the investigation of the Fountain disappearance. Garrett tells how he received five hundred dollars per month as an investigator until he became sheriff, and that in those first meetings in El Paso with Governor Thornton and others, such as Llewellyn and James Beard, he was given evidence they had collected in the Fountain case. He claims the evidence pointed to Lee, Gililland, McNew, and "an official of Doña Ana." No one in court doubts he's referring to Fall. He tells of asking Fall, and Fall agreeing, to visit Santa Fe to have him appointed sheriff, which resulted in the discharge of two county commissioners before he was appointed.

"Did you ever at any time, while sheriff of Doña Ana County, have any conversation with Mr. Lee to the effect that if warrants were issued for him, he was to surrender?"

"Not that I know of."

I wonder how his reply is supposed to square with Curry's story about the poker game in Tipton's Saloon.

"Do you remember telling Mr. Lee not to surrender to any posse of which Ben Williams was a member?"

"No, sir, but I told him I thought it would be unwise."

Fall sticks out his lower lip, looks at the jury, and nods. "What was the condition of affairs when you first went to Las Cruces?"

"Well, you fellows had been shooting at one another and cutting up."

"What fellows?"

"You and Lee and Williams and others." The courtroom spectators all laugh at that one.

"Didn't you tell me that Williams had a mania for killing?"

Childers is on his feet. "Objection! Hearsay!"

Judge Parker frowns. "Sustained. You know better than that, Mr. Fall."

Fall nods. "At the time you went to Las Cruces, political feeling was running pretty high, wasn't it?"

Childers is back up. "Objection! The witness is not being examined on politics!"

Fall tries to argue for the question. "Your Honor, I intend to show that—"

Judge Parker thumps his gavel. "Objection sustained. Get on with it, Mr. Fall."

Fall turns back to Garrett. "What was Lee's official position when you went to Doña Ana County?"

"I understood he was a deputy sheriff."

Fall looks at Judge Parker. "Your Honor, permission to question this witness as to his opinion of Williams, because Williams was a member of the posse that went after the defendants."

Judge Parker squints at Fall, pauses, and says, "Very well. Continue, Mr. Fall, but remember you walk a fine line here."

Nodding, Fall asks Garrett, "Is it not a fact that Ben Williams was a maniac on the subject of killing?"

"I told you he was a maniac, not to murder, but on the subject of killing."

"What did you say would be your course if given any warrants for the arrest of Lee? Did you not say that you would go after him by yourself?"

"Yes, sir."

"Upon what were these warrants based?"

"Upon affidavits."

"They were issued four terms after Fountain disappeared, were they not, and after the grand jury adjourned?"

"Yes, sir."

"Who made the affidavit before warrants for defendants were issued?"

"I did."

"At that time you knew what Jack Fountain and other witnesses would testify, did you not?"

Catron's voice rumbles, "Objection! Calls for conjecture and hearsay by the witness."

Fall snaps back, "Your Honor, the defense is attempting to show that evidence provided by the prosecution, and even what the witnesses would testify to, was known for over two years. It is, in fact, inadmissible. The grand jury did not think it valid then, and apparently neither did the prosecution. Therefore, it is not valid now. Furthermore, it is the intent of the defense to show that the object of the prosecution is not to discover the real murderers of Colonel Fountain but to fix the blame on the defendants."

Judge Parker shakes his head. "Factual evidence does not change with time, Mr. Fall. There is no statute of limitations on the evidence, and you know it. It does not support your supposition that the intent of the prosecution is to fix blame on particular defendants, whether they be guilty or innocent. Objection is sustained. Continue."

Fall looks disgusted. "All right. Then, tell us, Sheriff Garrett, when this evidence came into your hands, why didn't you apply for a bench warrant?"

"I didn't think it was the proper time."

"Why didn't you think it was the proper time?"

Garrett raises his brows and shrugs his shoulders. "You had too much control of the courts down there."

The entire room laughs; even the judge and attorneys smile. After several knocks by Judge Parker's gavel, Fall continues, "In other words, you thought I was the administration?"

"You came pretty near it."

I sit there thinking, *What a game of politics! If the trial had been held when Fall was a judge, Fall would have thrown the case out for lack of evidence. Lee's enemies waited until the Republicans were back in power, hoping to steamroll convictions on the same evidence.*

Fall cocks his head to one side and frowns as though he doesn't believe Garrett. "You base your conclusions on the fact that I procured the sheriff's office for you?"

"Well, you showed your strength then."

"What did you do when the warrants were sworn out?"

"Sent a posse out to serve them."

Fall then leads into a series of questions about who was in

the posse, which he called a mob, that included known enemies of Lee and Gililland. Questions follow about the attempt to take Lee and Gililland at Wildy Well. Fall brings out a large diagram that shows the house on which Lee and Gililland were sleeping, the shed roof close by upon which some of the posse climbed, and the nearby water tank, where Williams was stationed.

"Now, Sheriff Garrett, you say when you climbed up on the roof you hallooed, 'Surrender' or 'throw up your hands'?"

"Both Kearney and I hallooed it."

"Could you see Lee, and was he armed?"

"Yes, I could see him and his gun."

"Didn't you tell me that Kearney fired too quick, contrary to orders you had given him?"

"I told you I thought he fired too quick."

"What took place then?"

"I fired a few shots myself, and then it got to be a general skirmish. I fired two shots."

"Then what did you do?"

"I went to Kearney and assisted him off the roof. We had a little conversation with Lee. He said, 'It's a hell of a thing to order a man to throw up his hands and shoot at the same time.' I told him I thought Kearney had shot a little too quick. We talked a while about them surrendering. He said he didn't believe he'd surrender to me, as he had heard I intended to kill him. I assured him he would be perfectly safe in my hands and that any such story was false."

"Didn't he tell you something further?"

Garrett's face becomes mask-like. "I believe he asked me who had the best of the situation. I told him he did, that we were in a hell of a fix. Then he said that if we would pull off and give him a little time, he would promise not to shoot any of us when we got out from behind shelter. I doubted that and told him so. He said whenever he gave his word, he kept it. We drew off, and as we were leaving, he called out to me that if I'd fix a bond for him, he'd come in and surrender."

"Didn't he tell you that if you'd quit opposing his making a bond, he would surrender?"

"He seemed to be under the impression that I was opposing it, but I told him I had nothing to do with his bond."

There are a few more questions about what happened after the Wildy Well fight, and the jury is asked to retire because Fall wants to ask Garrett several questions that have been ruled inadmissible. Fall wants them to be part of the record. It's clear from the questions that Fall is laying the groundwork for future trials and appeals he expects to make for Lee, Gililland, and McNew. Fall asks Garrett about the political situation when Garrett first came to Las Cruces, and Garrett says he thinks it was out of hand on both sides.

When asked why he was so slow to attempt to arrest Lee and Gililland after he put McNew in solitary in Las Cruces, Garrett says he didn't want to see his posse shot up by Lee and his men, and he thought McNew would eventually break and tell the truth. Fall then asks about Garrett's opinion of McNew's veracity when he didn't break, and Garrett replies, "Either he was the most loyal man in the world, or he was innocent." Finally, Fall asks, "What did you know about the conspiracy to murder myself, Lee, and McNew?"

"Only that there were some leaders who would not be sorry if the three of you were gone." Fall has his fill of excoriating Garrett, and Judge Parker calls for midday recess.

I sit in the courtroom for a few minutes, still trying to sort through my thoughts from my interview with Lee. I think he killed Walter Good because he believed Good murdered George MacDonald, and the law ignored his plea for a hearing. I wonder what that means for this trial. Does that revenge killing define

Lee as a murderer or as someone who acted when he believed he didn't have any hope of finding justice from the law? He seemed to go to great lengths to try to work within the system and only took matters into his own hands when the system failed. I wonder what Lee learned about himself from that killing. Did Walter Good's blood make him more reluctant to take matters into his own hands, or quicker to become judge, jury, and executioner? Did it make him more likely to murder Colonel Fountain because he believed Fountain was trying to frame him and thus destroy a lifetime of work and threaten the prosperity of his family? Or was he less likely to murder Fountain because he found he could make the law work for him with the help of Albert Fall?

I jump when I feel a hand squeeze my shoulder. Looking up, I see the smiling face of Tom Tucker. "Tom! Where in the hell have you been? Green Scott nearly cut me a new one last night."

He sits down beside me and nods, his face grim, his eyes narrow slits. "I heard a feller say this morning some fool down to the dance hall had his coat lapel nearly sliced off last night. I never imagined it was you, though. I'm mighty sorry I wasn't there, Quent. I hope you shot the bastard."

"It was a close call. My pistol went off because his hand hit the barrel on his back slash. He got away clean, and I got a new-style coat."

Tom snickers and then looks serious again. " 'Fraid I got some bad news. Clayton and Greco are outta jail."

"Damn! When? How'd that happen?"

"They were set free last night. Ed Brown posted their bond, a hundred dollars apiece, and Judge Parker let 'em go. They left last night. I follered 'em halfway to the river. Looks like they was headin' straight fer San Marcial, but it'd be real easy fer 'em to loop back. I figure ol' Green Scott was tryin' to put the fear of Satan in you, or if he was lucky, kill you 'fore they got outta here. I talked to George Curry 'bout it. Told him you made enemies faster than Oliver Lee, and that there's at least four men we know of who'd be happy to have your gizzard fer supper. George said fer me to stay closer to you than stink on a skunk. That there's what I'm a-planning to do."

I look at him sideways and grin. "Thanks, Tom, that's very generous on your part, and Sheriff Curry's. Did you tell Sadie to pass the word along to—"

He grins. "Miss Persia? Why, I shore did. Sadie said she'd make certain Persia had something to protect herself with, or she'd put her on the stage outta harm's way. Now, how 'bout some dinner? It's hot in here, and it's gonna be a long afternoon."

I shake my head. "I'm not hungry. I need to finish writing up my story from my interview with Oliver Lee this morning, so I'll just stay here."

Chapter 30
Dr. Crosson and Carl Clausen Testify, 2 June 1899

The courtroom is filling with an unusually large number of women. They've come, I suppose, hoping to see the famous and handsome Sheriff Pat Garrett. A well-dressed young man sits down beside me. He sees my notes and sticks out his hand. "Hughes Slater, *El Paso Herald.* Are you a reporter?" he asks in a light New York accent that still has a little Virginia smoothness mixed with it. Hearing it brings back a flood of early memories that make me homesick.

I grab his hand and give it a firm shake. "Quentin Peach, *San Francisco Examiner.* Are you from New York? Virginia?"

He laughs, shaking his head. "I was born in Virginia and worked for a few years in New York. Then I moved out here to work as a railroad construction engineer in northern Mexico for Díaz and decided I'd get in the newspaper business. I just went to work for the *Herald.* You have a great ear for accents."

We both laugh. It's good to find a reporter who's about my age. We chat until the bailiff calls the court to stand for the entrance of Judge Parker.

With Garrett back on the stand, Barnes conducts a redirect examination for the prosecution. "Sheriff Garrett, can you explain why you obtained bench warrants against the defendants?"

Garrett crosses his arms and looks directly at Fall. "Because their attorneys had access to the grand jury room. If the defendants were indicted, the prisoners would have known it before my deputies could serve the warrants." Under Barnes's lead, Garrett tries to testify as to what Kearney, after he was shot, told him. He's stopped by an objection on hearsay evidence, and a question and objection on who shot Kearney are thrown out.

Barnes questions Garrett about his chief deputy. "Did you ever have reason to change your opinion concerning what you said this morning about Ben Williams having a mania for killing?"

"Yes, sir. I changed it before I employed him as a deputy."

As Garrett is excused, Slater and I write furiously. I wonder what caused him to change his mind about Ben Williams.

The prosecution calls Dr. Francis Crosson. Dr. Crosson is the chemist to whom Governor Thornton gave the blood and horsehair samples Van Patten collected. Crosson states that he has practiced medicine for eleven years and conducted extensive study in the analysis of blood. He describes the tests he conducted on the blood, including measuring its specific gravity, obtaining a spectral analysis, and tasting it to determine if it was salty. Crosson concludes from his analysis that his measurements show the sample has all the characteristics of blood. I note that the witness is careful not to say it is blood. I understand now why I saw Fall reading a college chemistry book and making notes a couple of days earlier.

Barnes gets Crosson to testify that the blood was not from a sore and that there was a lot of it. Fall objects to Crosson's estimate of how much blood there was. Crosson is temporarily excused, and John Meadows is called.

Meadows was a member of the first group to reach the scene and was in Van Patten's posse that later scouted the scene. He described the blood spot and how it was surrounded by a sprinkling of blood having a diameter of over eight feet, and how Van Patten had gouged up some of the blood and earth and carried it away.

On cross-examination, Fall attempts to discredit Meadows by getting him to admit he once went by the name of John Gray and had spent time in a Texas penitentiary for assault to commit murder. Meadows's testimony causes several rounds of laughter from the spectators, including the judge, when he denies ever being in that prison.

Dr. Crosson is recalled, asked a few more questions by Barnes, and then given to Fall for cross-examination.

Fall hovers over Crosson like an avenging angel, asking unequivocal questions about blood and how it reacts to different environments. Crosson, initially tense and nervous, appears to relax. I can tell from the growing smirk on his face that he's thinking he can handle this. Fall reminds me of a cat crouched in the grass, quivering in anticipation, waiting to spring on an unsuspecting bird.

Fall pounces. "Tell us, Dr. Crosson, what effect would salt in the earth, if there was any, have on your experiment?"

Crosson raises his brows and shrugs his shoulders. "I don't know. I didn't examine the earth for salt."

"And yet you swear this blood was human blood?"

Crosson straightens up, frowning. "I didn't swear anything of the kind. There is no human being who can tell human blood from any other kind of blood after the red corpuscles have changed construction. But I did swear that my conclusions were that the blood came from a human being."

Fall raises his brows and nods. "Oh, that's different, that's different. Now, is the specific gravity any conclusive test of blood? Can you tell by specific gravity whether blood is from a horse, a coyote, a rabbit, or a man?"

Crosson shrugs his shoulders and looks disgusted. "I don't know."

"I see. Well, would a piece of litmus paper show what kind of blood it was?"

"No. Litmus paper indicates whether the material is an acid or a base. I can't provide specific evidence that the blood was human blood."

"Will you undertake before this jury to taste samples of human blood, dog's blood, or rat's blood and tell which is human blood?"

"No, I will not."

"That's all."

Judge Parker asks, "Redirect?"

Barnes asks, "Why can't you swear the blood sample taken is human blood?"

Crosson shifts in his seat and sighs. "Blood testing is so difficult that the best experts in the world will not swear to it."

"No more questions, Your Honor."

Judge Parker looks at his watch. "Gentlemen, it's nearly suppertime. We will recess until seven p.m."

As Slater and I get up to leave, I notice a shiny wedding band on his left ring finger. "Hughes, are you married?"

He smiles. "Yes sir! I married Elsie McElroy in Washington, D.C., a couple of months ago."

The potential for revelation flashes in front of me. "Do you have any plans for supper?"

"No, I don't. What do you recommend?"

"The Ocean Grove Restaurant isn't fancy, but Tom Ying puts out a great meal."

Slater frowns. "The Ocean Grove—doesn't Sadie Orchard run it? Isn't it a bordello?"

I laugh. "The Ocean Grove is a hotel. There might be an occasional liaison going on there, but right now it's housing me, Judge Parker, members of the jury, and a couple of bailiffs."

Slater grins and nods. "Okay, let's go."

At the bottom of the steps, I introduce Hughes to Tom Tucker and explain that he'll be joining us. We stop at the telegraph station where I drop off my latest story.

We're lucky to find a table in the Ocean Grove Restaurant. I look around but don't see Sadie or Persia anywhere. Sam, the tall black woman who works for Sadie, takes our orders and disappears, soon to return with steaming cups of black coffee.

I take a sip of coffee, glance at Tom, and jump into the breach. "Hughes, we just met this afternoon, but it feels like I've known you for a long time. Mind if I discuss some personal business with you?"

Hughes's brows go up, and he smiles. "Ignorance has never prevented me from voicing an opinion. What's on your mind?"

"I've been reluctant to court a young woman here. She doesn't want to give her heart to someone who's going to leave on Sadie's stage and ride away forever after the trial is over. I've told her I want to be a front-page reporter, and it wouldn't be long before she'd feel like I'm neglecting her while I make a name for myself. I know you must want to be a top reporter, too, yet you've married. How did you reconcile being married and being a newspaperman?"

Hughes purses his lips in a silent whistle. Tom Tucker takes a slurp of coffee and wags his head at both of us. "Quent, you do know how to ask an awkward question."

Hughes ruminates for a moment and says, "I married because I love my wife and because I want to be the best reporter I can be."

I'm confused by his response, and it must show on my face because he adds, "This is hard to explain. Look, if you had only one arm, you'd never be able to do all the things you could with two. I'm not religious, but I've come to believe that we're designed in two parts—one male, and one female."

I try to grasp what he's saying. "You mean a couple with a lifetime commitment to each other is a completed thing—the whole is greater than the sum of the parts?"

Slater points his finger at me and grins in agreement. "Exactly! I think I'll be a better writer if I can understand a woman's point of view. That way, I learn to see the world differently and maybe see things I'd otherwise miss."

I nod. "Yeah, I guess I understand. That's deep, Hughes. But what about all the time you spend away from your wife while you're researching stories? That doesn't help a marriage, does it? It makes her second in your priorities, doesn't it?"

"No, I don't think so. Stories come and go, but she's always on my mind, and I always come back to her. I couldn't do what I do without her, and she knows it. Where did you get the idea that a man makes his wife second in his priorities if he has work that takes him away from her?"

Sam brings our plates piled with meat, freshly baked rolls, and fresh vegetables. I mull over Hughes's question as Sam puts the plates down. "I don't know. I guess I've always felt that way."

Tom just sits back in his chair grinning.

The insects and peepers are beginning to sing outside the courtroom windows when the evening session begins, and Carl Clausen is called to the witness chair. He was a son-in-law of Colonel Fountain. During the Apache wars, he was a tracker for the army and the colonel's militia. Now he's a house painter in Las Cruces. He describes how he and Luis Herrera followed the tracks of the horses from Colonel Fountain's buckboard, and when the trail from the overnight camp split, they followed the tracks of a large horse over Monte Carlo Pass in the Jarillas toward Lee's Wildy Well Ranch. He tells of the signs he saw suggesting the horse was ridden at night. It had been ridden straight into mesquites, and then backed away and around the thorn bushes.

Barnes asks Clausen, "Did you follow the trail to Wildy Well?"

"Yes, sir. I lost the trail a few times, but it pointed straight for Wildy Well. We needed water bad, and I hoped I might see some sign that would show who had recently ridden in there."

"What did you see as you approached Wildy Well?"

"The first party to come out of the house was a colored man, stepping sideways, a six-shooter in his hand. He stepped slowly until he passed me and then made a dash behind the water tank. A second man came out with a pistol in a holster and one stuck in his belt. He stood on the porch and didn't say anything when I asked if I could get some water."

"Was Mr. Lee at Wildy Well when you rode up?"

"Yes, sir, Lee came out wearing his six-shooter. I told him I was Carl Clausen and that my associate was Luis Herrera. I asked him if we could get water for ourselves and our mounts and fill up our casks.

"Lee told us to go on and get what we needed. He stood there and watched us get a drink and let the animals drink. Then we filled the casks. He says, 'You boys are a long ways off your usual roads. What are you doing way out here?' "

"And what did you tell him?" Barnes cocks his head to one side, as though to hear every word of the reply.

"I said, 'We're out here looking for my father-in-law, Colonel Fountain, and his little boy, Henry. It looks like they were waylaid over around Chalk Hill and taken in this direction. We wondered if you'd seen them or any strange horsemen over on this side of the Jarillas. You're a deputy sheriff. You know this country. Why can't you get your men and help us look for them?' "

"And just what did Mr. Lee say?"

"He said he hadn't the time and besides, 'what the hell are those sons of bitches to us?' He got on his horse and rode off toward the Jarillas, taking my back track. I lost sight of him in the distance and went inside to pay for the water. There were three men there, and as soon as I stepped through the door, they jumped up with their hands on their guns and confronted me. When we left, I measured the tracks of the horse Lee rode away on. They were the same as the ones we had followed across the Jarillas."

I recall Catarino Villegas's testimony that he couldn't tell if the horses they tracked were shod or not because the country was so rough, and I wonder how Clausen could know they were the same ones they'd followed across the Jarillas. I make a note to try to find out.

Barnes nods as he looks away from Clausen and stares at the jury. "No more questions, subject to redirect, Your Honor."

"Your witness, Mr. Fall."

Fall slowly lights a cigar, all the while squinting at Clausen. He approaches the witness chair, blows a puff toward the ceiling, and asks, "Did you or did you not, on the road down there to Lee's ranch, say to your companion, Luis Herrera, that when Lee came out to give you the wink, you'd kill him on the spot? Did you or did you not?"

Clausen looks surprised and shakes his head with short vigorous wags. "I'm sure I did not."

Fall takes another puff on his cigar. "Isn't it a fact that the Negro had a piece of lead in his hand he was using to stop up leaks in the water tank and you mistook the lead for a pistol?"

"It is not a fact, Mr. Fall."

"Was the horse you trailed over the Jarillas shod or unshod?"

"To the best of my knowledge, it was shod."

"Oh, I see, to the best of your knowledge. Well, was it shod or not?"

Catron, red in the face and almost spitting, shouts, "Objection! Mr. Clausen does not deserve to be interrogated in this manner."

With a smirk, Fall says, "I will interrogate the witness to suit myself, and I advise the heavyweight attorney for the prosecution to sit down."

Judge Parker pounds his gavel and frowns at Fall and Catron. "Gentlemen, there has been entirely too much harassment of the witnesses and bickering between the attorneys. You will cease such behavior in my courtroom. Enough!"

Fall turns to the judge. "No further questions, Your Honor."

"Redirect, Mr. Barnes?"

Barnes is up before Fall is fully seated. "Was this the first time you ever did any trailing, Mr. Clausen?"

Clausen smiles. "No, sir. I trailed in '81, '82, '83, '84, and at other times. In those days, Indians were plentiful, and a man had to be able to read signs."

Barnes scratches his chin as though trying to recall something. "Did you say Mr. Lee saddled the horse he rode away from the ranch?"

"No, sir, the horse was already saddled and hitched near the house."

I wonder what the question and answer are supposed to indicate.

The night session ends with Clausen's testimony.

Tom Tucker walks with me back to the Ocean Grove before heading to a saloon. The restaurant is closing when I return, but Sam is still there cleaning up. I wave her over before I step down the hall. "Hi, Sam. Where's Persia?"

"I think she's over at de Orchard Hotel with Miss Sadie. I think Miss Sadie gonna let her drive de stage agin tomorrah."

I thank her and head for my room. It's been a long day. I'm whipped, and Hughes Slater has given me a lot to think about.

Chapter 31
Branigan Testifies,
3 June 1899

In the morning, Tom Tucker is waiting for me. Slouched in a chair slurping coffee, he raises a baleful eye as I pull out a chair and sit down. "Thought you was gonna sleep all day, Mr. Peach." I look toward the kitchen—no sign of Persia. Tom shakes his head and grins. "Saw her on the stage with old Bill Reay this morning. She'll be all right. Sadie says she's got a natural talent fer handlin' the stage team."

After breakfast we trudge up the hill to the jail and courthouse. My watch shows it's more than an hour before court begins. Tom tells me he'll meet me at dinner recess and steps inside the courthouse's back door to the sheriff's office. I sit in the streaks of early morning sunlight between the jail and the courthouse. The grackles flutter about complaining as I read *The Advocate's* report of yesterday's testimonies.

A wagon rattles up with McNew driving Mary Lee to jail for her morning visit with her son. It's not long before the courthouse yard begins to fill with small groups of men having a final smoke and talk before going to the courtroom to find a seat. I fold my paper and head upstairs.

Ten minutes before the trial resumes, Hughes Slater slides onto the seat beside me. "Mind if I join you?"

"Good morning. Sit down. Glad to have the company."

He settles in and looks around the courtroom. "Did you see the piece in the *Examiner* about Governor Thornton?"

"No, why?"

"It's one of the worst examples of yellow journalism I've ever seen. It claims that Governor Thornton may have faked the blood and horsehair evidence. I hear he's is in a rage and says he's going to sue the reporter and the paper."

I look over toward the wall where I usually see Seymour. There he stands, a big grin on his face. He holds up his right forefinger and nods. I feel sick. His kind give reporters bad names.

Hughes sees him. "Is he the one who wrote it?"

I nod and wave Seymour over. "Peyton, meet Hughes Slater, who's with the *El Paso Herald.* Is that your piece in the *Examiner* about Thornton faking evidence? Hughes says Thornton's planning to sue you and the paper."

Seymour, shaking hands with Hughes, shrugs and grins. "He'll cool off. I'll play and lose a few hands of poker with him, and he'll forget all about it. Got to get back to my place before I lose it. See you later." I wonder what my future with the *Examiner* is if Seymour gets big bylines at the paper with that kind of writing.

A bailiff calls the court to order, so we stand as Judge Parker is seated, and the first witness for the day, Captain Thomas Branigan, is called.

Under Barnes's questions, Branigan tells essentially the same story Albert and Jack Fountain and others in the first posse told. Branigan's story carries additional weight because, between 1882 and 1885, he was captain and chief of scouts at the Mescalero Apache Reservation, whose agent at that time was W.H.H. Llewellyn. It is Branigan's conclusion that the child tracks found at the dry camp had been faked with the boy's right shoe. He says it was at that camp where he took measurements of the tracks of three men around the camp. He claims he saw the same tracks at other camps along the trail of seven horses from that camp and, the next day, found a set on Lee's dirt roof exactly like the one with the run-over heel he'd seen at the other camps.

Branigan also notes that Lee's horse's tracks also corresponded to those of the largest horse on the trail from the camp. He testifies that a little later, when McNew came to Las Cruces, he measured his tracks and found they were consistent with what he had measured while following the trail toward Lee's ranch.

Barnes makes a show of listening carefully to Branigan's testimony. "Now tell us, Captain Branigan, exactly how your measurements were made."

Branigan makes a tent with his fingers. "I measured the length of the track from heel to toe, across the widest part of the heel, across the width of the ball of the foot, and across the width of the toe. I had all these measurements written down and left them in the district attorney's office for safekeeping. Now it seems nobody there knows anything about them or where they are."

Barnes frowns and nods. "But you're certain the tracks you saw on the trail matched those you measured in the dirt on Lee's ranch roof and those of McNew in Las Cruces?"

"Yes, sir."

"No more questions, Your Honor."

I wonder how Branigan's measurements would compare to the pair of boots Ed Brown and Emerald James disposed of in San Marcial. Judge Parker nods at the defense table. "Your witness, Mr. Fall."

Fall, chewing on an unlighted cigar, approaches the witness, but looks at the jury. "How long have you been a scout and trailer?"

Branigan cocks his head in defiance. "Eighteen years."

Fall raises a brow and stares at him. "Don't you know that

it's impossible to measure a track in sandy soil after it has been made?"

Looking at the floor and speaking in a patient voice, Branigan says, "Well, some of them were almost perfect and others were deeper. Sand had fallen in the deep ones and partially obliterated them."

Fall began his favorite tactic of attempting to confuse the witness by asking rapid-fire questions, pointing out several times that because Branigan wanted the trail to lead to Lee's ranch, it couldn't have gone anywhere else. Fall disorients Branigan a time or two, but he generally sticks to his original story. He looks relieved when he is finally excused.

Next Barnes calls W.T. White, who explains that he and Dan Fitchett were driving a herd they were holding to Lee's ranch. He says they met a group of men who asked whose cattle they were along with other questions. The men passed on, and when they reached Lee's ranch, Gililland, McNew, Blevins, and Lee were there. White says, "McNew went in the house and got his gun when we came up."

Barnes asks a few more innocuous questions and turns the witness over to Fall for cross-examination. Fall asks about White's relationship with Lee, and White responds it's good, they're neighbors. He asks how long it had taken to gather the herd they were driving to Lee's ranch. White answers without hesitation that the herd had been building for nearly a week.

"Mr. White, in driving the cattle from Dog Canyon to Lee's Well, which is the best route?"

"The one we took."

"As you were going down, on which side of you was the posse when you met it?"

"On my right."

"Then the posse went on around the herd and went to Lee's Well?"

"Yes, sir."

Looking at Clausen's map stuck on the wall, I try to imagine where the posse might have met the herd. The only place I can see where they can come up on the right side is after the road from Dog Canyon turns south toward Wildy Well. I wonder why White was not driving the herd on the most direct line across the desert. It's something I'll have to ask Tom Tucker.

Barnes next calls Irving Wright, who testifies to finding Fountain's mare on the west side of the road covered by Van Patten's group. Fall doesn't challenge Wright's statement.

After Wright steps down, Judge Parker tells the jury to retire. The attorneys have an extended argument about the admissibility of the testimony of Charles Lusk concerning McNew's statement that Fountain was only prosecuting McNew, Lee, and Gililland to break up their partnership. Childers argues that the evidence as presented, although circumstantial, demonstrates a conspiracy between the defendants and that Lusk's testimony is proof of it.

It seems odd to me that the prosecution would want Lusk's testimony. If McNew and the others believe Colonel Fountain was only trying to break them up, then they couldn't have been too concerned that he had sufficient evidence to convict them.

Fall argues that a criminal death has to be proven and a conspiracy shown before the evidence is admissible. The arguments are long, and the courtroom is hot. I fight dozing off, even though it's not yet eleven o'clock.

Chapter 32
Kidnapped

Slater's elbow pokes in my ribs. He thumb-points toward the back of the courtroom. Tom Tucker stands near the door, waving his big paw for me to join him. Tom meets me at the foot of the stairs. Saying nothing, he jerks his head toward the back door. Outside, Tom heads for the street across the yard between the jail and the courthouse. I trot to keep up with him.

"Tom! What's happened? Where're we going?"

"They took Persia. Sadie wants to see us right now."

"Who took Persia? How—"

Tom is impatient with my slow wit. "You damned idjit! Some trash took her off the stage, give the regular driver a note, and disappeared. The driver nearly drove the team into the ground gettin' to the Lake Valley telegraph office. Soon as Sadie got the telegram, she sent fer us."

I feel sick. This is all my fault. Brown's boys wouldn't have bothered Persia if I'd just left town.

Sadie looks up, her eyes cold and filled with rage, as we rush in. Her hand quivers as she hands me the telegram.

> STAGE STOPPED 3 MILES NORTH OF HARLOSA SPRINGS. THREE MEN TOOK PERSIA. SAID SEND FOLLOWING NOTE FROM LAKE VALLEY: PERSIA WITH US. PEACH IN ENGLE BY MIDNIGHT. STAYS UNTIL TRIAL OVER. PERSIA OK. IF HE DON'T PERSIA AIN'T COMING BACK.

I hand the note to Tom Tucker and tell Sadie, "Of course, I'll go. What's the quickest way to get to Engle? Where is Engle anyway?"

Tom shakes his head. "You must be makin' Ol' Brown and his boys sweat. Engle is over the river about forty miles north and east of here, on the far side of the Fra Cristobal and Caballo Mountains, in the middle of big ranch country. Forget about findin' it. You ain't goin' by yourself."

"Why not? I can take care of myself. I know how to ride. I have to do everything I can to get Persia back. It's my fault they have her."

Tom snorts. "You got *cojones,* but this here country'll chew you up and spit you out if you ain't careful. My money says they're setting you up to git rid of you and Persia before you ever git to Engle. You're gonna disappear just like Fountain and the little boy—maybe even share the same canyon over in the San Andres. You'll have ta be smarter than them fer you and Persia to survive."

Sadie crosses her arms and nods. "Tom's right. Best thing you can do is let this old warhorse help you take care of those no-good bastards. How many horses do you need, Tom?"

"Four good saddle horses and a packhorse. You'll have to lend Quent a saddle and trail gear, and he oughter have a rifle to go with that peashooter you give him." He scratches his chin and looks at the floor for a moment. "Maybe Tom Ying can throw us some eatin' supplies in a sack? You do that fer us, Miss Sadie?"

She thrusts out her chin. "Why, hell, yes, I can. Tom, you go on an' get your gear, I'll fix Quent up with some of J.W.'s clothes and a rifle. I'll have Quent and your supplies ready in an hour down at the Ocean Grove."

Tom pulls down his hat. "Thanks, Sadie. See you in a bit."

Sadie points me down the hall. "Go down three doors and

take off your duds. I'll be along directly with some of J.W.'s trail clothes for you to wear."

I jump as she bellows, "Sam! Sam! Get your black fanny in here and help me!"

Tom squats by the back door of the Ocean Grove. With a cottonwood twig, he sketches a map in the dust. "The country says how we got to play this game." He draws a swerving line between two points. "This here is the stage road to Lake Valley. Persia was took off the stage about here. You might remember when we come over from Lake Valley there's a line of low mountains that runs alongside the stage road just off to the east. Them bastards will ride through a pass in them little mountains about here and head straight for the river. That's about a four-hour ride. Then they'll turn up river and head for Palomas Springs and use the ferry at Elephant Butte. Not far from there is a long winding pass up between the Fra Cristobal and Caballo Mountains that tops out on a road over to Engle, which is about fifteen miles off to the east of Palomas Springs. I'm guessin' they're gonna find 'em a good nestin' point in that pass and wait to bushwhack you. They must be figurin' you'll ride through about dark—easy pickin's for an ambush. Ain't no mistake. They mean to kill you. Brown's in a real sweat. Just when he thought he oughter be free and clear, a damned reporter that ain't got no dog in this fight could hang him out to dry, even if the politicos won't."

I nod and ask, "If they kill me, what do you think will happen to Persia?"

Tom shakes his head. "Dead women tell no tales. Think about it. If you don't go to Engle and the law comes after them, they can claim they were just taking her back to her uncle—no kidnapping at all. They'll tell her if she don't cooperate they'll kill you fer shore. She'll lie to protect you if she has to. When they're done with you, she's next, and I'm bettin' Brown told 'em they could enjoy her first, even if she is his niece. If you both disappear, they'll claim it's because you run off together. In either case, Brown is rid of you both and free and clear."

I can't argue with his cold logic. "What do you think we ought to do?"

He looks at me from under his brows. "First thing we're gonna do is to take care of the sons of bitches that took her. It's gonna give me a whole lot of satisfaction to put them boys away. Once they're out of the way, we'll set Mr. Brown straight. Miss Sadie fixed you up, didn't she? You could pass for J.W. Orchard from a distance. You all saddled and ready to go?"

I hold up the old model 1876 Winchester and point to the saddled pinto Sadie has lent me. "Let's ride."

Tom leads the way. He alternates the pace of the horses between a fast walk, a trot, and a fast gallop. The rusty red and brown massifs of the Caballo and Fra Cristobal Mountains loom before us in the golden glare of the midafternoon light. They are huge, imposing, breathtaking vertical cliffs, with occasional flashes of green near the river and on cliff ledges. I can't imagine how there can be trails and roads across them.

We water the horses in the greenish-brown Rio Grande. Its flow is fast and deep—too dangerous to cross at this point. Tom tells me to swap horses and ride the red one to let the pinto rest. He does the same with his pony, a tan mustang. We mount and turn south, following a cool and pleasant trail that twists along through the trees beside the river.

In a couple of miles, the river turns toward the west. On the east side, there is a wide swath where the brush under the trees is gone, a sure sign this spot has been used as a cattle crossing. Tom doesn't hesitate to ride into the river. I'm right behind him, expecting to get off and swim with the horse, but the water only comes up to the horses' bellies.

"I thought you said the best ford and ferries were in Palomas Springs or down toward Caballo."

Tom laughs. "They are. The local ranchers know about this ford but don't recommend it because it comes and goes, depending on the weather upstream. There's another pass through the Caballos close by and a trail leading over to Engle that'll get us around those bastards sitting in the main pass a-waitin' on you."

The pass through the Caballos is long and winding. There are several narrow ledges with two- or three-hundred-foot vertical drops. Tom tells me just to let my horse pick his way, and I'll be fine. The horse's sure-footedness doesn't stop me from breaking into a sweat every time I look down.

The sun is fading in diffused orange and purple glory behind the Black Range when we come out on the *Jornada del Muerto*, the Journey of Death, desert country. Off to the east, the jagged outline of the San Andres is just visible on the black horizon.

Throwing a leg over his saddle horn, Tom stops to rest the horses and have a smoke. The desert is already giving up its heat. The night will be cold. Not used to long horse rides, I'm saddle sore and my legs are cramping. "Where to now?"

"We got another couple hours to ride until we hit the Palomas Springs to Engle road, two or three miles after it leaves the pass."

"Then what?"

"I figure them boys is gonna be waiting on you close to where the pass pops out on this side. They'll stay there until maybe ten o'clock before they decide you ain't comin'. Then they'll saddle up and head toward Engle to git over to Brown's place. We're headed for a place where the road crosses a wash. We'll wait on 'em there."

"If Persia won't charge 'em with kidnapping, what are you going to charge 'em with?"

"I'll figure something out."

We ride until we hit the Engle road ruts winding toward dim lights twinkling far in the distance. The moon lights up the horizon behind the San Andres and soon rises big, yellow, and brilliant. At the bottom of a shallow wash Tom leads us off the road and around a bend. We dismount, unsaddle the horses, rub them down, and give them some water and grain.

"Quent, if you'll dig us a firepit a couple of feet deep, I'll go stir up some kindlin'."

The ground is sandy, and it's easy to scoop out a hole before he returns with an armful of brush. "This stuff will burn fast, but it's enough to make a pot of coffee. That pit will keep anybody from seeing our fire unless they're right on top of us."

The night is cold, and the coffee good. It goes well with Tom Ying's cold biscuits, bacon, honey, and corn fritters. Tom checks his watch. "Our friends ought to be here in an hour or two. Persia is likely to be ridin' between the first two. I want you on the south side of the road. I'll be on the north side. You grab her horse's lead rope as soon as we stop 'em and get her down here. She's gonna be cold and hungry. We'll stay the rest of the night here before we head back for Hillsboro."

"What are you going to do if they don't surrender?"

Tom frowns at me like I don't have good sense. "Whatever it takes."

Coffee finished, we kick sand over the fire and hunt up more brush we can use to make another fire when we get Persia back.

We take our blankets and walk back up the wash to the road. I find a place on the south side giving a clear view across the wash and down the road toward the Palomas Springs pass. Tom is on the north side, practically invisible behind a big, spreading soapweed. An hour passes, then two. It's nearly midnight before I make out four riders casting short, black shadows under the high moon. I feel the hair on the back of my neck prickle. I wonder when Tom plans to step out in the road to tell them he's the law and to put their hands up. I wonder what'll happen if they put up a fight and wish we could just shoot the scum and be done with them.

It isn't long before I'm sure the second rider is Persia. From the Mexican *sombrero,* I surmise the man in the lead is Greco. I can't tell who's riding behind her, but one of them is big enough to be Clayton. I pull the hammer back on my rifle a full click to safety. I hear Tom's rifle faintly click twice, one to safety, another to full cock.

The four ride down into the wash. Even in the moonlight, I can see Persia looks haggard. I grind my teeth, cursing the bastards who stole her.

A shadow rises in the bright moonlight.

The *sombrero* jerks toward it. "Wah?"

Flame and thunder come once, twice, three times. My jaw drops. I'm stunned, frozen in surprise. *Sombrero* is on the ground, not moving, his horse racing down the road toward Engle. Persia, her hands tied in front of her, is trying to hold on to the mane of her rearing mount. The two horses behind her are rearing and plunging. The rider behind Persia is rolling on the ground, groaning, his hands on a dark wet spot on his belly. The last rider, a wet spot on the back of his coat, is on his hands and knees, trying to crawl up the wash.

I run for Persia's horse and grab its lead rope. Tom runs up to the second man and stares at him a moment. I hear the lever on his Winchester, and then the roar of a forth shot. The shot is still ringing in my ears when there is a fifth shot. The man on his hands and knees isn't moving anymore.

Persia's horse settles as I reel in the lead rope. I see the moonlight sparkling in the streams of water rolling down Persia's cheeks, and I hear her say, "Thank you, God! Thank you, dear God!"

Tom runs down into the wash, catches the third horse, swings into the saddle without using the stirrup, and thunders past us as I reach up to help Persia dismount. "Gittin' the other horse. I'll be back!" he yells.

Persia is in my arms. She trembles, and I feel my shirt get wet as she buries her face on my shoulder. "You all right? Are you hurt anywhere?"

She grabs the lapels of my coat in her hands and looks in my face as I wrap my arms around her. "Now I'm fine."

We stand there holding each other. Then, rubbing her back, I help her up the wash to my blanket. "Stay here while I take care of business." She nods as she wraps the blanket around her, and I walk back down into the wash.

Sombrero lies on his back, a perfectly round, black hole dead center in his chest. The gutshot man has a second shot between his eyes, and the back of his skull and brains are splattered on the ground in a little halo behind him. I don't recognize him. The man who was on his hands and knees lies facedown, a bullet hole in the back of his head. I roll him over with the toe of my boot. The top of his head is gone, but there's no doubt it's Clayton.

The flood of nausea is swift, unexpected. I retch and vomit violently, my hands on my knees. I've seen bodies before, but the stench of death overwhelms me.

Persia stands up. I wave for her to stay put, and I walk down the wash about a hundred yards to retrieve the last horse. Its reins are caught in a mesquite bush. I tie the horse off near the bodies, and then I take Persia and her horse down the wash to the place where Tom and I have tied our horses. I give her some water and make a fire. With the coffee pot heating up, I give her

Tom Ying's sack of victuals, and I go back to the road.

I have Greco's body wrapped in a blanket and tied off on the horse when Tom appears leading the other horse.

Saying nothing, he slides off his horse and tosses me its blanket roll. He ties his horse to a bush and takes the blanket roll off the one he was leading and walks down the road into the wash. "Did you take the guns off Greco before you wrapped the blanket around him?"

I nod. "Yeah."

"Good. Be sure to do the same with the other two. Spoils of war. Greco's rig was fancy. You keep it or sell it. I'll keep the other two."

We wrap the other two bodies in the blankets. When we're finished, we sit down a minute to rest a little. Tom rolls a cigarette and lights up.

"Tom, mind if I ask you a question?"

"No, sir. You earned all the questions you need to ask this night."

"Why didn't you tell them to surrender before you started shooting?"

Tom wags his head. "Bunch of reasons. Mainly, they kidnapped a woman. Any man does that don't deserve no chance to surrender. He's gonna die. Whether by a bullet or a rope, he's gonna die. After them bastards murdered you, they was gonna rape her and slit her throat. They ain't getting any chance out of me, includin' a first one."

"But you're wearing a star. You're sworn to uphold the law."

"Yep, I am, and I did. They got all the judge, jury, trial, and execution they deserved. You agree with that, don't you? I saw where you puked over there."

I look at the ground and nod before I look back into his black eyes. "Yeah, I do. You won't get any argument out of me."

"Good. Let's throw these bodies over the horses and get down to the fire. It's right chilly, ain't it?"

Chapter 33
Ed Brown, Gravedigger

It's a long night. Persia sleeps by my side, but the horrors of the past day are heavy on us. I turn from one side to the other, restless, thinking of what might have happened. Trembling, startled by bad dreams, she awakens several times. Tom Tucker, wrapped in two blankets on the other side of the fire, doesn't move all night. The snores from under his hat drown out the calls of distant coyotes.

Before dawn, giving up any hope of sleep, Persia and I crawl from our blankets to build up the fire. Hearing us move around, Tom is instantly awake. He sits up, nods good morning, stretches, and yawns. After making coffee and eating bacon and biscuits, we load the horses and set off down the steep, winding trail toward the Rio Grande.

It's midmorning when we reach the river. The ferryman, eyeing the blanket-wrapped bundles draped over the horses' saddles, wastes no time getting us across the river. On the west bank, we give the horses a ration of grain and let them drink. Tom refills the canteens and water cask.

After dipping his bandana in the river, Tom wrings out the excess water and hangs it around his neck. "Quent, you reckon you folks can find your way back to Hillsboro without me? Just follow the road south an hour or two, and then swing west straight for the Black Range. You'll cross the road to Hillsboro purty quick that way. Ride at a good trot, and you'll be back by midafternoon."

"I'm sure we can, but where are you going?"

Tom nods at the horses. "I'm gonna take these here bodies to ol' Ed Brown fer plantin'. Before he does any diggin', we're gonna have us a little chat to be sure there's enough holes in the ground for ever'body. He just might need an extry one fer his own self. When I'm finished with him, I don't expect he'll be sendin' nobody in our direction or bothering Persia no more."

Persia, a frown on her face, shakes her head. "You're not going without me, Tom Tucker! That man tried to have me killed. I'm coming with you!"

Tom, his brows raised in surprise, looks at Persia and then me. "Quent?"

Persia's eyes flash, wide and angry. "What are you asking Quent for? He doesn't have any say over what I do. He can come if he wants, but I'm coming with you. Even if I have to follow from way back, I'm coming."

Feeling a strange mixture of pride that she has such spunk and fear that, if the guns come out, she'll be killed or badly hurt, I know I can't stop her unless I tie her up and throw her over her saddle. I nod at Tom. "Looks like it's going to be a three-man posse, Tom. I want to have a little eye-to-eye with the SOB myself."

Tom grins and pulls out his cigarette fixings. "You birds can come with me if you're of a mind, but I'm wearing the badge, and you'd best damn well do what I tell you, or old Ed is likely to fill us all full of holes."

Persia and I nod as Tom lights up.

"I'll lead. Quent, you bring up the rear and take the lead rope for the horses with the bodies. Miss Persia, you take the lead rope for the other pack animals and ride in the middle. I want us to stay at least a hundred yards apart in case there's an ambush. Think you can handle it?"

We nod.

"All right. I'm gonna stay close to the river. I figure about eight hours to Ed's place. That's about right, ain't it, Miss Persia?"

"Yes, sir, more or less."

We mount and ride the trail north along the river. A couple of miles north of Elephant Butte, the river widens and winds through the *bosque* along the river. I wonder if we'll all be alive by the end of the day.

We make good time. An hour before noon, we pass through the little town of San Marcial without having seen a soul except the ferryman all day. Tom turns east. After crossing the river, we stop to eat dinner and rest for a while in the shade of a big cottonwood. We unload the pack animals. The bodies are stiff and starting to smell. Finishing his dinner, Tom stretches out next to the cottonwood's trunk for a nap.

Persia takes her last bite of biscuit and says, "I'm in need of a bath. Will you go down the river a little ways with me and be a gentleman who guards my privacy?"

The thought of being alone with her makes me laugh with pure pleasure. "Yes, ma'am. I will, if you'll do the same for me."

She giggles. "Wonderful!"

A quarter mile upriver, we find a willow grove, the ends of its long, green wands dragging on top of the current. They form a green privacy wall around a calm pool. Persia disappears through the green wall while I keep watch for stray eyes and listen to her splash around. I'd love to see her bathing, but I'd never betray the trust she's placed in me. It's not long before she's back, her long hair wet and shiny black.

I take my turn in the river. The water is cold, refreshing, hard to leave. When I come out of the willows, Persia has her hair in long braids.

Walking back to Tom's shade tree, I hear cattle bawling off to the east. When we arrive at the cottonwood, Tom is already up and has the horses saddled. His jaw muscles ripple, and I know something's not right. "Tom, what's going on?"

"Small herd, maybe ten or twelve head, comin' this way."

"Okay, but why does your face look like a cloud filled with thunder and lightning?"

Tom pulls his big Winchester out of its scabbard and turns to me. "There's two drovers, and one of 'em is Ed Brown! The cattle'r gonna be thirsty. Brown and his *vaquero* will let 'em stop to drink. I'm gonna lay back in the bushes and wait fer 'em. I want you and Persia to stay back in the brush with the horses. I'll have Mr. Brown step down from his horse and send the *vaquero* on with the cattle to cross the river for town. I'm purty sure they're heading for the cattle pens in San Marcial, and Ed's probably plannin' to meet up in a San Marical saloon this evenin' with those fellers I kilt. He'll be wantin' to find out how rubbin' out you two went. Well, he's about to get a firsthand report. When the drover is out of sight, I'll call to you, and then we can have our little talk with Mr. Ed Brown. Give Persia a rifle from one of the dead men's rigs, and then you two get out of sight."

Knowing Tom doesn't need Persia and me to cramp his style, I pull the horses into the brush, where we can still see the action but not be easily seen. Tom steps behind the tree and waits. Persia and I check our rifles and pull the hammers back to safety. The cattle come closer. The air is hot and still, filled with mosquitoes and flies. The smell of death from the bodies is strong and sickening.

I see two red cows with white faces lope up to the river, splash in up to their bellies, and begin to drink. The rest come trotting up to stand in the water at the river's edge and drink. Right behind them are the two drovers. One is an old Mexican, his face lined from years in the sun. Hanging against his back is a wide *sombrero,* dusty and tattered from long wear. An ancient, scarred cap-and-ball revolver in a well-oiled holster rides on his hip. The other man is middle-aged with bushy brows and a black mustache under a bulbous nose. He wears a long-barreled Colt on a gun belt filled with cartridges. He and the Mexican stop at the water's edge to let their horses drink.

Tom steps from behind the tree and levers a round into the chamber. "Howdy, Brown."

Brown jerks his head toward the voice as his right hand reaches for his revolver, but recognizing Tom, he moves his hands to his saddle horn where Tom can see them.

"Well, I declare." Brown smiles as his eyes sweep the brush and river behind Tom. "What's doin', Tom?"

"Git off your horse, Brown. Send your man on with the cattle. We're gonna have us a little talk over here under this cottonwood tree."

Brown speaks to the Mexican and waves him on across the river. Appearing relaxed and affable, Brown swings down and leads his horse over to Tom.

"Take off that shooter and hang it on your saddle before you sit down here in front of me."

Brown flashes a toothy smile and nods. "Shore, Tom, glad to be friendly. Bein' Curry's deputy and all, I'm surprised to see you. I thought you'd be up to the big trial in Hillsboro. Wished I coulda gone." He hangs his gun belt from the saddle horn and loosens the cinch on the saddle before tying the horse to a bush.

From where Persia and I watch, I can see Brown's eyes, cold and calculating, searching for others who might be hidden in the brush. Taking his time, he gives no indication he sees Persia and me. He sits down cross-legged in front of Tom, tips back his hat, and pulls a sack of tobacco and papers out of his vest pocket. He begins to roll one under Tom's dark scowl. "What can I do for you, Deputy?"

"Brown, we're gonna reach us an understandin'."

"Why shore, Tom. Always glad to accommodate the law and help out old friends. You know I'm good fer that."

Tom doesn't move a muscle as Brown lights up. The he asks, "Smell anything, Brown?"

Brown sniffs the air and makes a face.

"Yeah, something's dead."

"What you're a-smelling is the three boys you sent to murder your niece and Quentin Peach."

Brown doesn't blink and slowly begins shaking his head. "What are you talkin' about, Tom? What boys? I used to be my niece's guardian, but now she's on her own working over to Hillsboro. I ain't seen her for months, maybe a year, and I never heard of Quentin Peach. Who the hell's he?"

Tom's rifle comes to full cock. A twitch ripples across Brown's face as the rifle points directly at the center of his chest.

"You and Miss Persia come on out here, Quent, and bring them horses with you."

Persia and I walk out of the brush and tie the horses to bushes. There are streamers of sweat rolling down Brown's face. Persia sits to Tom's right, crossing her legs under her. "Surprised to see me, Uncle Ed?"

Brown shows some teeth in his smile. "Shore am, child! You decide to come back home and live with me and Delia?"

As Brown speaks, he gives me the once-over while I study him. Persia surprises me with her steady voice. "I'm not stupid, you sorry excuse for a man. After I was kidnapped, I heard Greco tell Clayton you didn't care if they had a piece as long as I didn't come back. You knew all about it. You set it up, didn't you?"

Brown shakes his head. "I haven't seen Greco or Clayton since, oh, maybe March, and that's God's honest truth."

Tom squints at him and says, "I ain't listening to no more horse apples coming off your tree, Brown. I'd just soon kill you as look at you. You're gonna cover up them boys while I think on what I'm gonna do with you. There's a miner's shovel tied on the back of Arch Clayton's rig. What you reckon he planned to use it fer? Git it! There's a nice little clearing right over yonder in the brush. Dig three graves first, by then I'll decide if I'm gonna need you to dig a fourth un. Now move!"

Tom pokes the rifle barrel into Brown's chest so hard, Brown has to catch himself by throwing his hands back. Brown jumps up, twisting away from that rifle, and holds up his hands, palms out. "I'm gettin' it," he says.

Tom walks him over to where he wants the graves dug. "Git busy, Brown. Faster you dig, more likely I'll be in good spirits when you finish."

The earth where Brown digs is soft. He flails away with the shovel. Soon, his shirt is soaked and sweat falls off his face. He works for a couple of hours while we sit and watch. Tom squats, resting the rifle on his knee.

When Brown finishes the three graves, he stands up straight, stretches his back, and implores Tom, "Can't I have some water, for God's sake?" Tom pitches him a canteen. Brown drinks most of it and pours the rest over his head.

Then Tom thumbs back toward the bodies. "Get them men! Bury 'em! Now!"

"You gonna help me with 'em?"

"Hell, no! But I'm letting Mr. Peach go with you to watch you work, 'cause he's right eager to settle up. Now git!"

In another hour, Brown has the bodies buried. He's soaked in sweat all the way down into his chaps and looks like he's about to collapse from heat exhaustion. Tom asks Persia and me to saddle the horses while he waits in the shade of the cottonwood with Brown.

The horses saddled and the gear on the packhorses, I call out, "Ready to ride." Tom nods. His eyes cold and flat, Tom stares at Brown. "Ed, this here ain't a threat. It's the way it's gonna be. I ever get word anything violent happens to those two over yonder, you be ready, 'cause I'm comin'. Anybody ever comes after me with money in his pocket, you be ready, 'cause I'm comin'. Anybody follows us outta San Marcial, I'll come back, and you'll never see the light of another day. You been mighty lucky today. Do we understand each other?"

Ed sits staring at the dirt and nods. We mount and ease into the crossing. I look back when we're on the other side. Ed hasn't moved since we left. Tom lays a beeline for Hillsboro.

It's well past the middle of the evening when we finally walk the exhausted horses up to the Orchard Hotel. Sadie is sitting in a rocker on the Orchard's stoop, sipping tea from her china cup and reading a newspaper by the light of a lantern. J.W. sits on the steps whittling a block of white pine. A little black boy, Sadie's helper, Boots, sits on a nearby wall, trying to find notes on a guitar.

At the sound of our horses, Sadie looks over the top of her paper and laughs. "I'll be damned! Welcome back! J.W.! You and Boots put up the stock and supplies for these weary travelers."

Persia and I sit on the stoop step next to Sadie's rocker, and Sadie says, "I could hardly sleep a wink last night worrying about you. Tom? You all right?"

Tom stretches his back and grins. "I'm fine, Miss Sadie. Been a mighty long ride in a short time. We near rode all our horses into the ground. Wouldn't wanta do that again fer a while. Uh, is Nadine busy tonight?"

"Sunday is a day of rest, but I'm sure she'd be happy to see you. Walk down the hall there and knock on her door."

He smiles. "Don't mind if I do. See you folks in the morning."

I grimace, so saddle sore I can barely walk. Sadie looks at me and raises an eyebrow. I say, "We carried three bodies back to Brown and had a little talk with him."

"I knew Tom wasn't about to let those bastards get away." She squints at Persia, "Are you all right, honey? I mean, really all right?"

Smiling, Persia nods. "I'm all right. But if this fine man and Tom hadn't come after me, I'd be in some canyon in the San Andres, raped and with my throat cut. After the warning Tom gave my uncle, I don't think he'll bother me again." She hugs my shoulders. "I know I'll never forget what you did for me, Quent, and I'll never be able to thank you enough."

I look in her eyes. "There was never any other thought than to bring you back safe. I couldn't let anyone steal a piece of my heart."

Sadie smiles. I can feel my ears warm as I wonder why my tongue is suddenly so loose.

Persia frowns, looking confused. "What do you mean by that?"

I give Persia's hand a little squeeze. "Let me take you to supper tomorrow night, and maybe I can explain it to you."

"After all you've done for me? You can have all the supper dates you want, Mr. Peach." She gives me a peck on the cheek. "I'll see you tomorrow after court lets out."

Chapter 34
Llewellyn Testifies, 5 June 1899

Ben Williams is on the stand and maintains a professional manner, replying to Catron's questions with crisp answers. He testifies that in Lincoln at the grand jury meeting in January of '96, the indictments were found at the insistence of Colonel Fountain, and that he, Williams, had held warrants for the arrest of the indicted men.

Fall lounges in his chair, eyes narrowed, his head tilted to one side. After a short examination, Catron looks over the jury and says, "No more questions, Your Honor."

The room is still. "Your witness, Mr. Fall."

Fall shakes his head. "No questions at this time, Your Honor."

There's a gentle rustle through the courtroom as the crowd shifts in their seats, registering surprise at Fall not cross-examining his blood enemy.

Charles Lusk, the deputy over whose testimony there were long arguments Saturday and who Parker let testify while I was gone with Tom Tucker, is recalled. He's asked to confirm the exact words he claimed to hear McNew say about Colonel Fountain trying to break up his partnership with Lee and Gililland. Again, there are no questions from Fall. Lusk is excused.

Judge Parker calls for the dinner recess early. Hughes and I go out the front door of the courthouse, heading for the Ocean Grove. I haven't seen Persia all morning, and I'm anxious to visit with her.

We walk through the big, arched entrance of the courthouse just in time to see Governor Thornton not twenty feet away, red-faced and yelling at Seymour, "By God, I ought to shoot you. If I did, I'd get away with it, but I'm going to sue you and that goddamned rag you work for and bleed you dry!"

Seymour, white as wagon canvas, is holding up his hands at Thornton. "Governor! I'm sorry. I didn't have anything to do with the way the editor put out the story. He just made it sound sensational to sell more papers. There's no harm done."

"The hell there's not, goddamn it! I'm going to break you and that damned paper of yours!"

A small crowd has gathered. Seymour shakes his head. "Now, Governor, the paper was wrong, and it wronged me, too. Let's go down to the Union bar and play a little poker. I'm sure we can work this out."

Thornton glares at Seymour for a few moments. He says, "Stud!" before turning away and heading down the hill. Seymour practically runs after him.

As the afternoon session begins, Judge Parker asks the prosecution to call its next witness. Catron stands. "Your Honor, the territory calls Major William Henry Harrison Llewellyn."

Llewellyn, looking older and more worn out than a man should in his late-forties, is aided by a young man in a suit. Shuffling up the aisle to the witness chair, sweat runs in rivulets down Llewellyn's face. His hands have a slight tremor, and his skin has a yellowish tinge.

Llewellyn nods when he's reminded he's been sworn and must tell the truth. When he's seated, he asks for water. Catron pours him a glass. He greedily downs it in two or three long swallows and slumps back in the chair, wheezing like he's just run up the hill from Main Street.

Catron asks, "Major, can you continue? You look very ill."

Llewellyn uses his elbows to scrunch up straight and then squares his shoulders. He shoots a venomous glance toward Lee and Gililland and says, "Sorry. Just a touch of yellow fever I picked up in Cuba with the Rough Riders. My doctor is right over there if I need him. Your questions, sir?"

Catron nods. "Very well, Major Llewellyn. You're a member of the bar in Las Cruces, New Mexico Territory. Is that correct?"

Llewellyn hacks into his damp handkerchief. "Yes, sir. I have a law practice with Rynerson and Wade in Las Cruces. Prior to that, I was the agent on the Mescalero Reservation."

Wheezing and coughing, he mops his face and continues. "After living awhile in Las Cruces, I was elected to the territorial legislature and was speaker of the house of representatives. More recently, I left for Cuba as a captain with the Rough Riders, and returned a major. Mr. Roosevelt is a personal friend."

Catron says, "You were on good terms with Albert Fountain from what I understand. What did you think of his family?"

"I was on the closest of terms with my great friend and colleague, Colonel Albert Fountain. Albert had one of the closest families I've ever had the good fortune to know. He and his wife, Mariana, were more like a newly married couple than one that had been married for nearly forty years. Why—"

Fall is on his feet. "Objection! The defense has no intention of any discussion regarding Fountain family relationships."

Judge Parker frowns. "Mr. Catron, I fail to see why this testimony has any relevance. Can you enlighten us?"

Catron wears a faint smile as he answers, "Your Honor, allegations have been made in certain newspapers around Las Cruces and by persons I can point to in this court that Colonel Fountain and his lovely wife were not getting along too well, so he just took his little boy and disappeared. I intend to prevent any such claims from being made in this court. I intend to nip them in the bud."

Judge Parker nods. "Very well, objection overruled. Continue, Mr. Catron."

Catron turns back to Llewellyn and waits while he coughs into his handkerchief. "Now, Major Llewellyn, please tell the court about your actions after you learned of Colonel Fountain's disappearance."

Sweating profusely, Llewellyn coughs again. "Barela was driving his team like the wind when he came roaring up in my yard. He told me he had just come from talking to Jack and Albert Fountain at the colonel's home and of his despair at what he'd seen that morning. I asked Barela and my hired man to round up a quick list of men I prepared, thinking them best for a posse, and to tell anyone else who wanted to come that they were welcome. We left Las Cruces about midnight with around twenty-five men, including three in a buckboard.

"The next day, we came upon the Fountain brothers and their group, who were searching for signs of the colonel's buckboard Barela said had driven off into the desert. Van Patton searched for clues up and down the road near Chalk Hill while the rest of us followed the buckboard tracks out into the desert." Llewellyn goes on to tell the same version of events other witnesses told of following tracks and measuring tracks. He breaks into a coughing fit and then says, "I saved the measurements for some time and left them in the district attorney's office for future reference. No one there seems to know anything about them now."

Catron looks over his shoulder at the defendants. Llewellyn describes how the posse followed the trail across the north end of the Jarillas, but never says anything about the problems Henry Stoes mentioned to me of the trackers losing and finding the trail several times. He says the cattle herd Dan Fitchett was driving from Dog Canyon obliterated all signs of the trail six or seven miles from Wildy Well.

Hughes and I look at each other, frowning. Just looking at Clausen's map on the courtroom wall shows that can't be right and is inconsistent with what Joe Fitchett testified earlier. I see it is also inconsistent with what Henry Stoes told me about the cattle herd incident. It seems clear Llewellyn's bout with yellow fever is jumbling details in his mind.

Llewellyn never mentions the terrible suffering the posse members and their horses went through trying to reach Wildy Well. At Wildy Well, he says, Clausen called his attention to a man on a white horse in the distance. "We rode out toward the man, but he disappeared into the brush. When we found the horse's tracks, I examined and measured them. The trackers said, and my measurements confirmed, this was the same horse that went from the campfire on the south side of the Jarillas toward Wildy Well."

Llewellyn's coughing grows worse. Catron waits a couple of minutes, and then says to Judge Parker, "Your Honor, this concludes our questions for this witness. May we request a recess for the rest of the day in order to give him an opportunity to gain some strength before facing Mr. Fall's inquisition?"

Judge Parker looks at Fall, who nods his agreement. "Very well. Court is recessed and will resume at nine o'clock tomorrow morning."

Chapter 35
Second Oliver Lee Interview, 5 June 1899

Geronimo Sánchez and his guards go through their usual procedure for checking me for weapons. I'm let through the door to the prisoner cells, where Gililland is stretched out on his bunk. Lee watches me come through the door.

"Howdy, Quent. Fall said you'd be coming by. I didn't expect to see you so soon. What brings you?"

"I was hoping to get another interview."

Gililland begins to snore loudly.

"All right. What do you want to know?"

Flipping to a new page in my notepad, I ask, "Llewellyn appears to be your blood enemy. Why is he so anxious to see you hanged? Henry Stoes says Llewellyn wouldn't let members of his posse ride over to your ranch to get water and question you about your whereabouts the day the Fountains disappeared. Why not?"

Lee draws up his chair next to the bars and stares at the floor for a minute. "I remember it was a beautiful fall day in '92. I had men at work all over the range, and I was heading to Dog Canyon from Wildy Well when I saw a dust streamer out in the desert. Somebody was riding like a whirlwind toward me. I checked the loads in my guns and waited.

"The kid was from Las Cruces and had just about killed his horse carrying a message to me from Fall. He said the Republicans were planning to march the local militia down Main Street on Election Day, which was the next day. Fall said he needed me to help him stop the march, and that I needed to come with my men as soon as I could. I thanked the kid and gave him eight bits to ride on over to Wildy, tell the boys I said to meet me at Dog Canyon pronto, and then take care of his horse before getting himself one of mine in exchange."

I frown as I write. "What's the big deal about having a parade on Election Day?"

Lee raises an eyebrow. "It wasn't just any parade. Fall was outraged. The election he'd worked hard to win was about to be stolen right in front of his eyes. He'd been ranting all over Las Cruces and Mesilla that the Republicans were out to intimidate voters with their militia and steal the election. Of course, the Republicans maintained they were doing no such thing. They just wanted to be sure the ballot boxes weren't being stuffed.

"Regardless of how they put it, they were going to march and station armed men up and down the street where votes were being cast. Fountain had been the commander for the mounted militia for years. Llewellyn, who had been a speaker of the house in the territorial legislature, and Branigan were the foot militia's commanders. Fall beat the Republicans in the '90 election, and it looked like he was about to do it again. The Republicans weren't having it, regardless of how the majority of the voters might feel. Fall decided he had to fight fire with fire. Get the picture?"

I nod. It's beginning to sink in that politics in the territory is truly a blood sport. "So what happened?"

Lee crosses his arms. "It was late in the afternoon by the time I got ten or twelve men together, saddled fresh horses, and filled canteens. I told them all why we were going and what might happen. I said that if any of them didn't want to go with me, I wouldn't hold it against 'em, but they all came. We rode all night and got into Las Cruces just before dawn."

I shake my head. "It amazes me that you could cover sixty or seventy miles on horseback at night in ten or twelve hours. How'd you do that?"

Lee nods. "I wouldn't want to do it every day. We had some of the best horses in the basin. We didn't ride them into the ground, either. The trick to fast long-distance riding is to do intervals, fast walk, good trot, slow gallop. A horse in good physical condition can keep up a pace like that for hours."

"What happened when you got to Las Cruces?"

"First thing was to unsaddle, feed, and rub down the horses. It was just getting light when I told the men to ease into town, find a café, and get a big breakfast. They hadn't had any supper because we left in such a hurry. I told 'em just to drift into two or three places, two or three at a time. If they went barging in together, they'd get folks wondering what was going on, and tales could be spread that might alert the Republicans we were in town. We planned to meet after breakfast at Lohman's Store, across the street from the Masonic lodge, where folks were supposed to vote. In the meantime, I went over to Fall's house.

"Boy, was he glad to see me. He wasn't sure I'd make it before the Republicans marched.

"Lohman's place is a long, one-story adobe with a parapet along the roofline across the front. Lohman was a Republican, but he didn't like what the Republicans were trying to pull any more than Fall. Fall and I figured if we could get some men up on top of Lohman's with rifles, we could control what went on in the street.

"Lohman let us borrow rifles and cartridges he had for sale in the store and gave us access to his roof. We had a perfect field of fire up and down Main Street, and that parapet gave us great cover. We carried the guns, a couple of cases of cartridges, and a bucket or two of drinking water up on the roof and waited."

I give a low whistle. "You carried cases of cartridges up on the roof? You didn't really expect to get in a fight with the militia, did you?"

"Quent, if Llewellyn and Branigan didn't back down, blood was going to flow. It wasn't long after we settled down that Llewellyn and Branigan came marching up the street with the militia behind them. Before they got very far, Fall walked out in the middle of the street with his arms raised and yelled, 'Halt!' "

I ask, "What happened?"

Lee smiles. "They stopped. Their jaws dropped like trapdoors. Fall proceeded to give them a little speech about how the Republicans were trying to intimidate the voters with the militia and said he wasn't going to stand for it. He finished up with something like, 'Llewellyn, get the hell out of here with that damned militia, or I'll have you all killed.' Then he pointed at the parapet. The boys and me raised up and levered a round into our rifles. Llewellyn and Branigan knew we were ready to use them. They knew if shooting started, they were in big trouble with the governor for unauthorized use of the military in an election, and what was worse, blood was sure to run in the streets, in which case they'd be headed for prison for starting it.

"Being the smart military officers they were, Llewellyn and Branigan called retreat. In Llewellyn's eyes, my boys and I had humiliated and embarrassed him and Branigan in front of the whole town. Llewellyn must have been thinking then how he'd get even by killing or humiliating me in front of the world. Couple that with his belief that I had a gang stealing cattle, and I'm on top of his list of people to bring down.

"He and Branigan signed that bench warrant Garrett got after the grand jury threw out his evidence in '98. They claimed in the warrants they had followed trails and that other circumstances gave every indication McNew, Carr, Gililland, and I murdered the Fountains. Fall has since shown me letters showing Llewellyn wanted to have us assassinated. That's the way politics is played in New Mexico Territory."

I nod. "Yeah, I can see now why Llewellyn and some of the others want to see you out of the way. Thanks for the interview, Mr. Lee. There are one or two other things I'd like to talk with you about in the next few days, if that's all right."

Lee smiles. "It's Oliver to you, Quent. Come any time."

Leaving the jail, I see Tom Tucker coming out the back door of the courthouse. He looks rested and relaxed. "Tom! Got time for a question?"

He waves me over to sit with him in the shade. "Howdy, Quent. What's on your mind, my friend?"

"Well, first off, I didn't get a chance to thank you for all you did to help Persia and me. We owe you our lives. On the ride home, a question kept eating at me, but I didn't think it was the time or place to ask you. Just between us, why didn't you kill Brown?"

He shakes his head as he lights a cigarette. "I wanted to kill his ass mighty bad, except I thought if I killed him, then there would be a trial. You and Persia would have been in it with me. Oh, I'm shore I'd have gotten off, but you and Persia would have gotten some of my dirt on you. He ain't worth the trouble. Woulda been nice to plug him dead center and be done with him. He don't scare easy, so I don't know if what we did will stick or not. Know what I mean?"

I nod and say, "Yeah."

"You and Persia're gonna have to keep your wits about you. I think Scott has headed for parts unknown. Brady ain't got nothin' to lose by tryin' to kill you, and he definitely don't want to be tied to the Fountain murders and have half the country lookin' for him if you turn up anything new. I'll keep an eye on you as best I can, but you and Persia got to be watchful."

Chapter 36
The Prosecution Closes Its Case, 6 June 1899

Llewellyn is recalled to the witness stand. He isn't sweating like he was yesterday, and his shuffle has changed to a purposeful stride. The clerk reminds him he is still under oath before he sits down.

Judge Parker says, "Your witness, Mr. Fall."

Fall rises and walks to within two or three feet of the witness chair. I can see Llewellyn glaring at Fall, who turns and faces the jury to ask his first question. His voice controlled, civil, throws a roundhouse punch out of nowhere. "Will you please tell the jury, Mr. Llewellyn, your role in plots to murder me and the defendants?"

Llewellyn jerks back in the chair as if struck. Before he can say anything, Catron is on his feet. "Objection! The witness is not on trial here! This question is slander and a smear!"

Judge Parker brings down his gavel hard before pointing it at Catron. "Sit down, Mr. Catron. Mr. Fall, relevance?"

"Your Honor, we propose to show it was not the original intention to prosecute these defendants, but that they were after me, wanted to accuse me, got into this, and now can't get out."

Judge Parker studies Fall a moment, then sighs. "Very well, objection overruled. Just remember, Mr. Fall, you are balanced on a very fine wire. Witness will answer the question."

Catron's objection gives Llewellyn time to recover. "To my knowledge, there has never been any conspiracy to murder you or the defendants. And if there were, I certainly wouldn't be part of it."

Fall nods. "I see, I see. Then what of the plan by your posse to blow up the defendants' homes with dynamite shortly after the disappearance of the Fountains? You did lead such a posse, did you not?"

Llewellyn refuses to be intimidated by Fall's attack and innuendo. "I did lead posses in search of the Fountains soon after they disappeared, but the posses I led never had any dynamite. I think, Mr. Fall, you have obtained very bad information from uninformed, gossiping, lying witnesses."

Fall unleashes a flurry of swift jabs that keeps Llewellyn off-balance. "I'll be the judge of the value of my witnesses, sir. Is it not true that Jorge Manuel is an expert in the use of dynamite?"

"I don't know."

"Didn't you personally request that he join your posse?"

"I—"

"Wasn't the dynamite carried on a wagon you took with your posse?"

"There was no—"

"If not the defendants' homes, exactly where was the dynamite going to be used?"

Llewellyn is getting red in the face, but he answers in a steady voice. "There was no—"

Fall takes a new tack, all the while watching the jury. "Major Llewellyn, how many assassins did you try to hire in the plot to murder the defendants and me?"

Llewellyn's face is a thundercloud as Fall waits, his arms crossed. "There . . . was . . . no . . . plot! I hired no assassins to murder you, the defendants, or anyone else!"

Fall, nodding, steps back to the defense table where Lee sits, picks up a piece of paper, and hands it to Llewellyn. As he hovers over Llewellyn, Fall thunders, "How do you explain this letter to W.W. Cox where you say you want to ensure Fall, Lee, and the others have no chance of escape, and you agree to pay a fee of one thousand dollars?"

Llewellyn is shaking his head as he sees the letter. "When I saw how badly the investigation was going, I was willing to pay money out of my own pocket for detectives. This letter is about detectives I hired, and Cox knows it. It has absolutely nothing to do with a murder plot. It was to get the evidence needed to hang you and your minions, sir. Not assassinate you. When I saw no progress in gathering additional evidence by Pat Garrett, Perry, or the Pinkertons, I hired my own detectives to find it."

"Right." Fall turns back to the defense table, lifts another page, and hands it to Llewellyn as he takes the first page from him. "And in this letter here, you were hiring more detectives? These were not part of a murder plot? More detectives, you say?" He picks up several more sheets, each another letter, and passes them one by one to Llewellyn, repeating the same questions again and again.

Llewellyn looks at the letters and begins to slump in the chair. "Yes, more detectives. The detective agencies were not having enough success fast enough to suit me, as this letter here plainly says."

Fall frowns as he looks at the jury. "The detectives couldn't find any evidence, eh? Is that why you decided to manufacture evidence?"

Llewellyn glowers at Fall. "I've never manufactured evidence."

Fall takes a step back in feigned surprise. "Oh? Didn't you sign letters to the Pinkertons using W.W. Cox's name?"

Llewellyn flinches as though Fall has struck him again. "No! Now, I may have written a statement for the Pinkertons that said it was Cox's, but it was exactly what Cox told me—no less, no more—and he knows it. I have never manufactured evidence."

Fall takes a step and raises his brows again. "You've maintained the tracks you measured belonged to someone on the Lee ranch. Didn't you testify yesterday that the track you saw at Las Cruces was not the same as any of the three you saw near the blood?"

Llewellyn's jaw drops and his eyes grow wide with surprise. Catron roars out of his seat, "He did not!"

Judge Parker hammers his gavel to no avail.

Fall nods, clenching his teeth. "Yes, he did!"

"No, he didn't!"

"Yes, he did!"

"No, he did not!"

Fall takes a deep breath, glowering at Catron. "When you say that, you state deliberately and willfully what you know to be false."

Catron pounds the prosecution table with his fist. "This witness clearly stated yesterday the tracks they found in Las Cruces exactly matched those they found by the blood and on Lee's roof! I demand an apology from you, sir! You are besmirching the honor of this fine gentleman and witness."

The sharp rap of Judge Parker's gavel makes my ears ring. He roars, "Gentlemen, if you don't stop this now, I'll hold you both in contempt and fine you each five hundred dollars. Sit down, Mr. Catron! Continue, Mr. Fall."

Catron sits down, still very red in the face. Fall resumes skewering Llewellyn on the evidence he claimed he and Branigan had to justify a bench warrant after the grand jury determined there was insufficient evidence to try Lee, McNew, and Gililland. He comes back again and again as to why Llewellyn tried to hire killers to murder himself and the defendants. Llewellyn refuses to be intimidated by Fall and only occasionally becomes confused.

Finally, Catron has enough and stands to challenge Fall's

harassment of Llewellyn. "Your Honor! The prosecution requests that you instruct Mr. Fall to quit bullying the prosecution witness. This line of questioning is completely unprofessional and uncalled for."

Before Parker can answer, Fall replies. "I will interrogate the witnesses to suit myself, and I advise the heavyweight attorney to sit down."

Along with Judge Parker's outraged gavel banging, there is a roar of laughter throughout the courtroom. I think, *I would have paid money to see this show.*

At last, Fall says, "No more questions of this witness, Your Honor."

On redirect, Catron has Llewellyn make clear he has always maintained the equivalence of tracks he and Branigan measured at the buckboard, Lee's roof, and those of McNew in Las Cruces; he has been no participant in any plot to murder Fall and the defendants; and that when the bench warrants obtained by Pat Garrett for the defendants' arrest were obtained, he and Branigan had no doubt as to the evidence that could link the defendants to the murders.

By the time Catron finishes, it's past noon. Judge Parker calls for a dinner recess until two o'clock. Hughes and I head for the back door with the rest of the crowd.

When court resumes, a large bouquet of desert wildflowers, courtesy of the women who have been attending the trial, sits in a vase on the defendants' table. Albert Fountain is recalled and testifies he was the first of the search party to find blood and, in the excitement, thought he saw the colonel's tracks near the large blood spot; however, he decided upon reflection that he was probably wrong.

Fall waves away an opportunity to cross-examine. When asked to call their next witness, Catron stands. "The prosecution rests its case, Your Honor."

Before Judge Parker can instruct the defense to begin, Fall stands. "Your Honor, the defense requests you dismiss all charges. The prosecution cannot produce a body or even prove that one existed. All its evidence is purely circumstantial and is not incriminating at that. There is insufficient evidence to whip a yellow dog, much less for a capital murder trial."

Childers is on his feet, objecting to the motion and arguing that New Mexico Territory does not require a body to prove a murder has been committed. It only must be established that it is reasonable to expect that a murder has been committed.

Judge Parker agrees with Childers. "Motion to dismiss is denied. Mr. Fall, the defense will begin its case at nine o'clock in the morning. Court will adjourn until then."

Hughes walks down the hill with me as the shadows lengthen in the receding heat, and dust hangs in the idle air. We drop off our stories at the telegraph office. Belvedere Brooks hands me a telegram that he's just received. The telegram reads, NEED DIRT ON THORNTON AND CROSSON. FIND IT.

Hughes asks, "Bad news?"

I wag my head, feeling a sense of outrage. "My editor wants me to find some dirt on Thornton and Crosson. I guess Hearst is worried about a lawsuit over that piece of trash he published a week ago."

Hughes frowns. "Last week, Seymour managed to lose several large hands to Thornton, and by the time the game was over, there was no more talk of suing the *Examiner* or Seymour. I thought Thornton forgot about a lawsuit. What's the worry now?"

"I don't know. Newspapers aren't supposed to operate this way. I ought to tell them to go to hell. I'm not digging up any dirt on Governor Thornton or Dr. Crosson. I've got to think this over. Even if I quit, I'm going to finish this assignment."

Hughes smiles. "You're a rare bird, Quent, a man of honor. It's something the press needs nowadays. Don't worry, you'll work it out. Come on, I'll buy you a drink."

Chapter 37
The Defense Begins, 7 June 1899

There is a hush of expectancy as Judge Parker tells the defense to call its first witness. Fall rises. "Your Honor, the defense calls Deputy Sheriff Tom Tucker."

I hear the confident thud of Tom's boots approaching the rail. He stands straight and tall, his chin jutting out as the clerk reminds him he has already sworn to tell the truth.

Fall begins his examination with questions about Tom's relationship with the defendants, where he was the day the Fountains disappeared, and whether he is familiar with the big gray horse Lee rides. Tom says he's known the defendants since before the Good-Cooper War, that he was working on Lee's ranch the day the Fountains disappeared, and that he's familiar with the horse.

"Now, Deputy Tucker, can you describe this horse for the jury?"

"Well, sir, he's good size, maybe seventeen hands, and he's faster'n greased lightnin', and if Mr. Lee is on him, he can cover a mighty long distance without stopping. Mr. Lee knows more about horses than any other man in this country, and he trains 'em to perfection. That horse's real musc'lar in his rear quarters, even kinda makes his rear feet look bigger than the front ones. Oliver never had it shod. Thought it was better for the animal out'n the desert country."

Fall stands intently listening. "I see, I see. So are we to conclude from your statement that Oliver Lee's big, gray horse, the one the first posse tracked all the way over the Jarillas away from the abandoned buckboard, did not wear iron horseshoes at the time of the Fountain disappearance?"

Tom nods. "Yes, sir, that's 'xactly what I said."

Asking a few more easy questions, with Tom giving expected answers, Fall announces, "No more questions for this witness, Your Honor."

"Cross, Mr. Childers?"

Childers is out of his chair, ready to pounce. "Thank you, Your Honor. The prosecution requires just one point of clarification from this witness. In your testimony, Mr. Tucker, did you actually say Mr. Lee's horse had rear feet larger than its front feet?"

A shadow of confusion crosses Tom's face as he looks from Childers to Fall, Lee, and Gililland. He shrugs his shoulders. "Yes, sir, that there is what I said."

"No more questions at this time, Your Honor."

"Witness may step down. Call your next witness, Mr. Fall."

Pedro Gonzales is called next, followed by Jacovo Chavez. They each testify they were members of Llewellyn's first search party. They maintain there were no tracks around the campfire when it was first discovered and that the tracks measured by Branigan and Llewellyn were actually tracks of search-party members.

Joe Fitchett is called. He testifies that he met with Oliver Lee at the Dog Canyon Ranch the day of the disappearance. A.N. Bailey, employed by Lee, also testifies he and the defendants were at the Dog Canyon Ranch the day of the disappearance.

Fall then calls Dan Fitchett, who, along with W.T. White, drove a herd of cattle across the trail Llewellyn's posse was following. White had been a prosecution witness earlier. Fitchett states he had been at Lee's ranch on the afternoon of the disappearance. "I saw Mr. McNew and Jim Gililland at the Dog

Canyon Ranch close to sundown. I'd gone over there to talk to Mr. Lee about his plans for moving some herds around on the range. He didn't want to get backed into a corner like he was by the Blue Water outfit the year before."

Fitchett says he was also at Wildy Well when Clausen rode up to ask for water and help in the search for the Fountains. Fall crosses his arms and looks at the jury as he asks Fitchett, "After you delivered the herd to Wildy Well, what did you do then?"

"We were helpin' with chores and just kind of taking it easy. I told Mr. Lee about the men we'd run into drivin' the herd over and how they were asking all sorts of questions. We were thinkin' they were probably with Blue Water and up to no good. Year before, we'd almost gotten into a little war with the Blue Water outfit 'cause they'd brought in about five thousand head in '94 and was tryin' to take up the range Mr. Lee's herds and other ranchers like myself were usin'."

Fall looks at the floor a second. "Do you know why Oliver Lee was at Wildy that day?"

"I know he'd told me Saturday afternoon that he'd be down there to do a head count of the cattle after we brought 'em in and pay us for 'em. He'd brought ol' Ed with him to solder a leak in the water tank for the windmill.

"When we saw two riders comin' in, we didn't have any idea who they were. We was all a little on edge from them strangers stoppin' us and asking all sorts of questions and then seein' 'em ride off toward Wildy. Made sense that the two riders comin' in were part of the same group that stopped us. We thought they might be Blue Water people, so we all went inside and waited to see who they were.

"When they came up, we didn't recognize either of them. One of 'em hallooed the house and asked if they could get some water. Ed decided they wasn't gonna start shootin', so he went back outside with the bar of lead he was using for soldering up the tank, but he sure didn't waste no time getting to where they didn't have a clear shot at him if he was wrong about 'em."

Fall nods. "Then what happened?"

"Ed shamed us all by going out, so we all eased out. Mr. Lee came out and asked those fellers why they were wanderin' around the range. That's when they told us the Fountains were missin'."

Fall turns back to the defense table. "No more questions of this witness, Your Honor."

Childers gives Fitchett a hard stare. "Mr. Fitchett, you said you told Mr. Lee about being stopped and questioned when you were bringing your herd down to Wildy, correct?"

"Yes, sir."

"You also stated that you first learned of the Fountain murders when the two men, who we now know were Mr. Clausen and Mr. Herrera, rode up to Wildy Well and asked for water, correct?"

"Yes, sir."

Childers then asks a question that had crossed my mind. "Are you claiming, Mr. Fitchett, that the men who stopped and questioned you when you were driving the herd never mentioned that they were looking for the Fountains? Are you claiming Mr. Lee had not heard earlier in the day from your own mouth that the Fountains had been murdered?"

"Them riders never said anything about lookin' for the Fountains, and I didn't say anything like that to Mr. Lee."

With a little one-sided grin, Childers looks directly at the men sitting at the defendants' table. "Was Mr. Lee surprised when you told him the Fountains had been murdered?"

Fitchett frowns. "I told you I didn't tell him. I didn't know myself until those men showed up asking for water."

"No more questions, Your Honor."

Judge Parker tells Fitchett he's excused and tells Fall to call his next witness.

Fall tells the clerk to call Sheriff George Curry. From inside the rail, Sheriff Curry stands and takes three steps to the witness chair.

Led by Fall through a series of questions, Curry establishes he knows Jack Maxwell on a friendly basis and that shortly after the Fountains disappeared, Maxwell told him he had bunked with McNew at the Dog Canyon Ranch the night the Fountains disappeared and had seen Lee and Gililland after they ate that night.

When Sheriff Curry is cross-examined, Childers makes him admit he's been friends with Lee for years and owes him for a loan. The defense reinforces Curry's testimony by calling to the stand Bud Smith, who had worked for Maxwell. Smith claims Maxwell told him the same thing he had told Curry. The prosecution counters by making Smith admit he and Lee were longtime friends.

The last witness for the day is Joe Morgan. Morgan is Fall's brother-in-law, and at one time had been a deputy sheriff in Las Cruces along with McNew, Lee, and Gililland. I recall Ben Williams telling me Morgan was with Fall when they had tried to kill him. Morgan testifies he saw the defendants at Dog Canyon Ranch on the last day of January 1896, the day before the Fountains disappeared.

Childers tries to discredit Morgan's reliability as a witness, as Fall did with prosecution witnesses, by asking Morgan if he was indicted for murder in Clarksville, Texas.

Morgan says yes.

On redirect, Fall asks, "Were you ever prosecuted for murder in Clarksville?"

Joe shakes his head. "No, I was not."

Fall looks at Childers, the jury, and then Judge Parker. "No more questions of this witness, Your Honor."

Judge Parker pounds his gavel. "Very well. Court stands adjourned until nine o'clock tomorrow morning."

Chapter 38
Decision

All day, testimonies of the defense witnesses have drifted in and out of my consciousness. A dark cloud hangs in my mind as I walk down Hillsboro's streets. Hughes walks with me until he stops by the telegraph office. I continue down the street. I'm wrestling. *Do I finish this assignment and refuse my editor's order to find dirt on Governor Thornton or resign now just when I might contribute stories that are useful to the paper and my career?* I know deep in my core I have to leave the *Examiner.*

As the porch to the Ocean Grove comes into view, Persia sits there relaxing in a chair, enjoying the evening. Just the sight of her gives my heart wings, and the storm clouds of doubt in my mind give way to hope. I know I have to tell her about the telegram.

As I approach, she stands and gives me a big smile. Even from several feet away, there is an ephemeral whiff of cactus flowers carried by her perfume.

Despite my grin, she looks into my eyes and frowns. "What's happened? Are you all right? Have you seen Brady?"

"No, no sign of Brady, but I got some news last night. Let's take a walk down by the river where we'll have a little privacy."

She smiles, taking my hand, as we head across Main for the path leading to the Percha. At the riverbank next to a big sycamore tree, we find boulders pushed together that form a bench large enough to seat both of us. The little river burbles gently as the light starts to dim. Persia crosses her arms. "Tell me your news."

There is still enough light to read the telegram. I reach in my vest pocket and hand it to her. "I received this yesterday afternoon and have been wrestling with what to do ever since."

She glances at the six words and stares into my eyes. "What are you going to do?"

"I know I have to leave the *Examiner.* It's just a matter of when. Do I continue this assignment until I'm finished and ignore those instructions, or do I quit now?"

She sighs and shakes her head. "Thank God!" She takes my hand and squeezes it. "Quent, every man and woman lives by two codes: the one they actually live by and the one they say they live by. Nothing in the world can convince me that for you they're not one and the same. With you, what you see is what you get."

I slowly shake my head. "Don't you understand this could be a disaster for my career?"

She pulls me down to sit beside her and stares off into the dusk.

"Quent, as we live our lives, events will test how strong we are and how well we live up to our own codes. Sometimes we can't see those tests coming. A man never knows what kind of man he is until his honor is tested. This telegram is a test. Only an honorable man would answer the demand the way you plan."

It feels like the world has been lifted from my shoulders. "How do you think I ought to handle my answer?"

"Why not just send your editor a note saying you won't try to dig up dirt on Governor Thornton? If he fires you, then it's time to start looking for another job. If he doesn't fire you, then finish this assignment."

Early the next morning I'm waiting for Belvedere Brooks to open the telegraph office. He grins as he unlocks the door.

"Morning, Quent! Hot story to get on the wire?"

I shake my head. "No, just a short answer."

Belvedere takes it and reads, "No dirt from me on Thornton or Crosson." Smiling, he says, "Good answer. It'll be on the wire within the hour."

Chapter 39
Albert Blevins and Mary Lee Testify, 8 June 1899

Hughes eyes me and smiles. "You look a lot more relaxed today. Get your problem solved?"

I nod and grin. "Yeah, I sent a telegram to my editor saying I won't look for dirt on Thornton or Crosson. He can accept it or fire me. It doesn't make much difference if he does, because I'm quitting the *Examiner* after the trial anyway."

"What are you going to do?"

"Look for another paper. I'd rather push a broom than be a yellow journalist."

Hughes smiles. "Good for you."

The bailiff calls the session to order as Judge Parker enters the court. Soon the clerk calls the first defense witness of the day, Albert Blevins. Blevins is a Texas and Pacific Railroad fireman who owns a ranch near Oliver Lee's.

After Fall guides him through a series of background questions, he asks what the crowd has been waiting to hear. "Where were you on the afternoon of the first of February, 1896?"

Blevins projects an aura of muscular strength and has a no-nonsense look in his eyes. He pulls a big, gold pocket watch from his vest pocket. "According to my railroad watch here, I rode into the Lee ranch at two o'clock that Saturday. Mr. Lee and me were helping each other out. He was in the middle of rounding up his cattle and moving the herds down south for early spring grazing, and I come to help. I was expecting Mrs. Lee to tell me where I'd find Oliver, but him, Gililland, and

McNew was right there at the ranch house setting out grapevines for her. Oliver said they'd been puttin' off plantin' the vines, and Mrs. Lee was afraid they was gonna die if they wasn't planted purty quick. Mr. Lee said they'd ride out early Sunday morning to get up north and start pushing stock south."

I think that matches what Eva Taylor swore to. I wonder why Fall isn't reinforcing Blevin's testimony with hers, but it occurs to me that maybe he's holding her testimony for one of the future trials.

Fall says, "Tell us, Mr. Blevins, were you at the ranch when Mr. White and the Fitchett brothers showed up with the herd Mr. Lee bought?"

"Yes, sir. Oliver, Gililland, McNew, and me saw 'em coming in. They were all pretty nervous about who it might be with them cattle since they'd had a hard time keeping the Blue Water outfit off 'em the year before. McNew, he wasn't taking no chances. He went up to the house to get his gun."

Fall continues to question Blevins to fix a clear timeline of what went on at the Lee ranch during the weekend the Fountains disappeared. When he is satisfied, Fall turns Blevins over to the prosecution.

Childers and Barnes go after Blevins hard for the next three hours. Blevins remains cool and unflappable during their constant attempts to find inconsistency in his testimony. When they finally give up, it's twelve-thirty. Judge Parker recesses the court until two-thirty.

Hughes and I decide we'll settle for a cold beer for lunch while we work on stories. We find a table in the Union Hotel bar and start to work. I finish a page and glance around the room.

Sitting three tables away is an older man dressed like a cowboy. His eyes are slashes that begin too close to a big, hooked nose that has seen the wrong end of a fist more than once. A beer sits in front of him. When he sees me look at him, he nods and looks away.

I wonder if he's Brady. The next time I look up, the cowboy is gone.

The beginning of afternoon court sessions is always hard because the pull of the afterdinner *siesta* is strong. The spectators are usually quieter and much less alert than in the morning, late afternoon, and night sessions. However, when Fall calls Mary Lee to the stand, there is no hint of drowsiness anywhere in the courtroom.

Mary wears a black dress with long sleeves and lace collar and cuffs. McNew stands and extends a hand to help her up. She accepts it, but it's clear she doesn't need help. Nodding toward her son, she walks past the rail ramrod straight and stops in front of the bailiff, who reminds her she has sworn to tell the truth.

Fall's questions lead her through the events of the day, 1 February 1896. Her answers are clear. Finally, Fall asks who was at her supper table that evening. "Well now, there were Blevins and Maxwell, Oliver, Jim Gililland, Good-Eye Tucker, my niece Nettie, and her husband, Bill McNew, and their two children. Bill, he's a mighty fine man. Next to Oliver, I reckon Bill McNew is my favorite gentleman around the ranch. He's a good, upright man, and Oliver is, too. Oliver was always a good boy who minded his own business, but me and Mr. Lee taught him from the time he's old enough to walk to defend himself when others attacked him." She pauses and sighs. "No one knows how hard it is to survive and make a living on that desert unless they've tried it. A tough land makes tough men."

Catron watches the jury during her testimony. When she finishes, Fall smiles. He turns to Judge Parker. "No more questions, Your Honor."

"Your witness, Mr. Catron."

Catron smiles and shakes his head. "No questions at this time, Your Honor."

Judge Parker turns to Mary Lee. "The witness is excused. Court will take a fifteen-minute recess."

I have to smile. Catron is smart. He's not about to give the jury any idea that the prosecution picks on elderly ladies.

Chapter 40
Oliver Lee Testifies, 8 June 1899

When court resumes, Judge Parker tells Fall to call his next witness. Fall turns to the bailiff. "Your Honor, the defense calls Oliver Milton Lee."

His chair scrapes against the hardwood floor as Oliver Lee pushes back from the defense table. I glance around the room. Everyone's eyes are on Lee.

Fall crosses his arms and paces about as he questions Lee. Like his mother, Lee sits upright and relaxed in the witness chair. Soon Fall gets to what we've all been expecting. "Now, Mr. Lee, where were you on the first of February, 1896?"

Lee glances at the ceiling, takes a deep breath, and begins. "As usual, we were up before daylight. That time of year is busier than usual because we drive the cattle south toward Wildy to keep from overgrazing the north range. We were expecting the Fitchett brothers and White, who were driving the main herd and picking up the cattle being driven out of the canyons, and they had some of their own they planned to sell me.

"At breakfast my mother reminded me that the grapevines I'd ordered for her were going to die if we didn't get 'em in the ground soon. I'd been promising to plant 'em for her ever since I'd brought 'em back to the ranch from El Paso. I promised her I'd get out and get the boys started working the cattle, come back for dinner, and plant the vines in the afternoon. Bill and Jim had come in to help with the work, and there were several neighbors coming in, too, so I figured I could spare a man or two to help me, and we'd get it done in three or four hours. After dinner, Jim said he'd help with the vines, and he did.

"It was suppertime by the time we finished. It took longer than I expected, but Frenchy Rochas had taught me that when those vines are planted, we had to tote plenty of water and use plenty of cow manure around 'em to be sure they took good root. Blevins came in the middle of the afternoon. Jack Maxwell showed up about dark for supper. Joe Fitchett came by. He said the main herd was filling out about like we'd expected and that it ought to be coming by sometime the next day if the weather didn't get too bad. We had supper and did a few chores there at the house and then went to bed."

From a cigar he's just lighted, Fall blows a long puff toward the ceiling. "So from dinnertime until you went to bed, you, Gililland, and McNew were there in plain sight of everyone at the ranch house?"

"Yes, sir, that's right."

"Now what happened the following day, Sunday?"

"McNew, Gililland, and I got up two or three hours before daylight, had breakfast, and rode up north of the Cruces to the Tularosa road. About daylight, we were just getting a small herd started south when the stage came by, headed for La Luz and Tularosa. That evening the Fitchetts and White came in with the big herd. They stayed and had supper."

"Blevins and Maxwell were still there?"

"Yes, sir."

"What did you do Monday?"

"Monday morning we looked the herd over and did a rough head count, and the Fitchetts and White got it started for Wildy Well. I told 'em I'd be down to do a final tally on Tuesday. I spent the rest of the day catching up on some bookkeeping and making plans with Gililland and McNew to develop some more wells and ponds for the cattle and maybe buy some property up in the Sacramentos. Blevins left for his ranch after the head count. He'd been a good neighbor, and I appreciated him coming over. Maxwell left after dinner."

Fall continues to pace and smoke. "So, are we correct in assuming that on Tuesday, you rode down to Wildy to finish your business with moving your cattle south?"

Lee nods. "Yes, sir. The cattle were grouped up when we rode into Wildy Tuesday morning. Ed, one of my colored men, came with me to do some soldering work on the leaky tank we used with the windmill. Dan Fitchett told me about being stopped on the drive over by some men who questioned him about the herd. He said they rode past the herd and headed for Wildy after he talked to 'em. When the cattle came into Wildy, the drovers saw signs of riders around the water tank, and there were the remains of a fire they'd built, but the men were long gone.

"Dan's story about the men asking him questions and then somebody staying at Wildy for a while before they got there put us on alert. Earlier, a year or maybe a little longer, we had a little argument over grazing rights with the Blue Water outfit, and they weren't too happy with the way things turned out. I told the boys to keep a sharp eye out for strangers in case the Blue Water hands had come back and wanted to do some more arguing.

"About the middle of the morning we saw two riders coming in, so the boys scooted inside to wait and see if it was just those two and if they were friendly. When they came up, they hallooed us and asked for water. I recognized one of them as Carl Clausen, one of Fountain's sons-in-law. We eased outside. I told Clausen to go on and get his water, and asked him why he's way out in the middle of nowhere."

Lee crosses his arms and leans back in the witness chair. "He looked pretty tore up when he said Colonel Fountain and his little boy disappeared on the west side of the Jarillas Saturday afternoon. He got this know-it-all smirk on his face and wanted to know if I'd help look for them, since I was a deputy and knew the range and all.

"It took me back that he had the gall to ask for my help. The cattleman's association had been giving me a hard time courtesy of their attorney, Colonel Fountain. I knew if I helped 'em, I'd be accused of leading a wild goose chase. There wasn't any sign of strangers on the range after Fountain disappeared except for the men Fitchett had seen. Even so, I might have helped look for 'em because the boy was with him, but Clausen's smart-aleck voice got my dander up. He made it sound like I already knew what had happened to them."

Fall takes a puff on his cigar. "And did you know what happened to them?"

"No, sir. It was the first time I'd heard they were missing."

Nodding, Fall faces the jury. "So what did you say?"

"I told him not only no, but hell, no! I had other things to do than to go look for fools who'd managed to get lost. Clausen and his man weren't gone five minutes before I knew I had to be the prime suspect, since they were looking over range I normally used. I figured I'd better get into Cruces quick and find out what was happening.

"I went to Cruces by way of your mine at Sunol in the hope I'd find you there, but you'd already left for home. Since it was late, I stayed overnight and went on to Cruces the next morning.

"When I got to Cruces, I learned there was a rumor that warrants were out for me and some of my friends."

Fall nods and takes a long draw to blow toward the ceiling. "What did you do when you found out about the warrant?"

"I looked up Deputy Morgan so I could see the warrant, post a bond, and talk to my attorney. Morgan said he hadn't seen any such warrant and didn't know of one being issued. I went over to the prosecuting attorney's office, but Mr. Young said he hadn't seen one, either. Justice of the Peace Valdez hadn't seen it, and neither had Sheriff Ascarate. Even if there wasn't any warrant, I told the sheriff I was willing to come in any time they wanted me if he'd send word and let me know when. Sheriff Ascarate said a lot of people weren't thinking straight right then, and it was best for me to go on back home. He said he'd let me know when I needed to come in.

"Deputy Morgan told me he'd heard a rumor there was a posse out that included Ben Williams and a few others who were out to hang me. The word was they knew I had come into town and they were waiting in San Agustin Pass to ambush me. A lookout was supposed to be posted in town to ride out in front of me to let 'em know when I was comin'.

"I was thinking about staying another day or two and waiting 'em out, when I saw an extra edition of the *Rio Grande Republican* that had come out the day before. It was calling for me to be lynched. I decided I'd best get out of there until those town people got hold of their senses, so I took Baylor Pass to get home and left the posse waiting."

Most of the men in the room are nodding that what Lee did made sense. The Fountain brothers stare at Lee with crossed arms and a look that says they don't believe a word he is saying. Fall turns to the defense table and picks up a newspaper. I see the big, black headlines:

JUSTICE WANTED, RETRIBUTION AT HAND
WANTED—ONE JUDGE LYNCH

"Your Honor, the defense wishes to enter into evidence a copy of the paper to which Mr. Lee just referred. It's clear the lead article calls for lynching Mr. Lee for the murder of Colonel Fountain and little Henry."

Catron is on his feet. "Objection! That paper contributes no evidence relevant to the subject of this trial."

Falls turns, slapping the fold of the paper with the back of his hand. "I can point to the man in this room who wrote this article, and he wasn't the editor. This article was written before any real information had returned with the posses searching for the Fountains. It's a clear demonstration that Oliver Lee was the victim of political maneuvering by Republicans in an attempt to get me."

Judge Parker hammers his gavel and stops Fall's tirade. "Objection sustained. However, the witness may testify as to the impact the paper's articles had on him."

Fall, in disgust, tosses the paper back on the defense table. "Continue, Mr. Lee."

"A while later I heard the posse with Williams had warrants for the murders of the Fountains and they planned to kill me for supposedly trying to get away after I was taken in. I went back to Cruces several times after that, and Sheriff Ascarate told me the warrants had been withdrawn.

"Even so, I had to be especially careful where I went at election time. I figured the Republicans were anxious to get payback for the Fountain murders and the political maneuvers in which I'd been involved. I didn't come in when the last warrant was issued because there was more talk of mob justice."

Fall smokes and paces. "How was Kent Kearney killed at Wildy Well?"

Lee stares at the floor for a moment, then raises his eyes. "Jim and I didn't want to get caught and shot by Pat Garrett and his deputies when we slept in our bedrooms. We'd started sleeping on roofs where we thought we'd have some warning if the Garrett crowd showed up." He smiled and shook his head. "I guess we didn't choose very well. We were asleep on the roof of the ranch house at Wildy Well. There was never any call for hands up before we were fired on.

"I was awakened by two shots ripping into the roof just under my belly. I grabbed my rifle and shot at Kearney, who was mostly just a dark outline firing at us, and the light was just enough that I saw Pat Garrett's head ducking down just as I took a shot at him. Kearney shot twice before I hit him with my rifle. Garrett shot once and was talking while he was shooting. Jim and I both hit Kearney and figured we'd killed him. We made Garrett and the rest of his posse ride away, but we agreed to surrender if Garrett told the truth about what happened. After Garrett and the rest of the posse rode off, we took care of Kearney and made him as comfortable as we could while he was dying. He was bleeding bad, and we couldn't stop it." Lee pauses and sighs. He adds, "After a while, I decided I'd best wait for a new sheriff in Doña Ana County before surrendering."

Fall nods. "I don't blame you, Mr. Lee. Where were you after you returned from Las Cruces until the fight at Wildy Well?"

Lee shrugs. "We were at Dog Canyon Ranch almost every day after the Fountains disappeared."

"Did any law officers visit the ranch during that time?"

"No, sir."

"Thank you, Mr. Lee. No further questions at this time, Your Honor."

Judge Parker looks at the prosecution table. "Territory's witness."

Childers struts out from behind the prosecution's table, his left hand holding his left lapel. "Who told you Garrett had threatened you?"

Fall is on his feet. "Objection! The defense requests that it be allowed to make a statement to the court."

Judge Parker nods toward the bailiffs. "The jury is excused, subject to immediate recall." The bailiffs escort the jurors into a room at the back of the courtroom and close the doors. "Proceed, Mr. Fall."

"Your Honor, if Mr. Lee answers the question just put by Mr. Childers, a life will be in jeopardy. Mr. Garrett said in the presence of witnesses that he would whip any man who stated on the witness stand that he had threatened Mr. Lee. If the court will not protect my client and his interests, we will have to resort to other methods."

Judge Parker shakes his head. "You will have to use your own method. I'm sure Mr. Garrett will go to significant lengths to ensure the party to whom the witness refers is not harmed. If he is, Mr. Garrett will most certainly appear under warrant before this court. I will ensure that he will pay a steep price if he shows any contempt of court. Objection is overruled. Bailiffs, return the jury."

Fall looks at Lee and slowly shakes his head. Judge Parker hammers his gavel. "Clerk will read the question, and the witness will answer."

Lee's jaw muscles are rippling as he answers, "Albert Ellis, the colored barber in Las Cruces, told me Garrett had said that if he was given a warrant for Lee's arrest, then no one need fear Mr. Lee."

There's a low rumble of comments among spectators in the courtroom. Judge Parker raps his gavel several times. "Since I expect Mr. Childers will have a long cross-examination, court will adjourn until nine in the morning."

Hughes and I wait until the crowd clears before we leave the courtroom. He begins transcribing his shorthand notes into text readable by the telegraph operator. Hughes impresses me. I've read his summaries of the trial proceedings that have appeared in the *El Paso Herald* and admire them for their accuracy.

As Hughes and I leave the courthouse, there are more deputies than usual standing around the jail. Tom Tucker is one of them. He waves when he sees us and comes over.

"Howdy, boys. Been a long day, ain't it?"

Hughes and I nod. Tom has a ten-gauge Greener shotgun cradled in his arm. "What's going on?"

"Aw, the whole damn town is up in arms. There's a rumor floating around that some men are gonna raise hell in town and take Lee and Gililland out of jail and give 'em a free neck stretching. Course the Lee camp ain't havin' none of that, so they're down in the bars and saloons just waitin' for some fool to make a wrong move. If they do, ain't no doubt the Percha's gonna run red. Sheriff and the other law dogs are plannin' to nip the whole damn thing in the bud. Got your pistol, Quent?"

I pat the right side of my coat. "Yes, sir, right here."

"Good. I'd recommend you boys stay off the street and out of the saloons until we get things calmed down."

We give Tom a quick salute and head off down the hill. Hughes heads for the telegraph office, and I to the Ocean Grove to eat and spend time with Persia before completing another story I'm writing on Lee.

At the Ocean Grove, Persia reaches in her apron pocket to hand me a wrinkled telegram envelope. "Mr. Brooks sent this down to you about three this afternoon."

I tear the seal and open the telegram.

OK NO DIRT. ANYTHING ELSE ON LEE?

Chapter 41
Oliver Lee Returns to the Stand, 9 June 1899

After the usual warning that he is still under oath, Judge Parker turns Lee over to the prosecution. Childers begins with an apparently irrelevant question. "Mr. Lee, what do you know about your attorney, Mr. Fall, getting Pat Garrett appointed Sheriff of Doña Ana County?"

Lee relaxes and looks Childers in the eye. "I heard a lot of talk about it from a lot of people. Most folks thought it was strange that Fall, a Democrat, had to use his political connections in Santa Fe to get the elected sheriff to resign and the man the Republicans wanted appointed. I asked Mr. Fall why he did that. He said something like it was for the best and we just needed to get on with the investigation. I don't remember Mr. Fall's exact words."

"Didn't Mr. Fall want Garrett to get the job to keep Numa Reymond from having it?"

Lee shrugs. "I don't know anything about that."

"Weren't Fall and Reymond bitter enemies?"

"Reymond was a Republican. Fall was a Democrat."

"Given that Ascarate had stayed in office as sheriff over two years longer than he was supposed to, isn't it true Fall was afraid Reymond would take advantage of the sheriff's office to pay him back for all the harassment the Republicans had endured?"

Lee shakes his head. "I wouldn't know."

"Do you consider William Llewellyn, Martin Lohman, and

Numa Reymond against you?"

"Yes."

Childers lifts his chin and cocks his head to one side. He crosses his arms and takes a step closer to the witness chair. "Did you know Charles Rodius and Matt Coffelt?"

"Yes."

"Did you have anything to do with killing them?"

Fall is on his feet, his face red, as he shouts, "Objection!"

Childers smirks. "Question goes to how the witness deals with people who are against him. This witness murdered two men he claimed stole a few cows from him."

Fall shakes his head. "No, sir. The prosecution is attempting to introduce evidence based only on indictments. The character and credibility of the witness cannot be impeached with evidence not relating directly to this case unless a conviction was shown."

Judge Parker asks the bailiffs to retire the jury while the defense and prosecution argue their respective points. He listens intently as Fall and Childers duel. At last, he shakes his head. "Objection sustained. Bailiffs will return the jury." When the jury is seated, he says, "Continue, Mr. Childers."

"No more questions at this time, Your Honor."

"Very well. Redirect, Mr. Fall?"

Fall is up again, pacing back and forth in front of the jury. "Mr. Lee, how long have you been in business with me, besides any personal relationship as friends?"

Lee looks at the ceiling for a moment. "Oh, I guess we've had business dealings since about 1889."

"You stated to Mr. Childers you thought William Llewellyn, Martin Lohman, and Numa Reymond were against you. Do you think Numa Reymond is an enemy of yours? If so, why?"

The spectators in the courtroom seem to lean forward as one body, intent on hearing Lee's answer.

"A couple of letters, written by Bob Burch and Jeff Aiks, state that they had been approached and offered money to kill me and you."

"Objection!" Catron thunders, rising to his feet. "These letters are nowhere in evidence!"

Frowning, Judge Parker looks at Fall. "Objection sustained unless the letters can be accounted for. Do you have them, Mr. Fall?"

Fall turns to Lee. "Can you produce these letters, Mr. Lee?"

"No, sir. I don't know where they are. The last time I saw them, they were in your office."

Fall nods and looks toward Judge Parker. "Your Honor, I request that I be sworn in to testify as to the status of the letters."

"Bailiff will swear in Mr. Fall."

Catron throws his arms out, his fingers wide, and he shrugs his shoulders. "Your Honor?"

"Bailiff, swear Mr. Fall."

The bailiff swears Fall to tell the whole truth and nothing but the truth.

Fall looks at Judge Parker and then the jury. "If it please the court, I looked for those letters recently, turned my office files inside out, but could not find them. I have, in fact, seen the letters. They were dated June and July 1896. After they were received, I read them to the parties themselves."

Judge Parker stares at Fall for a long moment, and then slowly nods. "Very well, Mr. Fall. Continue with your redirect."

Fall turns to Lee. "Did the letters state who would pay the money?"

"My understanding was that Numa Reymond had offered to put up the money."

Fall nods. "Have you heard any talk about Reymond putting up that money?"

Childers shouts, "Objection!"

"Sustained."

"Besides Maxwell, have you heard of any other witnesses being offered money to testify falsely?"

"Objection!"

"Sustained."

Fall turns to Lee. "Are you aware of other threats made against you by these men?"

Lee nods. "Yes, sir. I've become friends with Mr. W.W. Cox, who was friends with Major Llewellyn for several years. Mr. Cox told me Major Llewellyn paid Jake Ryan to kill both me and you."

Fall's brows raise. "Oh? And how did he come to find this out?"

"Mr. Cox said he caught Ryan setting up an ambush, and he made him talk before he ran him off. Ryan told Mr. Cox he was supposed to be paid through the New York Exchange by Major Llewellyn."

Fall nods and says, "I see. No more questions for this witness at this time, Your Honor."

"Very well. Any more questions for this witness, Mr. Childers?"

"Yes, Your Honor."

Childers stands with crossed arms and frowns at the jury as he asks Lee, "How did you become a deputy sheriff?"

Lee smiles. "Well, there was a lot of talk around Las Cruces about how Ben Williams was throwing his weight around, making trouble generally, and bulldozing the sheriff. The citizens wanted it stopped, and when I went there, I didn't have any better sense than to let them appoint me deputy sheriff. Not long after that, I took Williams's guns off him because it was a town ordinance that he couldn't wear arms in town."

"So you were made a deputy to especially disarm Williams?"

"There was some talk about it, but I wouldn't tell him that."

Childers nods, still looking at the jury. "You said you had seen the letters from Burch and Aiks, stating they had been offered money to kill you and Mr. Fall. How much were they to be paid?"

Lee didn't blink or hesitate. "Five thousand dollars."

Childers' brows go up. "Who informed you Numa Reymond was going to put up the money to have you killed?"

Lee stares at the floor for several seconds. "I'm asking you, sir, not to ask me that. Of course, if you force the issue, I'll have to answer since I'm under oath, but this isn't about me. There are a lot of innocent people who could be hurt if I name names. I can say it has been stated that Reymond was to pay."

Childers stares at Lee and slowly nods his head. "No more questions for this witness."

"Witness is excused. Call your next witness, Mr. Fall."

Looking relieved, Fall nods his appreciation toward the prosecution table. "The defense calls Mr. James Wharton."

Hughes looks at me with raised brows. I shrug my shoulders.

A balding, middle-aged man wearing wire-frame glasses and a fine suit walks to the stand. Before he sits down, the bailiff swears him in.

Fall approaches the witness. "Mr. Wharton, where were you living and what was your line of work in January, 1896?"

Wharton answers in a rasping voice, "I lived in White Oaks, Lincoln County, New Mexico Territory, in January, 1896. I was the district attorney in Lincoln and called the grand jury Colonel Fountain attended."

"Now, what was Colonel Fountain's connection with the indictments handed down against the defendants during that term of court?"

Wharton presses his fingers together, making a little tent. "As far as I know, Fountain had nothing to do with procuring the indictments or trying cattle cases that were before the court."

Hughes and I look at each other, frowning. Wharton's testimony is a direct contradiction to the testimony of the Lincoln County grand jury foreman, Theodore Herman, who said Fountain was the driving force behind the indictments against Lee and McNew.

Fall rolls his cigar between his thumb and fingers. "That is at variance with evidence given by a previous witness. Can you clarify your statement?"

Wharton nods. "Certainly. Colonel Fountain was not before the grand jury during that term. Les Dow was presenting most of the evidence in the cases, and I consulted with him and others but not Colonel Fountain. As far as I know, Colonel Fountain had no court papers—I mean no official documents—in his possession when he left Lincoln."

"And for the indictments brought against the defendants by the grand jury, what happened when they came to trial?"

"They were dismissed."

"Did the prosecution of these cases depend in any manner upon Colonel Fountain?"

Catron roars, "Objection!"

Judge Parker calls, "Overruled! Witness will answer the question."

Wharton looks at the jury. "It did not."

Fall turns back to the defense table. "No further questions for this witness at this time, Your Honor."

"Cross-examination, Mr. Childers?"

Childers stays seated. "When was Les Dow murdered? Was it before or after the next succeeding term of court?"

Fall yells, "Objection!"

"Overruled! Witness will answer the question."

"I believe Mr. Dow was killed before the next succeeding term of court."

Childers looks at the jury and nods. "Thank you. No more questions, Your Honor."

Judge Parker turns to the defense table. "Call your next witness, Mr. Fall."

"The defense calls John H. May."

May is a rancher. He testifies to the good character and neighborliness of Lee and the others but doesn't say anything that adds to the relevant body of evidence. When May finishes, Judge Parker calls for a dinner recess with the afternoon session to begin at two o'clock. Hughes and I head for a bar where we can have a beer for lunch and write.

Chapter 42
Print Rhode Takes the Stand, 9 June 1899

My mind is filled with last night's supper with Persia. The smell of her, the flush of her cheeks, her wisdom. I can't concentrate when I write for thinking of her. My day feels incomplete when I don't see her. I think about what Hughes told me about men and women complementing and completing each other and wonder if Persia is the one to complement and complete me.

"Now, Mr. Fall—"

My consciousness drifts slowly back to the courtroom action. Albert Fall has called to the stand his brother, Phillip, who was a sheriff's deputy in Las Cruces when Lee came in after learning of the Fountain murders. Phillip testifies he told Lee he'd heard there were warrants out for Gililland, McNew, and Jack Tucker. He says he helped Lee try to find the warrants, but they were unsuccessful. His story is consistent with Lee's regarding their search for the warrants, except Lee claimed he'd heard there was a warrant for him, too, and that he had heard it from Joe Morgan. He says Sheriff Ascarate agreed to send him, along with Joe Morgan, Tom Tucker, Howard Ellis, and Lee, to Dog Canyon to search for the men and ask them to come in.

Phillip says they found Gililland and McNew at Dog Canyon and then went to Wildy Well looking for Jack Tucker. At Wildy, he says they found three deputies with a note from District Attorney Young saying the cases had been dismissed and there was no need for them to return to Las Cruces.

It's interesting to me that Phillip Fall's story doesn't quite match Oliver Lee's or Joe Morgan's testimony, and I wonder why.

Childers doesn't pursue the differences in their testimonies, and Phillip Fall is soon excused by Judge Parker. "Call your next witness, Mr. Fall."

Fall is staring at Llewellyn, sitting several rows back from the railing, when he says, "The defense calls A.P. Rhode."

The bailiff calls for A.P. Rhode. No one stirs. The bailiff calls for Rhode once more. There is still no response. Fall and Lee look over their shoulders. Fall frowns at first and then smiles. "Bailiff, make that Print Rhode."

The bailiff calls for Print Rhode, and there is motion from the backbenches. "Sorry! Thought you's after somebody else." There's a general chuckle in the courtroom. A short, stocky man stands and walks toward the rail. He wears a white shirt, leather vest, and a pair of new canvas pants. It's easy to see muscles rippling under his shirtsleeves, and broad shoulders keep the shirt's tight fit. He has the kinds of scars on his face I've seen on professional boxers.

Once sworn in, he nods and sits, easing back into the witness chair like he owns it. Fall, who is smoking a cigar, approaches and asks, "Where is your home, Mr. Rhode?"

"My home and place of business is my little ranch. It's 'bout ten miles from W.W. Cox's place."

"What is your relationship to Mr. Lee, the defendant?"

"We've known each other on a first name basis for a right good while. 'Bout a year ago, he married my sister Winnie. Reckon that makes us brothers-in-law. Old Oliver, he's a good man, a purty good boxer I'd say, and I'm proud Winnie took him for a husband."

Nodding, Fall takes another puff. "I see. Now were you at Mr. Cox's ranch on the eleventh of July, 1898?"

"Yes, sir. I was there, and so was several other neighbors,

helping W.W. brand stock."

"Did you see Mr. Lee and Mr. Gililland at that time?"

"Yes, sir. They helped out some and watched for a while. The shadows was gettin' long when they come ridin' up to the gate to leave. José Espalin and another of Garrett's deputies was there and seen 'em. They weren't tryin' to hide or nuthin', and Espalin knowed it. He come up to shake hands with 'em—just wanting to show 'em he weren't out to arrest 'em. They talked for maybe five minutes before Lee and Gililland rode off toward the east.

"Lee and Gililland was gone maybe ten or fifteen minutes when José come over and said there's somethin' he needed to tell Oliver, an' Jim and asked me to go with him to catch up with 'em. He's 'fraid if I didn't come, Lee might think he's chasing 'em an' either take off or fill 'im fulla lead. So I mounted up with him. We ain't rode but five minutes when he pulls up and says real reluctant like, 'Maybe I'd better not go.' I says, 'José you're worse than any woman I ever knowed about changin' your mind.' "

There's a ripple of laughter through the courtroom. Even Judge Parker smiles as he raps his gavel and calls for order.

Fall nods. "And then what happened?"

"Old José says, 'Look, Print, I'm Garrett's deputy, so I oughta be keepin' my mouth shut. But you ride on, and you tell him there's some men on the range with blood in their eye. He needs to be on the lookout.' So I said, 'Okay, I'll do her.' I caught up with Oliver and Jim after a while, an' I told 'em what José said. Ol' Oliver said they'd be careful."

Crossing his arms, Fall looks at the jury. "I see. What made you take *Señor* Espalin's warning so seriously that you'd chase after Mr. Lee and Mr. Gililland in the dark to tell them to watch out?"

Rhode scratches his chin and nods. "Well, for one thing, I

always thought old José was a straight talker, even if he did work for Garrett. We got along all right. Besides that, I'd talked to a feller shortly after Colonel Fountain and his little boy disappeared, and that feller was damn anxious to see Oliver Lee done in fer murderin' 'em. Knowing the feller like I did, I figured he's just passing gas. Ya know what I mean? Just lettin' off a little steam, but then W.W. found Jake Ryan sitting in the rocks with a thunder boomer, and from the tale he told W.W., I figured the gas done gone the other way."

Judge Parker has to gavel for order as the whole room laughs. When the laughter dies down, Fall continues. "And who was this fellow you had been talking to, the one you thought was . . . uh . . . just passing gas?"

"William Henry Harrison Llewellyn."

The courtroom is very still. I can see the Fountain brothers, sitting a row back from me, arms crossed, their faces scowling in disgust.

Still looking at the jury, Fall takes another puff on his cigar. "Is it not true that Mr. Llewellyn said to you that 'there was nothing he would not stoop to, to connect Lee with this case'?"

The jury's attention is focused solely on Rhode, who slowly nods. "Yes, sir, that's about it, word for word."

Fall looks at Catron. "No further questions of Mr. Rhode at this time, Your Honor."

"Your witness, Mr. Childers."

Childers takes his notes, his brow furrowed. "Mr. Rhode, you don't normally associate with Major Llewellyn, do you?"

"No, sir. Don't reckon neither one of us is very sociable. He's some damned old attorney, so I reckon he has to 'sociate with lots of fellers he don't like and who don't like him, but he don't 'sociate with me, 'cept if we see one another on the street we'll speak."

There are chuckles and nods throughout the courtroom.

"Well, if you don't normally talk with Major Llewellyn, when did you have the conversation to which you referred in your answer to Mr. Fall's question?"

Rhode scratches his chin. "Well, sir, let me see. It was a week or two after the Fountains disappeared. I seen some fellers camped out around an old adobe house next to the Las Cruces road down in the flats. They was maybe a couple of miles from my place, so I rode over to find who they was and what they was up to. Turned out it was Major Llewellyn and his posse. There was maybe five or six of 'em, and they was keeping low in the brush like they was tryin' not to be seen from the road. The major, he come ridin' out to meet me. That there is when me an' the major had our talk."

There is a long pause. Childers appears to be waiting for Rhode to go on, but Rhode is silent.

"What did Major Llewellyn have to say?"

"Oh, we passed the time of day a little. Llewellyn told me he's ridin' back to Cruces to see if Lee was in town. They'd stopped there and sent a man on who was supposed to watch Lee, and when Lee started out, the feller was supposed to come out ahead of him and tell the posse he was comin'. He said they was gonna lay there by them walls where they'd hid their horses and kill Lee when he came out. I asked him how long they'd been waitin' to get him, an' he said a better part of a day when the lookout came out from Cruces and told 'em Lee had gone out the other way.

"The major, he was hot to get Lee. Said his posse had tracked the horses that had stopped and surrounded the Fountain wagon all the way across the Jarillas to Lee's ranch at Dog Canyon. He said Lee and his boys was murderin' bastards, an' he wouldn't stop at anything to do those fellers. He pointed toward a wagon he had with 'em an' said there was dynamite in it. They was about to go back to Lee's place and take care of business. If there was any women in the house, he'd invite 'em out. If they didn't come out, then he's gonna throw the dynamite in an' blow 'em all up.

"I sat a spell with them fellers. Major Llewellyn was having a hard time makin' up his mind 'xactly what he's gonna do. One of the posse, Fowler, was gettin' tired of freezin' out in the wind. He says to Llewellyn, 'If you're going to do this job, you better get to it. If you ain't, I'm a-goin' on back to town.' I decided they had to figure out what they was gonna do, so I told 'em *adios* and rode on back home.

"Later that evenin' the posse come ridin' up to my place. Me an' Mrs. Rhode had done had supper, but there's a big pot o' coffee on the stove, so I told 'em to make a fire in the yard and offered 'em some. They's glad to get it. Major Llewellyn come in the house for a while. Said he's gettin' old and the cold was a-soakin' into his bones. Damned if he didn't say again, right there in front of Mrs. Rhode, an' I didn't appreciate it one damn bit, how he was gonna use his dynamite to blow up that murderin' bastard Lee and his womenfolk, if need be, in his own house."

About two-thirds of the courtroom spectators cheer when they hear this revelation of new evidence that Llewellyn and the Republicans are out to get Lee in the worst way. Judge Parker pounds his gavel and threatens to have the bailiffs empty the courtroom of spectators. With that, the cheers fall off quickly, but the smiles stay. Lee keeps a poker face, but I see him look at Fall a couple of times as if to say, *We told 'em, didn't we?*

Childers paces back and forth in front of Rhode. "Now, Mr. Rhode, did Mr. Llewellyn seem to have possession of his senses that day, the day he did all the talking?"

Rhode looks at Childers and shrugs. "He had 'bout as much senses as he ever had, I guess."

That riposte brings the house down. Judge Parker covers his

brow with his hand and looks at his desk. I can see his shoulders shaking. Fall laughs and slaps his knee. Even Lee smiles. Catron is the only one who isn't smiling. He sits with his arms crossed, giving Rhode a reptilian stare. Judge Parker raps for order and tells Childers to continue.

"Returning to the time when you say *Señor* Espalin was at the Cox ranch and asked you to give Lee and Gililland a warning, can you tell us on what evening that was?"

"Why, yes, sir, that'd be the night before the rumpus."

"The night before the rumpus? Can you define *rumpus* for the court, Mr. Rhode?"

Even from where I sit, I can see the mischief in Rhode's eyes. "Why, shore, be glad to. Rumpus is when Pat Garrett pert near had his rump shot clean off by Oliver Lee, and us was glad to hear about it. Rumpus!"

There is so much laughter in the courtroom I see some men wiping tears from their eyes. Childers concentrates on a window, I think to keep from smiling. Lee manages to keep a straight face, but Gililland is wiping his eyes. Judge Parker raps again for order, and the room soon returns to a low rustle of people shifting in their seats.

Childers looks at Judge Parker and shrugs his shoulders in defeat. "No more questions of this witness, Your Honor."

"Any redirect, Mr. Fall?"

"No, Your Honor."

"The witness is excused. Call your next witness, Mr. Fall."

Fall looks at the jury. "Your Honor, the defense rests."

Judge Parker looks at his watch. "Gentlemen, it is now nearly four o'clock. Mr. Childers, you have until seven-thirty this evening to prepare your rebuttal. Court is adjourned."

Chapter 43
The Prosecution Rebuttal, 9–10 June 1899

I slide into the seat next to Hughes just as Childers calls David Sutherland, his first rebuttal witness. Sutherland swears Dan Fitchett told him he went to Dog Canyon Ranch on the morning, not the evening, of 1 February 1896, and that Lee was setting out grapevines at the time. Sutherland also says Fitchett told him he didn't believe those boys were guilty because he had seen them in the morning at Lee's ranch.

The next witness, Pat Garrett, testifies that a conversation he had with Dan Fitchett was consistent with Sutherland's testimony. Tom Branigan, testifying next, claims that during the first half of February, 1896, he had camped in the flats about two miles from Print Rhode's house. Members of the camp included Carl Clausen, William Llewellyn, Jack and Tom Fountain, Ben Williams, and Fowler. Branigan claims he was at the camp most of the time and didn't see Rhode at the camp, but likely would have if he had come in at any time. He says he didn't hear, as Rhode claimed, Fowler tell Llewellyn, "If you're going to do this job you had better get to it, or I'm going back to town." Branigan grins when he says the group, which he refuses to call a posse, never put their horses in an adobe enclosure or hid in wait to kill Lee. He says they stopped at Rhode's house on the way to Las Cruces, and he was with Llewellyn all the time they were there. He says Llewellyn never went in the house or had any conversation with Rhode. Branigan says he is positive none of the conversation Rhode described could have taken place without him knowing about it.

I glance toward the back of the courtroom. Print Rhode sits in the same seat he had before he testified. His arms are crossed as he shakes his head.

Branigan is followed by Carl Clausen, who gives nearly the same testimony, except he more vigorously denies that Rhode ever came to their camp and that Llewellyn didn't talk to Rhode at his house. Clausen claims he and Llewellyn were side by side the entire time they were at Print Rhode's house. According to Clausen, the only person who went in Print Rhode's house was Ben Williams.

Fall requests that he cross-examine Clausen and is allowed to proceed. He paces up close to Clausen but looks at the jury. "The man Print Rhode said Llewellyn sent into Las Cruces to spy out Oliver Lee and give the camp warning Lee was on the way was Luis Herrera. Didn't Herrera have a note for Oscar Lohman asking where Lee was? And did not Lohman answer that Lee had gone out another way?"

Clausen's head makes quick, short shakes. "No!"

Fall smiles. "Did Tom Fountain leave the camp at any time you were there?"

Clausen lifts his jaw. "I don't think so, but he may have."

Fall takes a long draw on his cigar and casually blows it toward the ceiling. "Well, sir, you testified without doubt that Rhode never came into your camp at any time. Yet you are uncertain as to whether Tom Fountain went or not? How can you be so positive in one case and unsure in the other?"

Clausen shifts in his chair and crosses his arms. "Well, I might not have been at the camp the entire time. But I'm certain Rhode was never there!"

Fall nods knowingly at the jury. "No more questions, Your Honor."

Judge Parker looks at his watch. "Gentlemen, it's nearly ten o'clock. We'll resume at eight-thirty tomorrow morning. Court is adjourned."

Childers calls Jack Fountain as his next rebuttal witness. Jack, looking his usual earnest self, agrees with the rebuttal testimony of Branigan and Clausen.

Asked if he wants to cross-examine, Fall sits relaxed in his chair, ruffles his hair, and smiles at Jack. "Just so we're all clear, Jack, Mr. Clausen married one of your sisters, correct?"

"Yes sir."

"You are on a five hundred dollar bond as your assurance that you won't attack me for the murder of your father and brother, correct?"

"Yes, sir."

"And, in the Branigan camp, you always, I say always, had Llewellyn in sight—you were never away from camp gathering fire materials, never away from camp answering nature's calls? You always, always had Llewellyn within your sight?"

Jack looks at his hands folded in his lap. "Well, no . . . I mean . . ."

"No more questions for this witness, Your Honor."

Judge Parker excuses Jack, who frowns at Fall. José Espalin is called to the stand. Espalin's gaze nervously flicks about the room until Childers grabs his attention. "Now, Mr. Espalin, where were you late in the afternoon of 11 July 1898?"

"I was at the ranch of *Señor* Cox with another deputy, Clint Llewellyn."

"Did you see Mr. Rhode, Lee, and Gililland there at the time?"

"*Sí, Señores* Lee and Gililland were there a little while after we came up. They speak with *Señor* Rhode and *Señor* Cox before they ride off toward the Jarillas."

"That evening did you tell Print Rhode you wanted him to

go with you to speak with Lee in order to warn him that men were out to kill him or some such thing?"

"No, *señor.* I did not say this."

"You are certain of this, *Señor* Espalin?"

"*Sí, señor,* of this I am certain."

"No more questions for this witness, Your Honor."

Judge Parker gives Fall his chance at Espalin. Fall rubs his chin as he stares at the man. "About three weeks ago, did you have a talk with Don Pino and José Armijo about Lee and Gililland and the Fountain case?"

Espalin looks toward the ceiling as though thinking. "*Sí,* I may have had such a talk."

"Did you not tell these gentlemen that you had planned to get on the stand and help Lee and his boys? But after the fight at Wildy Well, Tom Tucker called you a goddamn sneak and coward, so you were going to get on the stand and swear against them?"

Childers stands. "Objection!"

Judge Parker looks over his glasses at Fall. "Sustained."

Espalin apparently feels bound to answer, squinting as he looks at Fall. "No, I was told Tom Tucker said I was a coward. I said I believed Tucker was straight, and he did not say it."

"Objection!"

"Sustained."

Fall nods. "How much money did you get off that Negro you murdered at Fort Selden three years ago?"

"Objection!"

"Sustained. Mr. Fall, stick to the facts of this case."

"Yes, Your Honor. Tell us, *señor,* for whom did you work in July of 1898?"

Espalin relaxes. "In July, 1898, I was a deputy for Doña Ana County Sheriff, Pat Garrett."

"When you were at the Cox ranch the evening of 11 July

1898, in your capacity as a deputy sheriff of Doña Ana County, did you not say to Oliver Lee *'Cuidado!'* as a warning when he said goodbye?"

"No, *señor,* I did not say this."

"Well then, when Oliver Lee and James Gililland left the Cox ranch on the evening of 11 July 1898, what did you do?"

Espalin shrugs and looks away. "Deputy Llewellyn and me went to Sheriff Garrett's ranch and told him we had seen Lee and Gililland leaving *Señor* Cox's ranch. He asked which way they were headed. I told him they were riding east toward the Jarillas."

Fall nods. "What did Sheriff Garrett say when you told him this?"

Espalin smiles. "He shakes his fist and says, 'Now I have the bastards. They're headed straight for Wildy Well. Get Williams and Kearney. Lee's not getting away this time.' "

Fall smiles. "No more questions of this witness, Your Honor."

"Witness is excused. Call your next witness, Mr. Childers."

Childers calls three successive witnesses who are familiar with Lee's big, gray horse. His questions are filled with minutia about the size of the horse's rear feet relative to its front feet. It's not long before the attorneys, judge, and spectators are rubbing their brows in boredom.

As Childers begins to question the third witness with the same set of questions, Fall stands, smiling. "Your Honor, the defense concedes that its witness, Deputy Tom Tucker, misspoke when he stated that it appeared that Mr. Lee's gray horse had rear feet larger than its front feet."

Childers nods. "Very well. No more questions for this witness, Your Honor."

"Witness is excused. Call your next witness, Mr. Childers."

"Your Honor, the prosecution calls Jack Maxwell."

Maxwell returns to the stand looking as though he'd rather

be anyplace else in the world. Childers gives Maxwell a moment to settle himself and throws him a couple of easy questions. "Mr. Maxwell, how do you know the defense's witness, Bud Smith?"

"Bud Smith used to work for me over to my ranch."

"Did he work for you during February 1896?"

"Yes, sir."

"Does he work for you now?"

"No, sir. He left a couple of years ago to work another spread."

"Now, according to Mr. Smith, after you came home during the first week of February of 1896, you told him about your stay at Oliver Lee's ranch during the weekend of 1 February 1896, when you went over there to help with Lee's winter roundup. Is that correct?"

"Yes, sir. I said a thing or two about it while we's having coffee."

"What exactly did you tell Bud Smith at that time?"

"I don't remember the 'xact words, but it was somethin' like them boys was gonna catch it cause Colonel Fountain and the little boy was murdered. I said Lee and his boys comin' in late for supper that Saturday night looked kinda strange to me. I wondered then where they'd been. I seen them worn-out horses the next day and really started wondering."

"That was all you had to say to Bud Smith? Just that, or words to that effect?"

"Yes, sir, that's about it."

Childers nods to Judge Parker. "No more questions of this witness, Your Honor."

"Your witness, Mr. Fall."

Fall advances toward Maxwell, takes a long draw from his cigar, and blows the smoke directly at Maxwell.

"Mr. Maxwell, let's review your testimony. You claimed to me during cross-examination that you got to Dog Canyon Ranch around nine on the evening of 1 February 1896. Correct?"

"Yes, sir."

"Now that time of year, sunset is around five o'clock and good dark is by, oh, quarter of six, is that right?"

Maxwell's eyes seem a little glassy as looks at Fall. "Yes, sir."

"According to the stenographer's notes, you told Mr. Childers you got to Dog Canyon Ranch just before sundown or about five o'clock. Which is it, Mr. Maxwell, what you told me or Mr. Childers?"

"Well, I guess you confused me. It was just before sundown."

"So you had enough light to see the grapevines Lee and his boys planted?"

"Yes, I did. Told Mrs. Lee I'd shore like to have a few grapes when they started producing, and she said she'd be sure I got some."

"Was the soil still moist around the grapevines when you saw them?"

"Yes, sir."

"So they had been planted no later than an hour or two before."

"Objection. Witness has no knowledge of when the grapevines were planted."

Judge Parker nods. "Objection sustained."

Fall smiles. "Were a large number of vines planted, Mr. Maxwell?"

"Yes, sir, I seen several rows of 'em."

"So when you were talking to Bud Smith, you didn't mention Mrs. Lee was going to be sure she'd give you some of the fruit from those grapevines?"

Maxwell licks his lips and looks out the window. "Well, I probably said something about that when I talked to Bud."

"I see. Did Mrs. Lee tell you how those vines got in the ground?"

"She said Oliver and two or three of the other boys had planted 'em that afternoon."

"Did that impress you? I mean that's a lot of hard work—digging all those holes, filling them back in, packing water to them. It's not nearly as much fun as riding or wrangling horses."

"Yes, sir. It impressed me that there was a lot of labor went into plantin' them vines."

"Did you mention that to Bud Smith, too? That it took a lot of labor to plant the grapevines?"

Maxwell shrugs his shoulders. "I probably did say something like that to him."

Fall nods. "So you told Bud Smith that when you got into the Lee ranch just before sundown, you'd seen where a number of grapevines had been planted, Mrs. Lee promised to give you some of the fruit, and that it had taken a lot of work to plant the vines. Didn't you say to Smith that you didn't see how those boys could have had time to be out murdering the Fountains?"

Maxwell looks at his hands folded in his lap and mumbles, "Yes, sir, I probably had some such conversation."

Spectators in the courtroom are all shaking their heads. Maxwell is now the best witness Fall has.

"No more questions of this witness, Your Honor."

Judge Parker nods toward Maxwell. "Witness is excused. Call your next witness, Mr. Childers."

"Your Honor, we call Mr. Irving Wright."

Wright steps out of a row and walks, as if in a trance, toward the witness chair. Childers asks him several questions, but his answers don't relate to the questions. Finally, Childers throws up his hands. "Well, do you know anything about it at all?"

"No, sir."

"This witness concludes our rebuttal, Your Honor."

Judge Parker orders the bailiffs to sequester the jury while he hears arguments on his charge to the jury. I see a dark frown fill Fall's face and puzzled looks on the faces of the defendants.

Judge Parker rubs his smooth chin in thought. "Mr. Childers, the court would like to first hear yours, and then Mr. Fall's arguments on what my charge to the jury should include."

Childers stands. "Your Honor, the prosecution believes a conviction for first degree murder might be in error because there is a possibility that the defendants, lying in wait, were not there for the purpose of murder, but to steal papers or kidnap Colonel Fountain, and Colonel Fountain, realizing the impending attack, fired the first shot and was killed by the returned fire. The jury should have the option, therefore, if they are so moved, to award guilt for the lesser crime for which they think the defendants are guilty, and not be forced to award for the crime for which they might believe the defendants were not guilty."

Judge Parker takes a moment to write a note before he turns to Fall. "An opinion on the charge, Mr. Fall?"

Fall stands. "Your Honor, the prosecution has not explored the various possible constructs of the evidence. There is insufficient evidence to do that. There has been only idle speculation by members of the various posses on the meaning of tracks or who wore the boots that made the prints they claim to have measured. The prosecution's evidence shows, if it shows anything at all, a cold-blooded, cowardly murder that deserves the ultimate punishment. This case is about the murder of an eight-year-old child, and the defendants are either guilty of outrageous murder, or they are not guilty. First-degree murder must be the charge to the jury."

Judge Parker stares at his notes for a moment. "Mr. Fall, the facts are open to several interpretations, and it must be left to the jury to decide. I will charge on all three degrees of murder, since under the New Mexico legal code, there is no manslaughter. The court will take a fifteen-minute recess and begin closing arguments."

Chapter 44
Closing Arguments Begin, 10 June 1899

R.P. Barnes's closing argument for the prosecution goes through the chain of evidence, piece by piece. The general thrust of his review is that, while some coincidences might be explained away, the totality of the evidence makes it certain the defendants murdered Henry Fountain. His presentation is pretentious and overweening, filled with quotations from Dickens's *The Pickwick Papers,* thus driving the translator crazy and leaving the jury without a drop of substance.

He comes to Mary Lee's testimony, testimony the prosecution did not dare rebut when she was on the stand. He dances around calling her a liar, but says, to the consternation of the interpreter, that in her testimony she had "laid a wreath of maternal duty on the altar of maternal love." The interpreter throws up his hands and asks Barnes to speak plainly. It takes two tries before the translator finally tells the jury that Barnes is suggesting Mrs. Lee lied to protect her son because she must have thought it was her motherly duty. I see several members of the jury raise their eyebrows and shake their heads when what Barnes is trying to say becomes clear.

To everyone's relief, Barnes concludes his argument. Judge Parker looks at his watch. "Gentlemen, it's close to the noon hour. We will take a dinner recess and resume court at two o'clock this afternoon. Court is adjourned." Hughes and I head for our usual bar to have a beer and catch up on our writing.

★ ★ ★ ★ ★

Judge Parker says, "Mister Fall, your first closing argument."

Harvey Fergusson rounds the defense table to stand in front of the jury. Unlike Barnes, his style is smooth, easy to follow. He speaks directly to the jury, even calling one of them by name. Fergusson's strategy is to rebut the prosecution witnesses, discredit them one by one, thus showing the weakness of the prosecution's case. He points out that the blood spot found by the posse cannot be related to Henry Fountain. The prosecution's own witness cannot prove the blood spot is even human blood. "You must be certain, not only that circumstances show these defendants committed a crime at the place and time charged in the indictment, but that a crime was committed. Does any of the evidence submitted show the crime beyond a reasonable doubt?

"Albert J. Fountain, a soul of honor, has not lent himself to the work of Llewellyn and Branigan. He testified that, to the best of his knowledge and belief, the tracks of a boy around the campfire were those of his little brother and were naturally made. Albert Fountain examined the tracks of the buggy and the horses with minute care, but he swore he saw no blood spot. Why was there no blood on the buckboard? Who drove the buckboard after the three men had surrounded the vehicle and Fountain had been killed? Did the boy drive? Then was he dead? Was the boy alive at the campfire where his tracks were found? Might he not have been abducted? The mail driver testified the blood was partly fresh nine days after the disappearance. Did he not see it soon after it had been spilled there? Was it there at all the day after the disappearance? There is nothing to show it was."

Fergusson attacks the track measurements, saying it's impossible to identify a man by his boot tracks in the sand. He pointed to the problems in interpreting the horse tracks around the buggy. The prosecution could not even show the tracks were made at the same time as the buggy tracks. He suggests it had taken very little for the searching posse to confirm their suspicions using the tracks.

Judge Parker holds out his hand, indicating Fergusson should pause. "Mr. Fergusson, it is now five o'clock. If you're at a good stopping point, we'll take our supper break and resume at seven."

Fergusson nods. "Thank you, Your Honor."

A breeze off the mountains makes the late afternoon air comfortable as Hughes and I walk down Eleanora Street toward the Ocean Grove for our supper. At Tom Ying's, there's already a crowd waiting around the door for a seat. Persia sees me, waves, and I point around to the back steps and raise my brows. She nods. Hughes offers to find us a place in a little cantina up the street. I tell him I won't be long, but not to wait for me.

I sit on the kitchen's back steps and wait. In five minutes, the screen door creaks open, and Persia sits down and leans against my shoulder. She's red in the face, and wisps of hair stick out of the bun on top of her head. "Sorry I'm so busy, but it's Saturday night. How did things go in court today?"

"It looks like the jury will be allowed to choose between three degrees of murder, the third being the equivalent to manslaughter. The attorneys are in closing arguments. I have to be back in court by seven, and it'll probably be very late before we finish. I was wondering if we might take a ride together some time tomorrow. I want very much to be alone with you for a while and tell you some things I've learned. Can we do that?"

She makes a face. "I suppose. I'll arrange to borrow some horses from Sadie. Maybe we can take an early evening ride up the Percha around four o'clock or so. How's that?"

"Perfect! I'll meet you at the Orchard."

She gives me a little hug before going back to work. I find Hughes up the street in a cantina. By the time we finish our enchiladas and beer, it's nearly time for court to start again.

The night session begins promptly at seven. Standing in front of the jury, Fergusson looks at each juror momentarily. "Gentlemen of the jury, I ask you to consider, what evidence there is against James Gililland. Who has testified against him? Nobody but Riley Baker and the Goulds, father and son, personal enemies of Gililland. They only testified as to an alleged remark that may have referred to some person other than Colonel Fountain. Even if it did refer to Colonel Fountain, it would fit many different interpretations in addition to the one forced upon it by the prosecution. Will you hang a man because three irresponsible men, two of them jailbirds, say the defendant said something that might be construed as self-incriminating?

"The prosecution had to get three such men to testify against Gililland because there were three tracks to fill and, since Lee and McNew did not fill the bill, they picked out Gililland. It was true those men were all indicted at that term of court, but there were fifteen or twenty indicted at the same time. Why did they pick out Gililland? Even if it had been shown Colonel Fountain had never prosecuted anyone else other than the defendants, would that have been sufficient motive for this heinous crime? As a matter of fact, this alleged motive applies to too many men in the territory, as we all know. There must be grave doubt in your minds as to the guilt of these defendants. The jury has got to be certain beyond a reasonable doubt that these two men killed little Henry Fountain at the time and place specified in the indictment. Can you say that?

"I am sorry to say that there is evidently a great deal of political and personal animus in this case. The defense did not bring it in. I was staggered by the showing made here of the state of affairs in Doña Ana County. Is it any wonder Lee was afraid to surrender to a posse under Garrett and of which Ben Williams was a member? The warrants issued by a justice of the peace were withdrawn, and, notwithstanding that, there had been four sessions of the grand jury where no regular warrant was issued for these men, but a bench warrant was issued and given into the hands of a militia company under Major Llewellyn, a fierce personal enemy of the defendants.

"Why was the sheriff ignored? The defendants resisted arrest simply to make sure they would not have to surrender to their personal enemies, possibly at imminent risk to their own lives, in order to get a fair trial. They finally made arrangements with the governor of the territory that they would be protected from violence, and the mad dog, Ben Williams, would be muzzled and kept out of the way.

"In Doña Ana County, there was a fearful state of affairs. The newspapers there were practically advocating mob violence against these defendants. In view of all the evidence, the jury must decide whether the existing state of affairs warranted Lee and Gililland wanting to keep out of the way of that mob.

"Sheriff Garrett, by his evidence that Kearney fired the first shot in the fight in July 1898, lifts all burden from Lee for the killing of Kearney. It has been shown here that Lee and Gililland were not given a fair chance to surrender. They were not given to understand that the men firing on them were officers of the law, armed with proper papers—instead they were fired on while they were asleep. Sheriff Garrett has proved himself an honorable man, but he did not appoint honorable men as his deputies. Why was it necessary for him to appoint Ben Williams, that 'maniac on the subject of killing,' and other thoroughly bad men on his posse, like this fellow Espalin, when there were so many good citizens in Doña Ana County who would have been willing to serve on the posse?

"I believe the death of Kearney should be laid not at the door of Lee but on the mad cry for mob violence and the outrageous persecution of these men in Doña Ana County that persistently has been raised since 1896.

"I salute the courage and tenacity of the defendant's lead attorney, Mr. Albert Fall, in the face of personal attacks by the prosecution. The prosecution's attempt to bring Mr. Fall into the case has resulted merely in showing the animus in the case more clearly. Everything demonstrated in this courtroom has shown Attorney Fall has been faithful to his client, friend, and business associate through thick and thin. Sheriff Garrett has testified he was told when he first came to Las Cruces that 'Fall was one of the men they were after.' I strongly believe a not-guilty verdict will set things right for Mr. Fall and set the stamp it deserves upon all this rioting and lawlessness tearing Doña Ana County apart.

"I'm willing now to give my client's case into your hands. Before you find the defendants guilty, you must be certain, beyond a reasonable doubt, that they killed Henry Fountain. No fair-minded man could see it. I am certain there can be no conviction." Fergusson then turns and says, "Your Honor, this concludes my remarks."

Judge Parker looks at his watch. "Gentlemen it's getting late. This court stands in recess until half past eight Monday morning."

Chapter 45
Bill McNew Interview, 11 June 1899

I have a drink with Hughes at the Union bar before heading to the Ocean Grove to write another story for my editor in the hope he won't fire me before I quit. It's ten o'clock when I enter the soft glow of the porch lantern, pull open the door, and start down the dark, quiet hall. On Main Street, a raucous Saturday night filled with miners, cowboys, and businessmen having a good time is in full swing.

In my room, I pull off my vest and shirt and throw open the window to let in the night sounds and cool air. Using the washstand as a desk, I write a summary of what I've learned in the last few days. As I try to fit all the pieces together, I realize the pivotal point in the conflict between the Republicans and the Democrats is the range war of 1894 between Lee and the Blue Water Company. It was the source of the confrontations between Lee and the city-based businessmen trying to make a profit with their big cattle companies, the cattleman's association that organized the big operators, and between McNew and Lee and Les Dow. Not a shot was fired, yet it seems to be a major reason Lee and his men stayed on guard around strangers on the free range in 1896. I decide to interview Lee once more and get his view of what happened when he confronted the Blue Water Company in 1894. I know that tomorrow morning Lee's breakfast visitors, his mother and the McNews, will probably attend the church less than a block from the jail. While they're in church, I should have time for an interview.

At midmorning, the church bell rings. Grabbing my notepad and pen, I puff up the hill in a brisk walk to the jail. At the jail, Bill McNew sits on the fill wall between the jail and the courthouse, whittling with his Barlow and waiting for his women and children to come back from church. The outside guard, usually Gene Rhodes, is nowhere to be seen.

McNew's ice-blue eyes study me as I approach. His ten-mile stare is enough to make anyone think twice before approaching him.

"Mr. McNew?"

"You came to the right place."

I hand him my business card. "My name is Quentin Peach. I'm a reporter doing background stories on the trial for the *San Francisco Examiner.* Your name is often associated with Mr. Lee and Mr. Gililland. I understand Sheriff Garrett held you in the Las Cruces jail for nearly a year. I'd like to write a story on what happened from your point of view. I've done a couple of interviews with Mr. Lee, and I think he'll vouch that I'll write my stories without twisting your words."

He continues to look me over. "Yeah, I remember seeing you in court. Oliver and Jim told me you talked to 'em a couple of times."

"Yes, sir, I did. I hope to talk to them again later today."

"I reckon if they'll talk to you, I will, too. What you write better be true. Might get ugly if it ain't. We on the same page here?"

"Yes, sir."

"All right. What do you want to know?"

"I understand Sheriff Garrett arrested you in Las Cruces in early April of last year. How'd that happen?"

McNew folds his Barlow and pockets it and his carving. Pushing back his hat, he stares toward the Black Range. "The grand jury was meetin' in Las Cruces the end of March in '98. It'd been over two years since the Fountains disappeared. Garrett had been on the case for about two years, and things were quiet. Bryan, the district attorney, told Fall that Garrett was ready to present his evidence to the grand jury for indictments in the Fountain disappearance. Since Lee and several of us associated with him were suspects, Fall told Bryan he'd get us to come into town to answer any questions the grand jury might have for us. Bryan said he thought that was a good idea. End of March rolls around, and Lee, Gililland, Carr, me, and a couple of others saddle up and ride sixty miles into Las Cruces.

"We waited around the courthouse for three or four days. There were no requests from the grand jury for us to answer questions. The grand jury adjourned for that term's session. Fall came out, said they looked at Garrett's evidence, and decided there wasn't enough to whip a yellow dog, much less issue an indictment against anybody for the Fountain murders. Our names weren't even mentioned."

"I guess you were relieved."

"Yep, sure was. I had a pregnant wife with three young children on a new spread up on the edge of the Sacramentos and needed to get back. I had stock that needed tending and range to look after, so outfits like Blue Water didn't come in with some underhanded trick to try and drive us off. All of us did. Main reason we came in for the grand jury was so, if we were indicted, we could post a bond and get on back home to take care of business. When Fall told us we didn't even have to post a bond, we felt like a black cloud that'd been hanging over us for two years was finally gone.

"Oliver was all the time working on new range deals down in El Paso, and Jim wanted to let off steam in a big way, so Oliver changed clothes over in Henry Stoe's store, and they caught a train down to El Paso. Carr and me, we wanted to get back home as soon as we could. There had been rumors about Williams and others planning to ambush us, so we decided to wait around in Las Cruces until it got dark before we traveled. We wandered around, looking in the stores. I thought I'd try to find some little presents for Nettie and the kids before I left.

"I remember I was looking in a store window at some dolls with china heads and fancy little dresses, when I saw the reflection of Pat Garrett and two deputies with shotguns behind us. He says, 'Hands up, boys, you're going to jail.' We weren't packing any weapons because of the city ordinance against it, so it was easy for him to arrest us. Our hands went up, nice and proper.

"I thought there must be some mistake. I said, 'Who are you after, Sheriff?'

" 'You, McNew, and Carr. I know Lee and Gililland have already run off and ain't in town.'

" 'What are you arresting us for? We ain't done anything. The grand jury didn't even mention our names when it finished today.'

"Garrett says through clenched teeth, 'Those boys on the grand jury ain't got much spine, and Fall has 'em under his thumb. I got a bench warrant from Judge Parker after the grand jury was done. Your killing days are over, McNew. Put the cuffs on 'em, boys. You fellows know where the jail is. Now get out there in the street and start walking. This town needs to see there's justice being done. I'll get Lee and Gililland soon enough.'

"It was embarrassing to walk down Main Street like that, but it was hell not to be able to get back home to my family. Since the grand jury hadn't brought any charges against us, I figured Fall would have us out of jail in a day or two. I was worried about Oliver and Jim—that they'd come back and Garrett and those deputies would do 'em before they had a chance to defend themselves. Jim went on home from El Paso. Oliver came back on the train, walked down the street big as you please, and picked up his clothes at Henry Stoes. Seemed like he was just daring Garrett to come after him. The whole town was speculating about why Garrett didn't try to arrest Oliver then. Most of them thought he was afraid of him, but others argued that Garrett just didn't want lead flying where innocent bystanders might get killed."

I flip a page in my notebook and ask, "What do think, Mr. McNew? Was Pat Garrett afraid to go after Oliver Lee?"

"I think Garrett was playing it cautious. He didn't want anybody killed in Cruces. But the rest of the time? Look at all the times Garrett let things waddle along until Wildy Well. He flat wasn't gonna face Lee head on. Knowin' Lee, I can't say as I blame him. I'd'a been real careful too, if I's in his shoes."

"That sounds like an honest assessment. What happened next?"

"Henry Stoes came by and visited us a couple of days later. He said Oliver told him, 'Pat Garrett will shoot me in the back if he ever arrests me, and he'll claim it was self-defense. I won't let them take me that way.'

"No sooner did Oliver get home than a ten-man posse from Garrett showed up. Oliver was standing on his porch, putting on his gloves. He had on his pistol, and he eyed each one of them. There wasn't a man among 'em made a move, and I'd bet half of 'em was peeing their pants. Oliver didn't say a word. He just turned, walked inside, and they sat there with their mouths open. Pretty soon Tom Tucker came out—old Tom, I bet he's grinnin' like a gut-eatin' dog—and said, 'Oliver ain't home! Ya'll git!' One of the posse members rode up and handed

Tom a note. It was from Fall, and it said Oliver was wanted in town.

"Next day, Oliver was in El Paso and sent word to Fall that if the court would fix him a reasonable bond, he'd come to Las Cruces by himself. However, he said he didn't propose to be taken to Las Cruces and put in jail for an indefinite period without a trial, and that's almost exactly what he told me later. Guess he knew what happened to me and Carr.

"So Lee wasn't there a week after Garrett arrested us, when we attended our pretrial hearing to determine if there was enough evidence for a trial. Fall figured if he could beat the prosecution at the pretrial hearing, we'd be home free and them damnable Republicans would leave us alone. If he didn't, we was gonna be in for a long, tough fight. So Fall brought out his best firepower. He got Judge Warren out of Albuquerque and the Socorro D.A., Daugherty, to help him."

I hold up my hand to interrupt him and ask, "The same Daugherty who's helping Fall now?"

"Yeah, one and the same. Daugherty resigned his job up in Socorro to work on the case because he figured he'd have work for a right good while. Events proved him right. The Republicans brought in their big guns, too. Bryan brought in Childers and Catron to help counter Warren and Daugherty.

"They went at it for six days, and just about ever' witness you've seen here in Hillsboro was at the hearing. That good-for-nothing Maxwell told the same lies he's told in this trial, and he even admitted that he was promised a share of the ten thousand dollar reward for his evidence. When it was all said and done, Fall moved that me and Carr be discharged on grounds of insufficient evidence.

"Parker ruled there wasn't enough evidence against Carr, but there was against me, and said I had to go back to jail and he wouldn't let me out on bond. That there was exactly what Lee was afraid of, and he got real careful where he went after that, especially when he found out a new posse of sheriff's deputies, made up of men from the Republican militia company and led by Van Patten, was coming after him."

"So you were in the Las Cruces jail for nearly a year?"

"Over a year."

"Tom Tucker told me a bench warrant is only good for one cycle of the grand jury, and if they haven't considered the case against you by then, they have to let you go. Over how many grand jury cycles were you held?"

"Four!"

"Four? So they kept you in jail illegally for over nine months. Why did they do that to you? That's not justice."

McNew takes the piece of juniper he'd been whittling out of his pocket and starts using his Barlow. "No, it sure as hell ain't. It was a sorry thing to do. I'll never forgive Garrett for stealing a year of my life, and then the Republicans wouldn't even give me a trial. They wanted to keep me in jail for another three months on a continuance."

I can only shake my head. McNew stops shaping the piece of juniper and looks over toward the Black Range. He meditates for a moment and turns to me. "Garrett kept me in solitary the whole time I was in jail. I couldn't figure out why for a while. I was behaving myself, not causing any trouble. After a while, I realized the deputy who was the jailer treated me right decent, and then Garrett, growling and snapping like a cur dog, would pay me a visit once or twice a week. They's just tryin' to get me to spill what I knew to the only friend I had in jail. Trouble was, there wasn't anything to spill.

"They wouldn't give me nothing so I could write Nettie, and I got no mail from her. I just about went crazy, worrying about her being out on the ranch by herself with those three kids and pregnant and all. Only thing kept me from going over the edge was the certainty that Oliver and Mrs. Mary was lookin' after her as best they could.

"The deputy kept trying to convince me I could get out and go take care of Nettie and the ranch if I'd just give evidence against Oliver that he done the murder or was in on it. I wanted out of that stinking jail mighty bad, but I wasn't going to lie. Them keeping me in jail was wrong. Me lying about Oliver would have been worse. Two wrongs never made a right.

"I found out after my hearing in Silver City about a month ago that the Pinkerton agent Governor Thornton sent to find evidence against us had put the idea in Garrett's head that, if he got me away from Oliver and in jail for a while, he could break me, and then I'd run my mouth like a fresh spring. It was a dumb idea. I ain't gonna lie—and nobody needs to lie—for Oliver Lee. When Fall got me a hearing date in Silver City, I guess Garrett decided he wasn't gonna break me, and they started treatin' me better. They suddenly found the letters Nettie wrote to me, and some of 'em was nearly a year old. They finally gave me paper to write to her.

"After I was freed in Silver City, it would have given me the greatest pleasure to blow that sonovabitch Garrett to hell and gone for all the grief he brought my family that year. Nettie lost the baby a few days after it was born because a cold rain got in on it and gave it the fever. My daughter nearly died from a fever. False rumors were started—some even saying Nettie was unfaithful to me—to try and run the help off our spread. She had to work herself to death keeping the spread up with only a hired man helping her a couple of days a week. I was in hell, and so was she, all because of Garrett and the damned bench warrant he got with evidence the grand jury threw out."

"What kept you from taking revenge for what he did?"

"Nettie. She made me promise I wouldn't do anything that might put me even close to jail again if I could help it. Garrett can go his way. I'll go mine. Somebody will kill him one of these days, and good riddance."

I hear the sounds of women talking, men laughing, and children running down the gravel of Eleanora Street. We look back up the street to the group out in front of the church, shaking hands and saying their goodbyes. As his three children come running for their papa, McNew and I shake hands.

He grins and says, "Don't forget our deal Mr. Peach." I nod and leave them to their visit with Lee and Gililland.

Chapter 46
Third Oliver Lee Interview, 11 June 1899

Hoping to find Persia and buy her dinner, I walk back to the Ocean Grove. She's nowhere to be found. The energy that seemed to fill Hillsboro during the week is gone. The few who remain from the trial crowd relax in cool peace under the big cottonwoods. I step into the Union Hotel bar, order a beer for lunch, and find a table to write McNew's story.

Before I can get started, I feel a folded paper crackle in my coat pocket. It's the story Gene Rhodes wanted me to review. I feel guilty that I haven't read it and decide now is as good a time as any.

It's a good story about a cowboy on the run, who risks his freedom for a family in desperate need. There are numerous unexpected twists and turns, and it easily holds my interest. After Rhodes polishes it up and fixes a few rough spots, it'll be publication quality. Writing suggestions on the manuscript's edge, I make mostly complimentary remarks. I think Rhodes has potential to do outstanding work. Checking my watch, I see it's one-thirty, time to visit with Lee and Gililland.

When the jailer's door clanks open, Lee looks over the top of his newspaper, sees me, neatly folds it, and stands in his socked feet to greet me.

"I have a few more questions, if you don't mind."

"What else do you want to know?"

"Putting my notes together, trying to make some objective

sense out of what happened to the Fountains, who was involved, and why it happened, one piece of the puzzle keeps showing up, and from more than one interview. It's your Blue Water range war in '94 and probably into '95. There doesn't seem to have been a shot fired, yet you came out on top. It seems to have played a major role in why you were blamed for what happened to the Fountains. I'd like to hear your side of what went on in '94 and '95."

Lee sits back in his chair. "All right, but I don't see it playing a significant role in the Fountains' disappearance, but maybe I'll understand your point of view when we're done."

"First, what exactly was the Blue Water Company?"

"It's kind of complicated. I'll give you some background history, and maybe it'll be easier to understand. Some small investors and I started the Sacramento Cattle Company in '87. It owned a few ranches about twenty-five miles east of Lee's Well up around Weed and a few on the Basin side of the Sacramentos."

"Lee's Well, the place not far from Dog Canyon?"

"That's right. In '89 Nations and Hilton came up from Mexico and bought the Sacramento Cattle Company and its stock for about thirty-two thousand dollars."

"Nations and Hilton? I don't think I've heard of them. Who were they?"

"They were just businessmen new to the territory out to make a lot of money off all the free grass the government land offered. After the sale and paying off my other investors, I had the working capital I needed to expand. The Sacramento Cattle Company became Hilton and Company. It was mostly backed by big-time investors out of El Paso, people like the Irvin brothers, Andrew McDonald, Frank Garst, and a few in Las Cruces, like Rynerson and Wade. Llewellyn and Catron might have been part of it, but I never knew for sure.

"Hilton assumed the sale of the Sacramento Cattle Company included all the ranches on the western slope of the Sacramentos, but I hadn't intended to sell Horse Camp Ranch, which had a good water supply. You know the rule—control the water, no matter how small the ranch, and you control the surrounding range. However, the contract was so vague it could be interpreted that either I owned it or Hilton did. So in '90, McNew moved onto Horse Camp and started developing it—all perfectly legal because it was government land and subject to claim by homesteading. Hilton and Company didn't realize what McNew was doing until '92 and tried to run him off.

"I signed an affidavit that I wasn't a party to the lawsuit Hilton brought in August of that year to get McNew off Horse Camp. McNew swore he was making improvements to the property with the intent of homesteading. Fall was our attorney in that lawsuit, too. He argued that since it was public land, I couldn't possibly have sold it to anybody, and McNew had a right to homestead it. We went to court in Carlsbad at the end of November in '93. Nobody representing Hilton showed up and we . . . uh . . . McNew won without a court fight."

"Why didn't Hilton and Company show up?"

Lee shrugs and smiles. "Their attorney claimed he had the wrong court date on his calendar. The problem was not that they had lost a lot to me and McNew. They hadn't, even though Horse Camp is prime real estate. Their real problem was that all the little operators saw that if they used the legal system, they could stop Hilton and Company from muscling them off what was rightfully theirs. Needless to say, the Hilton boys thought McNew and I had gypped 'em out of Horse Camp Ranch. They were madder than a stepped-on rattlesnake. I didn't care. There wasn't a thing they could do about it legally. I figured after what they'd done, driving off all those other folks, they were owed losing one.

"Charlie Hilton was the general manager of Hilton and Company. He wasn't a bad sort, but his loyalty was to his investors. They had enough money so they could buy big herds of cattle or goats, run 'em on government-owned range where the little operators had their herds, and overgraze the range. Come fall, the little operators' stock had had so little to eat, they didn't bring nothing at the stockyards. Blue Water herds were so big that, even if they didn't fatten up, they still made a little money. Come spring, the overgrazed range couldn't support new stock, so the little operators had to move on to find better pastures and leave all the work they'd put into homesteading. Guess who moved in to claim the remains? Hilton and Company didn't care. They could afford to wait until the range came back. They took possession of the abandoned homesteads with the water, and then they bought more stock so they could run somebody else off. They kept doing this and buying up abandoned homesteads with good water until they did it once too often."

The pages in my notepad are filling quickly. I'm thinking, *Chief says in nearly all confrontations to follow the money. Wealthy men defending their fortunes often do regrettable things, and their enemies are always someone who stays their hand.* I ask, "What happened?"

"Three months after Hilton and Company lost their lawsuit against us, James Smith killed Hilton in '94, about the middle of February. Smith was a small operator who had won a permanent injunction, fair and square, to keep Hilton off his land. He warned Hilton to stay off his property or he'd kill him. Hilton didn't listen and went back on the property to pick up some fencing he'd left when the lawsuit started. Smith shot him for trespassing. Smith got away with it, too—claimed self-defense. About a month after Hilton was killed, the cattleman's association was formed, and Fountain was told to take care of the little operators who were mavericking the big operator herds down to nothing. Branding stray mavericks is one thing; changing brands and claiming they were mavericks is another. That's pure rustling, even if you are just trying to survive.

"After Hilton was killed, the Hilton and Company investors formed a new company and started a big spread with headquarters in Blue Water Canyon on the headwaters of the Sacramento River. As the crow flies, Blue Water is about thirty-five miles from Dog Canyon. I figured it was far enough away so we wouldn't be stepping in each other's tracks. I didn't pay much attention to what they were doing. They made Frank Garst the new manager and told him to make 'em some money."

"And did he make them money?"

Lee shakes his head and grins. "I don't know. I do know that, because of me, they lost a lot when he was in charge."

"How's that?"

"Well, sir, in '93, we were just coming off one of the worst droughts that part of the country had ever seen. It hadn't rained worth spit since '90, and I can tell you it was brutal. Lots of operations went broke. To a man, farmers around Tularosa were done in, and most of the little ranchers in the Basin were wiped out, too. I'd been smart, building water ditches out of the Sacramentos, digging wells, and rotating where we let our cattle graze, so McNew, Gililland, and me had made it through when others were going broke. Cattle over in Texas had gotten dirt cheap, and the fall monsoons in '93 brought so much rain, the grass and brush were taking hold and coming back in a big way. I figured it was time to buy more cattle.

"We bought us a nice-sized herd in Texas. The cattle weren't in the best of shape, but we didn't lose any driving 'em back. They took to that winter range like ducks to a pond. The herd from Texas, what we already had, and neighbors' stock was about all the range could support without overgrazing. There was plenty of water in '94. In fact, there was a big wet-weather lake over by Cox's Well close to the north end of the Jarillas, so we didn't even need to pump much well water that entire season.

"About the end of April of '94 we discovered that the Blue Water Company had moved five thousand head right in there with our stock. It was all perfectly legal, since it was government land that hadn't been homesteaded. But with our stock and a few neighbors, plus that extra five thousand head from Blue Water, the range was going to be overgrazed and wiped out by winter. I wrote Garst three letters over the course of a month and had a man deliver 'em directly to him. Garst never answered. By the end of May, he hadn't done anything. Not only that, after the cattle were in place, he tried to run four thousand goats out of pastures up in the Sacramentos down onto that same range. They were gonna wipe us out big time."

I make a silent whistle. "What did you do?"

"We got lucky. Word came the goats were heading our way. When the goat herders tried to bring their goats down out of the Sacramentos to the Basin range, some neighbors and I met 'em before they got there. We made them understand those goats weren't going anywhere, and blood was going to be spilled if they tried to move further down out of the Sacramentos, so they turned around and went back home. Garst didn't try that again.

"It was obvious the Blue Water boys had me in a hole with their herd competing with mine for the grass and brush, and they were going to keep turning the screws until I was wiped out, just like they'd done with so many others."

"So how did you manage to make Garst move his herd?"

"Off the record?"

I nod. "Off the record."

"There wasn't a lot we could do. If we rustled branded animals and tried to change brands, all they had to do was look at hides coming out of our herds, and Fountain would have us in prison in the blink of an eye." He shakes his head. "Rustlin' was never an option anyway.

"The thing that saved us was Blue Water's hurry to even the score when they thought McNew and I had gypped 'em with the Horse Camp Ranch lawsuit. A large part of the cattle in the herd Garst brought in to wipe us out were unbranded mavericks. Most of 'em weren't even following their mamas anymore and were pushing yearling age. Garst's cowboys were afraid of me and my boys. They flat refused to stay on the range long enough to brand their mavericks with us out on the range every day."

"Why was that?"

"You heard Childers ask me about killing Rodius and Coffelt during cross-examination?"

"Yeah?"

"I knew those boys. There were good cowboys. They got desperate and stole some of my stock, along with a few head from my neighbors, and headed for Mexico. McNew, Tom Tucker, and I caught up with 'em just before they could cross the Rio Grande east of El Paso. I told 'em they'd taken some of our stock and started to cut ours out of their little herd. They shot first and missed. McNew, Tucker, and me, we don't miss. We had a grand jury hearing down in El Paso, and the killings were ruled self-defense. We never went to trial, but that didn't make any difference to the rumor mill. I was fast and accurate with a gun. Those killings made my reputation as a deadly killer worse."

"So you took the mavericks that weren't branded and put your brand on them?"

"That's right. By the code everyone on the range lives by, it's all right to do that. We were careful never to take calves still running with their mothers. Garst sent a man or two down once a week to check on Blue Water's cattle. It didn't take long for 'em to figure out their herd was shrinking, and they didn't have a clue how.

"When Garst had lost about a thousand head, he moved his herd out of there. We even helped separate our stock from his and kissed 'em goodbye. The big stockholders in Blue Water were mighty angry. Garst told 'em rustlers were bleeding them dry. No doubt, he was telling them we were the rustlers—they just couldn't prove it. We'd outfoxed 'em twice by then.

"We kept a sharp eye out when we were out on the range. You just never knew when Garst might send a bunch for blood. By '95, there were three range detectives working for Fountain trying to get some evidence about what we'd done with Garst's herd. They even had Williams get an indictment down in El Paso, claiming we stole cattle in Texas from Irvin, Garst, and MacDonald, so the Rangers could come after us, but the Rangers didn't do anything with the indictment for over a year, and eventually it was dismissed."

"So you think that's why those businessmen were so anxious to prosecute you for Fountain's murder when there were more likely suspects?"

"Yeah, I think that's it. And you know what? They're gonna lose on this one, too. The real losers are the Fountain family, because these men are so blind to the facts and so anxious to nail me, they've missed getting the people who *are* responsible."

From outside come the sounds of a driver calling to his team and slapping the lines. In his cell, Gililland stands and looks out his window. "Looks like the stage is coming toward the jail. What's going on, Oliver?"

Lee frowns and shakes his head as he tries to see out his window. "I don't know. I can't see."

The stage stops. There are voices of a man talking to the guard outside the door, and then the soft, sweet voice of a woman. Lee's jaw drops as he shakes his head. "It can't be! I told her to stay in San Angelo until this is over."

Before I can ask to whom Lee is referring, Geronimo Sánchez steps inside the door. "*Señor* Lee! Your *mujer y niño* are here to see you! *Un momento, por favor!*"

Lee looks dumbfounded, smiling, shaking his head in disbelief.

Gililland is grinning with me as Sanchez steps through the doorway, followed by a young woman with a baby in her arms. He steps to Lee's cell door, unlocks it, and pulls the door back. Under his breath, he says, "*Señor* Lee, I know you will stay here, *sí?*" Lee nods, gratitude in his eyes as he holds his arms out for them. "Winnie! How in God's name?"

She and the baby are through the door and into his arms. "I had to come, Oliver! I had to come show you your son!"

Lee takes the baby, swings him high, and he giggles. The look on Lee's face is one of pure joy.

Winnie, tall and willowy, her light, brown hair framing her kind face and dark eyes, laughs. "We were the only ones on the stage. The driver said Mrs. Orchard would fire him if he didn't bring me directly here."

Bringing the boy down to his chest, Lee hugs his wife and kisses her. I stand to leave, giving Lee and Gililland a little salute of thanks.

Lee sees me and shakes his head. "Wait! Quent, let me introduce you to my wife, Winnie, and my son, Oliver, Jr. Winnie, this is Mr. Quentin Peach. He's a reporter for the *San Francisco Examiner,* one of the very few I trust enough to talk to."

Winnie nods her head at me. "It's a pleasure, Mr. Peach."

"The pleasure is all mine, Mrs. Lee. I'm delighted I got to meet you and Oliver, Jr. Now, if you'll excuse me, I know you have a lot of catching up to do."

They give me a little *adios* wave, and I'm out the door, filled with the pleasure of the moment and thinking about what joy men and women can bring each other.

CHAPTER 47
RIDE ALONG THE PERCHA

I walk down Eleanora Street in the dust behind the stage, heading for the Orchard corral. The look in Oliver Lee's eyes when Winnie walked through the jailer's door with his baby in her arms, a baby he's never seen, thanks to Pat Garrett, makes my entire trip to the Hillsboro trial worthwhile. Lee's eyes are an epiphany, a sudden clear view of exactly what Hughes Slater and I discussed over supper. I know now what I have to do. It is what I've been fantasizing about and losing sleep over since Tom Tucker and I rode out to bring Persia back.

When I turn the corner for the Orchard Hotel, it's a little after three, nearly an hour before Persia agreed to meet me. Two horses are tied to the Orchard's hitching post. One is the sturdy, beautiful black and white pinto I rode when Tom and I went after Persia, saddled with a working cowboy saddle. The other is a big, glossy black, maybe sixteen hands high, and carrying a polished side saddle with two pommels. Persia, wearing an elegant lady's riding dress, is sitting in Sadie's rocker on the front stoop of the hotel. Looking up from a newspaper, Persia smiles. "Hello, Mr. Peach! Glad you could drop in today."

"Why, Miss Persia Brown, you look delightful and elegant. Can we leave early?"

"We can. I was just relaxing while I waited for you. When I asked Sadie if we could borrow a couple of horses, she insisted I dress the part and loaned me her horse and saddle."

I tighten the cinches and help her mount. She's a little

awkward adjusting to sitting with one leg draped over the top pommel and bracing her left leg against the leaping horn. Seeing my frown, she says, "It's okay Quent, I'm just not used to riding aside rather than astride. I'll be fine after we ride a little while."

Nodding, I swing up on the pinto. "Where to, madam?"

"We'll go up Main Street toward Kingston and then take the river trail just outside of town. It'll be cool in the shade."

The trail along the Percha is peaceful. As we look up through the tree branches, the sky is a translucent, deep-water blue on the horizons. Relaxed in each other's company, saying little, we follow the trail upriver for a couple of miles toward the Black Range. Like a high-speed kinescope, my mind is playing imaginary scenes of what I'll do and say when we stop. My heart pounds with anxiety, wondering what will happen.

The sun is sliding toward the Black Range when we find a grassy spot by a big sycamore. I help Persia down, let the horses drink, and loosen the saddle cinches before tying them off to a branch in the shade, where they can nip off a little grass. Persia runs a hand over her shiny black hair, before sitting down by me. She smiles. "This is nice. It's too bad we couldn't have done this last Sunday. But then, I guess I wouldn't have come with you last Sunday if I hadn't been kidnapped." She shakes her head. "Life sure is full of surprises. It's going to be mighty hard to see you go after the jury brings in its verdict, but I wouldn't trade the last week for anything. You've given me wonderful memories."

We've said little about my leaving since we came back from San Marcial. Now all my fancy and romantic images of how things will happen fly out the window. Speechless, I can only nod while I dig around in the recesses of my mind, trying to find an opening that will keep me from looking like an idiot.

My conversation with Hughes Slater has been much on my mind after seeing Oliver and Winnie together. There will never be a better time to share it with her. "I met a new friend a couple of days before you were kidnapped."

She looks at me, mischief sparkling in her dark eyes. "Oh? Who is she?"

I roll my eyes and shake my head. "She is a he . . . Hughes D. Slater."

"What does the *D* stand for?"

"DeCourcy."

She grins. "I didn't know you were interested in *those* kinds of friends."

I puff in exasperation. "Come on! I'm trying to carry on a serious conversation here."

She puts her hand on my arm and looks in my eyes. "I'm sorry. I'm being mean, and you don't deserve me acting this way. Tell me about Mr. Slater."

My heart skips a few beats. "Well, he's a little older than I am, but, like me, he was raised in Virginia. Like me, he worked on a paper in New York, and then came out West. He's worked for about two years in northern Mexico, as an engineer constructing railroads, and has just started working for the *El Paso Herald.* He showed up in Hillsboro a couple of weeks ago to write about the trial. So you have two young men here from Virginia via New York, both reporters, and both thinking that the Lee trial is their first big chance to become a widely read reporter."

Persia smiles. "Well, you two certainly have a lot in common. I hope—"

I shake my head, "Wait. Listen to me for just a minute. The similarities in our backgrounds aren't why I'm telling you about Hughes Slater . . . I don't want to get on Sadie's stage when the trial is over and leave you."

Her eyes widen, and her fingers cover her mouth.

"Persia, my writing career is just starting. I'll forever be chasing stories far from home or working late into the night at my desk. If you stayed with me, you'd be living alone most of the time. I didn't think it was fair for any woman to be married to a man like that. I tried to tell you that back on the bridge that night a lifetime ago. Instead of proposing, I said I wanted you to stay with me in Hillsboro so we could enjoy a few days together, perhaps be lifelong friends, but I just couldn't make love to you and then leave, even if it was with the best of intentions. And I thank God you wouldn't let yourself be used like that."

Her dark, beautiful eyes are fixed on me. Her hand, still resting on my arm, gives me a reassuring squeeze. "Quent, where did you get such romantic ideas? Have you forgotten my father was a rancher? If I were a rancher's wife, I might not see you for days or months on end. I'd have to live with the thought every day that I might be standing at your grave the next day.

"Don't you see? Frontier women are raised to expect their men to work long hours and be gone for long times. And they're raised to look after themselves. A reporter will spend a lot more time with his wife than a rancher will. I just don't—"

I hold up my hand and shake my head. "Please hush and listen for a minute. Hughes was married in March. We had a long discussion over dinner about marriage and newspaper reporting. I asked him why he married when he knew he'd be all over the map as a reporter and gone from home more than he was there. He said men are never complete until they find the woman meant for them and he expected he'd be a much better writer married because he'd be a complete man. The same thing applied to his wife being a better woman because she'd be complete with him."

There are tears at the corners of Persia's wide eyes. I take a deep breath and plunge ahead. "I know now I'll never be a whole man without you. I hope you feel you'll never be a complete woman without me. Persia, I'm fumbling around here like an idiot trying to ask you to marry me. I hope and pray you will."

Her arms are around me, her cheek against by neck. My arms enfold her. She says nothing. My eyes track over our little shaded grove, the horses, the great wilderness around us, and the bright sky above us. I want to see every tree, mountain, cactus, bush, and every blade of grass. I know I'll never forget this place or this time, regardless of her answer.

She kisses me with her warm, heart-shaped lips. It is a sweet, longing kiss that fills my heart with the pure pleasure of life. Her arms around my shoulders, she leans back and looks in my eyes. "You're never going to be rid of me, Quentin Peach. I love you and have since I saw you that first morning in the Black Range Café."

I hold her and look in her eyes. "I have so little to offer you. I don't even have an engagement ring. When we get back to San Francisco, I may not even have a job."

Holding my face between her hands, she kisses me again. "You're all I could ever want, and your love is all I'll ever ask of you."

The last rays of sunshine are falling across the Black Range when we walk the horses into Hillsboro and over to the Orchard Hotel. Sadie sits in her rocker, sipping tea and reading a newspaper. Boots sits on a fence rail, watching horses nip at each other and play in the back corral, and J.W. is enjoying a pipe.

At the sound of our horses, Sadie looks over the top of her paper and laughs. "I'll be damned! Welcome back, you two. Climb down from them horses and visit a spell."

J.W. grins as he stands and gives us all a little salute off the brim of his hat.

Persia and I sit on a rock wall next to Sadie's rocker. "Well, Persia, how'd you like riding like a lady? Ain't Old Black Joe a treasure?"

Persia grins. "He's a fine horse." Persia blushes and nods, still smiling.

Sadie lifts an eyebrow at Persia. "What's going on here? What do you know that I don't?"

Persia grins from ear to ear. "Quent asked me to marry him, and I said yes."

Laughing in the pleasure of a happy time, the two women look me over. I can feel my ears warm and turn red as I try to manage a proud smile. I'm glad it's nearly dark.

Sadie, her eyes twinkling, says, "I knew it! First time I saw you two together, I knew it had to happen sooner than later. You'll make a wonderful couple, and J.W. and I wish you all the happiness in the world. Let's have supper at the Ocean Grove this evening." She opens her little brooch watch. "It's a little after six. Let's meet for supper at seven, what do you say?"

Persia looks at me, and I nod. "We'd love to, Sadie."

Sadie waves Boots over and says, "Boots, run down to Tom Ying's house and tell him that I'm asking him, as a special favor, to make one of his best suppers for four people, and that I need it in an hour. We're going to celebrate Miss Persia Brown's engagement to Mr. Quentin Peach. If he needs help firing up that stove of his, you stay and help. Got it?"

Chapter 48
Sadie's Gift

At the Ocean Grove, I pay the clerk six bits for a hot bath. Enjoying the luxury of hot water, I reflect on what I've done in asking Persia to marry me. The realization that it's the biggest step I've taken in my life and all the things it means starts to soak in. I'm thrilled and more than a little amazed at what I've done. I'm flummoxed about where I can find her a classy engagement ring. The mercantile stores in Hillsboro won't have the quality I want. Perhaps I can take Persia on the train next weekend to Las Cruces or El Paso and find one there. I want all her other suitors to know she's promised.

Back in my room, I try to think what we should do about a wedding. Marry here with her friends around her? Go back to New York for a big fancy one my folks will insist on giving us? See a justice of the peace in San Francisco? My mind starts to swim in dizzying circles as I think about all we need to do to get ready and the decisions we have to make.

There's a gentle knock on my door. Glancing at my watch I see it's not long until supper and think it's Persia. "Come on in, it's open. There's time for a little kiss!"

Sadie opens the door, laughing. "Well, pucker up, luv! I'm ready!"

I jump up feeling like I've been caught naked in the middle of the street. "Sadie! I thought you were . . . I mean . . ."

She waves for me to sit down and shakes her head. "It's all right, Quent. I haven't had a proposal like that since I married

J.W. You make an old lady feel like a young woman again. Persia'll be along in a bit. I just wanted to speak with you privately and show you this."

She hands me a folded piece of lace. As I open it, she says, "I've had that ring for a long time—since my days in Kingston. If you like it, and it won't offend me if you don't, I'd like to give it to you for Persia's engagement ring. Will you consider accepting it?"

The lace unfolds in my palm. In the center, sits a beautiful emerald mounted on a gold band. I'm stunned. Catching the light, the stone is brilliant, the gold polished to a mirror finish. "It's beautiful, Sadie. I can't imagine a ring any better or more appropriate than this one. But I can't just let you give it to me. I'll pay you for it and be thankful you were gracious enough to sell it to me."

Sadie crosses her arms, raises an eyebrow, and frowns. "You do have your male pride, don't you? Only if I sell it to you, eh? I set the price and you buy, no matter how much?"

"Yes, ma'am! You set the price, and I buy, no matter how much it is."

"Very well! The price is one dollar! Pay up now."

"Please, Sadie, this isn't right. This ring is probably worth more than a year of my salary, and I'll be happy to pay it. I have some money saved."

"The price, sir, is one dollar! Consider the difference between its price and its value my gift to you two. You've won yourself a treasure, Quent. Now, do you have a dollar, or do I take the ring back?"

I carefully fold the lace back around the ring, slide it in my vest pocket, and give Sadie a dollar. When I get back to San Francisco, I'll have it appraised and send her its full value.

She smiles and motions for me to get my coat. "Come on.

J.W. and Persia will be here any time. Tom sent Boots back with a promise that he'd whip us up something special."

Supper is something very special. We're all in great humor. Even taciturn J.W. tells delightful stories of the stage line and Sadie's driving antics. Sadie's stories of her bordello on Virtue Street in Kingston make us laugh so hard, there are tears in our eyes. Tom Ying's eye-of-round roast *au jus* surrounded by crunchy vegetables and baked potatoes would be savored in Paris. Dessert is hot apple pie.

When we push back from the table, Sadie and J.W. leave Persia and me to go for a walk through the moonlit streets. Hand in hand, we turn west up Main Street toward the glimmering stars rising above the Black Range. An easy stillness has settled over the village.

I look for a romantic place in the moonlight where I might slide the emerald ring on Persia's finger. She's radiant, roses in her cheeks, black hair gleaming, her voice with a lilt I haven't heard before. She wears the blue dress she wore when I first took her to dinner only three weeks ago. As we walk and talk, I feel my heart swell with love and pride for the woman who says she'll be my wife.

The Percha is bathed in the glory of the rising moon when we reach the west bridge, so we pause to listen to the frogs and insects close by the burbling water. I take her in my arms and once more taste her sweet lips. She holds me as though she believes I will sail off into the starry night. "Persia, I love you. You make me feel like I'm the only man in the world."

"For me, you are the only man in the world."

I reach in my vest pocket and put the folded bit of lace in her hand. "Will you wear this? Wear it to remind you that I'm deeply in love with you. Wear it to show others that you're promised to me. Wear it because you love me."

She unfolds the lace and gasps when she sees the stone glimmering in the soft white light. "Quent! How on earth did you find such a beautiful thing here? Of course, I'll wear it, for all those reasons and many more."

The ring slides easily on her finger, a perfect fit. We kiss again, feeling the glow from the universe of stars in the warmth of our bodies.

Chapter 49
A Nightcap with Jack Fountain

I leave Persia at her Orchard Hotel door with a good-night kiss and a promise to visit with her at breakfast. When I walk through the door at Tom Murphy's Parlor Saloon, Jack Fountain sits with Hughes Slater at a table off to one side. They motion me over.

I can't stop smiling as I pull out a chair and sit down. "Hughes," I say, "I've asked Persia to marry me."

They both congratulate me, and Hughes offers his hand and adds, "That's great!"

"Maybe you'll be my best man at the wedding?"

"You have my promise on that, my friend. I'm honored. Say, we missed you in court last Saturday afternoon. Did your engagement have anything to do with that?"

At Jack's signal, a waiter in a white shirt, black vest, and bow tie appears at our table. "What will you have, Quent? I'm buying a toast."

"Well, thanks, Jack! Make mine two fingers of Jack Daniel's straight up." They order the same.

The waiter nods and heads toward the highly polished mahogany bar.

"No, I didn't leave to get engaged. Three men kidnapped Persia off the stage last Saturday and left a note for the driver to telegraph back to Sadie. The note said I had to be in Engle by midnight, or they'd murder Persia."

Hughes says, "What? They must have wanted you out of town

mighty bad! What did you do?"

"Sadie Orchard outfitted Tom Tucker and me to go after Persia. We outflanked and ambushed 'em as they were crossing the Jornada toward Engle, and we didn't take any prisoners."

They both pucker in silent whistles. Jack says, "Don't get me wrong, I'm mighty glad you got Persia back, and her kidnappers deserved to die, and I would have expected them to be killed if Tom Tucker was involved. Did you bring the bodies back here?"

"No, we took them back to their boss, Ed Brown, made him bury them. Tom promised him if there was ever any indication he was up to his old tricks again, he'd die. I'd like to talk to you about that, Jack."

Jack raises his brows. "All right."

Hughes takes out his notepad and pen. I hold up my hand palm out. "Hughes, let's keep this off the record for now."

He smiles and slides his notepad back in his coat pocket.

"Jack, my fiancée is the niece of Ed Brown. I assume you know who he is?"

Jack's face sets in a hard mask and he nods. The waiter brings our Jack Daniel's. Jack takes his drink in hand, leans back in his chair, and relaxes. Hughes lifts his glass and clinks it with Jack's and mine. "You and your lady live a long time, Quent, and don't be stingy producing your stories or your children."

"Thanks, fellows. I'm honored to have friends like you."

I take a swallow of my Jack Daniel's. The burn of the whiskey warms me all the way to my belly. "Jack, I had a long chat with Sadie Orchard shortly after I arrived here. From things her girls told her, especially one named Nadine, and other gossip she heard, she's convinced that while those two up in the jail might have known about the plot to murder your father, they had nothing to do with it. She believes Ed Brown was in on it up to his bottom pucker."

Jack nods. "Yeah, I've heard those stories, too. But they're just stories, desert gossip that won't stand up in a court of law."

"Jack, besides others, my fiancée and I are living proof that what Sadie thinks has a lot of credibility. After I heard Sadie's story, I started asking folks during interviews what they knew about Ed Brown. There was Governor Thornton, who got his story from Slick Miller sitting in prison in Santa Fe. He gave it enough credence that he hired a Pinkerton to work with Sheriff Bursum and the district attorney in Socorro to get Brown to talk, but he didn't break before they had to let him go. I asked Ben Williams about it. He'd heard the story, too, but didn't think Ed Brown had the guts to do it. I've heard others say Brown sometimes hired killers to get rid of his enemies. Besides all that, there are at least four days around the time your father was murdered, which he's lied about.

"To cap it all off, I was warned by three men, one of whom was a Mexican *pistolero,* to quit asking questions about Ed Brown's involvement in the Fountain murders. After the warning, they proceeded to beat the hell out of me. I missed the opening of the first Saturday of the trial because I was laid up from the beating. A couple of weeks ago, Green Scott, a friend of Brown's, tried to cut my throat in front of the dance hall across the street before I sent him packing with the pistol Sadie gave me for protection."

Jack slowly shakes his head. Hughes pats his coat pocket, reflexively reaching for the notepad he won't touch because I wanted our conversation off the record.

"My fiancée lived at Brown's ranch and took all the abuse from him she could before she left for Hillsboro. She can testify about things she heard at Brown's ranch after the murders and affirm that Brown disappeared from the ranch during the time of the murders. He was threatening her harm if she didn't come back to his ranch until Sadie set him straight."

Hughes laughs. "Yeah, I've heard Sadie keeps a pretty detailed record of the foibles and transgressions of politicians and other movers and shakers she's had business with. So you think Brown had something to do with his niece's kidnapping, despite Sadie telling him to steer clear of Persia?"

"Consider what happened last weekend! As sure as apples fall from trees, those three—and I know for a fact two of them have worked for Brown before—were going to murder Persia and me before I got to Engle. I think there's a strong argument, even without the involvement of Persia or me, that Ed Brown and friends are even better suspects than Lee and his bunch.

"I don't get it. Sheriff Curry says a man named Chavez y Chavez told him at the grand jury in Lincoln he was going to kill your father. A day or two before the murders, Chavez y Chavez was supposed to have been seen near Luna's Wells. Pat Garrett believed a woman named Eva Taylor was lying when she gave a certified deposition that, from a stagecoach window, she had seen Lee, McNew, and another man who could have been Gililland cross the road near La Luz early on the morning after the murders. Garrett didn't believe her, because if it were true, Jack Maxwell had to be lying. Eva Taylor didn't have any reason to lie. In fact, when she gave her deposition, she thought it would show Lee and the others were guilty of murdering your father and brother. So, what about it, Jack? Why are Lee and Gililland on trial here and not Brown or Green Scott or Chavez y Chavez or this character Brady who Sadie's best whore told her about?"

Jack takes another sip of his bourbon as he studies me. "The short answer is I don't know. I've heard some of the things you've told me, and not others. My father was an officer of the court for years, and he took a lot of bad men down in his time. I trust the officers of the court to do the right thing. I do know that after Fall used Lee and his cowboys to stop Llewellyn and Branigan from marching the militia to the polling places on election day in '92, Fall and my father were mortal political enemies, and, by association, so was Lee. Fall used Lee and his boys with those big guns on their hips to muscle people around in Las Cruces.

"I think Lee and Fall are trying to build an empire on government-owned land, and they'll stop at nothing to do it—even to the point of murdering old Frenchy Rochas, who lived close to him, or my father and little brother. You heard what that sorry-ass Gililland said about my little brother—no worse than killing a dog because he's half-Mexican? I'll never forgive him for that."

Jack points at his chest and speaks through clenched teeth. "Me, I believe Fall was the brains behind it all, and Lee did what Fall asked. I have to confess there's a difference of opinion in my family about that. Shortly after the murders, Fall got Albert in a room alone, and they had a long talk. Fall convinced Albert that he had absolutely nothing to do with the murder of my father. Albert can't stand Fall, but he believes him. Now I have a sister who won't even speak to Albert. My father and brother's murders have ripped my family in the guts in more ways than one."

Shrugging his shoulders and sighing, Jack says, "These other suspects you mention may be guilty. But it's the law's choice to decide who to prosecute. They've chosen Lee, Gililland, and McNew. I think the trial is fair. I'll abide by what the jury says, but regardless of what the jury decides, regardless of whether he's guilty or innocent, I'll never forgive Gililland for what he said about my father and brother."

I study Jack's face as he talks. As usual, he's talking straight. "I understand how you feel. What do you think of the prosecution's case?"

Jack leans his chair forward until it's sitting on all four legs. He shakes his head. "I think it's been awful. The evidence they've presented doesn't prove anything except that Lee didn't have any use for my father, and neither did a lot of others out in the Basin. Fall is crucifying the integrity of every witness, whether they deserve it or not. I understand he's just doing his job. Still, it's nasty, disgusting business.

"What I want to know is where are those witnesses Garrett promised who would get Lee and Gililland hanged? Catron says they're afraid to testify, or they've disappeared into Mexico because they're afraid. The best witness they have is Jack Maxwell? Damn! They couldn't convict a cockroach with Jack Maxwell's testimony!"

Hughes and I both nod. I say, "Jack, I had a long chat with Henry Stoes about the posse he was in that followed the trail around the Jarillas only to see it wiped out by White and Fitchetts' cattle herd. He claims even before the herd came along, Major Llewellyn wouldn't let them go and talk to Lee and ask to look around the place for signs of the bodies. I'd like to talk to Llewellyn and get his side of it and some other things I've heard. Would you be willing to ask him if I could interview him?"

Jack looks into his drink and shakes his head. "You're a straight shooter, Quent, but I don't think he'll talk to you."

"Why not?"

Jack looks at me like I've lost my mind. "Because of the story appearing in your paper about Governor Thornton faking evidence."

I'm indignant. "I didn't write that trash! It makes me ashamed I work for the *Examiner.* Look, Jack, if your side wants its views known, you need me to tell the straight story. Come on. Get old Llewellyn to talk to me."

Hughes swallows the rest of his drink and sits with his arms crossed, eyeing me. Jack looks up and nods. "Yeah, I know your stories are straight. Okay, I'll see if I can't get Llewellyn to talk to you, but don't count on it."

"Thanks, Jack. I hope you can work it out, and you have my word I'll write it the way he tells it."

Jack downs the rest of his drink and stands. "Gentlemen, I hate to leave such convivial company, but I have to see Albert about some business in Cruces. See you in court tomorrow. *Adios.*"

We wave him out the door. I take another long sip of my bourbon.

Then Hughes grins and says, "Quent, I have a confession to make. I'm not just a reporter for the *El Paso Herald.* I own it."

I'm astonished by his revelation that he bought it a month earlier. He says he likes my style and honesty and that he's enjoyed my stories. I'm the kind of reporter he wants on the *Herald.* The salary he offers, the potential for stories from a Wild West border town, and the opportunity to become an editor sooner rather than later tempts me to accept his offer and shake hands right then.

"Hughes, your offer sounds very generous, but I want to sleep on it and tell Persia what I'm thinking to get her wisdom. Can I let you know in two or three days?"

"Sure, that's fine. I know that even if you accept my offer, it might be a month or two before you can get to El Paso."

Chapter 50
Childers's Closing Argument, 12 June 1899

It's a restless night. My heart races between thinking about my fiancée and Hughes's offer, my mind constantly conjuring up visions of a family and a long career at a growing newspaper. At six-thirty, Persia rushes down the hall, throws her arms around my neck, and gives me a soft kiss.

Over breakfast, I tell her about Hughes's offer. She's ecstatic, but she's careful to emphasize that she'll be happy to go anywhere I choose. Soon the restaurant begins to fill with hungry men, and the other waitress needs Persia to help her. Kissing me goodbye, Persia promises to meet me at dinner recess.

Walking up the hill to the courthouse, I've never been happier. Shafts of sunlight thrust through the cottonwood branches to form pools of light I use as stepping stones in the road on the way to the jail.

As usual, Gene Rhodes guards the front of the jail sitting by the backfill wall steps. I wave and walk over to give him my review. "Gene! Beautiful morning, isn't it?"

He grins and holds up a palm in greeting. "Morning, Quent. Yes, sir, it's mighty fine."

I pull his story out of my coat and hand it to him. When he sees it, his brow goes up, and he gives a little bite to his lower lip. "You read it! Thanks very much. What did you think?"

"Enjoyed it. It's good work. There are some notes in the margins where it might need a little work. No doubt, you can sell it. Maybe you ought to set it aside, let your brain cook on it awhile, and then pull it out and finish it with fresh eyes. You have a great talent for telling stories. If you keep at it, you can earn your living as a writer. Look over my comments, and we can discuss them in a day or two, if you like."

"Quent, I'm gonna hold you to that. Thanks again. I appreciate it."

"I'm going on upstairs to find a good place in the benches and do a little writing of my own before court starts. See you later."

As the time nears for the trial to resume, there are only about half the number of spectators in the courtroom as there were on Saturday. As usual, Lee is immaculately groomed, and Gililland appears in good spirits. The attorneys on both sides of the aisle are comparing notes and talking softly among themselves—all, that is, except Childers, who sits off by himself, making notes in a legal pad. Daugherty, who chats with Fergusson and Fall, is also filling a legal pad as he scratches through some notes and adds others. Fall sits relaxed in his chair, eyes half-closed. His sunken cheeks show fatigue, evident from the sag of the wrinkles on his face. The long trial and constant mental gymnastics to outwit Catron have taken their toll.

Lee looks over his shoulder when the McNews and his mother come in, smiles at them, sees me, and gives a little nod. Gililland waves at a friend and begins writing a note. The Fountain brothers appear and take their usual pews. Jack comes over and whispers that Llewellyn won't do an interview. We shake hands, and I thank him for trying.

All the daily reporters who've mostly stood around the walls during the trial are in their places. Seymour gives me his usual salute. We probably haven't said ten words since I bought him a beer the night I arrived.

The bailiff calls for the crowd to rise as Judge Parker enters from his office behind the bench. After a few words with the clerk, he nods toward the prosecution table. "I trust everyone had a peaceful Sunday and a good day of rest. Mr. Catron, the record shows it's the prosecution's turn at a closing argument. I assume Mr. Childers will be speaking next."

Childers rises and approaches the jury, his face earnest, his right hand holding his coat lapel, his left holding his notes. After a few pleasantries about how appreciative the state is of the jury's time in doing their civic duty for a long and arduous trial, he gets down to business.

"Gentlemen of the jury, the defense has made a great effort to discredit the evidence given here by Dr. Crosson, the expert chemist who examined and testified as to the character of the blood found beside the road near the place where Colonel Fountain's buggy was first surrounded. He said the blood had every characteristic of human blood, and he believed it was human blood. All the other circumstances are such as to make it certain it was human blood. Nobody has shown that any other animal, such as a dog, coyote, horse, or jackrabbit, had died there, and it would have been a most remarkable coincidence if such a thing had happened at just that time.

"The murder of Colonel Fountain at that time accounts for the blood being there. Its presence cannot be accounted for through any other theory or supposition; therefore, it must have been Colonel Fountain's blood. The expert testified that the shedding of such an amount of human blood must have caused death; therefore, Fountain must be dead."

I find it strange that although Lee and Gililland are on trial for the murder of little Henry Fountain, Childers has yet to say anything about the boy's death. Pacing back and forth in front of the jury, Childers goes through a list of possibilities to account for the absence of blood on the buckboard: Fountain might have jumped from the buggy just before he was shot; he might have been on the ground when he was shot; he might have been shot and have fallen out of the wagon; or he might have been carried in a blanket from the place where he was shot and placed there to bleed to death.

Childers puts a fist against his waist and leans in toward the jury. "Mr. Fergusson has told you it would be impossible to measure or identify horse or man tracks, especially if the wind was blowing, and that there is absolutely nothing in such evidence. You well know the trailing of horses and men is an everyday occurrence in this country and that, to men familiar with the tracking of individuals or parties by such means, the work is easy and certain. It is utter nonsense to talk about obliteration of such tracks in a week, or even two weeks. If they are lost for a time, they can be picked up farther on.

"The absence of the measuring sticks, the bloody coins, the napkin, etc., introduced by the prosecution at the preliminary examination and considered so important by the defense that they say they are essential to prove certain statements, is far more damaging to the defense than to the prosecution. Why should we want to destroy this evidence? It's not so all-important as the defense seems to think, however.

"The defense claims that being indicted at the insistence of Colonel Fountain was not enough motive on the part of the defendants to commit the murder. There were too many men in the same fix. But there has been ample evidence introduced here to show they were, in fact, afraid of Colonel Fountain, and they were glad after his death.

"These men had no reason to resist arrest. They need not have been afraid of the sheriff. Pat Garrett is an honorable man. The defense has paid great tribute to his honor and honesty. The defendants would have been safe in his hands. They need not have surrendered to that man Williams, if they were indeed afraid of him, which appears ridiculous. No, they were afraid of a newspaper, a little four-by-nine sheet. Why should they be afraid on account of the utterances of an idiotic newspaperman? Was there not all the law and power of the territory on the side of order and safety? Lee went in and out of Las Cruces without fear up to March 1898. He was not afraid. McNew was in the custody of Sheriff Garrett for many months. He was not killed, or mobbed, or threatened."

Childers pauses to pour himself a glass of water and drinks it slowly, allowing his argument to settle on the jury. Finished, he turns back to speak to the jury in a voice thick with sarcasm. "The men Burch and Aiks, having been picked out to do foul murder for pay, must indeed be miserable men; they must be assassins themselves. But why did the defense not bring those men here to testify? And then there are those letters Lee said Llewellyn wrote to Cox. Why didn't Cox come here and tell about them himself? It is a wonderful thing that the most important letters in the case of the defense are missing. The Burch and Aiks letters are missing! What kind of evidence is this to bring before you?

"The defense lays much stress on the claim that it was only after the governor, by permission of the court, had agreed to protect them from violence and permitted them to surrender outside of Doña Ana County that the defendants were willing to surrender themselves for a trial. On the contrary, the governor arranged with these fugitives to surrender in another county simply to take away their last excuse for resisting arrest.

"The Maxwell contract was not unusual. It is all right to pay a detective to secure evidence in a case or to put in shape that which is already in his possession. When the governor offers a reward for a fugitive, it is the same thing. Shall men's hands be tied? It would be offering positive protection to criminals if money could not be used, by the proper authorities, to secure the criminals or evidence leading to the conviction of the criminals."

Childers then takes up the matter of the alibi. He considers the evidence of the different witnesses in detail, using Garrett's testimony on the Kearney fight, which was so highly praised by the defense, to show he must have been telling the truth when he said Dan Fitchett told him he went to the Lee ranch in the morning, not the evening, and saw the defendants setting out grapevines.

"Fitchett denied on the stand what he told Garrett because of the exigencies of the case. The perjury of one witness is fatal to an alibi.

"Jack Maxwell and the witnesses for the defense agree on every circumstance and happening at the ranch on Saturday, Sunday, and perhaps Monday, except that Maxwell says the defendants and McNew were not there Saturday night. Maxwell must be telling the truth, for the witnesses for the defense had every reason to misrepresent the true state of affairs. Maxwell was disinterested. Maxwell did not say to Bud Smith that it would be no use to try to fasten the crime on these boys for he saw them at the ranch Saturday night. Maxwell would have been a fool to make such a remark to either Smith or Curry, and the prosecution has here shown Maxwell could not have said anything like it."

Childers claims that the two Goulds and Riley Baker were quite worthy of belief. He impeaches Lee's story of the Kearney fight by again citing the defense's own praise for Garrett's honest and straightforward tale. The defense stood by Garrett but tells a different tale. Therefore, Lee must be wrong.

"As for the alleged fear Lee had of Garrett, that is all absolutely baseless. What about the man Ellis, the barber in Las Cruces? Why didn't the defense call him to testify? There's nothing whatever in what the Negro said when it is considered that Lee fully knew Garrett's character and knew he would be safe in his hands whenever he should surrender to him.

"Gentlemen of the jury, you are about to decide one of the most important cases ever tried in this territory. If you conscientiously believe that these men are not guilty of this murder, the interests of society do not demand their conviction, or the improper conviction of any man. If you are satisfied that guilt rests upon these defendants or either of them, it is your duty to convict. You cannot shirk this duty for any consideration of politics or personal friendship.

"To hold that you cannot convict of murder because the body cannot be found is to condone murder, to put a premium on crime. You cannot so hold. It is so easy in this country to waylay a man and conceal his body where it cannot be found. There is every evidence that these three men were the perpetrators of this crime. These men have wholly failed to explain any of the incriminating circumstances forming the web we have woven so tightly around them. However, instead of refuting our evidence, they have resorted to mudslinging and have raised the cry of politics. Is there any politics in this case? Was there then a political murder? We never heard of politics in this case until the term was injected by the defense.

"Gentlemen, leave out every consideration or issue but the one you are called upon to decide. Did these defendants murder the Fountain boy? That is what you must determine. I thank you for your attention."

Childers flops down in his chair, smiling, confident, as he eyes the defense table and the jury. He's been at it all morning, nearly three hours. Catron reaches over and gives him a strong handshake.

Judge Parker looks at his watch. "Gentlemen, it's approaching the dinner hour. We'll recess until one-thirty this afternoon. Court is adjourned."

Chapter 51
Daugherty's Closing Argument, 12 June 1899

Hughes and I find the courtroom is much more crowded than it was for the morning session. We take seats a couple of rows back from Mrs. Lee and the McNews. Lee and Gililland are already seated, awaiting their attorneys. Mrs. Lee drops a tatting needle that bounces on the floor, rolls under the benches, and stops under the toe of my shoe. I pick it up and move down the bench to the center aisle just as Fergusson and Daugherty walk by and sit down with Lee and Gililland. Fall isn't with them. Lee frowns, apparently concerned.

Handing Mrs. Lee her needle, I hear Lee ask about Fall. Fergusson shakes his head. "He's done in, Oliver. He said to tell you that Daugherty and I can handle the closings just fine, and he has to get some rest before he collapses. He's down at the Orchard and will be back tonight."

I turn to go, but Lee grabs my arm in a bear-trap grip. "Hold on just a minute, will you, Quent?" He lets go just as a bailiff, seeing what's happening, starts to rise out of his chair. He grabs a pencil out of Fergusson's vest, writes a quick note he tears off a legal pad, and hands it to me. "Do me a favor and take this down to Fall at the Orchard. It's important."

"Sure, Oliver, I'll be glad to."

"Thanks."

It's at least ten or fifteen minutes before court begins, so I won't miss much of Daugherty's closing argument. Walking fast, I'm in the Orchard and knocking on Fall's door in five minutes. There are sounds of springs in his bed creaking and feet shuffling toward the door before he opens the door. It's stunning how haggard Fall looks as he sticks his head out of the dark room.

"Mr. Fall! Sir, you look awful! Sorry to disturb you."

"I don't feel any better than I look. My head's pounding, and I'm weak as a poot." Holding on to the doorframe, he asks, "What are you doing here?"

I hold out the note from Lee. He opens the door wide for more light. As he reads the note, he seems to stand a little straighter. "Lee says he needs me back in court quick. Any idea why?"

"No, sir. He was very concerned when Fergusson said you were leaving the closing arguments to him and Daugherty."

Fall groans. "Damn it! Guess I'd better get up there and see if I can't put a little oil on his water. I'll get my boots and coat. Will you be so kind as to carry my satchel?"

"It'd be my pleasure, Mr. Fall."

Fall seems to gather strength as we walk back to the courtroom. By the time we get to the top of the stairs and down the aisle in the courtroom, we still have a couple of minutes before Judge Parker is due to start. Before I can sit Fall's satchel by the defense table, Fall asks, "What's the matter, Oliver?"

"Albert, I want you to make an argument before the jury. I don't care if it's ten minutes' long, just make it."

"I'm exhausted. I'm so tired I doubt I can even stand on my feet for ten minutes. I'm afraid I'll weaken the case trying to talk in this condition. These men here can do a much better job closing than I. You don't need me to do it."

Lee shakes his head. "Listen, Fall, they're trying to hang me for something I didn't do. You know what I'd do for you if you were in trouble."

Fall doesn't hesitate. "All right, I'll stay. Just let me sit down for a while and give me a tall glass of water." He slumps in his chair, his head bowed. Catron, who has waddled past the conversation to take his seat, appears to study with interest what's happening at the defense table.

I leave Fall's satchel beside his chair and take my seat next to Hughes just as Judge Parker enters the courtroom and the bailiff calls for all to rise. After checking with the clerk, he nods toward the defense. "Mr. Fall, I believe the remainder of the defense's closing arguments are next."

Fall slowly pushes himself up. "Yes, Your Honor. Mr. Daugherty will give the next argument."

"Very well, proceed."

Daugherty rises and approaches the jury. He leans against the juror rail as a rancher might lean against a fence to talk to a neighbor. His voice is calm and filled with reason.

"Gentlemen of the jury, it is not for the defense to determine the facts of the Fountain disappearance. We have only to show that the defendants had nothing to do with his disappearance or his death, if he, in fact, is dead. The territory has entirely failed to show that the defendants had anything to do with the Fountain case."

Daugherty pauses for an instant to look over his shoulder at the prosecution. "There has been much confusion in this case. These defendants are not on trial for the killing of Colonel Fountain or of Deputy Kearney. They are on trial for the killing of a little child. Fix that fact firmly in your minds.

"The imagination of some of the witnesses for the prosecution is of the dime-novel order. They can, it seems, tell all about the feelings and thoughts of people from their tracks. Of course, it was hard, under such a fire of questions as was poured out upon their witnesses by the counsel, for the prosecution to discriminate between what they knew and what they thought they knew."

He holds out an arm toward the prosecution table, the volume of his voice increasing, and looks directly at Catron, who glares back. "The prosecution brought politics and outside issues into this case to prejudice the minds of the jury. They try to make these men out to be murderers, desperadoes, and fugitives from justice. The defense has had to go, to a certain extent, into the facts about the real conditions at Las Cruces in order to show it was not for the murder of Henry Fountain but for personal and political reasons that these defendants were prosecuted. Don't charge this state of things to the defense. The prosecution brought it here, and we had to meet and disprove it. I'm glad the matter has been brought so prominently to the front, however, for it will give the jury an idea as to the real animus lying beneath this persecution.

"You have heard much about the *corpus delicti.* Understand me. It is not necessary, in order to convict for murder, that the body of the victim be produced. But it is customary to bring into court some part of the body or something that carries absolute proof that a crime has been committed.

"I never heard of a case where men were put on trial before a jury for murder where there was not a scintilla of proof that a crime had been committed. The proof that these men committed murder upon the little Fountain boy must be cogent and irresistible. You have no reason to believe a crime has been committed.

"They prove a buckboard disappeared off a well-traveled main road. Soon afterwards, Albert Fountain went along the road and examined every sign carefully. He didn't see any blood. Has there been any evidence that any fight took place, as was suggested by the counsel for the prosecution? Again, is it reasonable to believe a great pool of blood would be left beside the road, in plain sight of everybody passing, by men as desirous of avoiding suspicion as the perpetrators of this cruel crime are said to have been?

"On direct examination, that fine expert of theirs swore the blood was human blood. On cross-examination, his testimony was shaken, and he admitted that not by any or all of his tests could he distinguish human blood from animal blood. He finally refused to make even a guess as to which of several vials of blood contained human blood, although he had said he could tell by the taste. What kind of an expert is that? And yet they ask you to hang two men on such testimony!

"Mr. Childers laid stress upon the fact that we had not shown the blood was not Colonel Fountain's. We do not have to show any such thing. We do not need to show that every splotch of blood along a public road does not come from Colonel Fountain's body. What have we to do with spots of blood along a road? The prosecution must show the blood comes from Colonel Fountain if they want to prove him dead. Have they shown any such thing?"

Daugherty holds up his fist, using his fingers to count his points.

"You have no further to go than this: They bring an expert to testify that certain blood was human blood. They assert the blood was Colonel Fountain's. They say from this that Henry Fountain, the little boy, is dead, and they ask you to hang Oliver Lee and James Gililland for his murder. This is what they call their case. Does it convince you?

"Whatever you may think as to a possible motive for killing Colonel Fountain, there could have been no motive for killing that little boy. It is silly to assume Lee and Gililland would think that by killing this man and his little boy, they could escape all further prosecution, if they were indeed guilty of anything. Did all justice and law in the Territory of New Mexico depend, then, on Colonel Fountain? It is absurd."

Daugherty turns from the jury rail to look directly at the

prosecution table. "The prosecution attacked our witness Tom Tucker savagely. What has Tom Tucker done? He has never been convicted of an infamous crime. He has been an officer of the law a large part of the time and has a most honorable record. But the leading counsel for the prosecution, Mr. Catron, attacked him and tried to discredit him before you. I have heard of men high in the territory who have been accused of grave crimes, but an accusation is not necessarily truth against any man. It ought only to make these men more careful when they undertake to question witnesses on the witness stand.

"The prosecution wants to know why we do not bring on the stand the two men and one woman seen on the road by the mail carrier not far from the place where Fountain disappeared. Why don't they put these people on? It is not our business to put them on the stand. We don't care what went on along that road or who passed there. They must prove their suspicions, or they are absolutely worthless.

"Albert Fountain rises as one of the stars above the mass of untruth in this, not prosecution, but persecution. He comes and tells the truth. What motive would he have to misstate anything? Through him, the territory itself refuted its own proposition that the boy Fountain is dead. At the campfire, there were dozens of boy tracks made by both feet. Fountain says so. He was the first on the ground. Will you believe the first man there, or will you believe a man who was there after fifteen or twenty men tramped around the spot? If the alleged murderers tried to deceive with the shoe of the boy, why did they not do the same with Fountain's shoes? It is a silly story. Would not the men at least have obliterated their own tracks?

"After the agents of the prosecution had measured the tracks so carefully, would they not then have simply taken the measurements of a certain size cowboy boot? How many men wear a number-seven or number-six or number-eight-size boot in this territory? And yet the only thing they want conviction on is the tracks comparison and measurement. No man saw those defendants on the road. No one saw them kill Colonel Fountain. No one saw them bear the body away. No one knows that Colonel Fountain is dead. Certain tracks were measured. Conviction is demanded. The prosecution does not dare to introduce any of those measurements in this trial. Llewellyn says the measurements were put in a package and given to a detective. The detective—where is he? Gone! They packed up all their case and sent it out of the country. That is what it amounts to. We challenge them to produce their measurements. They rely on them as their case to take the lives of two men. They say, when asked to produce them, 'We have them not.' A wonderful chain of disappearances in this case, to be sure.

"Everything goes to show the prosecution in this case holds a preconceived opinion that these men did the deed, and the prosecution did all they could to fasten it on them. They did not show proper judgment or common sense. They made no effort to find the real criminals.

"Van Patton tracked the gray horse and found it. The others found nothing on the face of the earth but tracks on top of a house. The other members of the posse swore the gray horse went straight on in an opposite direction from that in which Van Patton found the animal.

"Did Oliver Lee have any motive for resisting arrest? Read the *Doña Ana Republican* four days after the disappearance. It says, 'If Colonel Fountain is dead, there can be no question as to at whose door the blame lies,' thus, in effect, charging Oliver Lee with the crime. That posse didn't want to arrest Lee and bring him in, but they wanted to carry his dead body to Las Cruces. That's what they wanted, and Lee knew he would have to protect himself from violence.

"I believe Print Rhode was telling the truth. They say

Llewellyn had denied Rhode's statement before and didn't have to be called in to rebut Rhode. Llewellyn did not deny the story. He was in the courtroom while those men were testifying. Why didn't the prosecution put him on the stand? Ah! He had all the witness stand he wanted.

"Those letters written by Llewellyn to Cox about a mysterious cattle-buyer were not explained by Llewellyn. Oliver Lee testified that Cox explained the letters to him fully—there had been a cold-blooded conspiracy to kill Fall and Lee for political and personal reasons, and the man Jake Ryan was to do the work. The prosecution asks why we don't put on Cox. Gentlemen, we are not trying Llewellyn. We don't have to put on Cox.

"The alibi of the defendants is absolutely conclusive. The prosecution could get absolutely nothing against the defendants' witnesses as to the alibi. By innuendo, they charged Mrs. Lee, the old mother of Oliver Lee, with perjury. They did it in pretty words, but the district attorney had to do it in order to open his attack. And then he put up against that lovely lady a man who had jumped from place to place all his life and had changed his name with every jump—a man who, when asked whether he had told the truth at a former trial, at which he testified under oath, replied that it was 'so long ago that he did not remember.' That is the kind of wretch they put upon this stand to charge this lady with perjury. The man with the two thousand dollar contract is, then, the only one out of the six men and one woman who told the truth. Does that look reasonable?

"Now are you going to take all this confused amount of what they call evidence and convict these men of the murder of Henry Fountain? Suppose Colonel Fountain and his boy should walk into this courtroom tomorrow? Where could you put your finger on a single iota of evidence that would be worth a thought?

"Gentlemen of the jury, now is the time to give Oliver Lee and James Gililland the justice they deserve. Based on the facts of this case, I believe you will, without a doubt, pronounce them innocent of the murder of little Henry Fountain. I thank you for your generous time and attention during this long and arduous trial." With that, Daugherty returns to the defense table. Lee leans across the defense table, and, nodding, whispers in Daugherty's ear.

Hughes and I look at each other and smile. Fall was right to tell Lee that Fergusson and Daugherty would do well with the defense's closing arguments.

Judge Parker looks toward Fall, who is slow to rise. "Mr. Fall?"

"Coming, Your Honor."

Chapter 52
Fall's Closing Argument, 12 June 1899

As Fall rises, the shuffle of bodies in the now-full spectator seats ceases. Without notes, Fall comes to stand directly before the jurors, and looks each man in the eye before saying, "Gentlemen of the jury, you are participants in a great system of justice. A system where men are supposed innocent until judged guilty beyond a reasonable doubt by a jury of their peers, upright citizens who know and understand the character of the men they judge and can discern what makes sense about them and what does not. When men are judged by juries, they are not subject to the whims of kings, the anger of dictators, or the political shenanigans of presidents. What a jury decides in a courtroom has the untarnished value of fact. It is an honor to serve on a jury, and I commend your efforts in this work here."

Fall nods toward Lee and Gililland. "These men wanted to be tried in Otero County. They did not fear being tried there. It is over the objection of these men that this case is given to a jury in Sierra County. We wanted to stand Jack Maxwell and the other witnesses for the prosecution up before men who knew Dan Fitchett, Oliver Lee, Mrs. Lee, George Curry, and the others. But the other side contended that, in Otero County, Oliver Lee and his friends had too much control over the courts and law officers. It would not be fair to try them there."

Sticking out his lower lip, he shakes his head at the jury. "Otero County has twenty-five hundred people! It is quite unreasonable, is it not, that one man should control that county after the manner of a king or a dictator? Do not mistake this fact. Oliver Lee wanted to be tried in a county where he was known. The territory wouldn't have it."

As he speaks, Fall seems to draw energy out of the hot, still air, and he stands straighter and moves deliberately. "I know the leading counsel for the prosecution will try to weave about this case an intricate web of alleged evidence in his effort to create a case. He will ask you to go outside the facts as they appear in the record and speculate and guess at things that might have happened. When he does this, I want you to measure him carefully according to the facts in this case."

Fall makes a fist and releases a finger each time he makes a point. "First, it is admitted by both sides that Lee and Gililland and McNew were indicted at the January term of court in 1896 at Lincoln, that there was nothing in those indictments, and that they were dismissed. The question is, were those groundless indictments a sufficient motive for the murder of Colonel Fountain and his little boy?

"Second, there is no evidence the defendants ever knew that Colonel Fountain was in any way instrumental in securing indictments against them. If these men had such a motive, why did they not murder Les Dow, who had the indictments drawn up? Why not the district attorney, who prosecuted them? Why does the suspicion not rest on every one of the seventeen men indicted at that term of court?

"Third, two horsemen are said to have been seen apparently following Colonel Fountain, and three others were later seen ahead of him. So says the prosecution. We do not dispute this. Why should we? We know nothing about those men and care less. There were other people in the vicinity to make the tracks. The prosecution has shown that. We don't know who made any particular set of tracks, and we don't care. They attempt to show that one set of those tracks left Luna's Wells and went toward Lee's Well by way of the Jarillas, according to one witness. This is the only one of the horses' tracks they attempt to trace to these defendants in any way whatsoever.

"Fourth, it is significant that most of the discoveries were made by witnesses from the second posse that went over the ground. You saw the prosecution try to break down the testimony of their own witnesses when they did not testify as the prosecution wanted them to.

"We did not make the trail. We neither know nor care who made the trail. I'm surprised Branigan and Llewellyn weren't willing to swear the name of the horse was so-and-so by the shape of his tracks. The prosecution testified that Lee's horse was full shod. The defense proved he was not shod. The defense showed the trailers used by the prosecution were all at sea and were swearing in the dark.

"Fifth, Mr. Childers told the jury—he was the only one who said so, and he was not sworn as to the fact—that the tracks measured on top of the house were Lee's tracks. How does he know that? Everything has gone to show that the measurements and statements of Major Branigan were open to great doubt. And yet in these footprints, about which nothing whatever is known, even in what is guessed at, there are many conflicts. This is all there is in the case against the defendants.

"As to the alibi: If you believe Maxwell told the truth, you must believe Blevins is a liar"—Fall hammers the jury rail with his fist—"that Bailey is a liar, that Joe Fitchett is a liar, that Dan Fitchett is a liar, that Oliver Lee is a liar, and that Mrs. Lee is a liar. If Maxwell told the truth, you must believe these five men and one woman are all perjurers, are worse than perjurers, are murderers, for they are implicated in the case. If you believe Maxwell told the truth, you must believe George Curry is a liar and Bud Smith is a liar. Now take your choice. Either all eight witnesses are liars, or Jack Maxwell is a liar."

Fall, infused with the fury of his argument, begins to pace back and forth in front of the jury. "The story the prosecution attempted to put up about Maxwell's contract is most foolish. The prosecution made Garrett swear the contract means exactly what it says on its face: He was to be paid to testify against these men. Can you doubt it? Before you can go into the case at all and speculate on what might be, you must believe Jack Maxwell is telling the truth.

"We had about sixty witnesses here on our side. We have introduced only ten of them. We discharged the others because the prosecution did not succeed in making any case against these defendants. The territory has not done its duty. It has not been hunting for the real murderers of Colonel Fountain and his little boy. It has exerted all its power and spent all its money to fasten the crime on these men. It has held these men without bail and has required them to come here and prove their innocence, saying to them, 'We shall not attempt to prove your guilt.' Gentlemen, that is the position in which we find ourselves."

The anger in Fall's voice is palpable, clear. "They say you may find a verdict of guilty of murder in the third degree. Then why in the name of God are these men being held without bond? I ask for no white mantle of charity for these men. I desire no vindication. I ask simply for stern justice. If the evidence in this case convinces you that these men murdered little Henry Fountain, you must convict! There is no alternative. If you are not so convinced, turn them loose.

"You are no doubt surprised to learn that such a state of affairs can exist in Doña Ana County. In many streams, there is a point at a sharp bend in the course where the water pauses in its onward flow and forms an eddy. Around the edges the slime gathers, and the froth and logs, along with dead leaves and all manner of floating filth. The moss and ferns grow dank, and the shadowy places are haunted by creeping things. Snakes come out of their hiding places and bask in the sun on the slimy logs, and if they are disturbed in their retreat, they sting the heel of the man who is so foolish as to venture there. Doña Ana County is just such a dead eddy.

"Under the territorial form of government, public officers do not hold office by the choice of the sovereign people, but are appointed by the federal powers. In Doña Ana County, there have gathered together, as does the slimy filth on the edges of a dead eddy, a lot of broken-down old political hacks. They bask in the sun of political preferment, like serpents stretched out on dead logs. They never earned an honest dollar in their lives, and do not know how to earn one except by serving the people, forsooth, in public office. It was in just such a dead eddy as I have described that there arose this plot for the persecution of Oliver Lee."

Fall's face is a thundercloud, his voice, a roar as he slaps the juror's rail, making everyone in the room recoil. "Gentlemen of the jury, the prosecution of Oliver Lee is the result of a conspiracy to send an innocent man to the gallows." In his fury, Fall points a long, straight finger directly at each man in turn. "The district attorney is involved in the conspiracy. The Honorable Thomas B. Catron is involved in the conspiracy! His Honor on the bench is involved in the conspiracy!"

No one breathes. Bursting through his shock, Judge Parker, red in the face, pounds his gavel and jumps to his feet. Every spectator favoring the prosecution jumps up, too, as if pulled by one string, yelling, "No, sir!"

Judge Parker continues pounding his gavel. "If the spectators do not sit down, I shall empty the courtroom! Mr. Fall, unless you withdraw your remarks about this court from the jury immediately, I shall send you to jail for contempt."

There are several audible clicks of revolvers from those favoring Lee at seats throughout the courtroom. Fall sticks out his lower lip, shakes his head, and says in a sarcastic voice, "Your Honor will not send me to jail for contempt until I am through addressing this jury. When I finish my argument, you may do whatever you wish."

I look over my shoulder. Todd Bailey and his friends are behind me, their mouths set in hard, straight lines, their hands on their holsters. Every other cattleman I see has the same expression.

Fear in their eyes, the reporters standing by the windows look down to see how far they might have to jump if shooting starts.

Judge Parker surveys the room, slowly sits back down, and flips the back of his hand toward Fall to continue. Catron glares at Fall. Barnes sits still and stares straight ahead. Childers peers around the room and shakes his head.

Fall resumes his argument. "From 1896 to 1898, there was no attempt made even to arrest these men. The prosecution has been in possession all that time of the same evidence that was brought here for you to consider. Why was there no indictment? Why was there no arrest? Mr. Garrett tries to explain it by alleging I was so all-powerful, I clogged every wheel of justice in the territory. He must wait before taking steps to punish these men for an alleged heinous crime committed in February 1896. Mr. Garrett affects to think all the power of the territory, all the influence and money of the Masonic lodges, all the influence and money of the cattleman's associations, all the money put up to convict these defendants by corrupt politicians and infamous scoundrels, could be and were successfully offset by me, and he had to wait for a change of administration before bringing these men to trial. So there was no indictment found or warrant issued until I had left Las Cruces and gone into the army to fight the Spanish with Mr. Roosevelt.

"It might have been more interesting or more satisfactory to some people if we had put on the stand all our witnesses and shown just what I believe to be the facts in this case. But it is not our business to find Colonel Fountain or his murderers and bring them here. It is absolutely nothing to these defendants whether any crime has been committed or not.

"These defendants are paying all the expenses of their defense. The territory does not help them out. It costs a lot of money to put sixty witnesses on the stand, but, more than all this, we do not propose to show our hand until we are compelled to do so. There are two more cases for us to meet. As long as this persecution persists, we want to hold something in reserve.

"Our defense is an alibi, clearly proved. Put yourself in the place of these defendants. The prosecution has made no case at all. Their contentions are sheer nonsense. The alleged case seems to need no defense. We have simply attacked their witnesses by their own means. You would not hang a yellow dog on the evidence presented here, much less two men.

"Mr. Catron said it had not been proved what the politics of these defendants are, except that they are murderers and, therefore, Democrats. We hurl it back in his teeth! He says there is no politics in this case. Does not his own remark establish this fact?

"We've been forced to prove that certain witnesses brought here by the prosecution are perjurers. If this case had been tried in Otero County, as we desired, this wouldn't have been necessary, for those men are known in their own homes as perjurers.

"For three years, we've been trying to get this case before a jury. That has been the fight—to obtain, not only a fair trial, but any trial at all, for these defendants. At last, we have our opportunity and are confident that you will do your duty, the highest appertaining to American citizenship, as befits men. We leave the lives of these two men in your hands."

Men stand and clap as Fall sits down. Red in the face, Judge Parker hammers his gavel, roaring, "Order! Order in this court, or I'll have you all thrown out." With a big smile, Lee grabs Fall's shoulder and mouths his thanks. Gililland looks around the courtroom, grinning and nodding as if he's just made the speech.

Order is soon restored. Judge Parker stares around the room, his threat to jail Fall for contempt apparently forgotten. He looks at his watch. "We're approaching suppertime. I don't want to interrupt Mr. Catron in the middle of his argument. Court is in recess until eight o'clock."

I head for Tom Ying's and my fianceé. Hughes is off to the telegraph office to send a partial report of the day's fireworks.

The Ocean Grove is not crowded when I walk through the door. Persia, Sam, and Ruth are working the floor. I know Sadie expects a big crowd from the spectators in to see the pyrotechnics between Fall and Catron. For Fall's part, they haven't been disappointed, and I doubt Catron's argument will disappoint them, either.

Persia waves me over to a table. The emerald on her finger flashes in the late afternoon light. It makes my chest swell with pride. She whispers in Sam's ear. Sam grins and waves at me. Persia sits down after giving me a modest peck on the cheek. "I can sit with you for a few minutes. Sam says she'll look after my tables until the place gets too packed for her to handle. How were the defense's closing arguments?"

"Daugherty was very good, but Fall was spectacular."

Persia asks, "Any mention of my uncle or those men who worked for him?"

I shake my head. "Only a reference that there were a lot of other candidates besides Lee and his men who might want Colonel Fountain dead."

She squeezes my hand. "What can I get you for your supper?"

"The usual will be fine as long as you can keep me company."

Smiling, she disappears into the kitchen, soon to return with a big steak, fried potatoes and onions, beans, and a large loaf of buttered sourdough bread.

Persia and I begin a conversation as she tries to decide what she wants for the wedding. All I want is a wedding that will make her happy. Sadie has offered to give her one, but Persia wants to know my opinion before she accepts. As I slice the juicy, brown meat, I tell her I think it's very generous of Sadie, but she has already been more than generous with the price on the emerald.

Smiling, Persia nods before holding up a forefinger. "Oh! Changing the subject. Guess who came in just minutes after you left this afternoon?"

I shrug and shake my head.

"Winnie Rhode Lee and her son. Winnie and I had the nicest talk. She's a sweet person and loves Oliver very much."

"No kiddin'! I wondered why she wasn't at the trial with Mrs. Lee and the McNews."

"She said Oliver was happy to see her but made her promise not to come to the trial and listen to all the stuff being said about him. She wanted to be there to support him but did what he asked."

Sam signals that she needs help. We stand, and Persia gives me another little kiss. "Catron is starting at eight. He'll be long-winded. Why don't you and Sadie come join us when you can?"

CHAPTER 53
CATRON'S CLOSING ARGUMENT, 12 JUNE 1899

By eight o'clock, the courtroom is packed, and there are fresh faces who have come to be entertained by Tom Catron. Hughes and I get there early. Lee and Gililland appear relaxed as Sheriff Kahler leads them to their seats. Catron stares at them in disgust as they walk down the aisle. Fall doesn't look as debilitated as he had at the Orchard this afternoon.

From among the spectators, the Fountain brothers, their mouths set in hard, straight lines, give me a little nod. The bailiff calls for all to rise as Judge Parker walks to the bench. Judge Parker looks toward the prosecution table. "Mr. Catron, do you have a closing argument?"

Catron rises and rumbles, "I do, Your Honor."

"Proceed, sir."

Catron, surprisingly agile on his feet despite his weight and age, approaches the jury rail. He growls, "Gentlemen of the jury, we have endeavored on behalf of the prosecution to present before you evidence to satisfy you as to the true state of facts. We have made no effort to bring into this case anything that might be calculated to appeal to your prejudice or passion or anything not directly connected to this case. Our opponents, however, seem to feel that they must do all this—that they must appeal to your prejudices and complicate this case with entirely irrelevant matters. They have striven by every means in their power to prejudice you, gentlemen of the jury, against not only the witnesses for the prosecution, but against the counsel on this side as well.

"I care nothing about the slurs and insinuations thrown out against myself. I have been in this country too long, and I'm too old a man, to take notice of such things. They need not think to hurt me or turn me from my course one hair's breadth by such attacks.

"I do not know what your political beliefs are, gentlemen of the jury, and I care less. It was alleged that politics have been brought into this case and that political animus against the Democrats is responsible for the bringing of these men before this court. The gentleman who just preceded me misquoted a remark of mine, made only by way of a joke or passing remark, and put into my mouth words I never uttered in order to prejudice your minds against the side of the territory. What I said was this: 'There is nothing showing that fact unless it may be that they being indicted for murder may establish that fact.' It will be seen that I did not mention Democrats and the defense has seized hold of this passing remark of mine and distorted it for the purpose of misleading you.

"I shall confine myself to the facts as I understand them. The keynote of this whole case is Oliver Lee's remark to Frank Wayne: 'Say nothing about what you have seen here; it may interfere with our plans.' This was but a short time before the disappearance of Colonel Fountain. But the defense says the remark could not have had any reference to anything connected with the indictments against these men for the reason that the men did not know at that time they had been indicted. However, on the twenty-fourth day of January, just one week before the day of the disappearance, McNew was in Las Cruces and gave bond for his appearance to answer the indictment brought against him at the same time as those against Lee and Gililland. Of course, they knew. They couldn't help knowing. So the indictments could have been a motive for the crime and could have excited that remark, contrary to the assertion of the defense.

"What did that language mean? Wayne had made no particular observations. What plans might be interfered with? Lee did not deny the remark, nor did he offer any explanation.

"One week before the first of February, the defendant Gililland came to McNew's house, where little Jim Gould worked, and got a fresh horse and a lot of cartridges. He said, 'If anybody inquires of me while I'm away, tell them I've gone to Roswell.' But he did not go to Roswell. He went to Lee's Dog Canyon Ranch. What connection has this with Lee's plans?

"Tom Tucker was there, too. He was a deputy sheriff at Santa Fe, three hundred miles away. What was he doing there? He had come down and then telegraphed back for his gun and saddle. Had this any connection with Oliver Lee's plans?

"Soon after, McNew went by way of Roswell to Las Cruces. He made the remark, referring to the indictments, that *they knew they could not convict us, but they were going to break us up,* or words to that effect. Did this have anything to do with those plans?

"Joe Morgan was there. He had probably not been taken into the plot, and he was sent away. If Tom Tucker had remained so far away from his post, it would have excited comment. They sent him away. Thus, they had the trio necessary to commit the crime."

Catron turned to stare at the defense's table. Fall glares back. "The defense says they have proved an alibi—that there was nothing to Maxwell's evidence against six other witnesses. If that were true, it would certainly be a reasonable doubt as to the guilt of these men. But when a reputable witness is corroborated by all the accompanying circumstances, those circumstances stand against all the verbal evidence brought against him. In this case, everything corroborates the statement of Maxwell that Lee, Gililland, and McNew were away from Lee's ranch on the night of February first. We have ample evidence to show the three men left Dog Canyon Ranch in plenty of time to reach Luna's Wells. Did they get there? This will determine Maxwell's truth.

"At noon on Friday, Fountain was at Tularosa. Friday night he was at La Luz. He stayed there all night. The three men had assembled in the vicinity. Plans were afoot that might be frustrated. On the evening of Friday, how easy to go down to Wildy Well and cross over to Luna's Wells. Blevins was brought from Texas to fix up the alibi of the defendants and make their trail complete. This being true, there are good grounds for suspecting all the alibi is fixed up."

Catron pauses a moment and looks about the room. "Joe Fitchett looked no man in the face when he testified. Mrs. Lee said Joe Fitchett had told her he was going back to his brother's house when he left the ranch. He didn't go. Why all this concealment? Dan Fitchett told Pat Garrett and David Sutherland he went to the ranch Saturday morning and found the defendants there. There is evidence he misstated the facts when he said he went there in the evening. Bailey's evidence is not reasonable, but it was necessary to build up the alibi. They fixed it so each man would say the others were there. When men of Oliver Lee's intelligence commit a crime, they take care to fix up all the details. All of this could have been done by the defendant, who is capable of committing a deed such as is charged against him."

Catron pounds the jury rail with his pudgy fist. "Not one of their witnesses alone would stand against one disinterested witness. But, in this case, all the circumstances help to overbalance the alibi."

Catron paces back and forth in front of the jury. Most of the jury members follow his every move but sit with crossed arms, as if they don't believe a word he's saying.

"Fountain was probably shot at Chalk Hill. Four hundred and twenty-five paces farther on, the road widened. Here the buggy was apparently halted and backed up. Suppose Albert Fountain did not notice it didn't stop. Does that prove it did not stop? There are plenty of other witnesses to prove the buggy did halt and back up. Every witness but Albert Fountain says it stopped there. What happened there? There are signs of someone kneeling behind the bushes beside the road. There is a great blood spot. Something was laid upon the ground.

"The buggy went on. A horse was led behind, and two men, one on each side, accompanied the buggy on horseback, one driving the buggy. Do you believe that blood is the blood of anyone other than Colonel Fountain? His buggy was left there on the plain, his horses turned loose. Pieces of his clothing and pieces of the boy's clothing were left there.

"They say he might have got out of the country. How? Did he fly? Had he wings? No, that is impossible. If Colonel Fountain and his little boy had gone out of the country, they would certainly have left some track, some mark, some memory, something to show whither they went. They would have stopped to eat or drink. Colonel Fountain would not have starved his little boy to death. No, he did not get away—except as he and his little boy were carried away as corpses.

"It makes no difference that the doctor could not swear the blood was human blood. You must draw the natural conclusion that it came from Colonel Fountain's body and that he was murdered at the spot. No other animal or human being could have put the blood there but Colonel Fountain.

"They say there could have been no motive for the killing of the little boy, even while admitting there was one for the murder of his father. No motive? Suppose the boy was alive at the campfire. Did not the little fellow know who killed his father? The murderers had to do away with the boy. He would have identified them without doubt. They could not conceal him with any safety to themselves. They had to kill him. They were determined to finish their work.

"Frank Wayne and Jim Gould were both cautioned to conceal certain plans. The buggy was run off to the side of the road, and two bodies were hidden and have never yet been found. Let us suppose Fountain was shot through the body, and then, still alive, placed in blankets, carried a little farther, then his blood after his jugular vein was cut. There is no need for any blood spots on the buggy to prove the man's death.

"If the boy was alive at the camp, there is no evidence he was living beyond the point. They killed him by some means that did not leave the stain of blood—say they strangled him or wrapped him in a blanket and smothered him. There is every evidence the boy is dead. If he is not dead, how under heaven can you explain his absence? They talk about the *corpus delicti*. Texas is the only state requiring the production of the dead body in order to prove the commission of murder. But these men are from Texas. They knew the law there and used all possible means to conceal the body.

"I care little for Van Patton's testimony or his theories. Competent trailers have shown what became of those horses. As to the horse tracks, remember Tom Tucker, who was so eager to testify that he swore the hind feet of Lee's horse were larger than the front feet, did not testify that the horse was unshod. The defense tried to discredit all evidence based on the measurement or comparison of tracks. They say horse tracks cannot be depended upon on account of them not being permanent. They say the sand blows so as to make such evidence very unreliable. These tracks were not all in the sand, of course. Some of them were in the soil, some in places seldom disturbed. Some must have been preserved."

Persia and Sadie ease down the row where Hughes and I sit

as the men slide closer together to give them room to sit next to us. Persia, taking my hand, gives it a squeeze.

Catron's thunder slowly seeps back into my consciousness.

"Albert Fountain, to whom the defense goes for corroboration, is not a very reliable witness. He has been contradicted in many respects, so the evidence of other members of the posse must stand against his. The defense said no search was made out beyond the herd of cattle. Llewellyn testified he investigated all the tracks around the herd of cattle in every direction and found the trail did not turn aside. Llewellyn and Branigan went to Wildy Well and measured the tracks. These men and the rest of the posse went back to Las Cruces through the second pass and identified the tracks made by three of the horses seen at the camp. Each track has some distinguishing characteristics.

"We have shown you that these three men are the only ones who could have reached the point from Wildy Well where Fountain was held up, where their tracks were found and measured. Of what account is their alibi? These men, having arranged with their friends to testify to certain facts, could have left the ranch at any time they wished in order to make connections and carry out their plot."

With my future bride by my side, I have an epiphany. Witnesses testified Fountain had three men in front of him nearly all day the Saturday he and Henry disappeared. If, as the prosecution claims, three men did it, then following Catron's arguments and witnesses, it had to be the same three who killed them. According to the map pinned on the courtroom wall, the Lee ranch is nearly twelve miles from the La Luz to Las Cruces Road at its nearest point, and nearly twenty miles from where the three men started trailing the buckboard.

A horse ridden hard might make seven miles an hour over long distances, if it is in good shape. That means Lee and the others would have taken at least about three hours to reach the road near La Luz. The three riders who made the colonel nervous all day could not have been Lee, Gililland, and McNew, because no one seems to dispute they were at the ranch that morning. They didn't have time to reach the road and trail the colonel and Henry all day if they were at the ranch in the morning. The evidence also indicates, and Pat Garrett and Perry believed, there were at least four, more likely five, involved—the shooter behind the bush, and the three who surrounded the buckboard. Why does Catron keep ignoring the fourth man?

Catron's stentorian voice pounds into my ears. "Carl Clausen's testimony about the evident fear of the five men he encountered at the Wells, including Lee, has not been contradicted. There are many other incidents showing these men feared something and were on their guard. Here were six, eight, or ten men. If they had no reason for fear, why did they leave themselves open to grave suspicion?

"At the Wells, they shoved a Negro out first. It made no difference to them if he should get filled full of bullet holes. In a few minutes, another one of these brave men slunk sideways out of the house and hunted a hole to hide in. By that time, Clausen still had not opened up his battery on the men, and Mr. Lee walked out with his hand on his gun and asked what the visitor wanted. He replied he wanted a cup to get some water. I ask you, is that the way innocent men act, men who have done nothing wrong or have nothing on their minds?

"Clausen asked Lee why he wasn't out hunting for Fountain's body. Lee made the remark, 'What is that to us?' Lee left suddenly and took Clausen's back track. Why?

"Lee went in the direction of the second pass and probably discovered that Clausen's trail went over the pass. Not knowing where the posse might be, he turned to the right and started over the Jarillas. Then, changing his mind, he circled all around the mountain to Albert Fall's Sunol Mine Camp, and from there made his way to Las Cruces. We have proved he did not go through the second pass as he said he did.

"None of the witnesses for the defense have testified that Lee's horse was not shod at the time. All that was asked for, and all that was given, was the general testimony that the horse was usually not shod. These witnesses may have testified truthfully, after having themselves pulled the shoes from the horse's feet, or the shoes might have been pulled off somewhere between Lee's ranch and Las Cruces. Lee evidently called John May's attention to the fact that the horse had no shoes at the time, or why else would May have remembered that seemingly trivial fact for more than three years? Is there any doubt Lee's was the gray horse in evidence all through this case?

"Fountain and his little boy have been killed. You must take this evidence and consider each point, each track in detail. Does the evidence point in a reasonable way to any other solution to the problem? Would it apply as well to any other state of things than that these men are guilty of murder as charged?

"There is no explanation why Gililland went to McNew's house for extra cartridges and a fresh horse, telling the people there he was going to Roswell, and then going directly to Dog Canyon. No explanation except that he had a plan that might be frustrated. The attempt to manufacture evidence is the best evidence of guilt.

"The little extra paper Lee saw when he rode into Las Cruces from Sunol Camp, the one calling for a lynching, never mentioned Lee's name, but he at once assumed he was the man referred to. He called upon the editor and wanted to know why such articles were published. Why did he take it upon himself to resent that abuse if he was not connected with the matter? He lived fifty-five miles from there. Ah, no! It was not for any public reason that he took notice of the article, but because the article shot straight home and hit the mark. He had not enough control of himself to stay in hiding, and he was weak enough to go and give himself away.

"Put all the circumstances together. Is there a single one not pointing to Lee and Gililland as the perpetuators of this crime? They abducted those people, spirited them away, and took their lives. Can you prove by these circumstances anything else? If they can point to any other state of things, then these men are not guilty. But if they all point one way, it is your duty to convict these men.

"We have proved these men continually avoided arrest. They have undertaken to show they thought their lives were in great danger if they came within range of the officers sent to apprehend them, and that it was safer to stay out of reach until they could make some agreement to be protected. Gentlemen, the evidence does not bear out such a fear. Their continual avoidance of the officers shows they were not innocent.

"Nobody believes Judge Fall is connected with this crime in any way. Something has been said about a scheme to vindicate Fall and find Lee not guilty. We do not make any innuendoes against Fall, nor have we done anything to justify any assertion to the contrary.

"Does not that alleged conspiracy to murder Lee and Fall seem to you to be pure nonsense? Do you believe Cox would be fool enough to go into any scheme with Llewellyn to conspire to murder Lee and Fall? Do you believe he would make public evidence of his own infamy if he had done so? Why was Cox not put on the stand by the defense? It is a rule of law concerning evidence that every fact shall be established by the best evidence to be procured. They put Lee on the stand to testify as to something Cox told him. Cox was here. Why did he not speak for himself? But they say we should have brought Cox to testify. We are not defending ourselves.

"Lee is swearing for his life, and has every reason to swear falsely. If Oliver Lee knew about all those plots and conspiracies against him, why did he not publicly denounce their authors? Can you doubt that the people would have risen and denounced the conspirators?

"Print Rhode's testimony concerning Llewellyn was flatly contradicted by Llewellyn himself and by many other witnesses. Is it reasonable to believe that a man like Llewellyn would hunt up such a one as Print Rhode and tell him a story of his own folly and crime and infamy?

"Garrett said, regarding the Kearney fight, that when he first looked toward the housetop, Lee had his gun pointed and was preparing to shoot. Lee states that when Garrett's posse commenced firing, he was only half awake and punched Gililland to awaken him."

Fall shakes his head and speaks up. "No, he didn't. He didn't say anything of the kind, Mr. Catron."

"Well, the facts are, in substance, as I state them. If these men were not guilty, why did they go up on that housetop with guns and cartridges and prepare to fight?

"If these men did not kill Fountain and his boy, who did kill them? If the circumstances do not point to these men as the murderers, where else do they point? Explain them if you can.

"Now you are to judge, upon all the evidence, whether these men are to be sent back into the country again, or whether they are to be punished as the perpetrators of this crime. Consider your act just as if someone sacred and dear to you had been destroyed. I leave this case with you."

Catron turns from the jury, returns to the prosecution table, and slumps into his chair. I check my watch. It's ten-thirty. He's been talking nonstop for two and a half hours. There is dead silence among the spectators. Neighbor studies neighbor for reactions to this last argument. Sadie sits with crossed arms, staring at Catron and shaking her head.

Judge Parker looks over the crowd. “There will be a five-minute recess before I charge the jury.” Several of the men head for the facilities out back.

I give Persia a little hug. “I’m glad you came.”

“You can thank Sadie. She wanted to see what Catron would try after she heard about the reception Fall’s speech got this afternoon.”

CHAPTER 54
CHARGE TO THE JURY, 12 JUNE 1899

The bailiff calls for the court to rise as Judge Parker returns to the bench. Lee and Gililland sit straight, their hands folded on the table in front of them. Fall lights a cigar and slumps back in his chair. The silence in the room is deafening as Judge Parker adjusts his wire-frame glasses and begins to read a long, formal document with twenty-eight points for the jury to bear in mind while reaching a verdict. While he drones on, I notice that most of the jurors' eyes appear to be glazing over.

At the conclusion of the reading of the charge, Fall stands and notes a few exceptions to his charge. When Fall sits down, Judge Parker looks toward the stenographer, who nods he has the record. "Very well, defense exceptions are so noted. Gentlemen of the jury, it is now ten minutes after eleven. It has been a very long day. I charge you to return to your sleeping quarters, and at nine o'clock tomorrow morning return here to begin your deliberations. Court is adjourned."

The bailiffs begin ushering the jury members down the aisle. The spectators wait for the jury to clear before they rise, and the prosecutors begin wearily packing their satchels, but before the bailiff can tell the spectators to rise for Judge Parker's exit, Fall is on his feet. "Your Honor!"

The courtroom is quiet as every eye turns to Fall. Judge Parker looks over the top of his glasses with a pained expression. "Your Honor, the defense demands that the jury be brought back now, tonight. We have suffered through eighteen days of this trial. There is no need for any more. The defense demands a verdict!"

Looking at his desktop, Judge Parker rubs his forehead as though his head is pounding. "Mr. Fall, you do realize how late it is?" Spectators all over the courtroom look at each other, most likely wondering what kind of trick Fall has up his sleeve.

"I do, Your Honor."

There is a long pause as Judge Parker stares at the ceiling and drums his fingers on his desk. "Very well. Bailiff, bring the jury back."

Chapter 55
The Verdict

Persia and I look at each other, frowning. We're ready for a nice walk in the moonlight. The jurors will probably take days to reach a conclusion. Sadie sits nodding and smiling, her arms still crossed. Hughes shakes his head, writing with fury, grinning all the while.

In five minutes, the jurors are walking back down the aisle, several frowning. When they're seated, Judge Parker says, "Gentlemen of the jury, the defense requests that you begin your deliberations now. I've agreed to let you begin your work in the hope that you can reach a verdict sooner rather than later. Retire to the jury room, select your foreman, and begin your deliberations. We await your decision. Advise us if you are unable to reach one this evening."

The jurors file back to the jury room, and the courtroom breaks into myriad conversations as neighbors discuss this latest imbroglio. I look at my watch—eleven thirty-five.

The Fountain brothers, Williams, Garrett, and most of the other witnesses from Las Cruces sit toward the back, arms crossed, jaws set, saying nothing. Jack sees me looking in their direction and gives me a little nod. Close by the Fountain contingent, Seymour smokes a cigarette.

Lee and Gililland look tired and apprehensive. The McNews and Mrs. Lee talk to friends standing around them. From the look in their eyes, I think Nettie and Mrs. Lee are frightened.

It's impossible to tell what Bill is thinking behind those blue eyes with the ten-mile stare.

In less than ten minutes the door to the jury room opens, and a bailiff comes down the aisle with a folded note. The room grows quiet. The bailiff knocks on the judge's chambers door behind the bench and disappears inside. Within a minute, he reappears, steps up on the platform, and announces in a loud, strained voice, "Ten minutes until the reading of the verdict."

Persia squeezes my hand and smiles. We won't be here much longer. I feel queasy inside, filled with feelings of relief marble-ized with dread. What if by some quirk Lee and Gililland are found guilty? Maybe Catron's oratory was more convincing than Fall's. Will the judge send them to prison or the gallows? Will the murder in the third-degree strategy work? I look over my shoulder and see Todd Bailey and his friends. Their jaws are set, ready to act, and I can tell by the looks on faces scattered around the courtroom, so are several others. Curry moves his chair closer to the defense table. Lee and Gililland sit straight and ready as Fall leans in to Lee and speaks in his ear while Lee nods.

I whisper in Persia's ear, "If they're found guilty, you and Sadie be ready to hit the floor. Lead will likely fly." She nods she understands and whispers to Sadie who looks over at me and smiles.

At eleven fifty-five, the bailiff announces, "All rise!"

Judge Parker takes his seat. "Bailiff, bring in the jury."

The door to a back room opens, and a bailiff leads the jury back. I think, *They can't have deliberated more than seven or eight minutes.*

The jury is seated. Judge Parker asks, "Has the jury reached a verdict?"

The foreman, Alexander Bentley, stands. "We have, Your Honor."

"Very well. Pass your decision to the clerk."

The clerk takes the decision and hands it to Judge Parker, who reads it, nods, and hands it back. "The defendants will rise and face the jury. The clerk will read the verdict."

Lee and Gililland, surrounded by their attorneys, stand straight, their hands folded in front of them, looking directly at the jurors, who look back unblinking.

"Case No. 2618, Territory of New Mexico versus Oliver M. Lee and James R. Gililland. We find the defendants Oliver M. Lee and James R. Gililland . . . not guilty."

For a brief instant, time stands still before cheers and old-time tent revival yells of *Hallelujah!* fill the room. Most of the spectators rush forward, crowding in to congratulate and make jokes with the grinning Lee and Gililland. Judge Parker, who doesn't even try to stop the celebration, leans over the bench to say something to the bailiff and leaves. The bailiff croaks in a shout, "Court is adjourned!"

Persia, Sadie, Hughes, and I are in the crush moving forward to shake hands and offer our congratulations. Looking over my shoulder, I see the Fountains are gone. I see Catron's back disappearing down the steps. At the head of the stairs, a lone, tall figure in a long, black frock coat leans against the jury room wall, smoking a cigar. Pat Garrett.

EPILOGUE

On the bright, sunny morning of 13 June 1899, Sadie and J.W. Orchard's two stagecoaches left the Union Hotel at seven o'clock crammed with twenty-three passengers. Among them were Tom Catron, Sheriff Pat Garrett, William Childers, and Albert Fall.

Judge Parker had refused to let Oliver Lee and James Gililland post bond and remain free until their trials for the murders of Colonel Fountain and Kent Kearney. However, at their request, Judge Parker did allow them to be jailed in Alamogordo under Sheriff Curry while the territory prepared its case. Before the end of the summer, Judge Parker agreed to let them post bond. By the end of August 1899, the territory dropped all charges against Lee, Gililland, and McNew.

Free at last, they immediately rode to Las Cruces, intending to pay their attorney fees. Finding Fall in his office in Las Cruces, they asked to pay what they owed him. Finding a slip of paper, he spent a few moments scribbling his costs before telling them, "Sixty-two dollars and twenty-five cents are my actual expenses. I saved you meal costs by eating at the chuck wagon." They begged him to let them pay what was "right." He refused. It is said that Lee eventually paid out over thirty thousand dollars to cover all his trial expenses.

In the years following the trial, Lee, Gililland, and McNew independently developed major ranches throughout the Tularosa Basin and in the Sacramento Mountains. They accomplished unbelievable feats of engineering with simple tools, horse-drawn plows, and shovels as they dug trenches to lay miles of wooden pipes to bring water to their herds scattered over the eastern side of the Tularosa Basin.

Oliver Lee died on 15 December 1941. He had served in the state legislature twice, held numerous civic appointments, and was a director of the Federal Land Bank for years. The Oliver Lee State Park sits by the towering walls of Dog Canyon and encompasses part of the original Lee Ranch a few miles south of Alamogordo.

James Gililland, the beloved Uncle Jim of his family, was a notorious practical joker who loved to play on the biases of those who believed he had got away with murder. He successfully operated the same ranch in the Tularosa Basin for over forty years. In his sunset years, he and his wife moved to Hot Springs, now Truth or Consequences, New Mexico. He died there on 8 August 1946.

Bill and Nettie McNew developed several ranches, their family members becoming well-to-do ranchers, businessmen, and one, an internationally recognized plant pathologist. Bill McNew died on 13 June 1937.

Despite the conflict between Yankee Republicans and Texas Democrats that Albert Fall claimed was the cause of Oliver Lee's arrest, he joined the Republican Party around 1902. He and Tom Catron became New Mexico's first U.S. senators in 1912. In 1921, Warren Harding appointed Fall Secretary of the Interior.

Later, Fall became entangled in the Teapot Dome scandal. He was fined one hundred thousand dollars and sentenced to serve a year in prison beginning in 1931. Released after six months in prison, Albert Fall was the only one to serve any jail time for the Teapot Dome scandal. He died, bedridden, in the Hotel Dieu Hospital in El Paso, Texas, on 1 December 1944 at age eighty-three.

Eugene Manlove (Gene) Rhodes appeared at the Apalachin, New York, home of widow May Davidson Purple on 18 July 1899, five weeks after the trial's verdict. He and May married less than a month later. Caring for May's parents forced Gene, May, and her young son to live in Apalachin for the next twenty-five years, where Gene farmed and wrote, and May typed his manuscripts. Many of his fourteen novels and novelettes and sixty short stories about the West were published in the *Saturday Evening Post.* May and Gene returned to New Mexico in 1926. Gene died at his home in San Diego, California, in 1934. He is buried at his old ranch in Rhodes Pass in the San Andres Mountains.

Sadie and J.W. Orchard divorced around 1902. In 1914, the Percha Creek flooded and wiped out many homes and businesses in Hillsboro. The flood was followed by an epidemic of influenza and pneumonia in 1918. During those years, Sadie became known as Hillsboro's "Angel of Mercy," giving her fancy dresses to line coffins for children and doing every job that needed to be done, from nurse to undertaker. After losing the fight with the Sierra County government against moving the county seat from Hillsboro to Hot Springs in 1936, she lived out her later years in Hillsboro running a hotel and dining room with Tom Ying. She died in Hillsboro on 3 April 1943 at the age of seventy-eight, although it is admitted by all who knew her that her age was a moving target, not easily hit.

Tom Ying continued to run the Chinaman's Café until his

death. When he passed away in 1957, his age was between one hundred five and one hundred fifteen.

Supported by Albert Fall and Lew Wallace, former New Mexico Governor and author of *Ben Hur,* Pat Garrett was nominated customs collector in El Paso by Theodore Roosevelt and confirmed by the Senate in 1901. Roosevelt refused to reappoint Garrett the next year; political sensitivity was not Garrett's forté. Thereafter, Pat Garrett's fortunes steadily declined until he was deeply in debt. He was shot in the back of the head while relieving himself at the side of the road near Las Cruces, New Mexico, on 29 February 1908. The same day, Wayne Brazel, one of two traveling companions, turned himself in to the Doña Ana County sheriff. He confessed to the killing, and claimed self-defense. W.W. Cox, one of Garrett's debtors and Brazel's employer, hired Albert Fall to defend Brazel. In a day-long trial Fall obtained an acquittal of the murder charges, still claiming self-defense. Subsequent investigators were convinced that Brazel did not shoot Garrett. The evidence suggested Garrett had been shot from ambush. Pat Garrett's son, Jarvis, believed his father was murdered by Carl Adamson, Garrett's other traveling companion.

Hughes DeCourcy Slater bought the *El Paso Daily Herald* in 1899 when he was twenty-five years old. He served as a reporter, publisher, and editor for the paper. In 1917, at age forty-three, he enlisted in the United States Army Infantry, and at the end of World War I returned to El Paso a captain. Thereafter Hughes was affectionately known around El Paso as Cap Slater. He bought a rival morning paper, the *El Paso Times,* in 1925. Retiring in 1929, he pursued lifelong interests in art, music, and sculpture, producing at least forty works of his own. He died on 22 September 1958.

Quentin Peach married Persia Brown in the little Union Church on Eleanora Street in Hillsboro on 18 June 1899. They took a honeymoon trip to San Francisco, where Quentin showed up at the *Examiner,* announced he had returned, and waited until he heard, "Peach!" Closing the door behind him, he told Chief he had married and was resigning. The old man sat speechless as Quent walked out. Such silence in the newsroom has not been heard before or since.

Quent accepted Hughes Slater's offer and went to work at the *Herald* in August 1899. His zenith as a reporter and writer came ten years later with the Mexican Revolution. The stories he wrote about Pancho Villa, a charismatic Mexican *pistolero* and revolutionary he befriended in an El Paso bar in 1908, were carried nationally by major newspapers and were later quoted by eminent historians who studied Villa's role in *La Revolución.* Living a long life with a distinguished career, Quent died in El Paso on 12 June 1959, sixty years to the day after the end of the Hillsboro trial. Persia followed him in death ten years later.

Ed Brown's wife, Delia, divorced him in 1902 and raised their four children to become respected members of the community in Alamogordo. Sometime after 1908, Ed Brown was struck and killed by lightning while riding his horse in a pasture.

The bones of Colonel and Henry Fountain have never been found, despite numerous searches for them. Many in the Fountain family, their supporters, and some reputable historians continue to believe Oliver Lee, Bill McNew, and James Gililland murdered the Fountains and got away with it. From the same facts, the Lee, McNew, and Gililland families and their supporters believe the trial was a political persecution. There are also respected historians who conclude Lee and the others probably were not guilty and believe there are other suspects at least as likely as Lee, McNew, and Gililland, if not more so, who murdered the Fountains.

AFTERWORD

The Additional Reading List presented at the end of the story contains well-written histories that summarize the trial. Yet, historians are hindered in their work by the fact that the trial transcripts were destroyed in the mid-1930s when the Sierra County Seat was moved from Hillsboro to Hot Springs and the Hillsboro Courthouse demolished. The only surviving written quotations from participants in the trial—attorneys or witnesses—are from newspaper accounts written by reporters attending the trial and from occasional notes made by the attorneys and others. These have been used and quoted extensively in this story.

Newspaper accounts of events leading up to the murders and the trial are often strongly biased by Republican or Democratic points of view. These accounts require the discernment of fact from opinion—an art, not a science, to say the least. Even surviving records of hearings and grand jury proceedings prior to the trial in Hillsboro demonstrate political bias through those who were selected for prosecution and by prosecution theories of what actually happened and why. Therefore, objective history can only speculate on the motives or likely actions consistent with the personalities of the defendants or those who tried them. Such speculation is done and is the business of fictional reconstruction such as presented in *Blood-Soaked Earth.*

At least five factors affected my telling of the trial story: first, the facts of the case and the background history going back as much as ten years before the trial; second, an understanding that nearly all written records of what was said in the trial are in fact, for the most part, synopses by reporters, which can leave out small but significant details; third, a detailed timeline of the events that led up to the murders and their subsequent investigation; fourth, ranch and town life in New Mexico Territory at the close of the last century; and, fifth, the personalities, interests, investments, and codes of conduct by the players in the trial. These factors show, and I believe *Blood-Soaked Earth* demonstrates, that the trial was not "shamefully loaded" as one reviewer of a recently published history of the trial claimed.

I conclude that Albert Fall, the lead attorney for Lee and Gililland, said it best: "What a jury decides in a courtroom has the untarnished value of fact." Lee and Gililland were judged not guilty by a group of men mutually agreed upon by the prosecution and the defense. The trial was conducted at a location the law said was unbiased either for or against the defendants. The jury in Hillsboro, New Mexico Territory, after listening to all the witnesses and evidence the prosecution and defense brought to the trial, decided in the span of less than eight minutes that Oliver Lee and James Gililland did not murder in any degree defined by the law, Henry Fountain.

This novel has presented a case for the person I believe did commit the Fountain murders and why the Fountain family and their supporters should be disgusted with the conduct of the murder investigation and the case the territory provided for the trial. In recent years some researchers have determined that the nephew of Oliver Lee, Todd Bailey, was the most likely culprit. There is no direct evidence to suggest this is true except that Todd Bailey was not at the ranch the night of the murders; he was dedicated (or was it guilt for his mistake) to Lee to the point of planning his escape; he was young enough to make horrific errors in judgment like killing the Fountains; and that near the Lee ranch, and in later years, stories in Bailey's family in Arkansas say he claimed he was responsible. The Bailey theory is like all the other speculation and circumstantial evidence for the case. The odds are we'll probably never know the identities of the killers.

ADDITIONAL READING

1. Gibson, A. M., *The Life and Death of Colonel Albert Jennings Fountain,* University of Oklahoma Press, Norman Oklahoma, 1965.

2. Hutchinson, W. H., *A Bar Cross Man: The Life and Personal Writings of Eugene Manlove Rhodes,* University of Oklahoma Press, Norman Oklahoma, 1956.

3. Keleher, William A., *The Fabulous Frontier: Twelve New Mexico Items,* The Rydal Press, Santa Fe, New Mexico, 1945.

4. King, Patsy Crow, *Sadie Orchard, The Time of Her Life,* PDX Printing, El Paso, Texas, 2006.

5. McNew, George, *Last Frontier West,* Privately Printed, 1985.

6. Metz, Leon C., *Pat Garrett: The Story of A Western Lawman,* University of Oklahoma Press, Norman Oklahoma, 1974.

7. Owen, Gordon R., *The Two Alberts: Fountain and Fall,* Yucca Tree Press, Las Cruces, New Mexico, 1996.

8. Recko, Corey, *Murder on the White Sands: The Disappearance of Albert and Henry Fountain,* University of North Texas Press, Denton Texas, 2007.

9. Sonnichsen, C. L., *Tularosa: Last of The Frontier West,* University of New Mexico Press, Albuquerque, New Mexico, 1980.

10. Pinkerton Reports of J.C. Fraser and W. B. Sayers, to Gov. W.T. Thornton, March 5—May 13, 1896, Ritch Collection # 1193, Huntington Library, Pasadena, California.

11. *El Paso Daily Herald* reports from the trial from 26 May

1899 to 13 June 1899. The articles by H.D. Slater in the latter portion of the trial are particularly useful and quoted extensively here for examinations and summation speeches.

ABOUT THE AUTHOR

W. Michael Farmer's in-depth historical research and southwest experience fill his stories with a genuine sense of time and place. His first novel, *Hombrecito's War,* won a Western Writers of America Spur Finalist Award for Best First Novel in 2006 and was a New Mexico Book Award finalist for Historical Fiction in 2007. He has published short stories in anthologies, and award-winning essays. His novels include: *Killer of Witches,* a 2016 Will Rogers Medallion Award winner, *Mariana's Knight,* 2017 New Mexico–Arizona Book Award winner for Historical Fiction, and *Blood of the Devil,* 2017 New Mexico–Arizona Book Award finalist for Adventure-Drama and Historical Fiction. In 2018 *Mariana's Knight* and *Blood of the Devil* were awarded 2018 Will Rogers Silver Medallion Awards for Western Fiction, and his book of historical essays, *Apacheria, True Stories of Apache Culture, 1860-1920,* won the 2018 New Mexico-Arizona Book Awards for Best New Mexico Book and Best History-Other.

The employees of Five Star Publishing hope you have enjoyed this book.

Our Five Star novels explore little-known chapters from America's history, stories told from unique perspectives that will entertain a broad range of readers.

Other Five Star books are available at your local library, bookstore, all major book distributors, and directly from Five Star/Gale.

Connect with Five Star Publishing

Visit us on Facebook:
https://www.facebook.com/FiveStarCengage

Email:
FiveStar@cengage.com

For information about titles and placing orders:
(800) 223-1244
gale.orders@cengage.com

To share your comments, write to us:
Five Star Publishing
Attn: Publisher
10 Water St., Suite 310
Waterville, ME 04901